The Last Encore

Elodie Colliard

This novel is entirely a work of fiction. The names, characters and incidents portrayed in it are the work of the author's imagination. Any resemblance to actual persons, living or dead, events or localities is entirely coincidental.

First edition

Editing by Dominic Wakeford, Britt Tayler & Julie Mianecki
Book cover and design by Leni Kauffman

ISBN 9781778137907

Praise for *The Last Encore*

"*The Last Encore* beautifully captures the push and pull of a friendship evolving into something more, the magnetism of the people we structure our hearts around when we're young, and the way returning to those people can feel like finally coming home. Full of heat, emotion, and endearing side characters, Josh and Avery's love story will break your heart and then put it back together. A delicious treat for fans of heartfelt romantic dramas." – **Ashley Winstead**, author of *Fool Me Once*

To Listen While Reading

<u>Listen to Josh and Avery's playlist</u>

- The Art of Starting Over – Demi Lovato
- Girl on Fire – Alicia Keys
- In My Blood – Shawn Mendes
- Count on Me – Bruno Mars
- Strangers – Jonas Brothers
- Always Remember Us This Way – Bradley Cooper & Lady Gaga
- Don't – Her
- One More Hour – Anthony Ramos
- Ocean Eyes – Billie Eilish
- Dress – Taylor Swift
- Forgiveness – Paramore
- Ease My Mind – Ben Platt
- Treacherous – Taylor Swift
- I Guess I'll Just Lie Here – Noah Reid
- Good As Hell – Lizzo
- I Feel It Coming – The Weeknd
- Close – Nick Jonas
- Father and Sons – Cat Stevens
- Adore You – Harry Styles
- The Luckiest – Ben Folds
- It'll Be Okay – Shawn Mendes
- Hold On – Adele
- Audition (The Fools Who Dream) – Emma Stone
- Wild – John Legend
- Malibu – Miley Cyrus
- Liebesträume No 3 – Franz Liszt
- City Of Stars – Ryan Gosling
- Clair de Lune – Claude Debussy
- Million Years Ago – Adele

Trigger warnings

Sexual assault, depression, anxiety, loss of a loved one

Author's note

Dear reader,

Thank you for choosing to give *The Last Encore* a chance. I felt it was important to take the time to talk a little more about the content warnings in this story.

It quickly became evident to me to include in Avery's background a reference to sexual abuse, because of my own experience. In today's society, and in the post-#MeToo movement, I wanted to be brave and share what I experienced through Avery.

Although this moment does not take up more than six pages in the book, the sexual assault that Avery experiences is described on page (208-215). The purpose of this is not to add shock value to the story, or to be disrespectful to victims of sexual violence, but to explain why some people, like me, like Avery, may have trouble living their intimacy. And it was essential to me that this scene occurs in my book, and not just be told in a conversation, or in Avery's thoughts. While it might be uncomfortable to read, not including it felt like I was silencing Avery's voice, and my own. It's time we hear these stories. That we read them.

Yet, the goal of the story is not to focus on Avery's recovery from what she has experienced in her past, but to explain her present behavior, and how she acts when confronted with intimacy. We all experience our traumas in different ways. I do not claim to speak for all victims of sexual violence, nor do I claim to offer a universal response to a very traumatic situation. I only share my experience, my story, in all humility.

Writing this piece of my own story was not easy, but in a way, it reconciled me with that part of myself that has lived in shame and silence for too long.

I hope that I have treated this topic with the sensitivity and care that it deserves, and that you, reader, feel safe and loved while reading this story.

With love,

Elodie

If you or a loved one have experienced abuse and need help, you can visit:

USA: RAINN (Rape, Abuse & Incest National Network)

Canada: Crisis lines for those affected by gender-based violence

To the women who feel like giving up: everything is temporary. No matter how bad things are right now, it shall pass. And tomorrow is another day to get back up and fight, just like we've always done.

And to Emily Henry, the Yogurt Queen of the Ohio River Valley, who made me want to write and tell stories in the first place.

One

The Art of Starting Over

"Shit, Simba!" The orange cat looked at her innocently from the kitchen counter, purring , as Avery inspected the cream top she'd just put on. *Great.* Her sleeve was covered in coffee stains and her favorite mug lay shattered on the floor. Her cat was giving her puppy-dog eyes, which was pretty ironic, considering.

"Don't look at me like that. Look at what you did!" She grabbed the nearest napkin and started to dab the silk fabric. Well ... that definitely made it worse. The stains spread in faint circles all around her arm, in an animal-style print, and her blouse was now wet.

"You, mister, are definitely going on the naughty list this year." Avery waved her finger in front of Simba, who proceeded to sniff, then lick the tip, clearly missing her warning. Avery rolled her eyes. Nothing could distract him from a good scratch under the chin or the prospect of food.

Already late, she opened her closet in the hope of finding another top that said she had her shit together. She could not show up to her first meeting with a new client with coffee stains all over her, but above all, she *couldn't* show up late.

She stripped down in one second and slipped on a burgundy cashmere sweater and a pair of dark jeans. Autumn was in full swing in Toronto, the air was cooler, and the leaves painted a burning picture all over the city, ranging from warm yellows to fiery reds.

Gathering her photography portfolio, Avery hurriedly tied her long brown hair in a (involuntary) messy bun while slipping on her boots. She was doing a maternity shoot with Claudia, a new client, and this meeting was supposed to set the tone for the rest of their time together.

"But you won't make a good impression, if you don't show up on time," she mumbled to herself.

This contract was an opportunity for her to show how talented she was to a different kind of clientele, a wealthier set. It came with a huge paycheck, significantly more than what she was used to, which barely paid the bills. She needed to be focused, sharp and professional, as she always strived to be. One look in the mirror, and Avery confirmed she was ready to head out. She grabbed her keys and flew out of her apartment.

Kensington Avenue was a small street in her neighborhood, always very quiet in the mornings. Avery loved this side of Toronto, home to the famous Kensington Market, which made her salivate every time she passed alongside it, the aromas of food from all over the world mingling together. The neighborhood was full of vintage shops and vibrant and colorful Victorian row-houses that looked like a kaleidoscope coming to life on the streets. It was loud, it was bright, it was alive.

She lived in a sky-blue house that her best friend Brooke had inherited from her parents, who'd gracefully agreed to let Avery stay there. After her awful breakup with Alex last year, not to mention the dreadful announcement her parents had delivered to her and her brother four months later, while she was still trying to make sense of her new reality, Avery had desperately needed a place to stay. Brooke offered her the small one-bedroom, as her parents were now living outside of the city. It wasn't perfect; the house had been empty and not in great shape, but it had been exactly what she'd needed at the time. Plus, she'd thought that there was something kind of poetic about living in a house in need of a little bit of love. She could have used some too.

♪♫

When Avery arrived in front of her new client's house, the knot in her stomach tightened. She couldn't count the number of times she'd driven to this part of the city, but even now, she felt like an intruder.

Bridle Path, one of the most ostentatious suburbs in Toronto, was nestled between the Don River Valley and lush, endless parks. It was also the place of all her childhood memories. Everything Kensington was, Bridle Path was the polar opposite. Big mansions, pools, tennis courts — anything opulent and over the top, it was here. Avery had never felt like she'd *belonged* in this place, home to a never-ending series of cocktail parties and fundraisers her parents used to throw when she and her brother Miles were younger. There were always people in their house, always something going on, because after all, you couldn't refuse an invitation from the great Dan Clark.

Her dad, you could say, had 'made it.' He was a world-renowned neurosurgeon for the Toronto General Hospital, famous for assembling brilliant research teams to work on Alzheimer's disease, while her mom, Rebecca, had stayed at home with her and her brother.

Dan had never been a family man, although Avery suspected that wasn't the picture he'd painted back when he and Rebecca had planned on starting a family.

Avery wasn't the kind of person to complain, but the fact was, the absence of her dad throughout her childhood hurt her. He was there when it mattered, at least, most of the time. Birthdays, Christmas, big milestones. But he'd missed out on her and her brother growing up, and wasn't that the most important part of all? He'd missed the time Miles fell off his bike on his first ride and scraped his knees and hands so bad Grandma had to take him to the ER. He'd missed out on the time Avery got home from school so upset after her first boyfriend dumped her in front of her friends, she didn't come out of her room for three days.

Sure, Avery remembered that she'd never felt lonely at Christmas, and when she looked at birthday pictures, she could always find both her parents surrounding her, smiling like they were proud to be there. But when she thought about it, all it did was remind her that the rest of the time, her dad wasn't there, and her mom, although physically present, was miles aways from her kids in the ways that mattered.

Avery knew her mom got tired of Dan's late nights and last-minute detours to the lab on weekends. On some days, she could see it on her mother's face – the exhaustion, sadness, anger, resentment – but after several years, it just became her daily life. One day, the switch flipped, and she was no longer able to take care of her kids anymore, because she just couldn't get out of her own bed. Avery's grandma Susan would come then and take care of them, to be there in the way nobody else had been. On other days/On good days, Rebecca would treat them to ice cream, or take them to see a movie, or just cook with them, and Avery held onto those memories as if they were the most precious thing she had.

And now, here she was, back in front of the memories of her childhood, looking at a million-dollar house as she took a deep breath and closed her eyes. *You can do it. You need to do it.* She just needed to ring the bell, do her work, and get the hell out of here.

"Good morning miss." A small woman opened the door thirty seconds after Avery rang, a warm and welcoming smile on her face. "Can I help you with anything?"

"Hi, um, yes. I'm the photographer, I have an appointment with Claudia Monroe this morning?"

"Of course! Follow me." Avery walked inside behind her, where massive stairs descended on each side of the grand hall. Everything was white and black, neat, and clean—nothing in here screamed 'home' or 'warmth.' Maria, the woman told her when Avery asked for her name, led Avery to the master bedroom, where her new client was buried under a huge pile of clothes.

"Madam, Miss Clark is here."

"Is it already nine, Maria ?!" A strand of hair emerged from behind the clothes, revealing a woman who looked like she'd already run two marathons this morning. "I apologize, I was sure I still had time before our meeting." She got up and a huge belly pointed right at Avery. "Nice to meet you. Please call me Claudia," she said as she held out her hand. Avery shook it, bemused by the situation and half-relieved she was not dealing with another stuck-up rich person.

Claudia was beautiful. Tall, lean, and elegant from her raven-black hair to her fingertips. Her clothes fell in clean, straight lines, with the exception of her round belly tightly secured beneath her dress. She had to be at least eight months pregnant, closer to nine if Avery had to guess. Her whole look was very rigid and stern, and would intimidate most people, but not Avery. She knew it was just a façade as soon as she saw Claudia's face light up when she smiled back at her.

"Nice to meet you too, Claudia, and please don't worry," Avery said, waving her hand. "I understand the struggle." She looked at the dresses laid out on the floor. Not an inch of hardwood was visible, and despite her own bedroom being approximately a quarter of the size of Claudia's, she had just as many clothes. She could relate.

"Let's move to my office," Claudia said as she walked out of the messy bedroom.

Avery nodded and followed her into the adjacent room. The contrast was shocking. The room was cozy and warm, full of throw pillows and blankets in calming pink, gold and white tones. In the middle of the room stood a white marble desk that probably cost more than her car. Claudia waved for Avery to sit down as she rounded the desk to sit in a glamorous rose-gold chair.

"So, let's get down to business," Claudia said, plopping her elbows on the desk. "My due date is coming up soon, as I'm sure you can see." She hugged her belly gently. "Lisa told me great things about your work and everybody I know is booked solid for the next month, so I thought why not go with someone new?" A small smile curved her lips. Lisa was the boutique owner Avery worked with when she needed gowns and other accessories for her photoshoots.

"I'm so happy that Lisa gave you my number," Avery said, returning her smile. Claudia seemed nice, level-headed and not too bossy. "Why don't you tell me what you have in mind, and I'll guide you through my process."

They spent the next hour hammering out every detail of the photoshoot. Color palette, locations, dress, mood, and style. They decided to set the date in two weeks, enough time for Avery to get the materials she needed, come up with a mood board and book a venue for the day. Claudia wanted to be photographed in a pumpkin field, as well as in her backyard for the more intimate shots. Nature was the central theme, and they agreed on a bohemian style for the dress that would go beautifully with the fall vibes. After finalizing the last few details, including pricing, Claudia walked Avery back to the door.

"I almost forgot to ask you!" She rolled her eyes. "This baby brain, I swear. Would you be available to do a second shoot on my due date? I'm planning on having my baby at home and I would love to have someone immortalize the moment. I mean, depending on how the first shoot turns out, of course, and if you're comfortable with that."

This was an incredible opportunity. The maternity photoshoot was already paying way more than Avery usually charged her clients, and now, Claudia wanted to hire her for the birth? She would actually be able to save some money to invest in her business.

"I would love that, Claudia," she said. "I'll keep you updated on next steps."

Waving goodbye, Avery hopped in her car, a big smile on her face. This could finally be what she'd been hoping for since starting her company straight out of college. Photography was her passion. She loved being able to connect with people, understand their desires, and let the emotions flow through the lens of her camera. She had the ability to see through people better than they could themselves, capture their essence and translate it into the photo, like time forever frozen in the moment.

This job was not just a job, it was who she was. Building her company from scratch had been a challenge, but one she'd willingly taken on. And even though it didn't pay the bills yet, even though every day was a struggle, she just knew she would get there someday—giving up was not in her DNA. If you asked Brooke, she would probably say that Avery was by far the most stubborn person she'd ever met, and she would be damn right.

Two

Girl on Fire

Avery pushed open the bridal boutique's door with one hip, her hands full of gowns and other bridal accessories, and the sound of tiny bells rang through the store. It was after hours, so the boutique was empty, but Avery had texted Lisa to let her know she had some stuff to drop off.

"Avery, is that you darling?" Lisa's voice called from somewhere in the store.

"Yep, it's me! Hi!"

Lisa's Creations was Avery's go-to place when she needed anything for her photoshoots. She'd stumbled upon it one day while strolling with her grandmother around St George Campus. The little boutique was hidden away in a small street and, at first glance, didn't look like much. The white façade was in need of a refresh; the ivy covering half of the front of the boutique hid the name, and the paint was peeling off. What had caught Avery's eye was the tastefully dressed store window full of details, like every object had its place. Her curiosity had only grown stronger after a quick search on the Internet told her that Lisa Hill owned the store. In the wedding industry, everyone knew Lisa, and worshipped the ground she walked on. She was a petite, refined woman in her fifties, whose tastes were never questioned and whose opinions were always respected.

The boutique, which looked so small from the outside, actually spanned two floors. On the ground floor, some of the biggest designer wedding dresses, from Vera Wang to Monique Lhuillier, were elegantly displayed on mannequins, although these were not the names clients came here for. Accessories, shoes and bridesmaid's dresses filled the back of the room, next to Lisa's couture studio. The upstairs was dedicated to fittings and the rest of the wedding dress collections, where Lisa catered to every need of her clients and their bridesmaids.

What had started out as small requests here and there for Avery's photoshoots had soon grown into a close partnership and friendship.

Avery set the box she was carrying on a pink cushioned bench and hung the dresses on one of the rods behind the front desk.

"Are you upstairs?" she asked.

"In the studio!"

She walked toward the back of the store and poked her head through the studio door. "Hi!" she said, beaming at Lisa, who sat buried under a thousand wedding gown sketches, her glasses perched on the bridge of her nose and her glossy black hair neatly secured in a low bun. She looked to be working on another design for her next winter collection, pencil in hand and measuring tape around her neck like it was just another piece of jewelry. This was Lisa in a nutshell.

"Hi gorgeous!" Lisa got up and made her way through the sketches and pieces of fabric lying all over the floor. She gave Avery a tight hug and a little pat on the back. The smell of Chanel n°5 lingered in the air, even after Lisa released her.

"I hung the dresses on the rack behind the desk and left the shoes with the hair clips and bracelets by the door— thanks again for the last-minute pick up!"

Lisa made a "don't sweat it" gesture. "Thank you, darling. Do you need anything else for the week?"

"Actually, yes," Avery said. "I have a shoot coming up and wondered if you had some flowy dresses in lavender or yellow I could borrow. Trying to go with something natural."

"Hmm ... let me see. Follow me." Lisa walked past Avery and didn't look back to check if she'd managed to make it out of the chaos that was her studio.

Within minutes, Avery found herself with a dozen different dresses in her arms. Lisa glanced briefly over her glasses at the designs she'd handed to Avery. "Okay let's see. We have some blackberry, deep, pastel, and blue lavender gowns," she said, ruffling through the racks "Ah! This is the one I was looking for. Dusty lavender is very on-trend right now." She handed Avery the long dress.

Avery nodded in agreement. "It's beautiful," she said.

They went through the same exercise with different shades of yellow, and Lisa even threw in a few olive dresses. "Trust me, it's a timeless and elegant color. Just in case you change your mind," she assured Avery.

Lisa wrapped the dresses carefully in their sleeves and placed them on the counter.

"Thank you so much, as always," Avery said, thankful that her friend always delivered. "I'll get those back to you by the end of the week, and the one I choose after the photoshoot next week."

"No rush, darling. Wedding season is over, demand is low right now. Which reminds me ..." She fumbled in one of the drawers and handed a paper to Avery. "It's not official until next week yet, so keep that pretty mouth of yours zipped, but you know the store has been doing really well over the past few years ..."

Avery scanned the document and widened her eyes. "Lisa, oh my god! You're going international?"

"It's about time! Everybody knows me already in New York. Just have to make it official now."

"I ... I can't believe it, wow! Congratulations!" Avery squeezed her tight. She had witnessed Lisa's business grow before her eyes since becoming a regular at the store, and although she was undoubtedly proud of her friend, she couldn't help but feel a little twinge of envy at her success. When would it be her turn? She was working as hard as Lisa, but was struggling to get more business. What more did she have to do?

"Thank you, dear," Lisa said, patting her arm. "Now, this is just one part of the news. Since I'm expanding in the States, I'm also hoping to go further here, in Toronto." Avery cocked an eyebrow, intrigued. Lisa gestured for Avery to follow her. "Come, sit, sit, I want to discuss something with you." Lisa sat on one of the luxurious velvet couches and patted the empty seat next to her.

"You know how I built my clientele here through word of mouth, right?" Avery nodded. "Good. So, that's what my boutique in New York will be. I want it to be selective, high-end luxury and 100% *my* designs." She raised a finger before Avery could interrupt. "That means broadening my horizons in Toronto. I owe everything to my clients here. Flip the page, darling." She gestured toward the document Avery was holding. Avery turned the page and read the rest of it. A photography contest? She frowned, not quite sure where Lisa was going with this.

"You're holding a contest?"

A small smile tugged at Lisa's lips, her eyes full of excitement. "Well, I'm not the one holding it—truly, my team came up with the idea and put a panel of judges together. I need to promote my store, you see, my designs. Everyone knows me in the industry, but the average Joe doesn't. I don't have any say in the contest itself, but I want you to enter it."

Avery had stopped listening, her eyes narrowing on one crucial piece of information: the contest not only offered her the chance to photograph one of today's hottest designer's winter collection, but it also gave the winner the chance to sign a one-year contract with the boutique as part of a 'wedding dress and photographer' package. As much as the idea excited her and awoke the competitor inside her, Avery was puzzled as to why Lisa hadn't just asked her to do it and offered her the partnership directly. She knew she was good at her job and she knew Lisa was aware of it too. Hadn't they worked together long enough for it to be the normal course of their professional relationship?

"Avery, listen to me," Lisa said, taking Avery's hands in hers, squeezing lightly. Avery snapped her attention back to her. "You know how much I love your work, but this is not a decision I'm making on my own. My team thinks we'll have better exposure holding a contest than me just choosing someone, *especially* someone close to me." She clapped her hands. "I just wanted to give you a little heads up, but that's all I can do. Makes the whole thing more fun, don't you think?"

Avery could picture it: her name next to Lisa's, the official partner of the Toronto boutique, her business bursting with requests. *This is it, Ave. this is your shot. Don't blow it.*

"Yeah, sure …" she said, still obviously in shock.

"I get it, it's a lot to process. But the contest is going live next week. You *are* going to participate though, right?"

"Of course, I'll participate, are you kidding?!"

Lisa smiled, pride plastered on her face. She got up and escorted Avery to the door. "Now, don't get your hopes up, darling. Again, I'm not the one deciding on the winner." She rested her hand on Avery's shoulder. "But I know you have it in you with how talented you are, so give them hell, okay?"

"Oh, trust me, I will."

"That's my girl." With that, she opened the door and wished Avery a good night.

What the hell just happened? Avery had only come to drop off some items, and she was leaving with a dozen dresses and the chance for her business to finally grow into something she'd always imagined it to be. She looked again at the paper Lisa had left her with. All the terms and conditions were listed, the judges, the criteria and the theme: "A Winter Wedding Wonderland." She was going to give her best, try her hardest. She *was* going to give them hell. She just needed to find a last-minute wedding to photograph. No big deal.

Three

In My Blood

A quick glance at the calendar on her fridge was enough to ruin the rest of Avery's day. The high she'd been on since the morning deflated as quickly as a burst balloon as heat rose to her face, her stomach tightening with nervousness. She couldn't believe September 21st was two days away, and suddenly, she felt like she could throw up.

Avery knew the signs all too well, and as soon as she started to feel dizzy, she laid her burning cheek on the cold kitchen floor while trying to breathe through yet another panic attack. She had become pretty good at managing her anxiety throughout the years with the help of her grandma, Brooke and her brother, who'd all learned to detect the signs and avoid certain situations they knew would trigger her anxiety. But the last year had been a challenging one. Avery felt like she was back to square one, like she wasn't in charge of her body anymore.

For as long as she could remember, she'd liked to be in control. She liked doing things her way, on her own terms, at her own pace, as having a routine helped manage her stress. Her anxiety had always been a part of her, something she'd learned to live with, side by side. It was almost like a scar—it might fade with time and care, but it would always be there. Although she'd learned to tame it, she knew it was always lurking in the shadows, close to the surface, ready to pounce the minute she let her guard down. She was the prey, and her anxiety was her number-one enemy.

Having a routine helped with her stress. She liked to organize her thoughts and feelings just so she could breathe a little easier.

Well, today was its lucky day. And right now, Avery could feel herself being pulled into the abyss, control slipping through her fingers as her anxiety tightened its grip around her chest, slowly climbing up her throat. Anxiety 1 – Avery 0.

She took her phone out of her jean pocket and dialed her emergency person.

"Brooke," Avery managed to get out, trying to breathe through it. "Can you ... please ... come over?" She dry-heaved, but at least the words were out, and Brooke didn't need anything more to understand.

"On my way," she said before hanging up.

Avery let her phone slip out of her sweaty palms onto the floor next to her and tried to focus on her breathing. *One breath in, one breath out.*

Brooke and Avery had met when they were babies— literally, the day they were born. Brooke's parents moved into the same neighborhood when her mother had already been pregnant, and she'd immediately bonded with

Rebecca. They weren't due to give birth at the same time, but Rebecca had gone into labor a month early.

How could they not become best friends after that? They'd grown up like sisters, always in each other's homes, never sleeping alone. They were together every second of every day, through heartbreaks and incredible highs. It was the two of them against the world.

A few other friends had come and gone, but no one really stuck. They were too intimidated by the almost mystic bond between Brooke and Avery, and every last one of them had gotten scared away, except Josh. And just like that, the iconic duo had become the inseparable trio. The memories tightened a string around her heart. She hadn't thought about him in a while, and even though things were better now, every time his face or his name popped into her head, she felt this uneasy feeling, almost like her chest was narrowing shut around her heart.

Back then, they'd been so close. Maybe closer than friends are supposed to be, but what did they know about love? They were teenagers, trying to keep their shit together like everyone else their own age, all while figuring out who they'd wanted to be.

Still, there'd been times where Avery had thought "maybe he should be something more." And she'd wondered if he had felt it too, during those long summer nights at the Toronto Islands, lying in the sand, cradled by the sound of the waves.

Or when Josh had held his first concert at the prestigious Toronto Conservatory, where Brooke and Avery had sobbed in the front row like proud friends, cheering for him just before he'd decided to wink at her. Had he felt it then, too?

And of course, there was that one New Year's Eve party, just before he left. The countdown to 2012 had begun and with a mischievous glint in his eyes, Josh had bent down as the clock struck midnight, and kissed her so softly on her lips, a mere brush of his mouth on hers—even though it had felt like he'd sucked the air right out of her. "Tradition," he'd said after breaking the kiss, while she had been busy struggling to catch her breath.

But before Avery could fully comprehend what that kiss had meant, Josh had announced his decision to leave for Europe, breaking the one promise he was not supposed to. Avery and Brooke had been crushed, like they were suddenly missing a vital part of themselves. They'd gone back to two, trying to figure out how to move on together, while somehow trying to fix the hole in their hearts Josh had created when he'd left them behind. What hurt the most, she thought, was that he'd never come back. Not once.

Avery heard her door fly open and a second later, Brooke barged into her apartment, snapping her out of her spiralling memory. She headed straight to the kitchen, not even stopping to check on Avery. She knew the drill. Avery watched as Brooke boiled some water, got the lavender essential oil and chamomile tea out of the cupboards, and filled Avery's favorite mug with the tea. While the water infused, she took a clean cloth and drizzled a few drops of essential oil on it. She found Avery still face down against the floor, hyperventilating, with Simba snuggled up against her belly.

"Ave, come here, let's get you seated." Brooke kneeled in front of Avery and helped her lean against the wall. She pressed the lavender cloth gently under Avery's nose, leaving a soothing scent for her to breathe in. She handed her the mug.

"Now listen to my voice." Brooke's voice was the most calming sound she knew, her tones as rich as honey. But in that moment, she sounded muffled, the sound barely reaching Avery's ears.

"Focus on my breathing, Ave. One breath in ..." She held her breath and Avery tried to do the same, her lungs burning with the effort. "And let it go now." She exhaled sharply. The second time was slightly better, and by the third attempt, she managed to take a shaky sip of her tea. Her vision was not as blurred as it had been five minutes ago, and she could now focus on Brooke's adorable face too. *That was better.*

"Okay, let's try to focus on something else, let's see ..." Brooke sat next to her, putting her hand on Avery's knee and squeezing gently. One way or another, Avery knew Brooke would manage to shift her attention. She always told these incredible stories, things that could only happen to her.

"Oh, I know! You won't believe what happened to me at work today," she said, mortified. Avery took another sip and the hot liquid burned deliciously down her throat. She smiled a little and took a deep breath. Her breathing was becoming steadier, her hands were less shaky.

"On a scale of 1 to 10, how much do I really want to know the story?" she said, her voice still trembling. *Bright side, at least you can talk like a functioning adult.*

"Oh, you do want to know, trust me," Brooke said with a playful smile. "I told you we had a new intern starting this week, right?"

Avery nodded. Brooke was working for a company that developed apps for small businesses using artificial intelligence, helping to make space for them in the e-commerce world.

"So, today was his official training session with me and I was supposed to show him how we use the company's software for day-to-day scheduling. Listen to this. Our software is called *Planned*, okay? So he opened up Google on his laptop and started to type "p" to download it, and I swear Ave, the first words that appeared in the search bar were 'porn MILF.'"

Avery choked on her tea, bursting into uncontrollable laughter. "What?!"

"I am dead serious. I swear Ave, I was *horri-fied*. I've never seen someone type that fast. I acted like I didn't see anything, but the rest of the day was so awkward."

"Hum, yeah. I mean the rest of the internship will be awkward. You know, you're basically a MILF to him."

"Oh my god stop!" Brooke slapped Avery's arm softly. "I'm only 28, thank you."

"Yeah, isn't he like, 20?"

Brooke made her *Okay, you're right* face. The one where she pinched her mouth into a straight line, trying to suppress a smile, because she knew she'd been busted.

"Nineteen."

Avery let out another laugh. "You should probably start wearing turtlenecks and sweatpants at work, you know, just in case."

"I would still look hot," she smirked.

Avery rolled her eyes. She realized her breathing was back to normal. The apartment was not spinning anymore, and the headache was vanishing slowly. That was her best friend's magic.

She took Brooke's hand. "Thank you," she whispered.

"Anytime." Brooke squeezed her hand. "Always together."

Brooke got up and patted Avery's shoulder. "I'm gonna get started on dinner, you take your time." Dinner was also part of the ritual, nothing fancy, just a big bowl of comforting noodle soup and chocolate chip ice cream.

While Brooke was busy in the kitchen, Avery slipped into more comfortable clothes, her dark blue sweatpants, and her favorite overstretched shirt with Simba's face on it. Alex had gifted it to her on their first Christmas together, almost eight years ago. In her bathroom, she gathered her long caramel hair into a messy bun and splashed cold water on her face, helping her muscles loosen up under the coolness of the tap's stream. She glanced in the mirror, catching the red sploshes on the skin at the base of her neck. She rubbed, as if it would do anything other than worsen it. The thing about her panic attacks was that they didn't go away the minute she could breathe again. They lingered in her chest, hovering around her stomach, for days sometimes, leaving her lightheaded and nauseous, like a reminder that they could ignite again at any moment.

"Ave, it's ready!" Brooke yelled from the kitchen.

The girls settled on the couch with their soup bowls, a wine bottle opened on the table. Avery pulled up a blanket and pushed some cushions behind her back when something occurred to her.

"Hey, am I keeping you from Alice tonight?" Avery hated the fact that Alice was alone tonight, because her girlfriend needed to take care of her poor, lonely best friend. The thought hadn't crossed her mind while she was hyperventilating on the floor, and possibly with good reason, but still. *How selfish of you.* "I didn't think about it B., I'm sorry if I ruined your evening."

She snorted. "Are you kidding? I'm home all the time. Alice was happy to have the house to herself, trust me." She picked a big chunk of noodles up with her chopsticks and looked at Avery. "What's up with you? What happened earlier?"

Avery knew the question was coming but that didn't stop her from wanting to sink into the cushions.

"My dad's thing is in two days. You know, the big shindig he invited me to? Before ... everything? I completely forgot about it. I don't want to go, I don't have a dress, and don't want to spend another minute with him and his snobby friends."

The Alzheimer's Gala was an annual fundraiser in Toronto that happened on World Alzheimer's Day, where hundreds of people gathered to drink, dance, and spend millions bidding to advance research on Alzheimer's disease. Avery's dad had attended this fundraiser for the past 25 years, and she knew how important it was for him, because of his close ties with the disease. His mother had been diagnosed with early-stage Alzheimer's. Avery didn't remember much about her, but she knew her dad had long suffered from seeing his mother go through it.

"You're still not talking to him?" Brooke asked.

"Nope, unless it's an absolute necessity. I'm just not ready to have a conversation with him. It's too soon."

Too soon, too hard, too unforgivable. You pick.

A few months after Avery's awful breakup, her parents had sprung the news of their upcoming divorce on her and her brother during a family dinner, like the most banal thing to say in a random conversation. *"Avery, honey, do you want more potatoes? How about a divorce between your mom and me with that?"*

But that hadn't even been the worst part. Oh no, her dad had never done things half-heartedly. The news might have come as a shock to Avery and her brother, but what followed had left her jaw on the floor. After a long pause and a bunch of remorseful glances, Dan had finally confessed he'd been having an affair with one of his colleagues for the last two years. *Two years.* While he had been telling them how sorry he was for how everything turned out, Avery hadn't been able to stop looking at the heartbreak in her mom's eyes as Avery had realized that her mom had sacrificed everything for a man who'd betrayed her.

Brooke pulled her out of her thoughts. "Are you actually thinking about ditching your father?"

Avery sighed. "No, I can't really do that." Not going to the gala would be the equivalent of dropping a bomb on her already damaged relationship with her dad and forgoing any chances of a peace treaty. It made her stomach twist just thinking about doing it. She couldn't bear knowing she would inevitably disappoint him, no matter how pissed she was with him at the moment. "Don't get me wrong, the thought has crossed my mind more than once, but that would mean the end of our relationship. This is too important for him. I can't get out of it, as much as I want to ..."

"So, what's our game plan?"

"Thought maybe you'd help me with this one."

"Of course you did. I'm the smart one, after all." Brooke winked.

She wasn't wrong. Brooke's mind was almost too advanced for the average human. Avery did not rule out the possibility that her best friend belonged to another species either, as her brain only understood numbers, complex technology, and borderline unsolvable problems, which was the perfect mix for her brilliant career in AI. Avery's situation was arguably less complex, but still needed her best friend's invaluable input.

Brooke sat up on the couch, her legs tucked under her. "Maybe we can take this one step at a time. When did you say the gala is?"

"In two days. Saturday."

"Okay so, let's meet tomorrow. You said you don't have a dress, right?" Avery nodded. "I'll take the day off. We can go have a nice day out together, shop a bit to find you the most gorgeous outfit, maybe get a manicure, have a coffee. You know, just *relax*." Avery liked the sound of that. Brooke knew her so well, she knew exactly what she needed, even when she couldn't figure it out for herself.

"What about your intern? Isn't he going to be lost without you?"

The face Brooke made was enough to pull a laugh out of Avery and raise her palms up. "Okay, okay, I guess he'll survive. That actually sounds perfect," she said.

"Great. And you don't have to go to your dad's house on Saturday. Text him that you'll meet him at the gala. You know how long those things are, but if you can manage to make it until ten, I can come and pick you up. Alice has a show this Saturday." Brooke's girlfriend was a professional ballet dancer, and Brooke had never missed a performance. Four hours. Brooke was only asking her to hold on for four hours.

"I think I can do it," she whispered.

"I *know* you can do it." Brooke took Avery's hands into hers and squeezed them. "I promise time will fly by. Remember to drink, but not too much. Just enough to be tipsy and enjoy the evening. You don't have to stay with Dan the whole time. Have fun, Ave. I promise to come and get you as soon as Alice is done. Then we'll have a sleepover at our place, it's been *forever!*"

They spent the rest of the evening binge-watching *Schitt's Creek* on Netflix while eating their chocolate chip ice cream and finishing the bottle of chardonnay. Simba kept going back and forth between Avery's lap and playing with something on the floor she couldn't identify from the couch.

Avery could feel her panic attack slowing down, even though her chest was still constricted. At least she was able to breathe steadily. And even though she was still apprehensive about the whole thing, the structure Brooke had provided helped her reorganize her thoughts and get a clearer picture of what lay ahead.

The girls kept close to each other on the couch, until Avery fell asleep on Brooke's lap around 1 a.m. Gently, Brooke lifted Avery's head and replaced her knees with a cushion. She got up and pulled the wool blanket they had knitted with Avery's grandmother one winter over her. Half-asleep, Avery heard Brooke feed Simba and slip out of the apartment quietly.

Four

Count On Me

"Nope, nope, nope." Avery shook her head vehemently. "This is not the one." She turned herself in front of the mirror, a mix of horror and disgust on her face. The *very* tight pink dress was way too short for this kind of event. Her breasts were almost spilling out of it.

"But you look so sexy, Ave!!" Brooke was looking at her with her puppy-dog eyes.

"B, come on. I can't wear this to a fundraiser gala, where I am accompanying my *dad*." She pulled on the super thin straps. "I feel like I'm naked. Please, let's go somewhere else."

Brooke put two firm hands on Avery's bare shoulders, looking her straight in her eyes. "Babe, this is the fifth store we've hit today. You've tried everything. Short, long, puffy, sexy, laced, sleeves. *Everything*. Are you trying to sabotage this whole operation?"

Was she? "I just haven't found the right dress yet."

Brooke made a face that said she wasn't buying any of it. "Well, I don't want to rush you, but tick-tock darling. We've got our spa appointment in an hour and a half. One more stop and we've got to go."

Avery sighed and went back into the fitting room to get her *appropriate* clothes back on. Maybe she was trying to stall a bit. How could she choose a dress when she was dreading the entire evening?

"Let's go." She took Brooke by the elbow and dragged her out of the store before she could pick another indecent dress.

They were shopping in Toronto's equivalent of New York City's Fifth Avenue. Bloor and Yorkville streets were lined with small, local boutiques and high-end designer shops, all the big names competing for attention.

The weight of her father's credit card in her purse was a constant reminder of her childhood and of how her father had sacrificed her and Miles for his work and status. There was no way she was going to use it. She would have to settle for a not-too-expensive dress and tap into her savings, all for an evening she didn't even want to go to. *Great, great, great.*

When they entered the next boutique, Avery already felt better. The small local store was refined and elegant. Long dresses hung on rails around the room, orderly and arranged by color, creating a beautiful rainbow of fabric. She scanned the hangers, looking for something to catch her eye, and settled on a gorgeous forest green backless dress.

"I'll try this one on," she told Brooke.

In the fitting room, she slid the satin dress on before spinning and taking a look at herself in the mirror. Avery was speechless. The dress brought out her green eyes and the golden accents in her hair. The thin straps were perfectly fitted on her shoulders and contrasted with the light tone of her skin. While her back was left completely bare, the dress fell flawlessly over her generous hips. In the front, the neckline followed the round curves of her chest, tracing a line to the parted skirt on her right thigh. Heat rose to her cheeks.

Was it too much? It had been a long time since she'd found herself pretty, but this dress definitely gave her a bit of that confidence back.

Loving yourself was a journey, one that had its ups and downs. Every day was a struggle when you were constantly reminded that your body didn't fit society's standards. Avery pinched her ass cheek between her fingers. Some days were easier than others. On those ones, she could look at herself in the mirror and think *So what if my belly isn't toned? Or my thighs are full of stretch marks? "They are the map of your body's history,"* her grandma used to say. *"Be kind to yourself."*

Right now, Avery was really trying her hardest to drill those words into her head. With all the courage she was able to muster, she left the fitting room and faced Brooke.

"Oh my gosh, Ave!!" Brooke sprang to her feet, both hands on her mouth. "You look gorgeous! Tell me you're buying it, please!"

Avery smiled. "I think I will. It's a little bit more than I expected to spend on a dress, but … I really like it." She twirled. "Do you think it's too much? Maybe I should go with something less revealing?"

"I mean, heads will turn, that's for sure." Avery went red again. Not what she was looking for.

"Maybe it's too much, then. I don't want the attention. Maybe I should go with something less shiny."

"Are you kidding? Look at you!" Brooke waved her hands dramatically at Avery. "Ave, you *have* to get this one. So what if people notice you tomorrow night? Don't you want to feel good about yourself? You're doing this for you, not for your father, not for the hundreds of men who will follow you all night like horny teenagers. This dress *screams* confidence. I will never speak to you again if you walk away from it."

Avery rolled her eyes. "Fine. But if the night is a disaster because of it, I will hold you personally accountable."

"I can live with that." Brooke smirked.

"Of course, you can."

Back in the intimacy of the fitting room, Avery turned to face the mirror and squared her shoulders, standing straight. *Yes, you can wear this glamorous outfit. You have nothing to fear because you are a confident woman, in control of her choices and her body.* She put her clothes back on and paid for the dress before she could change her mind.

The rest of the day flew by as Brooke had planned a full afternoon of treatments and pampering at a luxurious spa a couple of blocks down the street, letting Avery finally relax and try to forget what was waiting for her the following night.

♪♫

It was a good thing that Brooke had made them get their nails done the previous day, because it was one less thing for Avery to chew on. She'd woken up this morning, nerves on edge, with even Simba's purring against her chest doing nothing to help calm her anxiety. She was about to spend the evening with her estranged dad, and she couldn't wait for it to be over already.

As if Mother Nature had read her mind, the day's forecast was as grim as it could get, a typical fall day: gray skies and dark clouds. The wind was blowing the colorful leaves off the trees, painting the ground with the vibrant shades the sky was missing today. Avery spent the day lounging around her house, reading Emily Henry's latest book in bed, watching Netflix on her couch, and trying to keep herself busy with some chores and playtime with Simba. Around 3 p.m., the rain started to pour, and Avery simmered with excitement. She grabbed her rain boots and yellow coat and ran outside.

Her love for the rain was unmatched, though for those who didn't know anything about her, it would probably seem weird. It was so peaceful; the sound of drops hitting the pavement, the leaves, the grass. Everything around her seemed to slow down, to quiet. Even her own mind, used to working at 100 miles per hour, would stand still during a downpour. And who could tell then if her face was wet from rain drops or from tears? The rain was her best coping mechanism, but unfortunately, she could not conjure it on demand. So, when given the opportunity,

Avery had always seized it. And there she was, on her front steps, face up towards the thick clouds, smiling gently as the rain drenched her hair, her face and her yellow coat and washed her worries down the drain.

♪♫

Avery got out of a long and relaxing bath around 5 p.m., after a little incident involving Simba losing his balance and plunging head (and claws) first into the tub, scratching his way out. Her thighs were now covered in thin red cuts, courtesy of his royal catness.

Now, with hands shaking slightly, she started getting ready for the gala, carefully brushing her waves, and styling her long hair with pins and clips, so that it would gracefully fall over her left shoulder, leaving the other one bare. She slid on her satin dress and completed her outfit with a pair of gold pumps.

A quick kiss for Simba who was still and staring at the wall, as though hunting something, and she was out the door. Second thoughts and hesitation were not on the menu tonight, because she knew if she started thinking about it too much, she'd already be in sweatpants and back in her bed.

While she was waiting for her Uber, she shot Brooke a text.

Avery [5:20 pm]. On my way. Pick me up at 10 if you can
Brooke [5:22 pm]. Pick you up from where? (jk)
Avery [5:22 pm]. Ha. Ha.
Brooke [5:23 pm]. Try to have fun!
Avery [5:24 pm]. No promises. Tell Alice to break a leg tonight!

Brooke [5:26 pm]. Will tell her you said hi, but she needs both to dance

Avery laughed. There was truly no off-button on Brooke, and that's why Avery loved her.

Avery [5:28 pm]. What's going on with you tonight?
Brooke [5:29 pm]. Nothing! Just my usual charming and loving self
Avery: [5:30 pm]. Don't be late! Love you
Brooke [5:30 pm]. Won't even dream of it. Love you too

♪♫

The gala was held at the Paletta Lakefront Mansion, an impressive estate often used to host events of this magnitude because of its historical character and imposing presence. Avery had shot a couple of weddings and engagement parties there.

As soon as her Uber parked in front of the entrance, Avery felt nauseous. During the drive, she had texted her dad to let him know she was ten minutes away, so she shouldn't have been surprised that he was right there, waiting for her in the driveway, in his impeccable black tux that contrasted with his glistening white hair. She would have recognized his posture anywhere: tall and upright, one hand on his suit, the other in his pocket. He was dashing, all sharp points and clean lines.

Avery took a deep, slow breath, and another, before she got out of the car.

"Hi bug." Unsure of how to proceed, Dan took an awkward step towards her, his arms slightly extended. He had never been the hugging kind, so she didn't even know why he wanted to try now.

"Hi," Avery muttered. Her heart was beating so fast against her ribcage, it almost felt like she didn't have a pulse anymore. She accepted her dad's invitation and awkwardly hugged him back.

"I missed you." Her heart dropped. Had he ever said that to her? Ever? "I was thinking. Maybe we could get lunch together, tomorrow perhaps?"

Avery broke the embrace first, and took a step back, confused. "Um, no? The only reason I'm here tonight is because I told you I would be. That's it. It doesn't change anything else."

Dan sighed. "I want to work this out, bug," he said, gesturing between the two of them.

"There's nothing to work out, so don't waste your time." It was too much, too fast. Avery felt her anxiety slowly creep in, showing its face in her fingertips, steadily making its way up her arms, down her belly.

"I hope you don't mean that."

Her stomach, her chest, her throat, all began to burn.

"I'm sorry, I need a minute." Avery disappeared from view, away from prying eyes, before Dan could object. *Pull yourself together, Avery*. One breath in. One breath out. And again. And again. Her muscles started to relax, and air slowly entered her lungs.

She couldn't believe that he'd had the audacity to ask her out to lunch, before even thinking about apologizing for what he'd done to their family, and completely dismissing her feelings in the same breath, like she wasn't the more reasonable adult out of the two of them. The irony was too great not to laugh. Her anxiety dimmed and made way for a new kind of emotion, one she didn't feel often.

As she went back to her dad, she straightened up and gave him her coldest glare, bringing her tone to a chilling degree. "I am not here for you. I am not here for your questionable decision-making skills. I am here because I told you I would be, and I intend to keep my word. I will smile and shake hands and be an adoring daughter for the night. At 10 p.m., I will leave, and that will be the end of it. Work for you?"

Dan's throat worked harder. He wasn't used to being put in his place, and Avery knew he was really close to saying something back. *Let him try and I'll be out of his life before he knows it.* Thinking better of it, he nodded. "Sounds good."

"One last thing. I am not 'bug' tonight. You lost the privilege to call me that when you lied straight to my face for the last two years, or god knows how long."

As stoic and rigid as he could sometimes be, his eyes betrayed him every time. She could see the hurt she just caused in his warm hazel eyes. She knew which buttons to push, and which trigger to pull. And right now, he looked like she just ripped his heart out.

Dan cleared his throat. "Let's go then." And just like that, they were making their way into Avery's worst nightmare.

Five

Strangers

The mansion was already filled with people when Dan and Avery made their way inside. On her father's arm, she plastered a forced smile on her face and shook hands with people she was introduced to. "You've got a beautiful daughter, Dan." *Smile.* "You must be so proud of her." *Smile.* "She's very lucky to have such an extraordinary father." *Smile and nod.* The circus went on and on, and they hadn't even made it to the coat check yet.

As one of the longest-standing attendees of the gala and a renowned scientist, people were instantly drawn to her father. They all wanted a word, to show their face, crossing their fingers that the brilliant and highly selective Dan Clark would remember them when he assembled the next team for his forthcoming research.

Avery was already bored to death. How many people would she have to fake her enthusiasm to for the next four hours? The pair finally ran out of hands to shake and shoulders to pat in the grand hall and managed to make it to the attendant who took their personal belongings. As soon as she took her coat off, as predicted by Brooke yesterday, all eyes were on her. A rush of embarrassment quickly colored her cheeks as Dan looked at her with an emotion she couldn't quite read.

"Avery," he breathed. "You are absolutely stunning." Her father grabbed her hand and squeezed it.

"Thank you," Avery said, releasing her hand gently from his. She didn't want to hurt him more than she already had tonight, but she also knew what she could endure.

With her hands free, Avery stopped the first waiter with a tray and grabbed a glass of champagne, gulping it down like a shot. *There, better already.* She waved at her father, who was in a seemingly fascinating discussion with two middle-aged men, to let him know she was heading into the main room.

It had been a long time since Avery had attended this type of event, and she'd forgotten how stunning these evenings could be. The mansion was tastefully decorated with purple and white balloon arches, the colors of the Alzheimer's charity. Bouquets of white roses and lilies, and purple peonies and forget-me-nots were scattered all over the room; on the stage, along the rows of white chairs set up for the auction and on the small tables where people were drinking their cocktails, waiting for the evening to begin. At the back of the room, Avery spotted the bar next to the large French doors that looked out onto the vast, covered garden where the rest of the reception would take place.

The room was pure luxury and opulence. It reminded Avery of her childhood, when she and Brooke used to run wild among the designer dresses and tuxedos, stuffing their faces with sweets and dancing to the orchestra until they were both out of breath. Or when Josh danced with her when she was sixteen, cheek to cheek, to "Just the Way You Are" by Bruno Mars, while her parents were busy trying to convince their rich friends to donate large sums of money to fund a new research center for the Toronto General Hospital.

If she closed her eyes, she knew she'd be transported right back to that moment. Tonight though, she was alone, standing in a room full of people staring at her dress, or rather, staring at her. The attention made her head spin, and she realized she could use a second drink before the auction started.

A few moments later, she joined her father, who was already settled in their reserved seats. Glancing at her phone, she did some quick math. One hour down, three to go. With a bit of luck, the auction would take an hour or so, then dinner, and then Avery could start moving slowly toward the exit. As she put her phone back in her purse, she felt it buzz.

Brooke [6:55 pm]. Hope all is going well. Just know that I am thinking about you. The show is about to start here.

She smiled. It was good to have someone in her life that supported her the way Brooke did. She felt invincible.

Avery [7:02 pm]. As good as expected. Stuffing my face with shrimp and champagne. Wish I could be with you. Enjoy!

Tonight's auction mostly included art donated by private owners. Avery and her father were given an auction paddle to join in the bidding, although Avery was pretty sure she couldn't even afford the chair she was seated on.

As the auctioneer took to the stage, holding a microphone in his hands, Avery noticed the grand piano standing next to him, and she wondered how much it would be auctioned for. It *looked* very expensive.

"Good evening, ladies and gentlemen," the man on stage said, interrupting her guessing game and causing the room to slowly fall silent. "It is my great honor to be your host for tonight's auction at the 25th annual Alzheimer's Gala." A round of applause broke out.

"Thank you. As you all know, Alzheimer's disease and other forms of dementia affect almost a million Canadians every year. The toll that this illness takes on patients and their families who have to care for them is beyond measure. We've come together tonight, as we do every year, to raise funds to help scientists and researchers get closer to finding successful treatments." As another round of applause was heard, Avery glanced at her father, emotion all over his face. She knew he was thinking about his mother.

"But before starting the auction tonight, I have a little surprise for you." Avery turned her attention to the host.

"We haven't seen him in our beautiful city in a long time, but after several years travelling all across Europe, he has finally decided to come back home and grace us with his presence on stage. Ladies and gentlemen, please give a warm welcome to our very own Joshua Harding!"

Avery's heart jolted in her chest, tripping over its own beat. Was her mind playing tricks on her?

But if she doubted that she'd heard correctly, his entrance on stage confirmed it. Josh was here. In front of her. Waving at the audience. Her mind could not process what her eyes were seeing. She realized that her hands were shaking when she absently raised one to her mouth in absolute shock as her breath faltered, and her eyes filled with tears, threatening to ruin her makeup. She didn't know if they were tears of joy, anger, sadness, surprise or just a freaking mix of the above. All she could do was follow the lead of the other guests and applaud mechanically.

Her eyes followed him as he made his way to the piano. God, he was stunning. Avery knew what Josh looked like in a tux at 16, but Josh in a tux at 29 was simply breathtaking, all traces of the boyish features she remembered gone. That hurt, knowing she'd missed him becoming a man, the person he was standing in front of her. It felt like a loss she didn't know she had been mourning. In her mind, the memory of him was stuck with his too-long wavy hair always falling in his eyes, and his skinny body made for running the fastest in school. What else had she missed? What had happened to him during all those years apart? Being kept in the dark now that she could grasp the magnitude of the changes that ten years without contact looked like was suddenly unbearable. She used to know what he did every minute of every day, heard his voice go through puberty, saw his shoulders go from lanky to athletic. Now he felt like a complete stranger. What did he sound like now? Did he still gobble down sweet pastries in one big bite, afraid someone might steal the guilty pleasure right out from under his nose? Did he still have that mischievous spark in his eyes, the one that always promised trouble?

Avery had the sudden urge to run on stage and find out for herself. Ask him all these questions straight away. She needed to know who he was now and if the man he'd become was still the Josh she remembered. Kind and thoughtful. Goofy. And the best friend she'd ever had, next to Brooke. *Former* best friend, she corrected herself, reminded of the bitter truth that had been hanging all these years between them. He had left when he'd promised her he wouldn't. And he had never looked back. So ... that was that.

She pushed her unwelcomed thought away, and swept her eyes down his body. He was tall and lean, in an athletic way that came with years of running track in high school. *Guess he continued to run.* She could still distinguish the same silhouette, but with ten years refining and defining his frame. His chestnut brown curls were cropped shorter than they used to be, styled slightly to the side, so they wouldn't fall in front of his eyes, she assumed. His face was shaved, showing a strong jawline and high cheekbones Avery did not remember. She couldn't quite see his eyes from where she was and that was probably a good thing, because she remembered the carnage they could wreak on her heart.

Look at the mess you already are. Can you imagine if he raised those two ocean blue eyes to you?

She shook her head. She was mesmerized, gaping like a freaking fish. And since she was not meant to live under the sea, she remembered she needed air and took a deep, unsteady breath.

She wasn't sure how to handle the situation. Hell, she wasn't even in control of her own body right now. Josh couldn't see her from where he was, which hopefully gave her a bit of time to come up with a plan. Avery glanced at her father, who was focused on the stage, oblivious to her internal freakout. At least she was doing it quietly. She didn't combust or scream out loud because nobody was looking at her. This was good. *Small victories, right?*

Josh sat behind the piano and approached the microphone in front of him.

"Thank you everyone, it's good to be back." Avery's heart sank at the familiar sound of his voice. It was deeper, richer, vibrating through her rib cage like a double bass string. And yet, she could still hear the soothing notes that used to calm and ground her, all those years ago.

"This song has always been with me while I've lived in Europe, far from my family and my friends, and I would like to dedicate it to someone who always felt like home during my darkest and loneliest moments. Someone who reminded me of where I come from, no matter where I was, like an anchor to who I am deep inside. I don't know where in the world she is now, but Avery, this one's for you."

Dan shot her a questioning look, but she didn't have time to address it because Josh started to play and everything Avery thought she knew no longer made sense. The world around her disappeared as Josh stroked the first piano keys, his fingers flying delicately from one end to the other. It felt like she was in one of those old Hollywood movies, where everything turned dark, except for the soft glow of the spotlight showcasing the pianist. The ambient noise faded away, the camera focused on the artist before slowly shifting to the young woman in the audience, captivated by the music, and the man behind the piano.

The melody flew effortlessly from his hands to reach Avery, right in the little organ currently galloping inside her chest. An invisible thread connecting her to his music. There was a lot to unpack in what he had just said. She and Josh hadn't talked in years. But this song ... oh, she knew this song all too well.

Just before he'd left Toronto, Josh, Avery and Brooke had driven to his family home in Niagara-on-the-Lake to spend the fall break there. Josh's dad and sister had stayed in the city, and Avery's parents were busy as usual. The place was gorgeous, a sandy-white beach house that overlooked the immensity of Lake Ontario. A true holiday postcard, and their perfect paradise. During summertime, they used to run through the garden and jump into the lake at first light, only coming out to eat watermelon slices, or when their limbs were too tired to keep their heads above water.

But on that fall night, ten years ago, while Brooke had been busy cooking them dinner, Josh had settled behind the piano and started to play Franz Listz's "Liebesträume No. 3."

Tonight, it was "Liebesträume" that reverberated again in the room. It brought Avery right back to that October night. Her, slumped in the pillows on the floor, pumpkin spice candles and the fireplace warming up the night, the scent of homemade lasagna from the kitchen filling the air as Josh had sat behind the piano.

"Want me to play something?" he asked while she was plumping the pillows on the floor to make herself cozy.

"Always." Avery smiled. "But maybe we should wait for B?"

He settled behind the piano, brushing the keys with the tip of his fingers. "Nah. I think she's busy with dinner. Don't worry, I'll play again later."

Josh flashed her a smile before he started to play, and like every time he did, Avery couldn't take her eyes off him. There was something very intimate in playing music or singing in front of someone else, like you purposely let your guard down and chose to let the other person see who you truly were, your flaws and your weaknesses. Every time Josh played, and she had the privilege to listen, she saw his vulnerability shine through his every pore, and everything he wouldn't say out loud.

But tonight especially, emotions caught in her throat as she listened to the most romantic music she'd ever heard. The sweet melody rippled through Avery's body like little waves crashing against her heart, flooding her entirely with an unexpected feeling.

She wondered for a moment if Josh had intentionally played this song for her, but that thought was obliterated when for a brief instant, he looked up and gazed at her a little too long, heavy meaning behind his lashes.

Brooke came out of the kitchen with plates and wine at the same time, pulling Josh's focus away from Avery's eyes, and back on the piano, while Avery was left with her cheeks burning and a hundred unanswered questions.

"Damn Josh," Brooke said, "Who are you trying to sleep with tonight?" Avery almost choked on her own saliva. *"So romantic."*

"I felt inspired," he mumbled, but loud enough for Avery to have heard him.

The applause from the crowd snapped Avery back to reality, as Josh rose and bowed to the audience a few times. As he straightened up, his eyes caught Avery's and he froze there, mid-bend, something passing on his face she could not quite read. She held her breath, unsure of what to do, before he finally broke away and hurried off the stage.

Fuck, fuck, fuck.

She was not ready to face him. What were the chances of stumbling into him tonight of all nights, when she was already trying *so hard* to keep her shit together and be the good daughter her father expected her to be? What could she say to him, and more importantly, what could *he* say? Was he back for good? How long had he been back? Why hadn't he tried to call her all these years? Or had he? Did Brooke know? *Why had he abandoned her when she'd needed him?* So many questions, but she wasn't sure she wanted the answers.

♪♫

"I need to speak with some folks over there, are you okay by yourself?" her father asked after the auction ended.

Avery waved him off. "Yes, I'm fine. Don't worry about me."

She made her way through the crowd towards the bathroom because a little something told her she needed it. A quick glance in the mirror confirmed she was a total disaster. Her cheeks were flushed, and her mascara had run slightly under her eyes, giving her the infamous panda look. At least her hair was okay. She fumbled into her purse and dug out her travel makeup bag.

In that moment, she was grateful for her organizational skills. She splashed water on her face and proceeded to remove her makeup, because the last thing she wanted was to look like she didn't have her shit together. Not that she did, but she *needed* to look the part. Ten years without seeing him, and the first time *could not* be with her face all sweaty and looking like a five-year-old had done her makeup.

All freshened up and her make up carefully reapplied, she forced herself out toward the bar. If they were going to do this, she'd need to be a bit more buzzed than she was.

A glass of champagne in her hand, both elbows propped on the counter, Avery started to think about what she was going to say. "Hey Josh, remember me?" Nope, definitely not. "Long time no see, coward." Maybe a *tad* aggressive. "What's up, travel boy?" She facepalmed herself. *Way worse.*

"Avery?" The familiar sound came from behind her. She turned around quickly, startled by his sudden presence, and smashed her glass into Josh's chest. Champagne spilled all over his crisp white shirt.

"Oh my god, oh my god! I'm so, *so sorry*!!" She. Was. Mortified. *You just had to be clumsy tonight, Avery.*

Josh looked a bit stunned by the turn of events as Avery hurried to grab several napkins and started to dab them on his shirt to absorb the liquid. Under her shaking fingers, his chest was hard and sharply defined, and she *knew* she definitely shouldn't be noticing. *Bad idea, bad idea. Red alert. Abort.* But she didn't stop until Josh gently caught her wrists and pulled her hands off his shirt. Well *that* definitely made her freeze. She looked up.

"It's fine, it's fine." He smiled slightly, her wrists still burning from the contact of his fingers on her skin. She wondered why she felt like this. Like the simple sight and touch of him would destroy her. She thought maybe it was because she hadn't seen him in years, and the last thing she expected to see tonight was Josh in a tux, playing a song she'd held so close to her heart for years in front of hundreds of people. No, *this*, she definitely hadn't planned.

"Would you mind waiting for me here, while I go clean up?" *As if I could move of a damn bone in my body right now.* She nodded.

"Of ... of course," she stammered.

"Thanks." Josh started to turn away but stopped dead in his tracks and faced Avery. "Please, don't go anywhere. I'll be right back."

It took him fifteen minutes to return, his shirt impeccably clean, like nothing had happened. Avery was standing at the exact same spot he'd left her, the one difference being that her glass had been filled.

"I always have a spare in the car," Josh explained, as Avery gazed at his shirt, surprised. He hesitated, clearly uncomfortable. *Stop staring, you creep.*

"Um … Do you want to get out of here? I know it's weird, but I'd love to talk somewhere quieter."

Before Avery could answer that yes, she would love to run away from this party, the music started playing and the guests were ushered on to the dance floor, surrounding them and giving them no way out. Several guests were looking quizzingly at them, probably wondering what the handsome and talented pianist was doing with an ordinary woman like her. Panic ran through her body as she understood the apologetic glint in Josh's eyes. He extended his hand, palm up.

"I don't think we can leave *now,*" he said, sounding as thrilled as she felt. She didn't want to do this at all, too many memories resurfaced at the idea of dancing together.

"I guess we can't," she finally said.

She let her hand fall in his and Josh led them to the middle of the room. Carefully, he slid his hand down her back, and Avery shivered. Surprise registered in his eyes when his fingers brushed her bare back. The touch was too intimate for someone you'd last seen when you were still a teenager. The body was a beautiful and fascinating thing, able to memorize details and store them away, like it had a mind of its own. As Josh held her close, her body responded to his citrus scent, his familiar touch and his warmth, like a dormant fire brought back to life. But at the same time, it knew something was different, like years apart had altered the memories of him.

She discreetly raised her eyes to scan Josh's face and was immediately taken aback by the toughness in his features. He was looking straight ahead, lips drawn in a thin line, brows knitted together like he was trying to solve a mystery happening at the other end of the room. His jaw was clenched tight, highlighting the sharp lines there. What was she supposed to make of this? She wasn't comfortable with the situation either, but at least she didn't look disgusted by it. She was tempted to step on his foot, just so he could justify looking so irritated.

But despite the stiffness of his touch, his hand still firmly placed on the small of her back, Avery could feel the tenderness of his skin on hers, and she knew he felt it too.

Mid-song, the tempo of the music picked up and unexpectedly, Josh twirled her around, and before her brain could register what was happening, she lost her balance and came crashing against his chest. Both hands on her waist, Josh steadied her.

"I'm ... I'm so sorry!" She was burning red right now as her pulse quickened and panic crept in.

"No, no, it's me, I'm sorry, I don't know why I did that, it was stupid." He passed a hand in his hair, leaving a mess in its wake. She pushed herself out of his embrace and put some distance between them. *Dial down the clumsiness for god's sake, Avery.*

"I think we've danced enough for another ten years," she laughed stiffly, trying to defuse the tension. He gave her what she could only assume was a forced smile because his jaw still looked like it was ready to snap. Seeing him so aloof, unable to even crack a real smile at *her*, his once upon a time best friend, broke something in her. She suppressed bitter laughter. And here she thought he had done all the damage he could. Clearly, their friendship hadn't survived the test of time, and that reality check was like a punch in the gut. With all the courage in the world she could summon, Avery straightened up, put a brave face on, and tried not to let her emotions show on her face.

"Well, it was nice seeing you again, Josh. Enjoy the rest of your night." She turned around and walked away, tears threatening to spill out. *Hold it in, don't you dare cry over him.*

How could he still have this effect on her, ten years later? It wasn't fair. It had been a silly teenage crush then, and it was a complete disaster now. Their friendship was in limbo, like a big cosmic joke reminding her that all she was good for was being left behind.

"Avery, wait," Josh called behind her, but she didn't slow her pace down. "Would you please stop ... Avie, *please* wait a sec."

Avie. The sound of his nickname for her made her stop instantly. Nobody had called her that in *years*. The last time she'd heard it was the day he had left, when he'd told her he was going to miss her. *"So fucking much, Avie."* She swallowed past the lump in her throat.

Josh caught up to her easily, grabbed her hand, and Avery could not hold it in any longer. Tears rolled freely down her cheeks, and this time, she wasn't able to stop them. She didn't want to. He turned her around and his eyes softened when he saw her crying. Josh tightened his grip around her fingers and drew her back against him, tightening his arms around her shoulders.

"I'm so sorry Avie, I'm so sorry," he mumbled into her hair. He repeated those words again and again, until her sobs began to ease.

"I didn't expect to see you here tonight," he continued. "It caught me off guard and ... and ..."

Nestled in the hollow of his neck, Avery inhaled the distinct scent of his golden-brown skin, aware of her own heart pounding against his chest. His hands were drawing small circles on her back, attempting to soothe her but really, all it did was set her on fire. Josh took a big breath.

"And it's been so long. I don't know where to start, how to apologize, what to say or what to do."

"I don't know either," she confessed.

Josh moved her away from him, just enough to be able to look at her.

"How about I take us to my favorite place? No fancy shrimp, no champagne, no small talk. Just us."

"No champagne?" Avery pretended to pout. He chuckled, the sound rich and sweet to her ears.

"Alright. Wait for me by the entrance, I'll join you in two minutes, okay?"

"Okay," she murmured.

Avery watched him make his way to the bar and gasped as she saw him dip behind it and grab two bottles of champagne as discreetly as he could.

Quickly, she texted Brooke that she didn't need her to come and pick her up after all, and that everything was fine, before putting her phone on silent because she just knew her best friend would blow her phone up.

Josh walked over to her at a quick pace, the bottles in hand.

"You have absolutely no shame, do you?" Avery said, amused. "How old are you?!"

"Shhh quiet, act normal." He placed his hand on her back and guided her toward the door and as soon as they were outside, he started laughing.

"Okay now, run!"

Six

Always Remember Us This Way

"**Y**ou want to go to the islands … now?"

They were standing in front of the Toronto Island ferry gates, the streetlights flickering and giving the empty harbor an eerie atmosphere worthy of the best horror movies. It was almost 9:30 p.m. and the champagne was starting to wear off. Avery was more and more aware of the fact that she was alone with someone she barely knew anymore, and apparently about to hop on a boat to head to some deserted place where the only living creatures around would be beavers and minks. *Abso-fucking-lutely great decision-making skills there, Ave.*

Josh smiled a devilish grin. "Come oooon, where is the reckless and spontaneous Avery I know?"

At that, Avery stared at him dead in the eyes. "You *knew*," she corrected, because she couldn't help herself. She had the right to be petty. "Last I checked, we haven't talked in ten years, so I wonder what you think you still know about me, Josh."

"Touché." He ran a hand through his hair and slid it down his face, rubbing his impossibly square jaw. "Remember when we used to go to Ward's Island beach every time we needed a break?" Avery nodded. Of course, she remembered. She was surprised he did though.

Josh looked at her desperately. How the fuck could she resist that. "I just want to hit the pause button for a few hours and talk like we used to. Can we do that, Ave?"

He took a step closer to her and placed both hands on her arms, the light pressure of his touch sending shivers down her spine. "I know it's a lot to ask. Trust me, *I know.*"

His eyes searched hers pleadingly, sadness seeping in the electric blue of his irises. "Please, Avie," he whispered, and Avery could actually feel her heart break right here, right now.

Don't say it. Do not say it. Do not — "Okay." *Damn it.* "Let's go before I change my mind."

"Thank you," he whispered.

The boat trip to Ward Island was silent, the only sounds coming from the waves splashing around the ferry. The lights of the city reflected in the calm water, giving the lake the feel of an impressionist painting with the purple, orange and yellow colors blurred by the little ripples of water. Avery cast her gaze on the beautiful city ahead.

Toronto. The New York of Canada, as she's often called.

And yet, where New York City was an endless bustle, the city that never sleeps, Toronto was a unique blend of tranquility and urbanity, where the people lived a quieter, more carefree existence.

Avery had always thought of Toronto as a big, warm hug. One you'd gladly jump into when you needed a little bit of solace. Everyone was embraced here. Diversity was celebrated, and she'd never felt a sense of community like this anywhere else. The number of times she'd run to her downstairs neighbors, or the ones across the street to ask for a pint of milk because she'd forgotten to buy some at the store. Or how every time Mrs. Pradhan from two doors down the street cooked butter chicken, Avery always ended up with some for her lunch.

The city looked so big from here, but the reality was, it had always felt small. Just one giant family.

And that was also why she had never understood Josh's decision to leave. Who would want to give up a city like this, where everyone was someone, part of an ecosystem that relied on acceptance and kindness?

She watched as Josh stood against the boat railing, his back to her, admiring the beautiful city skyline and looking lost in his own thoughts. It was a full moon tonight, the soft light outlining his broad shoulders underneath his tuxedo jacket as both of his hands were braced tightly on the railing.

The last time she'd seen him, he was telling her and Brooke goodbye, and to this day, she could still remember the pain she'd felt that afternoon.

"I'm sorry, you're doing what?" Shocked was the understatement of the year. Avery's mouth suddenly went dry. She forced herself not to cry, because there had to be a perfectly reasonable explanation for what she'd just heard come out of Josh's mouth.

"There's nothing left for me here, Avie. I need a change of scenery, and fast." Josh had texted their BFF group chat today, asking them to meet after school at their usual spot in the city, away from the end-of-day hustle and bustle of the financial district. From the lawn of the old University of Toronto, they could make out the city skyline and the emblematic CN Tower. It was a peaceful and unusually warm day for February, although every inch of the lawn was still covered in snow.

But right this instant, there was no longer anything peaceful about this place, because Josh had just dropped something major on them, with no warning in sight.

"This is completely ridiculous," Brooke said, looking him straight in the eyes. She was pissed, and Avery knew all too well that Pissed Brooke was not a version of her best friend she enjoyed seeing. She was certain Brandon from their physics class still remembered to never, ever say to a girl again that she was "too pretty to like science."

"You know that, right? Surely, you must know that this is completely INSANE." Brooke got up on her feet from the bench she and Avery were sitting on, dragging her boots in the snow as she paced around them. Avery, her polar opposite, sat still, completely numb to what she had just heard.

"Listen, guys, I have to do this," Josh said. "I cannot stand to be here anymore, I need to go."

"You cannot stand to be here anymore? Are you for real right now Josh?"

"I didn't mean it like that Brooke, and you know it!" The accusatory tone in his usually warm voice caught Brooke off-guard.

"I just don't understand how you can be telling us that you're moving to Spain. Senior year isn't even over for another four months! Help me make sense of it, please."

Avery watched as the unbelievable scene unfolded right in front of her. It felt like she was on a night out with her friends to the theater, and was a spectator to a really, really bad play. She couldn't mutter a word, couldn't even think straight, because all she'd heard was that Josh was leaving, and that could just not be. Because if he was leaving, he was breaking the promise he'd made to her on Brooke's sweet sixteen, the only promise that mattered to her, and the one he'd sworn to never break.

"I don't want to leave you guys, but I have to do this for me. I have to put myself first. I cannot spend another minute in my house and ..." His voice, the voice that was usually so full of confidence, started to shake. "I need to make her proud."

He turned to face Avery, his eyes desperately searching hers and imploring her to understand him, understand his pain, his impossible decision, but she knew that deep down she could not, because she just wasn't that strong. He hadn't even left yet, and she was already unraveling, losing a vital piece of herself, one that she hadn't given him permission to take.

Brooke was still standing up, bouncing her leg nervously.

"When?" It was barely audible, and it took everything she had, but Avery needed to know.

He winced. "When what?"

"When are you leaving?" Josh's features twisted in pain, guilt plastered on his face. Avery knew how to read him perfectly. She had spent an unhealthy amount of time *studying every line and every corner and had memorized each intricacy on his beautiful, flawless face. When he took a deep breath, he finally revealed the whole truth.*

"Tomorrow."

"Tomorrow?!" *Brooke shouted.* "Jesus Josh, thanks for the heads up! How long have you been planning this for?"

"A while, I guess." He put his head in his hands and let out a labored breath. "It's only been finalized since December."

"That was two months *ago." Brooke would never forgive him, Avery knew it. "Wow, I guess Avery and I should feel lucky you're not skipping town on us, huh?" She gave Avery's shoulder a little tap. "Ave, say something for fuck's sake."*

All eyes were suddenly on her, but all Avery could hear was the loud ringing in her ears, hindering her every thought. His mind was made up, what could she possibly say that would change anything?

"Why?"

Josh kneeled in front of her and took her hands in his, gently massaging the back of them. Avery could sense that he was trying to reach something inside her, to make her feel what he was feeling right now, but her shock was overtaking every cell in her body. Her walls that had never been up when it came to him had risen firmly, faster than a snap of the fingers.

"You know why, Avie ..." His voice was soft, heavy with regret and unspoken truths.

"No, we don't!" Brooke cut him out sharply.

"Yes, you do!" Josh yelled and stood up. "You think this is easy for me?! Leaving you guys behind, my little sister? I got

accepted into the piano program at the conservatory here and I'm turning it down, you know why?"

There was no stopping him now. His voice cracked and tears rolled on his cheeks. "Because it's too fucking much. I see her everywhere Brooke. Every inch of this city is tainted with her perfume, her laugh, the sound of her heels on the pavement, and it's unbearable. I cannot spend another second in a room she used to spend her days in, trying my damn best to make her proud despite the fact that my own father doesn't believe in me, and not completely lose my shit over the fact that she is gone. My life is a constant reminder that I will never see her again. I can't breathe anymore, it has to stop. It has to stop, because if it doesn't ... I will," he said, slamming his hand against his chest.

Brooke fell completely silent, stunned by the outburst that was so unlike him. Josh shifted his attention to Avery, still kneeling, his knees bumping against her legs.

"Avie, please, please say something. Tell me you understand."

When he took her face in his sweaty palms, tears still running down his cheeks, she thought that seeing him like that would have torn her apart and ripped her heart to pieces. The agony in his eyes was excruciating, but all she felt was utter emptiness. She wanted to beg him to stay, to scream at him for even thinking about leaving her, but her mind was blank and her body lifeless. Avery pulled herself out of his touch and slowly stood up, staring into space.

"I guess ... goodbye." It was effortless. All she had to do was breathe.

"Goodb … goodbye?! That's what you have to say to me?" He glanced at Brooke who still looked upset, arms crossed over her chest, before he turned back to Avery.

And then something changed in his eyes, she could tell. Maybe he was giving up, maybe he was accepting that they would never be okay with his decision, but Avery could see that this moment was about to end, and it would be the last time she would see him.

In one swift motion, Josh stood up and brought Avery with him, closing the distance between them as he crushed his body against hers, every inch of them connecting. She was limp in his arms, completely lost in his scent and his tears that were dampening her hair, even though she felt her body coming alive under his desperate touch. Josh pressed a long kiss to her temple, where a few strands of wet hair were beginning to stick. His lips trembled against her skin.

"I will write when I'm ready."

She laughed—she didn't know if it had been out loud or in her head, but she laughed at the hollowness of his words. "I'm gonna miss you so fucking much, Avie," he whispered, so only she could hear. When his mouth moved close to her ear, his hot breath penetrated her like a million little daggers. "Please, forgive me."

He pulled away as suddenly as he had embraced her, leaving her cold and her body aching at the loss of his warmth.

Avery watched him gather his things and make his way toward Brooke. As he was about to hug her one last time, she took a step back.

"Don't."

"Brooke, come on. Please." Trying to reason with Pissed Brooke was a waste of time.

"I can't, I'm sorry. Hope you find what you're looking for over there." She walked toward Avery and slid her arm around her waist, holding her firmly against her. It was just the two of them again. "Don't call us." Brooke's last words had the effect of a slap in the face. Avery watched as his whole body took the blow. Josh nodded silently, gave Avery one last loaded look, and walked away. And it just about broke her.

Avery brushed away a tear on her cheek as the boat reached the deck. Ten minutes later, they were on the beach, the faint muddy smell of the lake floating in the air, Toronto's skyline behind them, and nothing but darkness ahead. This place held a lot of memories, and Avery was caught off-guard by the images that came flooding back in.

All of a sudden, it was like they were fifteen again, sitting on this beach, without a care in the world. Josh burying his feet in the sand with Avery's head on his stomach while they both looked for the constellations they couldn't see back in the city. They would talk for hours, Josh about his relationship with his dad, the weight of his expectations and his mother's legacy, his Mexican roots that left him more often than not lost in his identity.

They would tell each other stuff they wouldn't dare say out loud anywhere else, or to anybody else. Avery would open up about her anxiety, her mom's depression and her father's absence, while Josh played absently with the waves in her hair. Brooke would join them too sometimes, and they'd spend the night dreaming about their future, laughing so loud at Josh attempting cartwheels their lungs hurt, eating smores and falling asleep in a tangle of sweaty and drowsy bodies to the lulling sound of waves.

When Josh's mother passed away, this beach became their own little oasis, the only escape from the excruciating pain Avery knew he felt every single day.

She would listen to him talk for hours about his mom, and what made her who she was. How the sound of her laugh still resonated with him every day. How he'd kept one of her scarves that still smelled like her, honey and lavender. Josh would come alive every time he talked about her love for music and the grace she exuded when she played the piano, the one thing that still connected him to her, he used to say. But he would also talk about his complete disbelief that she was truly gone for good, sobbing into the slope of her neck, his body vibrating with pain.

And as she looked at him now, walking in front of her, the boy who'd wept in her arms so many times all those years ago turned around and stared back at her with the same eyes, only now with some wrinkles at their corners, and the same smile, only now with a more masculine and defined jaw. The sight took Avery's breath away, and all her nervousness with it, because it was him. It was Josh, and despite all the years and miles that had come between them, she knew how easily she could fall right back into old habits. It was kind of fitting, come to think of it, to be back here tonight, after ten years apart, ready to untangle the intricacies of their lives.

"You coming?" Josh called.

Heels in her hand, and the hem of her dress in the other, she sank her feet into the cold sand and walked to where Josh stood.

"Here, let me." He shrugged his tux jacket off, his biceps flexing under his shirt and stretching the fabric. She couldn't help but stare, transfixed by the movement, while Josh laid his jacket on the sand, waving for her to sit down.

"You didn't have to do that," she said, but still appreciated the thoughtfulness behind his gesture.

"Couldn't ruin this gorgeous dress." He smiled softly as he sat next to her. "So ..."

"So ..."

Josh chuckled, fiddling with a little rock between his fingers. "I guess a good start would be an apology." His eyes found hers, reaching to take her small fingers in his hands. "I'm profoundly sorry, Avie. For so many things, I don't know where to start, honestly. I'm sorry for running away and leaving you behind, and I'm sorry for disappearing on you and not reaching out during all those years."

He shook his head as his thumb drew small circles on the back of her hand and all her focus was narrowed down to this one simple touch.

"You don't know how many times I picked up the phone to call you, how much I missed you. At first, I was telling myself I needed a break from my old life, I needed to heal and start fresh somewhere new. I thought you would have never answered anyway after our goodbye." *I probably wouldn't have.*

"And then, next thing I knew, it'd already been several years, and I couldn't just text or call you out of the blue after being radio silent for all this time. I had no right to do so, to disturb your life because it fit my schedule. I thought you had probably forgotten about me and moved on at that point anyway ..."

Josh sighed, looking down at their intertwined fingers. "I know I hurt you, Avie. And I'll probably never forgive myself for that. But I was in a really dark place back then. I wasn't myself, I needed to get away."

Avery was stunned by his confession, confused by the fact that he *had* thought about her, when she had all but convinced herself that he'd left without looking back. She wasn't sure if she was supposed to feel better knowing she meant something to him, or furious that he had never tried to show it to her.

Slowly, she pulled her hand from his grip, trying to regain a bit of brainpower in the process, but those piercing blue eyes that were shining like a beacon in the open sea were fixed on her, intent on reading her most intimate thoughts.

"Listen, Josh." *Pull yourself together. Hadn't he brought some champagne from the party?* "I'm not gonna sit here and tell you that everything is fine, because even though it was a long time ago, and we've both moved on, you left *me*," she pressed her hand against her chest, "me and Brooke, for that matter, without even trying to reach out to us, after all we'd been through together."

Pain reflected in his eyes and she knew he understood the weight and meaning of her last words. *That's right.*

"Now that I've had a lot of time to think it over, some part of me understands the reasons why some part of you felt like you needed to flee the country to rebuild yourself, and I appreciate you acknowledging how deeply you messed up by leaving the way you did. But what I'll never get is why you stayed silent for all those years while I was here, wracking my brain about what I'd done wrong. Over and over again, I asked myself what I could have done to make you stay. If I had done something to make you mad and not reach out. Did you stop for one second and think about what it could do to me? Why, Josh? Why did you never text or call me?"

"I told you I—"

"Oh, cut the bullshit, please, give me some credit here." Avery's chest was rising and falling hard now. She needed to know. She also needed a drink. *Where was that damn champagne?!*

"Okay." He closed his eyes and pinched his nose between his thumb and index finger. "Okay, alright. You want to know the truth? I couldn't *stand* the fact that you hated me, Avery. Because I know you did, okay? And you probably still do, and who can blame you? I *know* what I did when I left. I didn't realize it right away, because I was consumed by grief. But I couldn't help but replay that day I told you and Brooke that I was leaving, again and again. I felt like I was missing a big piece of the story because I couldn't understand why you, of all people, would react the way you had. And that's when it clicked. I am sorry, Avery. I know I broke my promise to you. I will never forgive myself for doing it and forgetting about it." Josh blew out a ragged breath, like he was finally free of the burden he'd been carrying. When he spoke again, his voice was steadier.

"But don't go blaming only me in this situation either. Nobody forbade you from calling me, by the way," he railed. "My number was the same; you could have reached out too."

Avery took the blow full force. Yeah, she could have, she wasn't going to deny that. But unknowingly, she had wished so hard that he would be the one to make the first move since he had been the one who'd broken their hearts. She had wanted him to come crawling back to her and beg her to forgive him. Blame it on her pride.

As if reading her thoughts, he added, "I have never needed space from *you*. I needed to be by myself for a bit, but not forever." Josh sighed, calming down. "I didn't call you because it was easier for me to never deal with the reality that I had lost you." His voice cracked on the last words, along with Avery's heart, for the tenth time already tonight.

Why did it feel like just yesterday that Josh had packed his bags? It made no sense to be *this* shaken up. She was over it. *She was*. And most importantly, she was pissed off at him for showing up like this.

But at the same time …

At the same time, she was drawn to him like she had never been to anybody else. She was not supposed to feel this good about the fact that he was here, so close to her. And she should *definitely not* be noticing the way his shirt hugged his biceps as he leaned on his elbows, his legs stretched out in front of him.

"I don't know what to say, Josh. To be perfectly honest with you, I'm not sure I want to revisit that time of my life. You and I shared some special years together when we were kids, but we're not the same people anymore. I'm not … mad. I was just hurt, and now …" She raised her eyes to his before drifting back to the lake, sighing. "This was a mistake; I shouldn't have come here."

She started getting up, but Josh grabbed her hand, halting her and forcing her to turn to him. She yanked it back, the burn of his touch too intense for her to handle. She saw the sting of rejection on his face. *Why can I still read him so well?*

"Look, I'm not going to stand in your way. But just for tonight, can we please put everything aside? Just for tonight, Avery?" *No, no, no, not the pleading eyes.* "And then tomorrow, we can go back to our lives. I'll be out of your hair, and we can act like tonight never happened. But right now ..." Josh turned to grab the champagne bottle lying next to him, a small smile stretching his lips. "Right now, I just want to enjoy the moment. Especially if it's the only one I'll ever get."

Avery watched as Josh tilted the bottle slightly, removing the foil wrapping and wire cage. With a firm grip, he popped open the champagne, the cork sliding with ease next to her. His attention back on her, Josh offered her the bottle.

"So ... what do you say?" His eyes glittered with the playfulness Avery knew too well, sending her heart into overdrive. She grabbed the champagne and took a big gulp, letting the alcohol warm up her blood. *Finally.*

"Fine," she said, gently wiping her mouth with the back of her hand. "What do you want to talk about?" She handed the bottle back to Josh, who was watching her with an amused air, one eyebrow arched.

"What?"

He raised his hands up. "Nothing! Okay so let's see, where to start?" He took the bottle from her hands. "What are you doing now? When I left, you were thinking about getting a bachelor's in art, correct?"

Avery was about to respond, but the sight in front of her left the words stuck in her throat. She watched as Josh placed the bottle's neck against his mouth, wrapping his lips around it, where Avery's had been seconds earlier. His Adam's apple bobbed when he swallowed the champagne, his tongue slightly darting across the bottle's lip so he wouldn't miss a drop. She followed every movement like a dog after a treat, the pulse in her wrists quickening at the R-rated images flooding her mind. *Get a grip, Avery.*

"Hum, I ... I'm ..." She cleared her throat. *Why is my mouth so dry?* "Yes," she finally let out. "I graduated from U of T in 2016 and now I have my own photography business." No matter how many times she said this, Avery still felt pride radiate inside her. She was her own goddamn boss.

"You did? Wow, Avie, I'm impressed." He took another sip of champagne. "I mean, don't get me wrong, I'm not surprised at all. You've always had this fire in you. Nobody could stop you once you had that damn camera in hand." He chuckled. "Do you remember when Brooke suddenly decided she wanted to skinny-dip in the freezing lake when we were at my parents' house? When was it? I knew it was freaking cold. I bet she was happy you snapped a few pics."

She choked back a laugh. "OMG she was so drunk that night." Avery smiled at the memory of her best friend running straight to the icy water and the pure shock on her face that followed, forever engraved in her brain *and* the many, *many* photos pinned on her bulletin board in her office. "I'm glad we convinced her to keep her underwear and bra on, though. Can you imagine her horror if she'd seen those pictures sober?"

He laughed a full laugh that made her heart leap. "Please, no."

With warmth filling his gaze, Josh handed her the bottle back. "Cheers to you being a badass woman."

The words stung a little, because she'd spent the last three years working nonstop, sacrificing every other aspect of her life to build her business and so far, it wasn't paying off. She was still in debt, still not making enough money to rent her own apartment, and barely had a social life. She had been fighting so hard to do what she loved, but she had to admit that she was starting to get tired of not seeing the results she wanted.

"I'll drink to that."

She took the bottle from him, her fingers brushing against his, a jolt of electricity coursing from her fingertips up her arm. And if she remembered anything about Josh, it was that he used to slightly part his lips every time he was caught off-guard, and right now, as she watched him do just that, she wondered if he had felt it too.

She took another heavy swig of champagne, forgetting for a moment about the bottle going back and forth between their lips. "What about you? What happened to you in Europe?"

"Ah ... not what I expected would happen, that's for sure." Josh shook his head, his gaze fixed on the horizon.

"You don't have to tell me if—"

"No, I do. It's just a hard truth to accept. I spent my time between Spain, France and England, and none of it went anywhere. You know how sometimes you *know* you shouldn't get your hopes up, but you just can't help yourself because you want it to work out *so* bad?"

Avery nodded. "Been there, done that." *Still there, still doing that.*

"Who hasn't, right? Well anyway, I did a few gigs here and there in Madrid before moving to Paris. I got offered a teaching job at the Paris Conservatory and even though I enjoyed it, was it really what I wanted to do with my life? Truthfully Avie, I think I was at rock bottom. I was living in a maid's room that I paid a fortune for, so small that I could shower and stir my eggs at the same time."

"That bad?"

"Yeah, that bad. And you know, I thought that being in a different country would help me figure out who I was, not being surrounded by either my Mexican or Canadian family." Josh blew out a breath, still fiddling with a small pebble in his hand before tossing it into the lake. "Turns out it was worse. *Way worse*. People can be very … intolerant, or ignorant sometimes. The years in Paris were the worst, being called names or being told to go back to my country. I was just a naive 19-year-old who thought the color of his skin wouldn't attract too much attention since nobody in Canada had seemed to care, and *that* had been a problem for me too at that time."

When he glanced at Avery again, his eyes were wet, his expression full of hurt and regret. *Please don't cry,* her heart couldn't take it. "I just wanted to make her proud, you know? I wanted to show her that her legacy would live on through me, that I was capable of keeping it alive."

His voice broke under the weight of his words. Avery instinctively grasped his hand in hers, applying a gentle pressure to the smooth surface. His hands had always been an object of fascination for her, his delicate skin, his long but firm fingers always moving with grace, certainly because of the years of playing the piano under them.

She didn't have anything to say that would make him feel better because it was not what he needed right now, so she just kept massaging the back of his hand with her thumb, encouraging him to continue and showing him that she was listening, and with a shaky breath, he did.

"After four years, I finally called it quits and moved to London. I met some people and finally made friends after seven years between Madrid and Paris. One guy knew the director of the London Symphony Orchestra. I got hired as a backup pianist and did a few nights per week. I kept thinking my luck would change, but it never did. And you know, my father was starting to get old, and ... I missed home." He raised his blue eyes to hers and added, "And I feel now that I'm exactly where I should be."

She watched as his gaze slowly slid to her lips, causing Avery to part them, her breath coming out ragged, her heart pounding like ten bass drums in her ears. *What was happening?* The air suddenly felt very thick between them, wrapping around them like maple syrup coating apples slices in September. She saw his chest rise and fall, straining the fabric of his shirt in the process. He was going to kiss her, she knew it, and when he raised his eyes to hers, she saw all the intention on his face. Carefully and slowly, he leaned in.

Her mind was racing, torn between closing the last distance between them and give in to something she knew she had thought about, or pushing him away, the resentment and hurt still lingering in her broken heart. Plus, they were best friends, weren't they? *Had* been best friends. If Josh was back for good, Avery couldn't risk losing him all over again over some stupid, probably out-of-this-world mind-bending kiss. *Those gorgeous lips.*

But chances were, his stay in Toronto was just temporary, and he would probably be gone in a few days. Either way, her brain was screaming *bad idea,* waving red flags, and sounding the alarm, but her treacherous body was already thinking about the feel of his mouth on hers.

Avery felt the warmth of his breath caress her lips, the delicious smell of champagne she wanted to lose herself in, as he closed the distance between them. But before they could do something they would both regret, Avery cleared her throat, a raspy sound hanging in the air.

"I ... um ... it's getting late, Josh. Maybe we should head back," she said, a strain in her voice.

He stared at her for a second, not moving an inch from where he had stopped, before putting some much-needed distance between them.

"Yeah." He ran a hand through his already messy hair and let out a quiet sigh. Was he ... disappointed? "Yeah, you're probably right. I have to help out my dad at the restaurant tomorrow morning."

Change of subject, perfect. "Oh, I didn't know you were working there?"

"Well, you know my old man. Never misses a chance to rope me into the family business," he said sarcastically, shaking his head.

This new piece of information made Avery wonder if he was planning on staying longer than she'd originally thought, but before she could give it any more thought, Josh stood up, brushing the sand off his pants and held out his hand. She grabbed it, careful not to lean into him.

"Thank you for tonight, Avie. I'm so happy I got to see you again," he said softly, brushing a strand of hair off her shoulder. She shivered at the touch of his fingers on the thin skin there, sending a wave of heat right down her spine.

"Are you cold?" Frowning, he grabbed his suit jacket and wrapped her up in his intoxicating smell. *Is this man trying to kill me*?

"Thanks," she croaked. It took every ounce of strength she had to follow him to the boat, wondering how in the hell he'd made her feel like she was sixteen again.

Seven

Don't

As soon as Josh disappeared around the corner, Avery dug into her purse to retrieve her phone and reality hit. It was half past midnight and as predicted, Brooke had blown her phone up. Ten missed calls, seven voice messages and 23 texts.

Brooke [9:12 pm]: What happened? Who is driving you back?
Brooke [9:35 pm]: Are you still at the fundraiser?
Brooke [10:28 pm]: We're done at the show–please text me so I know you still alive
Brooke [10:56 pm]: OMG Ave I totally got it. You totally went home with a cute guy there. You sexy little minx. I knew this dress would get you laid. Hope you have the best sex of your life–please still text so I know you're okay

And so it went on for another 19 texts of a mix of eggplant emojis and worried messages, making Avery blush and chuckle. If only Brooke knew. She shot her a text to reassure her.

Avery [12:20 am]: I'm fine, I TOLD you I was fine, silly. Can I stop by your place or is it too late?

She hadn't even had time to lock her phone when Brooke's answer chimed.

Brooke [12:21 am]: SHE'S ALIVE. Coming to yours–Alice is asleep and tired after her show. Meet you there in 20. Better be ready to spill the beans!

She chuckled and put her phone back in her purse, right after ordering a taxi. It was surprisingly warm for a late September night, probably the last hurrah of the summer. She could easily walk the way back to her place, but it was past midnight, she was slightly tipsy, and it was completely dark outside. There was no way in hell she'd risk it.

A needy and hungry Simba welcomed her as soon as she stepped inside her house, purring against her legs, and leaving a trail of fur behind.

"Hey Simb." She crouched to scratch behind his ears. "I know you're hungry, let's get you fed!" Avery's little shadow followed her into the kitchen, where she popped open a can of raw fish and spilled the contents on a little plate. Simba was waiting by his usual feeding spot, his tail swishing in delight at the prospect of food.

"There you go, little monster."

While Simba devoured his meal, Avery took her coat and shoes off, and changed out of her party dress into something a little comfier. She untied her hair from all the bobby pins and rinsed her face. Back in the kitchen, she opened a bottle of wine and slouched on her couch. What a fucking night. She wasn't even sure she hadn't dreamt the whole thing, but the fatigue in her bones and the slight buzz she felt coursing through her veins answered the question for her.

She didn't know how she was going to approach The Josh Situation with her best friend, because the last time they'd spoken to each other, things hadn't gone down well between the two of them. But that was ten years ago, and things had changed since then. They were not teenagers anymore, and they had all moved on, even though seeing Josh tonight had awoken something in her she'd tried to bury deep inside.

She heard keys jingling in her front door and Brooke appeared a second later, bottle of wine in hand, dressed in nothing else but her Christmas pajamas.

"I didn't know it was a sleepover kind of night," Avery said, a smile on the corner of her lips.

"Listen, you ghost me all night and then text me at midnight saying you're free to talk." Brooke kicked off her shoes and slouched on the couch next to Avery. "I was not going to change for you, ma'am."

She eyed the bottle of wine already opened on the low table and grinned. "I see you already took care of the drinks. Well, since I don't know how long this will take, good thing I brought reinforcements."

Avery shuffled nervously with her blanket and sat straighter, the panic slowly getting to her.

"Alright, out with it. What happened tonight, where were you?"

And so, she told her everything. And while she was telling Brooke about the most surreal night of her life, she saw her best friend's face go from utter and complete shock, to what she could only read as surprise and … curiosity? She didn't seem angry though, so that was good, at least.

"Trust me when I say I have had my fair share of surprises over the years but this one …" Avery shook her head. "This one might just take the cake."

She studied Brooke, who had stayed silent so far, lost in her thoughts. "Well, that's a first."

Brooke snapped out of whatever she was thinking and stared at Avery. "What?"

"You. Saying nothing. I'm not used to you staying silent for more than five seconds. Any comments? Anything to ask?"

"I'm sorry, I just don't know where to start. I just can't believe he's back." Brooke closed her eyes and exhaled. "Alright, I'm gonna ask this, I just have to. Are you 100% sure it was him?"

"Am I 100%…*what*, really B.?! Of course, it was him!"

"I don't know!" She shrugged. "The guy is 10 years older, who knows what he looks like now. For all you know he could be bald and rocking a dad bod."

Avery rolled her eyes. "I'm choosing to ignore that. Yes, it was him. Even if he had changed physically, I'd think I could still recognize him." She cleared her throat before adding, "And not that it matters, but for your information, those 10 years do look good on him."

Brooke gasped and grabbed Avery's hands, squishing her fingers in the process.

"Avery Clark! Don't tell me Josh is the guy you spent the night with!"

She blushed and tried desperately to get her hands back, but Brooke was holding firmly onto her. Technically, she *had* spent the night with him, but not exactly how her best friend meant. And the visual of Josh sprawled naked in her bed sheets made her grow very, very hot. *Nope, nope, nope. Focus.*

"Of course not! I mean, I did leave the fundraiser with him, but we went to the islands and spent the evening there with some champagne from the party."

"Don't tell me he snagged a bottle again." Avery couldn't help but smile at Brooke's intact memory of their former best friend. "This guy ... always getting himself into trouble."

They stayed silent for a while, both reminiscing about the past in their own heads and unsure where to take the rest of the discussion. Avery hadn't had time to properly put her thoughts in order after tonight and was still in a state of shock. She wasn't even sure she could explain her evening to herself, because how could she even make sense of both the shattering sadness and deep exhilaration he provoked in her? For years, Josh had been the first person she'd said good morning to and the last she saw when she closed her eyes at night. He had been the one she had shared all her secrets with and confessed her hopes, fears and dreams to. And he had been the only one who'd known how deeply broken she had been and still was. That moment that had led to him vowing to never leave her side. And in a blink, he'd ceased to exist in her small world.

So, to see him back in the flesh again? Yeah, there were definitely some conflicting feelings there.

Brooke finally released Avery's fingers, turned white from her friend's constant pressure, snapping her back to reality.

"I'm just having a hard time believing he's here, you know," Brooke said. "So, what did you guys do till midnight?"

"We just ... talked, I guess. He asked what I was up to, I did the same and you know, just regular catching up."

She wasn't sure how much she wanted to share with Brooke yet, because she needed to figure out how she felt about it first. It had been so easy to fall back into old habits, feeling so relaxed in his presence. She flushed, remembering how she'd leaned against him on the way back, his hard body against her naked back, his suit jacket loosely hanging on her shoulders, the only piece of clothing separating her skin from his shirt. She blamed this careless moment on the too-many champagne sips she'd had, in trying to drown her nerves. Was it wrong that she wanted to keep him to herself, just for a little while longer?

Avery downed the rest of her glass and poured herself another one as Brooke watched, one eyebrow raised. "Wow, okay, I get it, it's a lot, but maybe go easy on the pinot?"

Avery stared at her dead in the eyes, an *are you fucking kidding me* expression on her face.

"Yeah, no okay, you're right." Brooke followed her lead and swung the wine bottle directly to her lips. "So, what's our game plan here now?"

Avery snorted. "Who the fuck knows? He probably ran out of town already."

That seemed like the most plausible scenario, one that'd happened too many times in her life. She always gave her all to people she cared about, because she didn't know any other way. She loved hard and fast, and always ended up with her heart broken and alone. So why would this time be any different?

Brooke took another gulp of wine and handed the bottle to Avery. "Ignoring that. Do you plan on seeing him again?"

"Yes?" She shook her head. "No. No, no, no, no." Ughhh, did she have to decide *now*?

Brooke was looking at her, amused. "Well, I haven't had the pleasure of seeing him, so if you don't mind, I'm gonna say the answer is 'yes.' Gimme your phone."

Avery narrowed her eyes. "Why?"

"I assume he gave you his number, yes?"

"Maybe?" She definitely should have said no but she was just incapable of lying. She had no poker face, especially when it came to Brooke.

"Give it, c'mon," Brooke said, holding her palm up.

Avery wasn't sure if it was the buzz of the wine starting to work its magic or the fact that a small part of her wanted to know what her best friend was up to, but in this moment, she felt reckless and handed her phone to Brooke.

Brooke gave her the phone back a second later and typed out a message from hers. "Alright, let's see ... how much should I make him feel guilty?"

"Zero!" *See?* She was already regretting her careless decision.

"Okay... aaaaand done!"

"What did you say?" As she asked, her phone chimed.

Brooke [1:52 am] to *The gang is back together* **group chat: Hi Joshua Harding. It's Brooke Pierce, remember me? Tall, blond hair, former best friend. Ring any bells?**

"OMG B. You did *not* just send that."

Despite being completely mortified by her shameless best friend, Avery was also kind of intrigued and eager to see Josh's response.

"It's way too late right now anyway, he must be—"

Ping

Joshua the traitor [1:54 am] to *The gang is back together* **group chat: Hey Brooke! Still cracking jokes, I see. Guess news traveled fast haha. Hey, Ave!**

Why wasn't he sleeping? He should be sleeping right now. The only reason Avery could think of to justify the fact that Josh was still awake was because, like her, their evening together had sent his brain into overdrive. And she didn't like how giddy that made her feel.

"Ave, what should we say?" Brooke asked, buzzing with excitement.

She ignored her question. "I can't believe you created a group chat! And the *name* you gave him?!" She was mortified. How was she going to explain that to him? It was almost 2 a.m. You'd think she'd have better things to do at this hour.

"Oh, come on. Relax. I'm gonna tell him we should get drinks tomorrow."

Avery gasped and swatted her arm. "Don't you dare!"

Before Brooke was able to send something else, both their phones buzzed.

Joshua the traitor [1:55 am] to *The gang is back together* **group chat: Do you guys want to get together Saturday for drinks? Let's say 5 p.m., at the Good Fortune?**

"Well, well, well. Looks like *someone* wants to see *someone* again." Brooke smirked. "I guess we're going out Saturday night!"

Brooke started to type frantically on her phone. Panic spread through Avery who tried to snatch her phone away from her reckless fingers, but she was too fast.

"Brooke, come on, I'm not ready to—"

Ping.

"You can't be serious right now."

Brooke flashed her toothy smile.

Brooke [1:57 am] to *The gang is back together* **group chat: We'll be there. Don't even think about cancelling.**

Joshua the traitor [1:57 am] to *The gang is back together* **group chat: Wouldn't dream of it. See you guys Saturday!**

Avery stared at her phone in horror, wondering what the hell she just had done.

Eight

One More Hour

Waking up the next day, or rather, a few hours later, was its own kind of nightmare. Avery had a massive headache pounding against her temples, and was still in her sweatpants, one too many pairs of legs tangled with hers in her bed. After blinking several times to try and clear the thick fog her mind was plunged into, she assessed that the legs in question belonged to her best friend, and not some rando she forgot she'd brought home last night.

Squinting past the bed, she took in the state of her bedroom. It looked like a tornado had passed through. *What the fuck did we do last night?*

And that's when she saw the pile of photos under her favorite Beyhive sweater. She narrowed her eyes.

No. No, no, no, no *they did not.* She sprung to her feet a little bit too fast, and immediately felt the dizziness take over. She gripped the edge of her bed to stabilize herself, Brooke still snoring soundly on her stomach, unaware of the total chaos around her.

How in the holy hell had they managed to find this box last night? Because if there was one thing she was sure of, it was that this particular box had been hidden under piles and piles of bags, shoes and anything else that would do the job of keeping it away from her.

Lying on the floor were the contents of that aforementioned box, objects and photos retracing their teenage years that Avery had snapped at the time. She'd always had her camera in hand, often annoying Brooke in the process, ready to capture and immortalize every ounce of happiness she'd felt with her best friends. Little did she know that all those years later, those souvenirs would come back to bite her in the ass.

She started gathering the memorabilia when she stumbled upon one particular photo that made her pause. She ran her fingers over the photograph, smoothing the curled ends. She didn't remember seeing this one, perhaps because she wasn't the one who had captured the moment, but she knew exactly where and when it had happened.

She was more than a decade younger in it, seated at her grandmother's kitchen table, laughing at some dumb joke Josh must have told her. It was summer 2009, one of the rare summers where Josh wasn't visiting his father's side of the family in Mexico. Brooke was out of town for school break, working at a kids' soccer camp, and Avery and Josh had decided then to spend this particular week with Avery's grandmother in the suburbs. Her grandma must have taken the photo without her noticing, because the rawness of the moment pulled hard at the strings of her heart.

The photo was angled in a way where Avery could see Josh looking at her younger self, his eyes sparkling with something she couldn't quite put her finger on. Like he was captivated by the sound of her laugh and couldn't look away. His gaze was so intense, she felt it in her tingling skin and her heart beating just a little bit faster.

Ridiculous.

She hadn't even known this photo existed until right now, and here she was, getting all worked up over a moment that had happened ten years ago. She really needed to get a grip. Seeing him again had messed with her head, that's what it was. Plus, she couldn't remember the last time she had sex, which in itself was quite disturbing, and, let's face it, sad, but now, out of nowhere, she'd found herself in front of a very, *very* attractive 30-year-old. Life was unfair. And downright cruel.

She closed her eyes, inhaled, and slid the photo in her purse. She finished cleaning the rest away and put the lid back on, storing the box back in her closet where she hoped she would never see it again.

After a long, hot shower that (mostly) cleared her hungover brain, and a much-needed cup of coffee, Avery slipped on her coat and wrote a quick note to let Brooke know she'd left for a boudoir session with a client. She grabbed her phone on the nightstand, accidentally brushing against Brooke's. Her best friend phone lit up, showing Alice and Brooke on the screen an ... a text from Josh.

Josh the traitor [2:23 am]: I know Brooke, I'm not planning on it. You need to chill. See you Saturday.

Confused, and let's be honest, a tiny bit jealous, she put the phone down, and stared at Brooke, weighing her options.

She could wake her up and ask why the hell Brooke had a separate text convo with Josh or what this text was about. They were definitely in the middle of a discussion here, but Avery didn't have any memories from last night except that they'd all agreed to meet at some fancy bar Saturday. After agreeing to that, she had needed to drown her anxiety about the prospect of the three of them being reunited, so she and Brooke had gone through the wine way quicker than they should have.

Or, she could let it go and maybe bring it up later with Brooke. *Or not.* Brooke was allowed to speak to whomever she wanted, right? It was none of her business. She didn't have any right to feel this bothered by it. But the fact remained—she was.

Her mind was relentless, building a million different scenarios over this simple little text that she knew deep down probably meant nothing. *But*, her little inside voice said, *it could also mean something. Remember when Alex hid all those things from you when he was in D.C? All those separate text chats he kept on the side?*

Avery groaned and shook her head. *No.* She was not about to get into this now. She was going to forget that her best friend was talking to their former best friend on a separate thread, and focus on the rest of her day, which, when she glanced at the time on her phone, she needed to get to. ASAP.

♪♫

What to wear to a best friends' reunion that screamed "successful and accomplished grown ass woman who is independent and doesn't need a man to be happy?" Avery had been weighing her options for the past hour, and had several outfits laid out on her bed, but none were jumping out to her. She wanted to look good, but not so good that it would be like she was trying too hard. What about the denim skirt that fell mid-thigh? Maybe... no, too casual. She eyed her go-to black dress. Yes, but no. That was an emergency choice. Last resort. She didn't want Josh to think she'd just thrown it on and that she didn't care. Because she did care. It wasn't every day that you were reunited with your childhood best friend.

After a few more unsuccessful tries, Avery settled on a pair of cream high-waisted rolled-up trousers and her favorite black top with a neckline that plunged just below her breasts. Tucking it in her pants, she twirled in front of the mirror, assessing her outfit. *Not bad.* And with her hair tied up in a high ponytail that left her shoulders and neck bare, the whole look was definitely sexy, but not in a provocative way. She let a few brown strands down to frame her eyes, making the green around her irises glow a honey hue. Texting the group chat that she was on her way, Avery closed her door, and stepped out into the coolness of the night.

When she arrived at Good Fortune, a small bar in uptown Toronto, Josh was already waiting outside. She just needed to cross the street. He hadn't seen her yet, so instead of going straight to him, Avery used this stolen moment to fully take him in. *Dear god, he was hot.* Standing next to the door, Josh was wearing slim black pants that hugged his long legs, and a deep red shirt that clung nicely around his biceps and broad shoulders, with sleeves rolled up to his elbows. *Fuck.* Why did men have to make a big show of their forearms like that?

His hair was messier than the night of the fundraiser, making a memory of a sweaty and tousle-haired Josh after track practise flash behind her eyes. Avery resisted the urge to run to him and slide her hands in his beautiful hazelnut curls. From where she stood, he looked a bit more like the Josh she knew, wild and spontaneous, only older, and *definitely* sexier.

Okay, here we go. Avery crossed the street that separated her from the bar, and as soon as Josh's eyes found her, his face broke into a huge, toothy smile, revealing perfectly aligned teeth.

"I wasn't sure you were gonna show up!" he said, wrapping her in a tight embrace that took her by surprise. Her body was pressed against his, drawing her into the hardness of his chest as warmth radiated from him and wrapping her in his citrusy scent. The electricity crackling between them was undeniable. She could feel it crawl under her skin and shoot straight down her spine, leaving a trail of shivers along the way. She needed to let go before she did something she knew she'd regret.

"Well, here I am." Avery smiled, taking a necessary step back. "Do you know where Brooke is?"

"Oh, you didn't get the text?"

Avery frowned. *No?* She was pretty sure Brooke hadn't sent a text, or she would have remembered it.

"She said she was running a bit late. She should be here in thirty minutes or so." Hesitating, Josh gestured toward the door. "Wanna get inside?"

Clutching her coat tight against her, Avery nodded and followed him inside, but not without double checking her phone first. Nope, that's what she'd thought—no message from Brooke.

Inside the bar, it was as though they'd been transported back in time to a 1970s Miami Beach clubhouse. The flamingo pink walls and palm leaf wallpaper surrounding green and terracotta leather couches recalled late nights at the house in Niagara-on-the-lake, dancing close to Latin music from Josh's dad's old vinyl collection, sweat from the summer heat sticking to their skin. And despite being a cold autumn night, Avery could feel the warmth of the atmosphere buzzing inside her. Unless it was because Josh kept on stealing glances over his shoulder while he made his way through the crowded place.

They settled in a small corner at the back of the bar, where the lights were dimmed and the music softer. Avery shrugged her coat off her back, not noticing right away that Josh was standing still, his jacket in his hands. His gaze slowly trailed down her body, taking in every inch of her exposed skin, and Avery felt every second of his eyes on her like a soft caress mapping out the path, and leaving her aching to be touched.

When he raised his eyes to her face, lips slightly parted and cheeks flushed, she thought she was going to explode. He grinned, like he knew exactly how she felt. And maybe he felt it too. It was a second too long, and dammit, it took everything she had to stay where she was and not throw herself at him like some desperate teenager.

You seriously need to reel it in, Ave.

The truth was, she kind of was desperate right now. Her sex life this past year had been DOA, and seeing Josh looking at her like that, like he was craving *her*, made her feel little tingles deep in her belly, moving in a treacherous direction. God, she needed to get laid already. But *not* with her ex-best-friend.

Josh cleared his throat, swallowing loudly. "I like the shirt," he rasped, his voice like gravel, scraping at her skin. He gestured toward the bar where a man with aviator Ray-Bans was mixing a pink and green cocktail. "I'm gonna get us some drinks. Tequila still a favorite?"

"Mmh-hmm, yep. Perfect." *Yes, alcohol, what a great idea right about now.*

"Be right back."

A few moments later, Josh placed a watermelon margarita in front of Avery and sat down on the green couch in front of her, a gin and tonic in hand. Anxious, she took a big sip and felt the alcohol burn down her throat. At least it had the effect of calming her nerves instantly.

"So, did you make it home okay the other night?"

"Yep, no problem."

"Good. Good," he repeated. "It was kind of late, so I hope nobody was waiting for you." Was he fishing for information on her dating status? *Still as subtle as ever, I see.*

"Well, he was a bit hungry when I arrived but nothing a few cuddles and food couldn't fix." Oh, she was enjoying the look on his face. Surprise, with a dash of disappointment, was that what it was? "My cat is pretty needy," she clarified, deciding to put him out of his guessing game misery, a small smile tugging at her lips.

"Oh!" He chuckled nervously. She saw relief washing all over him, the muscles of his neck relaxing. "So, no special man, or woman, in your life then?"

"No, not really. I mean, I do have Brooke. She's a little firecracker, so she definitely keeps me busy. But I don't do relationships anymore."

Josh cocked an eyebrow. "Anymore?"

Oh shit. Did she say the last word out loud? *Damn you, big mouth.*

"Yeah, well ..." She waved her hand like it was no big deal. Josh didn't need to know the full story anyway. "Let's just say that I've had my fair share of disappointment and heartbreak, and I'm not interested in re-living any of that."

Josh visibly tensed and mumbled something under his breath before saying: "I'm sorry, Avie. I didn't know."

"Ah, don't worry about it. I have my business to focus on anyway—I don't need the distraction." She cleared her throat, the question burning her tongue. "What about you?"

"What about me?"

"Is there a Mrs. Harding somewhere?"

Josh laughed. "God, no. Not married." His gaze met hers for a second, before returning his attention to his drink. "Waiting for the one and all that, you know? I honestly don't have time for that anyway. Between helping my dad at the restaurant, working on my career and my sister's wedding I—"

"Wait, wait, wait, pause." Somehow his evasive answer to her dating question wasn't what had caught her attention. "Julia is getting married?!" Avery hadn't seen her in forever. They used to get along so well when Josh was still around, but they'd lost touch over the years. They still texted each other 'Happy Birthday' or 'Merry Christmas,' but they weren't as close as they used to be.

"Yeah, she is! This December. I'm her best man."

"Oh my god, I can't believe it. Is she still with Paul?"

"They're inseparable—it's almost annoying."

Avery laughed, but the sound died in her throat instantly when Josh raised his glass and set his entire focus on her.

"To high school sweethearts." The pause that followed before they clinked their glasses together held a thousand meanings, all of them unsaid but understood as if they'd been shouted. *To what we could have been.*

She clinked her glass to his, still holding his gaze. Only a table separated them. Would she fit there, in the small place between the edge of the table and Josh, if she were to climb it and straddle him right now? Would he cup her ass with his strong hands? Would he run them through her hair? She was leaning dangerously closer to making a decision and finding it out. *What are you thinking?*

She snapped back to reality and cleared her throat. "How are the wedding preparations going then, best man?"

Josh was still looking at her, like he was trying to understand what the hell had just happened. *Oh, you know, just your average horny 28-year-old who hasn't seen a penis in a year. Focus, geez.* Lucky for her, Josh snapped his fingers, realizing something all of a sudden.

"Shit, I almost forgot to ask you! Would you be free to photograph their wedding? Their photographer bailed on them a week ago and Julia is going to lose it if I don't find someone fast."

"I—"

"Hiiiii, gorgeous!!" The chirpy sound came from behind Avery and could only belong to one person. Brooke gave Avery the tightest and warmest hug she'd ever received, making it really hard for her to breathe. She was definitely putting on a show, and it wasn't hard to guess for who.

Brooke was dressed like she'd just come from work, fitted pants and a cream blouse tucked in the front, paired with her blue good-luck blazer. She must have had an important meeting today. Her blond hair was neatly tied in a ponytail, her bangs framing her flawless face. She looked like she just hopped out of the shower, fresh and smelling good, not like she rushed through work and traffic to get here. *Lucky genes.*

Avery patted her arm. "Okay, okay, hi B. Let me go." She tried to wriggle out of Brooke's embrace and when she finally set her free, Brooke turned to Josh and held out her hand. When she shook his firmly, Josh flinched. "Joshua. Nice to see you again."

"Likewise, B." His smile faded as soon as Brooke's sharp retort came out of her curled lips.

"I'm sorry, it's Brooke to you."

"*Brooke!*"

She turned to Avery and mouthed *what?!* She mouthed back *stop it* although it was doubtful Brooke would obey. She settled in to the booth next to Avery. "I'll take what Avery's having," she said to Josh. Both amused and a little bit scared, Josh nodded and headed to the bar to get the drink Brooke had so nicely asked for.

She turned quickly to Avery and grabbed her by the shoulders. "Oh my god, when did Josh become so *hot*? And I'm not even into guys but damn, he is fiiiine."

Avery rolled her eyes. "Can you behave for one night, please?"

"I'm just sayin'. I have eyes. And so do you. And so do the two girls standing next to him at the bar apparently ..."

Avery followed Brooke's gaze where two women were whispering and giggling together while clearly checking Josh out. *Sigh.* There was no slowing Brooke down. Once she was focused on something, she always had to see it through. "So? Fill me in! How long have you guys been sitting here for?"

"I don't know, twenty minutes maybe? Thanks for the heads up by the way," Avery said while picking her drink up. It was almost to her lips when Brooke snatched it from her fingers and took a big sip.

"Hey!"

Brooke stuck her tongue out and Avery laughed, shaking her head.

"What? I couldn't risk you bailing on tonight, could I? *'Well, turns out I have to go to Miles' house tonight because his dog is sick,'*" she said, imitating Avery.

"Okay, okay, I get it. Also, I don't sound like that."

Brooke straightened up and placed her hands on Avery's lap. "Okay, now S-P-I-L-L."

Avery groaned, both annoyed at Brooke's insistence and the fact that her best friend could read her so well. Could she be honest with her when she wasn't being completely honest with herself?

"Will you stop already, god you're such a child! There's nothing to say!"

"Um, I beg to differ ma'am. I saw how he looked at you," she said, wiggling her eyebrows.

Avery crossed her arms on her chest. "Oh, yeah? And how would that be?" *Stop giving her ammo.*

"Like he'd prefer you be naked."

Avery blushed instantly. It wasn't like she hadn't thought about it. Their two bodies flushed together, sweat dripping down his spine, their lips swollen from hungry kisses, his toned arms braced on either side of her head.

"You're thinking about it, aren't you?" Brooke teased, pulling her out of her thoughts.

"Shut up," Avery muttered. She needed a change of subject when she remembered what Josh had told her a few moments earlier. "Get this. Julia is getting married and she needs a photographer for her wedding."

"No way!! Julia's getting married?!" Brooke screeched. "I thought she hated weddings. Is it with Mr. Boring-what's-his-face?"

"His name is Paul. But yes." Avery needed her full attention right now. "She needs a pho-to-gra-pher for her wed-ding in De-cem-ber." She was enunciating slowly so her best friend would understand what she was trying to get to. And when she'd finally caught on, she gasped.

"The contest, oh my god!!"

"There she is."

"You're gonna say yes, right?"

"I don't know. Yes? I'm not sure. It doesn't feel right to not talk about it first with Julia. I want her to know and understand that I'm going to use her wedding photos for a contest."

"What contest?" Josh was back at their table, sliding the margarita over to Brooke.

"Um ... yeah, so, I—"

"Avery has a shot at winning a one-year contract with a bridal boutique, but she has to submit your sister's wedding photos to be able to enter the contest," Brooke said in one breath. Avery flipped around and stared at Brooke and her sheepish smile. Was it possible to murder someone just by looking at them? Because she was sure as hell trying right now. When her eyes found Josh's again, he was looking at her with amusement and ... was it, tenderness?

"You need Julia's photos? I'm sure she won't mind at all," Josh said. "We can double-check with her tomorrow."

"Tomorrow?" The question came out of both Avery's and Brooke's mouths.

"Ha, yeah. I'm supposed to report back to Julia about the photographer situation tomorrow at our 'weekly wedding prep session,'" he said, air quoting the last bit. "So honestly, you'd be doing me a huge favor by coming with me to meet her." His hand was stroking his chin and the movement of his fingers on his scruffy jaw mesmerized Avery for a second.

"I think I should be able to make it if it's after 6 p.m. I have to meet with my brother beforehand."

"Great! We'll make it work. I'll text you the address."

They spent the rest of the night chatting, drinking, laughing, and drinking some more. Even Brooke was starting to warm up to Josh as the night was coming to an end. Avery had caught them in an intense discussion after she came out of the bathroom earlier, but from the way Brooke had relaxed after that, even cracked a smile at Josh (a smile!), Avery had deduced that whatever they had needed to work through had been settled.

Being together again, Avery felt her world tilt back on its axis. Despite the lingering bitterness in her heart, tonight was like they had picked up right where they left off ten years before. She hadn't been this happy and content in a long time.

As the bar started to clear out in the early hours of the morning, servers called for last rounds. Brooke's hair was no longer in her ponytail; strands sticking to her sweaty face and neck. Avery's straps kept slipping down her shoulders, and Josh had undone the first buttons of his shirt after his third drink, revealing the hard lines of his chest. Happiness flowed freely between them.

Drunk but elated, they gathered their belongings and headed for the door, as best as they could. Of the three of them, Brooke was definitely the drunkest, leaning against Avery with her arm around her waist, while smooching her neck. At some point during the night, Avery had noticed Josh swapping his gin and tonic for some ginger ale, which explained why he was able to walk straight and trailed close behind, making sure neither of them hit a chair or a wall.

As for her … Avery was drunk on both alcohol and happiness, and that was the most dangerous mix of all. But she quickly realized it wasn't nearly as dangerous as Josh's hand gripping her bare waist to keep her from falling headfirst when Brooke stumbled against the legs of an unexpected chair, nearly dragging Avery down with her.

The possessive touch sobered her up instantly. She stood up sharply and turned to Josh, his eyes dark, and his hand still clutching her hip. Avery watched as his chest rose up and down while his fingers flexed slowly against her skin. Her gaze moved from his fingers to his lips and very carefully, she drew closer to him. Everything around them stilled and disappeared, only Josh came into focus. Their lips were only inches apart. Avery rose on her tiptoes, her fingers digging into the flesh of his arms for balance. It was impossible to ignore the throbbing pulse between them. She was going to do it. She was going to kiss him. His breath flew across her lips and as she leaned in, Josh lifted his chin and kissed the top of her forehead instead. In her eagerness and current state, Avery hadn't factored this outcome in.

Too late.

She was already in motion and couldn't stop the humiliation she was already feeling. Like a slo-mo scene, her lips crashed miserably against his Adam's apple. As drunk as she was, it still wasn't enough not to feel the shame flood her body and consume her on the spot.

Oblivious to what had just transpired, Brooke was passed out on the table next to them, gently snoring.

"I'm sorry, I ... I don't know what came over me, I'm so drunk," she stammered, trying to disappear inside her coat.

"Avie, listen to me." Josh reached out and cupped her face in his hands, tilting her so she would look at him. He didn't seem pissed or weirded out. *I'll take it.*

When he finally spoke, his voice was soft and warmer than usual, hot caramel melted around dark chocolate.

"I know you're drunk. You probably won't remember any of this tomorrow when you wake up, so I think it's safe for me to say this. I've been dying to kiss you all night and bring you back to my place and kiss you some more." His thumbs were brushing her cheeks softly. "But I won't do this when you don't even know what you're agreeing to. Okay?"

All she could do was nod. Josh sighed in relief as he wrapped his arms around her, pulling her flush against his body and pressing another kiss to her head. "Next time, I hope," he whispered in her hair.

And Avery prayed that if she had to remember one thing and one thing only tomorrow morning, it was this conversation.

Nine

Ocean Eyes

Everything was hurting today. The sun was too bright, the temperature too cold and what was it with everybody shouting? *Ugh.*

Well, maybe Avery was exaggerating a little bit. There was no *actual* shouting, but everybody was so cheerful and in a good mood, and nobody seemed to notice that all Avery wanted was a bit of quiet. And also, a bed. And blackout curtains, if it wasn't too much to ask.

She'd woken up this morning with a raging headache and massive hangover, her second in a week. She hadn't partied like this since her early twenties, and clearly, she was paying the price today.

And as the responsible adult she definitely was, she had to face the consequences. The day had been packed with scouting locations for Claudia's maternity shoot, but as if she hadn't had enough trouble functioning properly already, all of her plans had fallen through when in the late morning, a blanket of snow had covered every inch of grass in sight. And it was only early October.

She hadn't had a minute to slow down. After a quick call to Claudia to confirm the changes in both location and theme, she had to take all the dresses back to Lisa and leave with another selection, look for new places, beg to schedule visits the same day to avoid falling behind schedule, and all this before 4 p.m. if she didn't want to be late for her dinner with her brother. *Breathe.* She needed to breathe.

Suffice to say, it wasn't the ideal day to be hungover. And on top of her stressful day at work, her mother had called her in tears to announce that she had just received the divorce papers. And between that and the pile of unexpected surprises that had fallen into her lap, Avery hadn't begun to clear the thick fog in her head from the previous night's events.

Exhausted, she closed her car door and turned the heat to maximum. Fuck, it was cold today. The sun was almost set by 4 p.m., and as much as she loved the season, it was a rather depressing sight.

She texted Miles to let him know she would be at his place by 4:30, dropped her seat as low as possible, and closed her eyes.

"Come on Avery, think," she mumbled.

Why did she have to drink so much last night? She remembered getting pretty cozy with Josh at one point in the night and Brooke chanting "Shots!" but that was pretty much the extent of her memories. She did have an uneasy feeling that she had gotten a little bit *too* cozy with Josh though.

Had they kissed? Avery dismissed this thought instantly. No, that was completely absurd. They would never do something that stupid. They were friends, and things were slowly getting back to normal between them. Why would they risk losing each other all over again?

Plus, she would never agree to start something with someone as unreliable as Josh. He had broken her trust once, and she would not give it back to him that easily. He was probably planning his next trip at that very moment, and she was not about to leave everything behind for a guy. Not again, and certainly not after seeing firsthand the disaster of her parents' marriage.

She always put the people she loved first, but who put *her* first? It was time she started prioritizing herself for a change.

But why did she feel like they'd kissed, then? Why could she still feel the brush of his lips on hers?

Come on, Avery, use your brain cells. This was clearly going nowhere, and she needed to get going if she didn't want to be late. Frustrated, she abandoned her thoughts for later, straightened her seat and put the car in first gear.

♪♩

"Hello, hello!" Miles welcomed her on his front steps, arms wide open, ready to engulf her in his warm embrace. Avery happily ran into it. She loved her brother's bear hugs. Miles was an impressive guy. At six-foot-three, he was her favorite teddy bear with walls of muscle from spending too many hours on the rugby field.

"Hi." She breathed a sigh of relief against his chest, his familiar scent soothing her on the spot.

He patted her back and dropped a kiss on her head. "Tough day?"

"Something like that, yeah."

Miles released her and raised an eyebrow. He looked just like a young version of their father, with the same dark hair he used to have, neatly trimmed on the sides and slightly longer on top, a stark contrast to the light color of his skin. The only notable differences that kept Avery from having anxiety every time she looked at her brother were his brown eyes and his thick but short beard.

"Let's get inside and you can tell me all about it," he said.

She'd barely gotten through the door when Happy, her brother's golden retriever, raced towards her and leapt at her full-speed.

"Ouch, hello Happy." She laughed, trying to get away from the dog. "I'm glad to see you too!"

She joined her brother in the kitchen and slumped on one of the stools at the counter while Miles made them drinks.

"No alcohol for me, please," Avery muttered. A pleasant whiff of lasagna filled the house when Miles opened the oven. It had become a tradition every time she stopped by. He knew how much she loved it.

"Oof, rough day *and* rough night?" Miles chuckled. "What happened to my little sister to make her drink so much?"

Avery loved her brother. He had always been there for her, and god knows she had needed him. When Alex had told her he'd met someone else in D.C. while she had been in the middle of packing to move there with him, it was

Miles who'd picked up the pieces and taken care of her before she'd moved in with Brooke. When they'd found out about their parents' divorce, it was Miles who'd forced their father to stop calling her because Avery was having panic attack after panic attack. And back when Josh had vanished overnight, he had been there every day to reminder her she was loved.

Miles was her rock, simple as that.

Avery groaned. "I've been dealing with so much shit today for a client, but this afternoon I finally signed a contract for the photoshoot's venue, so ... yay?"

Her brother laughed. "You don't sound so sure."

"It's been ... an interesting few days, let's put it that way." Miles crossed his arms on his chest, waiting for her to continue. She could discern some of his tattoos peaking out from under his sleeve.

"Ugh, okay." She massaged her temples. "Josh is back." There, she'd said it. Now it was out there, no take-backs.

Miles stared at her. "*Josh*, Josh? Josh I-broke-your-heart-and-left-for-Europe Josh? That Josh?"

If she had to take a shot every time her brother said "Josh," she would end up worse than last night.

She sighed, knowing she would not get away with it easily. "Yes, *that* Josh."

"Well, I hope you told him to fuck off," he scoffed.

"Yes, I did ..." she said, nodding her head vigorously.

"Good." Miles grabbed some plates from the cabinet behind him and settled them on the counter.

"... at first ..."

"Avery..." Miles groaned and shook his head.

"What? We just talked. I'm not letting him off the hook that easily, trust me."

Sometimes she felt like a child being lectured by her parents, and she was tired of always having to justify herself to her brother. The concern was appreciated, but she needed him to have more faith in her judgment.

"Do I need to remind you how devastated you were after he left? How long it took you to rebuild yourself when your best friend abandoned you like you were nothing more than a girl he went to school with?"

She sighed. He was right. But what her brother didn't know was the reason *why* it took her so long to open up to someone again, to friends or to love, to be able to stand on her own two feet without faltering. To Miles, it had been a breakup between two best friends, who were each other's world when they were kids and teenagers. To her, it had been a brutal betrayal.

"I'm not getting my hopes up, I know he's gonna leave soon."

Miles raised an eyebrow. Again. "What would you get your hopes up for?" He slid a knife and cutting board to Avery. "Can you put the salad together please?"

Avery turned the same color as the tomatoes she was holding in her hand. Was she *that* easy to read? She really needed to work on her poker face. Miles was still looking at her, waiting for her to answer.

"Well, you know ... like ... because ..." She gestured frantically with her hands. "I wouldn't want us to become really good friends like we were and have him disappear on me again." She watched Miles take the lasagna out of the oven, and her mouth watered.

"Uh huh, friends, sure. Like you guys were 'friends' the first time too?"

"First of all, you're way too old to air quote words," she retorted. "Second, we *were* friends, I don't know what you're insinuating." She felt an odd sensation in her belly. *Nope, not exploring that.*

"Friends don't look at each other with lovey-dovey eyes."

"*Oh my god* Miles, what are you, thirteen?" Every. Single. Time. They always acted like teenagers together, pushing each other's buttons to see who would crack first. Well, not tonight, Satan.

"I don't even get how you would remember the way I looked at my *best friend* ten years ago."

But this reminded her that she still had that photo of them she'd found in her souvenir box. "Hey, do you remember this?" She handed the photo to her brother.

He only glanced at it before answering. "Yeah, it was at Grams'. I've seen it somewhere." Miles shook his head.

"What?"

"Nothing."

"*What?*"

Miles sighed and scrubbed his beard. "I just, I don't know, at that time, when I was seeing you guys together all the time, I remember thinking that he'd be the one to stick, you know?"

"What do you mean?" Avery's voice quivered on the last word, rattled by what he was implying.

"Come on, Ave. It was so obvious. He was *so* in love with you. I was so sure you guys would get married and everything. Never in a million years would I have thought he'd go and do what he did. Which is why," he waved his knife in her direction, "we don't like him, and we won't do anything stupid. Right?"

She didn't know how to respond to either of those things, so she just rolled her eyes at him, making sure he saw how annoyed she was.

It hadn't been 'so obvious' to her. They were best friends and always had been. Just before he left, maybe something could have happened, but those were all hypotheticals. And her brother's opinion didn't make it the truth.

And if he wanted to continue lecturing her like she was a child, she was going to act like one. "You haven't talked to me about your work in a long time. How's it going with Riley?"

Despite his beard, Avery saw her brother's cheeks color pink. *Tit for tat.* "Any progress on that front?" She couldn't help herself and gave him her brightest smile.

Riley was Miles's co-worker and long-time crush. They both worked in public affairs and had started at their firm roughly at the same time, and her brother had been head-over-heels for her since then. Only, Riley was married to one of the firm associates, but not happily, from what Miles had told her.

She knew her brother too well to be confident that he would never act on it or push Riley to do anything, but her heart still clenched at the idea that he was waiting for her on the sidelines, hoping for something that would probably never happen.

Who knew her brother would end up being the most romantic of the two of them? *Who do you think you're fooling with your love-is-dead charade?* her inner voice whispered in her ear. Avery brushed it off.

"Not nice Ave, not nice." He gave her a full plate of lasagna and Avery dug in, burning her tongue in the process.

"Fuck, it's hot."

Miles laughed. "Karma." Carefully, he blew lightly on his fork and took a bite, making a whole show of it.

"Don't think you're off the hook with the Josh thing, but I'm going to answer you," he said, "because that's the adult thing to do, and someone has to be the mature one in this family." He winked at her, and Avery answered by sticking her tongue out. *Kids.*

"Her asshole of a husband called her out in front of the entire office last Friday for some stupid shit one of her clients did." His leg started bouncing. "It wasn't even her fault."

"What happened?"

"One of her clients had a cyberattack recently, so she spent *hours* prepping him for a press conference, practice and all, the whole shebang." Miles scoffed. "The guy went *completely*—and when I say completely, Ave, I mean like, in another galaxy—off-script during the Q&A with the journalists. They ate him alive."

"Oh, shit."

"Yup. Sean lost his shit when he found out and pinned the whole thing on her in front of everybody. And I watched it all happen and couldn't do a single fucking thing to get her out of there." He took a deep breath and laughed dryly. "So yeah, that's how it's been going."

Avery chewed on her lip. "I mean ... I'm sure she could have said something *herself*. She doesn't need you to save the day, you know." She took another bite. "Given that we're in 2022 and all that."

"I know. Ugh, *I know*!" He ran his hand down his face. "I just feel—"

"Useless?" Easy to provide a word when she was feeling the same way.

"Yeah ... that. She's the fucking smartest person I know—what does she see in this guy?"

"Well ... second-smartest, because obviously," Avery waved at herself, "me."

Miles rolled his eyes. "You're such an idiot, you know that?"

She beamed at him, making him laugh. "But a cute one at least. Speaking of idiot, have you heard from Dad today?"

"Yeah, he texted. I know the divorce papers went through. Finally." Avery was relieved that she had managed to divert the conversation from Josh, but she was not sure their parents' divorce was a better subject.

"Mom must be a complete wreck." She really needed to go see her, but given that she was having a hard time juggling her own life right now, she wasn't sure she'd be of any help.

The disconnect between her and her mother had grown exponentially over the past few years, as her mother drifted in and out of depression. It was hard for Avery to accept this change in their relationship, after being so close to her for so long. But as challenging as it was, she was still her mom, and so Avery made a mental note to call her after the meeting at Julia's.

They ate the rest of their dinner while catching up on each other's lives.

"How's the vow renewal photoshoot coming along?" Miles asked while chewing on lasagna.

"It's going. I'm shooting it in January. I actually have a meeting with them tomorrow to go over the final details. I'm telling you Miles, they are *the* cutest."

Avery was smiling just thinking about it. She had met Luc a few months ago at a wedding she was shooting. After being introduced to his husband, they had asked her if she was free to photograph their vow renewal for their ten-year anniversary ceremony. They'd talked for *hours* and had clicked instantly. They had no limits or budget restrictions and wanted to go all out. That was when she'd known she wanted to be the one to photograph them and give them the most special gift she could by capturing their beautiful love. She was the woman for the job, and it had only taken three glasses of champagne and a few solid moves on the dance floor to seal the deal.

"And then, I have a maternity shoot coming up and oh!" Avery muffled in her purse to find the document. "Look." She handed the pink piece of paper to her brother. "Lisa from the bridal boutique gave me that a few weeks ago."

Miles studied the flyer. "A contest?"

"Yes! Ugh, I *need* this. It would mean having a permanent contract with the boutique for a whole year. Can you imagine the portfolio and the client base I could build off this?"

She felt her excitement soar at the prospect. She had worked so hard those last few years to get her company off the ground, and she knew she was good at what she did, but talent wasn't enough in this industry. It was word of mouth that could make or break her career. She told her brother about her meeting with Julia later tonight, which he took fairly well considering the amount of time she would be spending with Josh.

As she was putting on her boots to leave for Julia's, Miles placed his two large hands on her shoulders, forcing her to look up.

"I'm only going to say this once, so listen to me, please." His voice was soft but tense at the same time, making Avery's throat grow tight. She knew her brother's concerned voice all too well.

"Don't give him anything he cannot give back, okay?" His eyes searched hers. "Please, Ave. I know you better than anybody, and I don't want you to end up heartbroken again. He did enough damage when he left, and I don't want you to relive that. Promise me."

She nodded, but Miles didn't let go. "I need you to say it."

"Ugh, fiiine Miles, I promise. Happy?"

The dog's ears perked up and he began to wag his tail. Miles chuckled and hugged her goodnight. "Yeah, happy."

♪♫

Avery turned right onto Kennedy Avenue, the street Josh had texted her. The brick houses in the residential neighborhood of High Park North weren't as flashy as those in the area she'd grown up in, but they had the homey charm Avery had always craved. In front of each were small yards already full of Halloween decorations of all sorts, from zombies risen from the dead to creepy smiling pumpkins.

As she drove up Julia's street, searching for 1763, Avery's heart pounded harder against her chest—the question of whether she and Josh had kissed or not still haunted her. Maybe she should try an experiment and jump his bones to see his reaction. She shook her head at the idea of having him between her legs. *Wow, Ave. Really went there fast, didn't you?*

When she saw the house, she slowed down, parked in the small driveway off to the side and turned off her car. Julia had decorated her house tastefully, with cool white lights strung across the porch illuminating the path to the entrance. No signs of witches or skeletons trying to break free from the ground, but a few paper bats hung in the trees and twirled with the wind.

She closed her eyes and blew a few breaths out, trying to quiet her growing nerves and slow her heart rate. Tonight would be fine. She adored Julia and—worst-case scenario—she and Josh had drunk kissed. So what? No need to make a big deal out of it.

A knock on her window made her jump. Squinting, she spotted Josh on the other side, waving at her. *Jesus.* Her heart was already hammering at the thought of seeing him. Could this man give her a break?

"Hi" he said, the sound of his voice muffled by the window.

Avery opened her door gently, forcing him to move out of the way.

"Hey," she said, getting out of her car and trying miserably to catch her breath. "You scared the shit out of me!"

Josh grinned from ear to ear and Avery had to grip the car door to avoid collapsing from the assault.

Closing the small distance between them, Josh picked her up, his strong arms encircling her waist and having no trouble lifting her up to his height.

"Hi," he said softly, the warmth of his breath tickling her neck and leaving a flicker of déjà vu. He used to pick her up just like that before, when he came back from a long period of time without seeing her, usually after visiting his family in Mexico.

Avery molded herself a little more closely against him, lacing her arms around his neck. Josh froze for a second, but quickly recovered and drew her closer to him, as if he could not get enough of her. It took her by surprise, the familiarity of his gesture, and the ease with which she sank into it. Like a habit one never breaks. A reflex.

"Hi back," she whispered.

His smell, his warmth, his body, all of him drove Avery on high alert. She was entirely drunk on the feel of him against her, despite the layers of clothing that kept their skin apart.

Her heart nearly exploded in her chest when his fingers brushed against her bare skin and squeezed her waist, her coat lifted by his arms holding her firmly against him. She heard him draw in a sharp breath and wondered if he was understanding the small but noticeable shift in the air too.

Slowly, he shifted her away from him, just enough to look at her, their noses almost touching. Keeping one arm tightly placed around her waist, Josh lifted his other hand and cupped her cheek, the roughness of his fingers on her skin making her dizzy. She felt like wax melting under a flame.

The tenderness with which he looked at her was enough to make her want to cry. She *missed* him. She missed him looking at her like that, making her feel safe and loved. She missed him feeling like home. *A home that threw you outside and locked the doors after promising to be your sanctuary*, her inner voice reminded her, but she pushed the thought away. Not now. Not when it felt so good to find a little piece of herself back. For a split second, Avery considered leaning in and feeling his warm lips on hers, she wanted to know his taste, wondered if it would feel as natural as being held by him. *Just do it. Do it before you come to your sense. Do—*

"Josh?"

Julia's voice startled them. They leaped away from each other, the loss of his body immediately making her shiver in the cold. In the darkness of the night, Avery hoped Julia hadn't seen how close they'd been to kissing. Good thing she had interrupted them. She didn't trust herself enough to have done it on her own, and that was definitely the smartest thing to do. *What did you just promise to your brother? Josh is going to leave again, and you know it.*

Josh cleared his throat, his eyes still locked on Avery. "Yeah Jules, I'm here with Avery! She needed help with …"

"My equipment," Avery whispered.

"Her equipment! Coming!" Josh mouthed *thank you.*

"Well, hurry up guys, it's freezing out here!" Julia said. When they heard the door close, his attention returned to her.

"You okay?"

"Mmh-hmm, yep. Let's go inside, your sister's right. I'm gonna lose a finger soon."

Josh ran his hand through his hair but made no attempt to move, his eyes still locked on Avery. After a long pause, he sighed.

"Yeah, you're right. Come on."

He reached for her hand, interlaced their fingers and led her to the front door. Standing on the porch, a wicked smile on his face, Josh brought her fingers he was holding to his lips and planted the lightest of kisses. *How much strength does this man think I have?*

He pushed the door open and stood aside as Avery walked into probably the longest evening of her life.

♪♫

They were all gathered in the living room, Josh, Julia and several bottles of wine, with food and wedding binders spread all over the floor.

Sitting on the rug, her legs tucked underneath her, Avery listened as Julia gave her the rundown of what was left to do for the wedding, but her focus desperately wanted to shift to Josh, whose attention hadn't faltered one bit since they'd come in. It was straight on her.

"... this is where the guests will arrive." Julia pointed to a map of the venue. "They will be seated here after checking the seating chart by the door." Avery was trying her best to nod and punctuate Julia's explanations with "umm" and "I see." She *was* listening. Okay, she really wasn't.

The space they'd chosen to host their wedding was a gorgeous 19th century barn outside of Toronto, which gave the perfect boho-chic feel, but was actually expensive as hell. Avery could already see how stunning the photos were going to be. She'd use the vintage wood of the barn and the snow to compliment the deep greens and neutral colors chosen by the bride and groom.

As she tried to shift her attention back to Julia's explanations, her mind kept wandering between Josh's lingering gaze and the absolutely unreal place she found herself in. Julia had welcomed her as though they'd seen each other just yesterday, and had wrapped her arms around her. Avery had to admit that it was good to see her familiar face again, and so she had no trouble returning her embrace.

Unlike her brother, Julia had followed in her father's footsteps and ran the marketing department of his two Mexican restaurants in Toronto. She was always dressed like a total boss in Avery's memories, pencil skirt and killer heels, so it was quite a contrast to see her tonight with her black hair up in a high bun and dressed in a grey sweatsuit, sitting on the floor with a glass of wine in hand.

"We are having a 'no phones during the ceremony' policy, so that should make your job easier," Julia continued.

"Thank you! It will definitely be better for me, and better photos for you guys too." She hated having to work around phones at weddings. *The. Worst.*

Her gaze shifted to Josh. He was sitting on the couch, one ankle crossed over his knee and his arms spread out on the back of the couch, looking so relaxed, and Avery thought for a second that the space next to him would somehow fit her body perfectly.

"Girl." Julia stirred her from further inappropriate thoughts. "I am *so* happy you're the one photographing our special day. Josh knows how much stress this whole debacle has caused me." She eyed her brother, but Josh smiled, pretending he hadn't heard her.

"Yeah, he knows what I'm talking about. He's just being a good, supportive brother and best man right now." She patted his knee.

"That I am," he said knowingly. "Hey, is Paul joining us tonight?"

"Yeah, he had a late meeting, but he should be here soon." She looked at her phone. "Actually, let me call him real quick to see if he's on his way. I'm starving and he's bringing Lebanese from our favorite place." She got up and moved to their bedroom, closing the door behind her.

Which left Avery to deal with her fantasies and a guy who didn't seem to want to give up. The silence in the room was deafening. She could actually hear herself breathe and noticed the sigh Josh let out as he leaned in, his elbows on his thighs.

"Can we talk about what happened outside?" he said, his intense blue glaze fixed on her.

"Did we kiss last night?" she said at the same time.

His laugh cut through her, straight to her heart. *That goddamn sound.* "You go first."

"Did we kiss last night?" she repeated.

"If you mean did you kiss my neck, then I'm afraid I'll have to go with yes."

The smile in his voice was unmistakable, and did nothing to stop Avery from flushing red, vaguely recalling the awkward moment. "Oh my god ..."

"Don't worry, I won't hold a boozy night out against you. Honest mistake," he chuckled. "Plus, you're this tall." He held his hand just under his chin, drawing Avery's gaze to where she didn't want it to linger. "So, it was bound to happen at some point."

Alright well, except for the fact that she was currently trying to come up with various ways to Houdini herself out of here and avoid further embarrassment, at least they hadn't *kiss* kissed last night.

"Okay, my turn," he said, all serious again. "I want to talk about what happened in the driveway."

This man had no filter. She was pretty sure it wasn't even a word in his vocabulary. It was all honesty, all the time, which was in a way reassuring, but dang, she could use a bit of withholding sometimes. You know, because of heart attacks and all.

"There's nothing to say, Josh. I got carried away, I'm sorry. I don't know what happened. It won't happen again." She could not bear to look at him, because she knew he would call her out on her bullshit.

What she'd felt outside during the *minute* they were tangled up in each other, was more than she had ever felt with *anybody*. Even the chemistry she'd had with Alex hadn't come close to the electricity that had run through every nerve ending of her body when Josh had gripped her waist and made her feel his clear intentions.

He swallowed hard, his jaw twitching like he was about to break. "What if I want it to happen again?" He paused, then whispered, holding her gaze. "What if I want to see what happens next?"

His questions sent Avery into a dizzying swirl of thoughts. What *would* have happened next if Julia hadn't interrupted them? He would have probably kissed her breathless—Avery could tell from the hunger she'd seen flashing in his eyes, despite the dim light of the driveway. And she had already been this close to grinding against him. *How embarrassing.*

Her breath caught in her throat at the idea of wrapping her legs around his waist and fully feeling him against every intimate part of herself.

Instinctively, she wet her bottom lip with the tip of her tongue, and when her eyes met his, she watched as his chest rose and fell hard, his eyes slowly drifting down to the movement she had just made.

"Don't do that, Ave."

"We're friends Josh," she managed to say as firmly as she could, ignoring his warning laced with want. She knew they were veering dangerously close to another territory, which she could not allow. Under no reasonable circumstances.

"Is that what we are?"

Before she could come up with an appropriate lie, Julia swung the bedroom door open.

"He's two minutes away," she said, plopping down on the couch next to Josh. "What were you guys talking about?"

Your brother wanting to feel me up?

"I was just inviting Avery to my show next Sunday night," Josh said before Avery could stammer and make a fool of herself. *His what now?* He hadn't said anything to her about a show.

"Oh great!" Julia turned to Avery. "I can't believe the conservatory asked him to play. Ugh, how talented is he?" She rested her head on his shoulder and ruffled Josh's hair, making him look exactly how Avery pictured he'd look if he'd just woken up, still drowsy with sleep. *Great*.

"What's the show for?" she asked.

"The conservatory is having a party to honor its most prestigious members, and our mother was one of them," he said, his voice thick with emotion. "Since she's no longer with us, they invited me a few months ago to pay tribute to her." Josh closed his eyes and heaved a deep breath.

Still propped against her brother, Julia gently patted his chest. "He's going to be amazing, just like he always is, and Mom would be beyond proud."

Avery's throat tightened at the sadness that clouded Josh's face. All she wanted to do was let her guard down, to hell with the consequences, and snuggle up to him, soothe him, anything that would lift an ounce of the pain she saw surging through him.

"I'd love to come," was all she could say. Julia gave her a grateful smile.

They heard the front door open and Paul, Julia's fiancé, appeared in the living room. He was dressed in a grey blue wool suit jacket, a light blue shirt tucked in navy blue slacks. The look gave him business yet laid-back vibes at the same time.

"Babe!" Julia leaped off the couch to greet her fiancé. "How was your day?"

"Busy, busy." Paul scanned the room. "Hey guys! Avery, nice to see you again!"

"Hi Paul, good to see you." Avery smiled, while Josh waved from the couch.

Julia gestured toward the papers sprawled on the low table and the rug. "We were talking about wedding stuff. Josh *finally* found a photographer. Guess who it is?"

Paul laughed, his eyes landing on Avery. "Well, unless Josh finally convinced Avery to go out with him, I would say that's the reason she's here."

An awkward silence filled the room. Avery's cheeks burned from the sudden scrutiny.

"*Paul!*" Julia slapped his chest playfully with the back of her hand. "Don't mind him." She rolled her eyes.

Paul leaned in and kissed his fiancée's forehead. "While you guys finish talking about this, I need to discuss something with Josh real quick."

Josh arched one eyebrow, clearly not privy to what Paul wanted to discuss with him, which made Avery nervous for some reason. They disappeared in the kitchen, leaving her thoughts to wander.

"Avery? Did you hear what I said?" Julia snapped her back to the living room.

"I'm sorry, I was—"

"Oh, don't worry," she waved casually. "It happens to me sometimes too when I have too much on my mind."

"Do you know what that's about?" Avery nodded toward the kitchen, frowning at the closed door.

"Not sure." Julia shrugged. "Maybe Dad's retirement?"

David was retiring? *Oh.* Knowing the expectations he'd had on Josh when he was just ten, Avery couldn't imagine what he needed from him now. But what did Paul have to do with it anyway?

"So, while we're still on wedding details, I've been wanting to ask you something else," Julia said.

"Sure, ask away! I actually had something I wanted to talk to you about too."

"Oh, well, go ahead!" Julia beamed.

"Okay, well." Avery took a deep breath. *Here it is, make or break.* "There's a photography contest happening right now and if I win, it could really help me get my business off the ground. The only thing is that I would need to use your wedding photos to be able to compete. I completely understand if you don't want to. It's your wedding, after all."

Julia stared at her, her face lighting up with each passing second. "Is that what you wanted to ask me? Are you kidding me? Of course, I don't mind! You're telling me that the whole world will see my wedding?" She pretended to think. "Hmmm, yeah! More spotlight on *me!*"

Well, maybe not the whole world, but definitely more people. Relief washed over her at Julia's response. She had just secured her place in the competition, and was one step closer to her dream.

"Okay, my turn," Julia said.

Avery straightened, feeling invigorated. "Lay it on me."

"I would love for you to come to my bachelorette party and rehearsal dinner."

"I ... well, sure!" Avery blurted out, surprised by the request.

"Great! This makes me *so* happy. I've missed you so much." She threw herself at Avery. "Okay so let me see …" She fumbled through her notes. "The bachelorette party is on the Saturday, November 29th, and then, we're leaving for Niagara-on-the-Lake on December first, rehearsal dinner is the Friday, and wedding the next day, the third. Sound good to you?"

It took her a couple of seconds to process the information Julia had just sprung on her and connect the dots. Seeing the confusion on her face, Julia clarified, "Oh yeah, we're doing a family/close friends pre-wedding party week at the house. I'm so excited, it's going to be *amazing*," she sang.

Oh. *Ooooh*. Four days. With Josh. Sleeping in the same house. This could not possibly be good.

"I'll send you a formal request tomorrow so you can issue me an invoice for the photography service. Thank you so much for doing this, Avery," Julia said, reaching out for her hands. "You don't know how good it is to see you again, especially after how everything went down between you and my brother …"

The air in her lungs grew tighter, causing her to strain for oxygen.

"Listen," Julia continued, "I don't know what's happening between you guys right now, but between us, let me say this. He was a mess, Avery. When he was in Europe, there wasn't a single time when we talked where he didn't ask me about you. When we," she gestured between them, "lost touch over the years, he was devastated. He didn't say it, but I just knew." Julia squeezed Avery's hand gently.

"And when he came back to Toronto, oh my god, I was *so* happy. Losing our mom and his career setbacks, you don't understand the toll it's taken on him. When I heard that he ran into you, and seeing how he is now? I feel like I'm getting my brother back, like he's coming back to life. I don't know how to explain it, but I know you have something to do with it.

"I know that there's a chance he'll leave again, but to see him like this is enough for me. I thought I had lost him for good."

Avery was trying so hard not to burst into tears as they filled her eyes. Fuck, she was so tired of the crying mess she'd been every damn day for the past week.

What Julia just said had blindsided her. She was drowning in the waves of her pent-up emotions, resentment towards the years of silence, and the undeniable connection between them that had never faded. And even with all that, she'd never felt more vibrant.

"I ... I don't know what to say." Avery's lips quivered.

Julia offered her a soft smile. "You don't need to say anything. I just wanted you to know."

The guys chose this moment to come out of the kitchen. Josh's demeanor had drastically changed from when he'd left the room. He looked withdrawn, on edge. Avery quickly wiped her eyes with her sleeve, not wanting any questions from him, but she hadn't been fast enough.

"Are you okay?" Concern was written all over his face as his gaze kept darting back and forth between Avery and Julia.

Avery sniffed. "Yes, everything is fine. It's just super late, I have to get home." She hurried to collect her things.

"Thanks for everything Julia. I can't wait to chat more about the wedding soon."

She gave Julia a quick hug, paused in front of Paul and nodded at him.

Finally, she stopped in front of Josh. "Thank you for thinking of me for your sister's wedding. I truly appreciate it."

Josh stared at her dumbfounded, unaware of what his sister had just sprung on her. "Let me walk you to your car."

"No, don't bother, I'm fine."

"I want to." Avery knew he wouldn't budge, so she nodded and walked briskly to her car.

Outside, Josh caught up with her easily. "Okay, Avery, wait a minute, what happened inside?"

She hated lying but she also didn't want to go through this tonight. So, she went with a half-truth. "Nothing, I'm just really tired from the past few days and need to get some sleep."

Josh raked a hand through his hair, still not letting it go. *This damn stubborn man.*

"What did my sister say?"

"What did Paul say?" she countered. His body went rigid at the mention of Paul. Apparently, he had no more desire to talk about him than she did about Julia.

She sighed. "I had a great time tonight, okay?" She stepped closer, knowing that it was about 98% a bad idea. From where she stood now, she had to look up, his tall frame towering easily over her.

"Hey." She placed her hand under his razor-sharp jaw, forcing him to look at her. She failed to consider the burning sensation she would feel from her fingertips, traveling all the way up her arm, and right to the little organ pumping all those feelings in her chest. She exhaled and looked at him.

"I mean it when I say I had a great time. Thank you for helping me go after my dreams."

As if her arm was a completely independent limb from the rest of her body, acting on its own accord, her hand traveled south, brushing the collar of his shirt, and landing flat against his pec.

Shocked by the intimacy of her gesture, she yanked her hand away, but Josh wrapped his fingers around her wrist before she could completely remove it, pressing her hand back to his chest, over his heart. Avery felt it race under her palm, and understanding slowly settled between them. When she parted her lips, Josh's gaze immediately slid there, both of them going a little bit breathless.

Avery broke the silence. "I have to go."

"Can't you stay tonight? Julia and Paul have two guest rooms, and I'm not entirely relaxed about you getting home so late like this. Please," he rasped.

"I ... I don't think that's a good idea Josh."

Slowly, she retrieved her hand and shoved it back into her pocket. She needed some space from his mind-numbing scent. "But I would be happy to come Sunday night, if you really want me there."

"Of course, I do. I'll call first thing in the morning and have them put your name on the list."

Avery nodded. "Perfect, thanks. Can you add Brooke's too?"

"Sure thing."

She rocked back on her heels. "Okay, well, I think it's time for me to head out."

"Okay," he whispered, his eyes still and always locked in hers. *Ugh, how were they supposed to say goodnight...*

Against her better judgment, she went with the hug. Josh wrapped his arms around her softly, his hands rubbing her back. When she broke away, there was so much warmth in his eyes that she thought she was going to melt on the spot.

"Good night, Avie."

"Good night."

He leaned down and planted a soft kiss her cheek, hot breath caressing cold skin. "See you Sunday."

Ten

Dress

Avery hadn't slept all night and had been on a pacing marathon since 7 a.m. Her nerves were shot, her emotions were on edge, and her anxiety was close to getting the best of her. On the menu today, stress cleaning, stress eating and stress Netflix binging. *Everything was fine.*

The good news was, her house was spotless, she had no more junk food since she'd eaten every last chocolate chip cookie she could find, and her Netflix watch list had shrunk considerably. *Silver lining, right?*

She checked her phone: 5:15 p.m. *Ughhh.* Why did Brooke always had to be late? Especially today of all days. Although to be fair, she wasn't aware of the latest development in the Josh and Avery saga because if she had been, she would have already been there. And they'd probably have gone through at least a bottle of wine already.

You gotta relax. What did your therapist say? One thought at a time, one thing at a time.

Today was Sunday, the day of Josh's concert, which she had told him a week ago she would attend. And *that* was after the fact that they'd nearly kissed not once, but twice in the span of four hours. You know how they say you have to think before you act? Yeah, well ... next time?

And then, because he was apparently perfect and sweet and everything a woman could ever want, he had texted to check if she had made it home okay. Now, she was breaking into hives from all the stress the past week had caused her. *Everything is great. You're not spiraling at all.*

How could she have let it go this far? She hadn't been in control of her body that night when she had casually laid her hand on his chest, as if she had done it a hundred times before. The gesture had felt natural, familiar. And the only plausible and completely reasonable explanation Avery could come up with was that he had simply bewitched her with his intoxicating scent and his captivating eyes.

Sitting at the kitchen island, she bounced her leg nervously, eyes locked on the front door. She was still in her bathrobe, fresh out of the shower, but at the rate the sweat was building up on her nape and trickling down her back, she was going to need a second one.

Her phone pinged and startled her out of her intense focus of trying to make Brooke appear on the spot.

Josh [5:20 pm]: Names are on the list for tonight, front row seats, so you guys won't miss a thing. Can't wait to see you in a few hours. xx

Her heart pounded loud in her ears. *Nope, you're not going to do that, Ave. You're not going to overanalyze the text.* He was just letting her know that seats had been reserved and that he was looking forward to seeing them. There. Straight to the point.

Although …

She could not rip her eyes from the 'can't wait to see you' and the tingling sensation it created in her fingers. And then, well, there was the matter of the two kisses at the end of the text, which, come on. Who sent two kisses to a friend? Even if you'd known that friend for close to twenty years, two kisses was pushing it.

But she would only make those observations if she was going to overanalyze it, which she wasn't, so there was no valid reason for her heart to be doing this weird thing in her chest.

Her front door rang. "Finally," she mumbled, rolling her eyes. Didn't Brooke have keys?

"Where the fuck have y—" she started, opening the door, only the man in front of her was definitely not her best friend.

"Avery Clark?" The man was holding a package.

"Hum … Yes?"

"I have a delivery for you. Can you please sign here?" He pointed to a dotted line on his receipt. "Thank you. Have a great day!"

Avery took the package inside, racking her brain to figure out when the last time she'd ordered something was, and almost slammed the door in Brooke's face.

"Hey! Careful!" Brooke yelped.

Avery spun around. "I'm sorry, I didn't hear you! Are you okay?" But then frustration and her nerves took over, and she didn't let Brooke answer.

"Where the fuck have you been?" Avery repeated, but this time to the right person. "We're supposed to leave in 30 minutes, you're almost an hour late, and I am *still* naked under here." She gestured towards her robe. "I told you I needed your help." She did. She really *really* needed it.

Brooke was already ready and on top of her game, nothing surprising there. Her blond hair, which she'd curled a little, was flowing in glamourous vintage Hollywood waves down her shoulders. She'd settled on a black satin dress, slit on the side just below her knee, which contrasted in a dramatic way with the light color of her hair. *Always making a statement.* At first glance, the look appeared simple, but the results were flawlessly chic.

"Well, hi to you too, wow." Brooke blew out an annoyed breath, and walked past Avery, making herself at home. "Someone needs to relax."

Sometimes, her nonchalant, easy-breezy attitude had a way of getting on Avery's nerves. *Especially* when there was so much at stake, when she was feeling like shit and ready to burst.

"I would be if you'd been here on time," she replied.

Avery settled the package on the kitchen counter.

"Alright, I'm here now, what's up?" Brooke nodded toward the package. "What's this?"

Avery shrugged. "I don't know, I just got it."

She opened one of her kitchen drawers and took out a pair of scissors. Gently, she cut through the package's tape and pulled open the flaps. There was a card with her name on top of a second package wrapped in white silk paper.

She looked at Brooke puzzled, and took the card in her hands, her fingers shaking slightly when she recognized the handwriting. *What did he do?* She slipped her index finger under the lid of the envelope and opened it.

Avie,

You could wear ripped jeans and an oversized t-shirt and still be the most beautiful woman in the room.

But I hope you'll accept this small present and wear it tonight. When I saw it, I knew it was made for you.

Yours,

J.

Her heart slammed against her rib cage and her breath caught in her throat. Was she on fire? Had the world ceased to exist?

"What is it?" Brooke asked.

"I don't know yet," Avery whispered, too low for B. to have heard her. She unfolded the paper and took out a gorgeous dress that made Brooke gasp.

"Avery, what is *this*???"

Avery couldn't answer her, too focused on the fiery crimson red dress she was holding at arm's length.

Running out of patience, Brooke picked up the card.

"Avie, you could wear ..." Her eyes continued to roam the note, before she gasped again. "Is this from *Josh*?!" She nearly screamed saying his name, in an Oscar-worthy performance.

Avery rubbed her forehead and muttered: "It appears so." The idea that Josh had thought of her when he'd seen this dress, that he'd felt it was *made* for her, like he'd imagined her in it, sent a rush of warmth through her. She imagined him walking around town and stumbling upon the dress in a window, entering the store, oddly selecting the right size and paying, the cashier probably asking who the lucky lady was. And apparently, she was.

"Avery, hellooo, back to earth." Brooke was snapping her fingers in front of her face.

"Sorry," she said while checking the time. "Can you help me put it on? I'll fill you in while I get ready."

They both went to her bedroom so Avery could snag a pair of underwear and a strapless bra, then headed to the bathroom. She stripped naked, nothing Brooke hadn't seen a hundred times before, and slipped them on.

Brooke was already back to her line of questioning. "Okay, so help me understand. I left you guys at the bar, where you categorically said you didn't want anything to do with him and here we are, going to his concert tonight, in a dress that he *bought* and *sent* you in one of the most romantic gestures in the history of rom-coms."

She crouched and held the dress so Avery could step inside. "What am I missing here? This screams hot sex to me."

At the mention of sex with Josh, Avery flushed three shades of red. Perfect, that way she could match the color of the dress.

"Oh my god Avery, you secretive little bitch." She stood up, leaving the dress hanging mid waist and swatted Avery's arm.

"Ow!"

"When??"

"We didn't, calm down!" *But what we did in the driveaway was basically foreplay.* She inhaled and let the truth out. "We almost kissed."

Brooke gasped, her hand flying to her mouth.

"Twice," Avery added reluctantly.

Brooke shrieked. "*WHAT*?!" Another swat.

"Stop it!"

"I can't *believe* you didn't text me the minute it happened."

"There's nothing to tell, B. We got confused for a second, that's all."

Brooke huffed out a laugh. "*Twice*? One time I could *maybe* understand, but twice in a night? Sure, if that's what you want to call it. But apparently, he didn't get the message," she said, retrieving the dress that had fallen on the floor. "Seriously Ave, maybe you should consider this."

She helped her slide on the off-the-shoulder sleeves that hung low on her elbows.

"I really, *really* don't think it's a good idea, B. We are not on the same page, and even if we were, there are too many things in our way for this to ever work out." Her fear of abandonment, her trust issues, her anxiety, his unpredictability, the fact that he was unreliable ... Should she go on?

"And if you don't think? What if you just *feel*, babe? What does your heart tell you then?"

Ah, her heart. The most unreliable organ in her entire body. The one that sped up every time Josh smiled, making his left dimple and the crinkles in the corner of his eyes appear. His whole face lit up whenever his eyes found her, and her heart had been a goner every time.

The same one that skipped a beat when his gaze pinned her on the spot. The very same that flipped over when he put his hands on her, the only person who made her feel safe this fast in the hands of a man. Yeah, if she trusted her heart, she'd probably have her answer.

From behind her, Brooke leaned her chin on her shoulder and hugged Avery, looking at their reflection in the mirror. "I know you've been through a lot with Alex and your parents. I *know* Josh was an asshole for leaving the way he did. But you're stuck in the past, Ave. The Josh you see today is not the one who left ten years ago. You've changed, right? It's only fair to give him the benefit of the doubt. And he is not Alex. Or your father."

Tears were beginning to pool in both of their eyes. "You're miserable, and you have been for a while now. You should try and be happy sometimes, Ave. I swear, it's worth it."

But was it really worth it to risk losing Josh all over again? To have her heart ripped out once more? To be rejected and feel even more unlovable than she already did? Was it *that* worth it? She didn't have any answer to those questions, and that terrified her. Enough to not take the risk. *Better safe than sorry.*

Leaning against Brooke, they stayed like that for a few minutes, rocking in each other's arms.

"You have to zip me up," Avery whispered in the quiet of the room.

"Oh my god, yes, sorry." Brooke pulled up the zipper and looked at Avery in the mirror, letting out an impressed whistle. "Wow, girl you look … Wow."

Yeah … she really did. Josh had taste. The dress was simply breathtaking, highlighting every single curve of her body. The long A-line gown fell perfectly on her hips and flowed generously at her feet like a cloud. The revealing heart-shaped neckline plunged slightly in a triangle between her breasts, following the lines of her chest. As for the off-the-shoulder sleeves, they gave the impression that Josh had spent the evening trying to undress her, a thought that immediately sent her head spinning.

And the skirt … If the slit in Brooke's dress reached her knee, Avery's almost touched her hip, bringing the extra touch of glamour.

"Well, that man knows what he's talking about. It does fit you perfectly," Brooke said. "C'mon, let's do your hair and makeup real quick before we head out."

Brooke used her *Voluptuous Red* lipstick to match the color of the dress, and a light touch of mascara to perfect her eyes. As she lifted Avery's long hair into an elegant updo, she let a few strands frame her face, while leaving her shoulders completely bare. Hadn't she said she'd needed her bff?

"I'm gonna order a taxi while you put your shoes on," Brooke said.

But a knock on the door interrupted her final touches. *What now?*

"Is Josh picking us up?" Brooke asked as she headed towards the entry.

Was he? "I don't think so."

She joined Brooke at the open door, where a man in a suit she didn't recognize was waiting.

"Hi, can I help you with anything?"

"Ms. Clark?"

Brooke and Avery exchanged glances. *What the hell?*

"Yes?"

"Good evening, my name is Jack. Mr. Harding asked me to drive you to the conservatory tonight."

Mr. Harding. Again, the question needed to be asked: *What the hell?* Josh had really gone all out tonight.

Brooke burst out laughing, gripping Avery's arm to keep her from falling. "Is Josh loaded? If you don't have sex with him Avery, I will. Alice and I have some renovations coming up in the apartment."

She dragged Avery by the hand, still laughing, as they climbed into the car. It was only 6:30 p.m., but the night was already shaping up to be full of surprises.

♪♫

Their entrance at the Royal Conservatory Hall revealed that they were definitely dressed appropriately for the occasion. Everyone was looking their best, bow ties and long dresses as far as the eye could see.

After confirming that they were indeed on the list, they slowly made their way into the auditorium, going down the steps to the front row. Avery felt out of place when she found the two seats labelled with their names. The same sensation that she felt during the gala resurfaced, and small beads of sweat trickled on her forehead. She dabbed a tissue lightly on her face and neck. *Breathe, everything is fine, it's just Josh, and you're here to support him.*

"Are you okay?" Brooke lowered her voice, concerned.

"Yeah, I'm fine, just a little hot."

Brooke winked. "That would be *the Josh effect.*"

Avery rolled her eyes. "You know I'm not the best at social gatherings. I'm feeling very ... inadequate."

"Well, your dress screams everything but inadequate, babe."

"You know what I mean."

"Yeah, I do." She patted her knee. "Relax, we're just here for our boy, okay?" Avery nodded. She couldn't imagine how Josh was feeling right now. A small part of her wanted to meet him backstage, to see how he was holding up. He had to be thinking about his mother.

The two seats next to her, reserved for Julia and Paul, were still empty when the lights dimmed, and the evening began slowly. According to the program, Josh was scheduled to perform just before intermission.

The girls listened to one performance after another, clapping when necessary. At one point, Brooke asked her if they served free booze during the show, making Avery giggle, which earned them a few pointed looks.

After the fourth number, Julia and Paul finally showed up, discreetly slipping between the seats and greeting Brooke and Avery with warm smiles.

"You look sensational," Julia said.

"Thank you," Avery whispered before seeing the gorgeous midnight blue dress Julia wore. "Oh my gosh, so do you!"

As they finished seating themselves, the director of the conservatory addressed the audience. "The performance that follows is a very special one for the conservatory family." Avery's heart sank. She knew what was coming. "One of our finest pianists, Nora, sadly left us too soon, twelve years ago. I am honored to welcome to the stage tonight her son, Joshua, who is carrying on his mother's legacy. Ladies and gentlemen, please welcome Joshua Harding."

Josh walked on stage, looking impossibly handsome in his custom-made tuxedo, his wavy hair perfectly styled.

While he greeted the audience, Julia leaned towards Avery again. "Josh requested that you be backstage for the performance." She slipped her a badge in her hand.

"What?" Avery was confused. "Why?"

"I don't know, he didn't say. I'm just the messenger!" She winked at her. "Go, go!"

Badge in hand, she stood up and apologized. Brooke mouthed *what are you doing?* and Avery replied *backstage* the same way. When she saw Julia explaining, she took a more deliberate step before Josh began to play.

She showed the badge to security, who opened the doors for her and stood behind the curtain just as Josh sat down at the piano, facing her. The movement must have caught his attention, because he looked up and their eyes met. Josh's gaze slowly roamed up and down Avery's dress in an appreciative way, taking her in. He swallowed heavily.

Her eyes locked on him, he began to play his mother's favorite piece, "Claire de Lune." The emotion in the room was palpable, because of the significance of the moment, but also because of Josh's exceptional talent, brushing the piano keys with a masterful hand. He wasn't just playing the song. He was living it, letting the melody flow through him and into the room.

Avery knew him like the back of her hand, and ten years without any contact hadn't erased the memories of his face, his expressions, the way he frowned when he was concentrating, or how he gritted his teeth when he got emotional.

She wanted to run to him and soothe the line that had formed between his brows with her thumb, to tell him that it was okay, that he could cry and let go, be sad. That she would be there to catch him, this time.

And as if on cue, she watched as tears slid down his cheeks. It took real effort for Avery to keep her feet planted where they were. Every part of her was itching to get to him. She hadn't realized she was crying too until her own tears fell on her arms, which were clasped tightly under her chest.

Thunderous applause vibrated through the auditorium when the last note sounded, and Avery saw everyone on their feet, not a dry eye in sight. She applauded as well, not at all surprised by the sheer power and talent of this man.

Josh thanked the audience from his seat and returned his attention to Avery. Only his gaze had completely changed. She saw the same hunger in his eyes that she had seen in the driveway the other night. With no warning, he picked up the microphone in front of him.

"Thank you very much. Thank you. My mother was an esteemed member of the conservatory, an incredible pianist, but most importantly, she was the best mother a son could ever dream of." Avery heard a few 'aws' from the crowd. "Tonight, I have the pleasure of sharing this tribute with my sister, but also with someone very dear to me." His eyes shifted back to Avery, and he spoke to her, as if it was just the two of them in his country home, her sitting on the rug, and him behind the piano. "This one's for you."

It was the second time she'd heard him say it, and still, she was not prepared when his fingers flew across the piano keys again, playing the first few notes of the very same song he'd performed at the gala. The one he'd said made him think of her. Helped him through his dark days. The notes tore through Avery's heart. Josh was playing their song, while keeping his gaze focused on her. There was no question this time as to what he was doing or what he was trying to say.

That was it. The last piece that broke her resolve. She couldn't keep pretending he didn't affect her.

She watched him play, mesmerized by the way his shoulders tensed when he hit the notes, how the vein in his neck swelled every time his eyes traveled up and down her body, how his jaw tensed when she tucked a loose strand of hair behind her ear, making her very core clench in response. It was like a chain reaction, like they were playing an invisible game.

Josh was giving her his full attention, like they were the only ones in the room and *wow*. She was *not* in control anymore. Her mind wandered to places she'd forbidden herself to go, like how it would feel to have his hands on her, to feel him hot and hard between her legs, how soft his lips would be on every inch of her body, how perfect she would fit under him, the pang of anticipation making her insides melt. She had never allowed herself to think about it because she knew how disastrous the results would be, but right now? Right now, she just wanted to let go, and give up the control she needed when her emotions were in play.

So, when Josh played the last note, quickly bowed to the audience, and turned back to her, his intentions oh so very clear, it was only logical that she nodded softly, giving him the permission he desperately wanted.

She saw his entire body tense in anticipation as his eyes went completely dark. He rushed off the stage and didn't slow down one bit when his body collided with hers. Eagerly, he backed her up against the nearest wall and finally, *finally* crashed his lips on hers. There was nothing tender about this kiss. It was all rushed hands, wet lips, craving and impatience. She was caught between the wall and Josh, and her hands moved quickly to undo his bow tie and the first buttons on his shirt.

Josh wrapped his long fingers around the nape of her neck and inclined her head, granting him better access, and Avery failed to contain the tiny sound that escaped her mouth as she opened to let him in.

The husky grunt that came from his mouth as their tongues collided could have made her come on the spot. This was the doing of a starved man. Desperate to get closer, Avery clutched Josh's hair as if she were holding on for dear life, marvelling at his scent, his taste, his power over her.

"You want more?" Josh asked roughly and all she could do was nod. *Yes*, she *needed* more.

He lifted her leg and wrapped it around his waist, the slit of her dress sliding up, leaving it completely bare. His hand went roughly up her thigh, cupping her ass underneath her dress as his fingers brushed under the line of her panties, her skin sizzling like a hot wire under his touch. *Fucking hell.*

She gasped against his mouth. His touch screamed 'mine,' and if he ventured a few inches lower, he would find evidence of how exactly his she was.

"Avie," Josh groaned. "What are you doing to me?"

It was less a question than a plea. Had she passed out? The feel of his hand against her skin, gripping her so tightly against him was indecently arousing, and she forgot for a minute that she was in a room full of people. *A room full of people. Oh my god.*

"Josh," she managed to get out. But Josh wasn't listening, his erection pushing hard against her belly, his hand sliding down her neck, contouring the curve of her breast and gripping her waist.

She laid her hands flat against his pecs and tried to push him away gently.

"Josh," she repeated.

He groaned again, and reluctantly broke their kiss, both of them panting.

"I know, I know."

Their chests heaved up and down, completely breathless.

She was still standing with her back against the wall, half-wrapped around Josh, half-naked, and beyond turned on. With his forehead against hers, one hand still firmly placed under her ass, the other on her waist, Josh was trying to come to his senses.

"I *knew* this dress would fit you perfectly," he said, a smile on his lips. Avery laughed, still dazed and drunk by the feel of him. She could still feel him hard between them.

Josh released her from his grip and helped her regain her balance. They were a fucking mess. His hair was all disheveled, his shirt completely untucked, his lips swollen from their kiss, and Avery had absolutely no desire to see what *she* looked like.

"Here, let me." After getting himself in order, Josh came closer and adjusted her dress, and the strands of hair that were fluttering wildly around her face.

His thumb lingered on her cheek, stroking it tenderly, then slid to her bottom lip, applying just enough pressure to part them.

"I love that look on you." He leaned in, and pressed a kiss to her lips, soft and sweet. "Wild and turned on." Another kiss. "I have a lot on my plate next week. What do you say we have dinner together next Saturday? My place, 6 p.m.?"

Avery nodded. "Yes."

She knew exactly what she was agreeing to, but for some reason, she wasn't afraid.

Josh flashed her his handsome smile, dimple and all.

"Perfect." He kissed her again. "Now go, because I have to stay here until the show is over, and I don't know if I'll be able to control myself if you keep looking at me like that."

He kissed her again, then moved down to her neck. Avery tilted her head and moaned, shivers running down her spine. He was driving her crazy.

Moving back up, he kissed her just below her earlobe. "And this isn't really the place I want to be inside you for the first time."

Well, that would do it. Gone was her sanity, because there was no way Josh just whispered those dirty words to her. He kissed her one more time.

"Okay, now go."

Avery couldn't really remember how she'd found Brooke afterwards, if she had explained what had happened, or how she'd gotten home. She somehow found herself in her bed, the smell of Josh clinging to every corner where his lips had been.

She could easily trace with her fingertips the path of his kisses, because her skin was still oversensitive, bringing her back to that very moment where he'd devoured her.

But in the back of her restless mind, Avery knew that once she came down from her high, panic would take over. So, she closed her eyes and forced herself to sleep, hoping to delay the inevitable for as long as possible.

Eleven

Forgiveness

Avery was fidgeting nervously with her phone while waiting at the high-end restaurant her dad had picked out for lunch. Of course, he couldn't have gone with something less flashy, somewhere where she would have been more comfortable, because Dan Clark never thought about anyone else besides himself. And prestige was everything to this man.

So there she was, waiting at the table the waiter had seated her at, near tall, squared windows, watching as the rain poured outside. How ironic that the weather was as miserable as her mood. She only had one wish: to run outside and let the rain work its magic.

She should have been feeling pretty elated after what had happened with Josh last weekend, and their date tonight, but the idea of seeing her father today dimmed the bubbling joy she felt inside her.

A waiter came to her table and filled her glass with water. She offered him a tight smile as he was leaving, her leg shaking under the table. *Ten minutes*. He had the audacity to be late to a lunch *he'd* invited her to. Should she leave? Five more minutes or she was out. For good.

As she was slowly gathering her stuff, ready to bolt as soon as the clock ran out, a familiar silhouette stepped through the restaurant's front door. His authoritative frame towered over the poor waitress, who turned and pointed to Avery. Her father's eyes found her and suddenly she wanted to crawl under the table and drape the tablecloth over her, like they used to do when she and Miles were kids. The thing was, she was not six years old anymore, she was a grown-ass woman, and she could certainly face her liar of a father. Straightening up in her chair, she mustered all her courage and blew out a sharp breath while her father made his way to their table.

"You can do this," she murmured to herself.

"Hi, bug. Sorry, I got delayed at the hospital. Meeting with some donors ran longer than expected," he said, as he sat down, clearly not hoping to get any warm welcome from his daughter. As usual, Dan was immaculately dressed. The expensive cut and midnight blue sheen of his suit accentuated the straight, sharp lines of his features. She watched carefully as he undid the button of his suit jacket and adjusted his cuffs before crossing his hands on the table.

"Thank you for agreeing to meet me here. I know we're not on the best terms right now, and I wanted a chance to explain my side of the story."

Avery scoffed. *Wow, off to a great start, Dad.* "Your *side*?" The guy had lived a double life for years. It was plain and simple, there was no other "side" to it.

Dan raised his palm. "No, you're right. I'm sorry, it was a poor choice of words on my part. What I meant to say was, I just want to be able to get everything out on the table and move on."

Very business-like meeting. No emotion, no smile. *Just get it over with.*

"Are you ready to order?" the waiter interrupted, iPad in hand.

"We haven't—"

"Actually, if you don't mind, bug," he said, silencing her with a wave of his hand before turning to the waiter. "We'll have the Oregon trout and a bottle of white Chablis Grand Cru 2018."

He dismissed the waiter with a "Thank you" and turned his attention back to Avery, who was staring at him with a stern face.

It was always the same with him—he was a master in the art of belittling. Calling her a pet name in front of people she didn't know, as if she were still ten years old, ordering her food for her, as if she wasn't capable of making her own choices. She. Was. Fuming. The worst part was that she knew he probably hadn't even notice because he was too focused on himself to care about his demeaning behavior toward his own daughter.

"Don't call me that in front of people," she said, her voice ice-cold.

He shrugged. "Habits. Sorry, bug."

Seriously? "It's fine." It wasn't, but there was no point in wasting her breath.

Dan cleared his throat. "So, look. I want to start by apologizing. I know I hurt you and your brother, and that's the last thing I ever wanted to do. I should have owned up to it from the start, and dealt with my mess myself, but instead I let it drag on for too long. I'm sorry." He delivered his monologue like one of his speeches he did for investors: like a well-oiled machine, straight to the point, no nonsense, no feelings.

Dan reached across the table and placed his hand on Avery's. The contact repulsed her and she pulled her hand away and tucked it under the table instantly, frantically massaging her fingertips between her thumb and index. Anxiety and anger were starting to get through to her, she was trying to cope with a mechanism Dr. Kant had given her.

"I miss you, bug." Dan sighed. "I know I screwed up, okay? I know I should have come clean to your mom sooner."

"Sooner?" she scoffed. "No, no. You should never have done it in the first place. How can you not see that? Please, the least you can do is take responsibility for your actions. Frankly, it's pretty fucking unbelievable that your 28-year-old daughter has to be the adult here."

Her father opened his mouth but closed it just as quickly, thinking better of it. Good. If he thought Avery would fall for his typical bullshit, he was clearly mistaken. This time she was going to stand her ground. She owed it to her mother.

The waiter came back with their plates, the smell of tarragon and caramelized shallots filling the space between them as he placed their food on the table. She took a bite of fish and the tender flesh of the trout melted deliciously on her tongue. At least she was getting a good lunch out of this.

"Look, I can't undo the past here. What is done is done and I take full responsibility, trust me," Dan said. "But I don't regret where it led me." Avery stopped eating and stared at her father. "Your mom and I grew apart, bug. We were too different in the end. I was miserable."

"*You* were miserable?" she scoffed again. This had to be the joke of the century. Was she being pranked? Where were the cameras?

Avery waited for him to answer but all he did was hold her gaze. She shook her head.

"Unbelievable. You couldn't be more self-centered if you tried. Mom gave up everything for you. *You're* the reason she's not the person she used to be." Her leg was shaking again, nerves were taking over. *Breathe.*

"Here's what's going to happen, Dan," she said, trying to steady her voice. "I know the divorce will be finalized soon. You're going to leave the house to Mom and—" She raised her hand as he started to open his mouth. "I'm not done yet. The house goes to Mom because *she* has been the one making it a home all our lives." Her father simply nodded.

"Second, I think Mom deserves to be generously compensated for raising your children by herself and giving up everything she loved for you, don't you agree?" She took a sip of her wine. "Those are my terms if you ever wish to hear from me again."

It took him a little while to wrap his head around the requests she had just made. Her mother would never have made them herself, she was too proud for that, but Avery wasn't above it.

"Okay," he simply said.

Okay? Just like that? It was not in her father's nature to accept something without some sort of negotiation. He had to be in control of the situation, have the upper hand. Something was off. She was waiting for the other shoe to drop.

And there it was.

Dan reached inside his jacket and pulled out a small ivory envelope that he slid across the table, his hand still resting on top of it.

"There's another reason I've asked you to meet today." Was he ... nervous? This could not be good. "Meghan and I are going to announce our engagement at a little family gathering after the divorce is finalized and I was hoping you'd be there. I ... I would also appreciate it if you could keep this to yourself. I haven't told your mother yet."

Avery was stunned, paralyzed by the punch she had just received.

"You're fucking kidding, right?" She raised her voice, unable to contain the rage that rapidly made her blood boil.

"Avery, please," her father said, casting furtive glances around. Of course his image was what was important to him right now, not the fact that he'd dropped this bomb on her.

She felt the tears welling up. *No, no please.* She didn't want to cry. She was furious, but her emotions rarely knew the difference between anger and sadness, and she loathed that part of herself. She didn't want to look weak, especially at that very moment when all she wanted to do was stand up to the man who had lied and torn their family apart.

"I think we're done here." She rose from her chair, snatched her coat and bag, and didn't let him get another word in.

♪♫

Avery slammed the door at Josh's apartment and let out a frustrated cry.

"Avie?" Josh poked his head out from his bedroom door.

She jumped. "Oh, sorry, I thought you'd be helping your dad at the restaurant." *Shit.*

"No, uh, something came up."

He frowned, a concerned look on his face as he took in her distraught state. "Is everything okay?"

Avery guessed what a mess she must look like right now. She had heroically held back her tears in front of her father, but as soon as she had stepped outside the restaurant, the flood had poured down her cheeks, blending in with the driving storm. Not even the rain had soothed her this time.

And so, she'd run to the only person she wanted to see. Josh had sent her his address after the night at Julia's, along with a text that said '*Keys under the mat in case you ever need anything and I'm not home.*'

Avery had brushed it off, thinking she would never have any use for it, but here she was, standing dripping wet from tears and rain in the middle of Josh's welcoming kitchen, with him watching her carefully, brows furrowed. *Great.* She'd thought she would have had the time to gather herself before he came home.

Her mascara had most certainly run down her face. She could feel her eyes all puffy and red, and her hair sticking to her forehead and dripping from the rain. And if she had done it right all the way, she probably had a few red patches on her skin caused by her anxiety. So, to sum it up, she was hot as fuck right now.

"I'm fi-fine." A long shiver shook her from head to toe. Her clothes were soaked too, and the cold temperatures were unforgivable this time of year.

Josh crossed the room in three big strides and wrapped her in the warmth of his arms, his scent flooding every one of Avery's senses and soothing her on the spot. He was only wearing a thin black shirt, and Avery could feel every single muscle of his chest pressed against her. As he drew small circles with his fingertips up and down her back, trying to quell the sobs that were building back up, she felt her strength slip away, knowing Josh would catch her if she let go.

"Come here, let's get you out of these damp clothes, you're gonna catch a cold," he said, slowly entangling himself from her.

"I'm o-okay."

"Avery," he warned. "Don't be stubborn right now, please. Let me help you. Come here."

She didn't have energy to fight him so she let him guide her to his bedroom, every fiber of her being shaking from the cold and exhaustion. Josh sat her at the foot of the bed and crouched down in front of her, taking her foot and gently placing it on his thigh.

"Is that okay?" he asked, pointing to the zipper of her boot.

Avery nodded and Josh began to remove her shoes, and then her socks. Placing them next to him, his hands grazed her thighs as he moved them up to grab the hem of her shirt. He looked at Avery to make sure she was all right with it, and when she nodded again, he slipped her shirt over her head and dropped it on the floor.

She heard him draw a sharp breath and saw his jaw muscles twitching as his eyes roamed furtively over her exposed skin. She shivered again and Josh snapped out of it.

"Let me get you a shirt."

He dug into his drawer and pulled out one of her favorite shirts of his, the one she had bought him when she'd returned from a school trip to France. On it was drawn a piece of toast with a beret and a mustache with "French Toast" written underneath. She couldn't believe he still had it. Josh helped her to put it on, his knuckles sliding along her sides.

"Sorry," he said.

"It's fine." She offered him a tight smile, but she was pretty sure it looked nothing like it.

Pulling her to her feet, he reached for the button on her jeans.

"Is this okay?"

Avery nodded, her heart pounding against her chest. Slowly, he unbuttoned her jeans, hooking his fingers into the loops of the waistband, and pulled them down her legs. The wet fabric clung to her skin and the task proved harder than it should have been. Josh squatted back down, his breath hot and quivering against her bare legs.

If he'd looked up at her, his mouth would have been flush against her underwear, but thankfully, he remained focused on the task at hand.

While gently holding the back of her calf, he lifted one leg then the other out of her jeans, rubbing her ankle with his thumb. Her hands were gripping his broad shoulders and she felt the tension growing in his muscles. Even if she was the one in pain right now, she wanted to soothe every knot with her fingers, kiss every inch of his skin, but now was not the time to give in to something she'd been craving since the concert. *Or way before.*

"Let's get you under the covers." His voice came out hoarse. He pulled up the covers and Avery slid under them. All she wanted to do was sleep. Every bone, every muscle in her body ached.

Josh stepped away for a second to get a towel, and when he returned, he settled on top of the covers and proceeded to dry her wet hair. The repetitive movement lulled her slowly to sleep, but sensing the weight shift beside her, she reached for his arm and pulled it over her waist.

"Stay. Please."

Josh didn't say a word, but he laid down next to her, bringing her against him, her back against his chest and his palm resting on her stomach. There, in his arms, Avery could finally relax slowly and breathe a little easier. Her own personal haven.

"Better?" he asked. He buried his head in the hollow of her neck, breathing her in like she was the one soothing him, which was a ridiculous thought.

"Perfect," she whispered and finally let herself drift off to sleep.

♩♫

"Avie. Avie ..."

Josh was panting in her neck as his palms raked her ribs, squeezing with just the perfect amount of pressure. *Yes.* She trailed her fingers down his arms, letting them linger a few seconds on his biceps, appreciating the hard muscles under them.

"Avie ..." His breath grew hotter, closer. She moaned under his touch.

"Avie, wake up."

She jolted awake. *What the fuck.* Where was she? What time was it? How long had she been asleep? Who was *touching* her?

Seeing the confusion and anxiety on her probably groggy face, Josh said. "Hey, hey. It's just me, don't worry. You're at my place Ave, you're safe."

She breathed a relieved sigh before another thought rushed to her mind. "What time is it? What happened?" And fuck, had she just been sex dreaming about Josh? She facepalmed herself.

"It's just after 5 p.m. You've been sleeping all afternoon, since you came back from your lunch with your father," he said, stroking her bare knee.

She dropped her eyes to his hand and her mind flew back to the dream she'd just woken up from. The both of them under the covers, sleek with sweat, his breath panting in the nape of her neck while ... Oh god. Had he *heard* her? Her face burnt red.

Misinterpreting her embarrassment for something else, Josh cleared his throat and pulled his hand away.

"Sorry," he smiled. "I, uh ... I helped you change because you were soaked from the rain. I didn't ... I didn't do anything ... I'd never ..."

"Oh, god no, I know!" She massaged her temple, trying to articulate some coherent thoughts through her sleepy, dream-sex-hazed brain. "I'm sorry, it's coming back to me slowly. My brain is still sleeping, apparently."

He let out a short laugh, visibly relieved. "It's okay. It seemed like you were having a nice dream though," he smirked, a little bit cocky.

Heat rushed to her face, again. Would he notice if she crawled under the covers and never came out? Or maybe she could just disappear. Change her identity, dye her hair, move to another country. All valid options.

"Did you ... hear anything?"

He chocked back a laugh. "You mean ... other than you moaning my name?"

"Oh my god. Oh my gooood," she grumbled. If she'd been embarrassed before, now she was mortified. Time travel wasn't a thing yet, right?

Josh laughed as he placed his hand back on her knee, giving it a little squeeze. "Don't sweat it. I'm actually flattered. And a bit jealous of Dream Josh, not gonna lie. Listen, I didn't want to wake you up but, um ... your brother kept calling and I thought maybe something was wrong, so I picked up and now he's coming over."

"He's *what*?!"

Oh, god. *No, no, no, no, no.* She would never hear the end of it, and she really didn't want to have to explain herself to her brother, *especially* not in front of Josh. Who he hated. Well, maybe 'hated' was a strong word, but he really, really didn't like him.

"Should I have not told him where you were? Are you guys okay?"

She shook her head. "No, no, everything's fine, it's just ...." She inhaled. "Miles is not very ... fond of you right now."

Surprise painted his face. "Oh."

She cringed. "Yeah ... and I haven't really talked to him since, you know, the show, so if we could keep whatever this is, between us, that would be nice."

Avery hated this. She hated that she had to ask him to lie to Miles, but she knew Miles would go all big brother on Josh, and she could not handle that right now. He had better keep the testosterone on the low.

His eyes traveled back and forth between hers, trying to understand the reasons behind her request. His jaw flexed and after a beat, he said, "Sure. No problem."

His tone was clipped, and Avery wondered why he was reacting like that.

"I'm sorry, I just don't have the energy to deal with him right now."

"It's okay," he said, but his eyes kept wandering everywhere but on her face.

Avery was about to ask him why he was acting so strange when the buzzer of the front door made her jump.

"Is that already him?!" She was still in his bed, wearing nothing but her underwear and his shirt. It looked really, *really* bad.

"Yeah, he said he was he wasn't far from here." He got up and walked towards the door before stopping just outside the bedroom. He offered her a little smile. "Maybe put on some pants quick?"

Yes. Pants. Great idea. She stumbled out of bed but when she grabbed her jeans, they were still drenched from her little walk in the rain.

Think, think, think.

She hurried to open one of his drawers when she heard Josh say: "Coming!"

She grabbed the first thing she found, his sweatpants, and threw them on. Oh, god. They were too big for her, and she didn't know if it was really better than her in her underwear, but it was too late to do anything about it because she heard her brother's voice from the front door.

"Avery?"

"Coming!"

She reluctantly walked to where Miles and Josh were standing. She didn't know what she was most worried about—her brother slowly taking her outfit in with a dumbfounded expression on his face, or the fact that he looked ready to punch Josh any second. Josh was a tall man, but Miles easily had several inches on him, which didn't reassure her. *One fire at a time.*

"Heeeey." *Light and breezy. Cheerful. Good.* "What are you doing here?"

Miles scoffed. "What are *you* doing here?" He nodded to her clothes.

Avery crossed her arms over her chest, very uncomfortable to be having this discussion with Josh next to her.

"I just stopped by to say hi to Josh while I was in the area."

"And *that's* how you say hi?" he mocked. He turned his attention to Josh, who had remained silent so far. "What's your game here?"

Avery was shocked Miles had the audacity to throw the question in Josh's face. She was about to say something, but Josh put his palms up, clearly taken aback by the turn the whole thing had taken.

"Hey, Miles, look man. Nothing happened. Avery just came by to chat and then she fell asleep and ..."

"Sure," Miles quipped.

"Miles," Avery warned, her patience slipping through her fingers like sand. She turned to Josh, feeling absolutely awful to put him through this, especially after what he did today for her. "I'm so sorry."

Josh merely nodded, avoiding her gaze. Perfect. Just fucking perfect.

"You," she said to her brother, her anger bubbling as if it was a volcano about to erupt. "Outside. Now."

She opened the door and waited for him to step through, before closing it behind her.

"What in the *fuck*?!" she snapped.

Not fazed by how pissed she was, Miles took an accusatory tone. "You promised to be careful Avery! You promised. Do I have to remind you what he put you through?"

She ignored his question. She did not want to hear this *again*. It was not his freaking business. "Why were you so hell-bent on calling me?"

"Dad told me about lunch. I just wanted to see how you were doing and when you didn't pick up, I got worried. Clearly, you're doing great."

She rolled her eyes. Enough of this bullshit. "I came here after lunch *because* of how terrible lunch was. I was drenched from the rain, and exhausted, and Josh just gave me some dry clothes and I fell asleep right away. I literally just woke up, dumbass."

That at least had the effect of shutting him up. "Oh? Nothing to add? No one to be rude to? No more accusations to make?"

"That's all? You didn't ..."

"Oh my god, Miles! My sex life is none of your fucking business."

He pinched the bridge of his nose. "I know. I'm just looking out for you, Ave. Don't we have enough shit to handle with the parents?"

"I can take care of myself. Honestly, I'm really embarrassed for you right now."

Miles laughed, but not the laugh that Avery loved. No, this one was full of bitterness, as if he had taken a bite out of a very sour grapefruit.

"Well, if you don't need me then, don't even think about calling me when he breaks your heart again and you pull the same 'nobody loves me' bullshit, okay?"

His words made her want to throw up. He was using her fears, her anxieties, her past against her, and he knew very well what he was doing. An aching knot stuck in her throat as the tears began to well up.

Seeing that she was about to break down, Miles' features softened immediately, giving way to remorse.

"Ave, I'm sorry, I didn't mean that." He tried to pull her into a hug, but she stopped him short.

"Oh, I think you did. I'm gonna go apologize to Josh and go home. I'll call you later."

Without another glance, she spun on her heels and shut the door in his face.

Inside, Josh was waiting propped up against the table, arms crossed. He was still not looking at her, which was truly the worst part of the whole thing. He had never avoided her eyes before.

"I'm going to go home, I think it's best if we reschedule dinner ... I'm sorry about my brother, he's ... a little bit too much with the fact that you're back. He's just worried about me." She walked over to him and placed her hand on his forearm, the touch of his skin like a band-aid on her sore heart. "Thank you for today." She stood on her tiptoes and dropped a kiss on his cheek before grabbing her coat and leaving.

In the elevator, she realized she hadn't changed and was still in the oversized sweatpants and t-shirt. *Fuck.* Worst day ever.

Twelve

Ease my mind

Two weeks had passed since her brother stormed Josh's place, but Avery could have sworn it had been longer. She and Miles had texted and called each other since then, ending with the agreement that he would respect her decisions and not go all papa bear on her. And even if Josh had assured her multiple times that he was fine, her busy schedule had made it hard for her to properly make sure he was not still pissed-off after what had happened.

Claudia's maternity photoshoot, which was supposed to happen a week ago, had been delayed at the last minute to today because of scheduling conflicts on Claudia's side, which, if Avery was honest, worked out well for her. The last few days before a photoshoot were always a frenzy of last-minute emergencies, cancelations, and an overall perpetual state of nervousness, so she'd at least had a bit more time to deal with them.

And so, it was with weariness coursing through her muscles, and an unsettled feeling that he was hiding something from her, that Avery knocked on Josh's door, eager to start their long overdue date night.

"Avie!" Josh said when he opened the door. Should she kiss him? They hadn't kissed since the show, hadn't even talked about it, and she wasn't sure where they stood or what the proper etiquette was. *Awkward.* She went with a hug. *Safe.*

"Hey," she said, breathing in his scent. He stepped aside to let her in.

She was not prepared for what she saw once she walked through the door. Josh had set the table for two and lit candles all around, the dancing flames creating a very cozy atmosphere. She recognized one of his favorite pianists, Khatia Buniatishvili, playing in the background on his record player. A bottle of red wine was open on the table—her favorite, Avery noted. On the stove, a pot was simmering, and a faint aroma of duck tickled her nose.

"Josh," Avery whispered, lifting a hand to her mouth, stunned. "I— I can't believe you did all this."

"Well, it's a date, isn't it? Here, let me take your coat."

Avery removed her coat on autopilot and took off her shoes. When she straightened up, Josh was standing inches away from her, his commanding frame towering almost a foot above her. Close to fainting from the overpowering proximity, Avery clutched tightly at the strap of her camera bag. So far, he looked happy to see her, but she knew her mind would not rest until she'd made sure of it.

"Are we okay?"

His beaming smile warmed her heart and ... someplace else too. He took a step closer. "We are. I'm sorry I closed off that day with Miles. It just … took me by surprise. But we're more than okay."

Gently, Josh tilted her chin up. "One thing I haven't stopped thinking about though, is kissing you. I haven't been able to concentrate on anything else than how your lips feel on mine." He chuckled. "If I don't kiss you right now, I'm scared I'm going to go fucking crazy, so please tell me that it was not a one-time thing, and you still want this."

"It was not. I still do," she whispered.

"Thank god," he said and without saying anything else, he dove for her mouth, his fingers curling into her hair and holding her firmly against his mouth.

Avery couldn't contain the whimper that escaped her when his lips made contact with hers, coaxing her mouth open, and gliding his tongue inside. The sound reverberated between them and ignited something in him, all of his restraint slipping away. He growled against her mouth, tilting her head back so he could taste her deeper, before leaving her mouth gasping and trailing down along her jaw, nipping her neck, his thumb placed under her chin to grant him better access.

"The things I want to do to you," he murmured against her skin. "Dirty, dirty things, Avie."

She couldn't speak, she couldn't breathe, she couldn't move. She wanted to know those things. Wanted him to show her exactly what those things he had in mind were.

"Do it," she heard herself say.

He chuckled, low and sinful. "No, not now. I'm gonna take my time." He kissed his way up her neck. "Savor you."

When he stepped away, they were both panting and dazed by the sparkling energy sizzling around them. Josh was staring at her, his hair messed up by the fingers she had run through a few seconds before, his gaze going back and forth between her eyes and her swollen lips; he looked like he was going to pounce any second.

She cleared her throat, but nothing came out.

"So," Josh said, walking back to the kitchen, like he hadn't just turned her world upside down. "How was your day? Oh, before you tell me, would you like a glass of wine?"

Anything to calm her nerves. "Yes, please." *Maybe a little bit less desperate, Ave.*

Josh smirked, pulling out two wine glasses and opened the bottle sitting on the table, not without Avery noticing how his arms flexed under his shirt while he twisted the corkscrew. *Since when had opening a bottle of wine become sexy?*

Josh poured the pinot into the glasses and handed one to Avery.

"Cheers," he said. "To our first date."

"Cheers." She smiled, butterflies fluttering in her stomach.

"So, how was your day?"

"Oh, yeah. Pretty busy honestly. I had the photoshoot I was telling you about, with Claudia." Josh nodded. "She was *gorgeous* and comfortable with the camera, which was great for me. I can't wait to show her how the photos turned out."

Josh jerked his chin toward her camera. "Do you have them here?"

"Uh, yeah?"

"Can I see them?"

Well, that was new to her. Her ex had never asked her to see what she was working on and when she did show him, he would lose interest very quickly.

"Sure, I just don't have my computer with me."

Josh rounded the island. "No problem, I'll go get mine."

A few moments later, he set the computer down in front of her, while Avery pulled out her memory card, inserted it in the slot and opened the photoshoot files.

"Okay, come see," she said.

Josh stood behind her, his arms coming around her waist and his chin resting on her shoulder. His hot breath gently caressed her neck, while his thumb softly grazed the bare skin under her shirt, distracting her from the task at hand. *Focus, Avery.*

"Um, so, we did the photoshoot at this gorgeous hotel." She pulled open the first photos. "Claudia wanted to wait before taking her maternity photos because she wanted her belly to be as big as possible. Look."

Claudia looked incredible in the shot. Standing on the side, you could see how round her belly was under the light and transparent tulle fabric of her dress. Avery had selected a long-sleeved, off-the-shoulder fluffy crimson gown that pooled around Claudia dramatically. The dress was purposely see-through to highlight Claudia's belly and long legs. The train of the dress was Lisa's masterpiece, which Avery had played with repeatedly, like it was its own prop.

She had also asked Lisa to add some ruffles on the sleeves as well as on the end of the skirt to create more texture, and per usual, Lisa had delivered.

"Wow, how did you do *that*?" Josh pointed at the train flowing in the wind. Avery had to admit she was pretty proud of it, because there had been no wind involved.

"I used a high shutter speed, which means my camera was set to take a lot of photos in a small amount of time. One of the makeup artists helped me by throwing the train up and I used this setting and shot wide open to get a better focus on Claudia. See how the background is a bit blurry?"

"Wow, that's *so* cool," he murmured, visibly impressed. "So, do you always have a team with you?"

"Depends on the client and their budget but usually, yes. Hair and makeup are always with me throughout the day, in case the client needs touch-ups or if we have a wardrobe change, as was the case with this one." She opened another photo; one she had taken of Claudia inside in the bathtub.

"Claudia wanted some shots in a milk bath. So, see, we changed her dress for a white lace one that clung to her figure, and decorated the bath with various shades of purple flowers. I took the photo from above to accentuate the shape of her belly and make it the focal point of the photo."

Avery continued to show the day's photos, explaining to Josh how she'd worked with Claudia throughout the photoshoot and how she would edit the photos afterwards, working on the light, and contrasts. Josh kept going back and forth between nodding his head along to her comments and punctuating each photo with "oooh's" and "wow's."

She loved seeing him like this, awestruck by her work, genuinely fascinated by what she was showing him, soaking up every word as if she was doing an oral essay on Chopin. He was asking her so many questions, like he was ready to take notes every time she got all technical. It was such a difference between what she was used to that she had to take a mental beat to fully appreciate the moment.

When she was done rambling, Josh, his arms still curled around her waist, his thumbs still tracing circles on the thin skin of her hips, remained silent for a few moments before humming with satisfaction in the hollow of her neck.

Avery giggled. "What?"

"I'm just …" He tightened his embrace, spreading his palms wider on her skin as if trying to cover every inch of her. "I think you're incredible, that's all. Claudia, and all the other people you do this for, they're going to have those beautiful photos and memories of such important moments of their lives, and it's all thanks to you. *You* gave them that."

Hearing Josh say out loud exactly why she was passionate about photography, to figuring her out so effortlessly after discussing it with him for less than an hour, made her want to hold on to him and never let go.

She turned her head, brushing her nose with his, and kissed him. She would have thought kissing Josh would be strange after years of close friendship, but she couldn't have been more wrong. It was as if they had denied themselves the possibility but were always meant to get there one day.

♪♫

"You had chocolate all over your face!" Josh burst out laughing.

"So did you!" Avery was bent over laughing, tears rolling down her cheeks.

"Because of you! You had decided that was the perfect moment to hug me!" Josh said, outrage all over his face.

Avery shook her head, smiling fondly at the memory. "Brooke's mom was so mad when she saw how dirty the kitchen was, my god."

"At least we had a half-decent chocolate cake."

"The one and only," Avery laughed.

When they were still in high school, Brooke, Josh, and Avery had gone through a phase where they'd attempted to recreate the winning *Great British Bake-off* cake of the week, with varying levels of success. The infamous chocolate cake had been the last one of these, as Brooke's mother had banned them from her kitchen after she'd found chocolate on almost every white wall of her kitchen.

Let's just say that the process had gotten a little out of hand when Brooke had booped Josh's nose with chocolate, and with Josh not being the type to take it lying down, things had escalated pretty quickly.

He chuckled, taking a bite of the delicious dinner he had cooked for them. "We had some good times, the three of us."

"We did," Avery agreed, lost in nostalgia. For a few minutes, they remained quiet, leaving the melody of forks and knives to fill the void of silence.

"So," Avery cleared her throat. "Now that you're back ... do you miss Europe?"

Josh leaned back against the back of his chair, looking like he was pondering his answer to the question. He rubbed his jaw, nearly taking Avery's mind off the question she'd just asked.

"Some days, yes. To be honest, it was nice for me to be free from the constant pressure of my father, you know? It felt like I could finally be who I wanted to be, take the time to find myself, make mistakes, without hearing my dad tell me 'I told you so' or 'you should be honoring your legacy.'" He snorted. "Hard enough for him already that I decided to change my last name to my mother's when she passed away."

He sighed, threading his fingers through his wavy hair. "I had some good times in Europe. Sometimes I thought 'this is it, I finally got it,' but it was always short lived. Most of the time though, I felt like a stranger living my own life. Sometimes, I still do."

Avery frowned. "What do you mean?"

Josh sighed again, this time with a lot more weight behind it. "I didn't really understand it when we were teenagers, but I do now. This feeling of never belonging anywhere because I'm too white to be Mexican, but too dark to be Canadian. I'm constantly living in this in-between where people here constantly ask me where I'm from, and when I visit my family in Mexico, they barely acknowledge me because I don't know anything about my own culture. Because I've lived in Toronto almost my whole life. And I can't help but think my father resents me for it, and that it's in part the reason why he wants me to take over the restaurant so badly. So that I can prove to him that that I have a shred of his 'Mexicanness' in my blood."

Avery listened as he continued spilling his emotions, her fingers aching to reach him and hold him tight against her. "I don't know how to be who my father wants me to be. But I don't want to deny that part of me either. I want to make him proud. I want him to be proud of his Mexican son." His voice cracked as he swallowed the last words. "But I don't know how to be that to him."

Avery didn't know what to say because she couldn't possibly know what he was going through. To her, he was Josh, and he was enough and perfect just the way he was. But she knew it was a naive way of seeing things, and it pained her that he was going through something he had no real control over.

"I take it there is still no improvement with him?"

"Not really." He let out a sigh that spoke volumes. "He's still the same grumpy old man he was when I left, that wants his only son to step up." He rolled his eyes. "I was hoping things would be different after ten years apart, but guess I was wrong. He still wants me to be someone I can't be ..."

His last words echoed in her mind and clicked the last pieces of the puzzle together that Avery had not been able to solve since the fight with her brother.

"Wait ... was that why you were so pissed when I asked you to lie to my brother when he came over?"

He scrubbed a hand through his curls. "Yeah ... look, I understood. But I'm tired of being asked to be someone I'm not. I feel like all I do is hide who I am, what I love, who I want to spend my time with. If your brother can't deal with the fact that I want to spend time with you, honestly, why should I care? Why should *you* care? You're your own person."

Shit. She hadn't considered this angle. She had panicked in the moment because she hadn't had the strength to handle her brother. And she had put that on Josh and let Miles go completely ballistic on him.

"I'm sorry. I … I know it's not an excuse, I just … Miles can be a bit overprotective sometimes, and I guess I thought quickly, and I didn't think about you or …"

Stretching his arm across the table, he rested his hand palm up, inviting Avery to place hers there. When she slipped it in, the rough pads of his fingers gently caressed her skin.

"It's okay. We're past it, okay? But I need you to hear this, Avie. I don't regret coming back. I don't regret bumping into you, and I certainly don't regret what's happening between us right now. Do I wish I had done things differently and picked up the phone while I was away? One hundred percent yes. But my decision to come back here is the best one I've made in a long time and this?" He nodded toward their laced fingers, squeezing her hand once. "It's been the easiest choice I've made in a long time, and one that's been on my mind for fucking forever. Long before I even left."

His confidence behind his words had her swaying. There was no harshness in them, just simple truths and the certainty of his decisions. Could she be that brave?

"I'd be lying if I said I hadn't thought of us this way over the years either," she managed to say between a few faltering breaths. She tipped his hand and smoothed his skin with her thumb. "I'm very glad you're back, and I'm happy to be here with you tonight."

His gaze flickered to her, warm and soft. "I am too. I wish you could have seen the places I went, the moments I lived. It's such a permanent part of who I am, and it's crazy that you don't know about it. I want to tell you. Everything. And maybe one day, I'll take you."

"I'd really like that," she murmured.

Josh smiled, something flickering in his eyes. "I'm happy to hear it." He let go of her hand and bit into a slice of meat. When he looked back at her, he frowned. "What's on your mind?"

Annoying mind reader. But he was right, she had a lot on her mind, especially because her anxiety wouldn't leave her alone, even during a date.

"What are you going to do now with your career?"

If Josh could read her mind, she could definitely read his body. The slight shift in his shoulders, the faint bounce of his chest, his Adam's apple bobbing harder, the muscles in his biceps tensing, and his fingers drumming on the table told her everything she needed to know.

He had no idea.

"Not an easy answer," he chuckled nervously. "I'm … in between right now, I guess? I'm trying this new thing called 'taking it one step at a time,' don't know if you've heard of it," he said, grinning.

Avery laughed, the sudden tension between them vanishing as quickly as it appeared.

"I'm afraid my mind doesn't work that way," she said.

"I love how your mind works," he replied as naturally as if he had just announced that tomorrow would be a sunny day.

She frowned. She hated how her mind worked. She hated being anxious, overanalyzing everything, getting all worked up over small things, having her fears and emotions take over, feeling *powerless* in her own head. People had called her lunatic, crazy, emotional, and once: *hysterical*. Nobody had ever said they loved her mind. "You do?"

He looked at her, confused. "Of course, I do. I know you get anxious sometimes, and you don't find it easy. But it's a privilege, Avie, to feel like you do. To live every emotion to the fullest. To care so deeply for the people you love. I think it's beautiful, and I love that I can still read every single thought on your face." He smirked, proud of himself. "I'm fluent in Avery Clark."

She cocked an eyebrow. "Are you now?" A challenge. *Do I really want to go there?*

"Sure am," Josh said, his smile growing wider. "Graduated in 2012. I have to say, I lost my touch a bit but y'know. It's like riding a bike; it never goes away."

Avery's cheeks painted a deep shade of crimson at the image of Josh riding ...

"I didn't mean it like that," Josh said, amused, as he witnessed the blush on her face. Avery's eyes went wide. *How the fuck did he—* "Told ya." He shrugged, hiding his smile in his glass of wine. "Fluent."

Josh took a sip of wine, his tongue darting out and licking his upper lip. *That should not look so indecent.*

"You remind me of my mom sometimes," he said. "How restless she could be when she was passionate about something." He looked down at his plate and for a moment, neither of them talked, letting this little truth float between them.

"Speaking of moms, how's Rebecca? I haven't seen her since I've been back."

At the mention of her mom, Avery's chest pulled tight. "She's ... she's good."

Josh stared at her with his 'cut the bullshit' look.

"Okay, *fine*. Remember two weeks ago when I came to your place and ended up sleeping in your, um, bed?"

Josh's ears turned a slight shade of pink. "I do."

"I'd just had lunch with my dad. We're not really on speaking terms right now. He uh ... they're getting a divorce. He cheated on her."

"He *what*?"

Josh's reaction was not surprising. He adored Rebecca, and the feeling was mutual. He'd often had dinner with them on school nights, and when his mother passed away, he had found in Rebecca an unconditional motherly type of love, a confidante. Josh's father had been devastated by grief himself, so Rebecca had stepped up to the plate. Avery knew his love for her ran deep.

"Yeah ... between our dads, the race for Father Of The Year is incredibly close," she sneered. "She's been a bit out of it for a few years now, before we knew about the affair, but the announcement made things worse. Her doctor finally diagnosed her with depression last year. I think putting her life on hold for a man who betrayed her after more than twenty years of marriage was a slap in the face."

Avery saw the guilt and disbelief painted on Josh's face. "Shit, Avie. I didn't know, I am *so* sorry."

"Nothing to be sorry for, you couldn't have known. Well …" She stopped just in time. No need to rub salt in the wound.

"She's still adjusting to her meds, and the divorce should be finalized next week. Hopefully, we can put the whole thing behind us soon. I want her to start living and do the things she didn't get the chance to do before. Like maybe opening her own design firm, like she always dreamt of doing."

Josh exhaled sharply, pinching the bridge of his nose. "It's a lot to take in."

She reached for his hand. "Don't beat yourself up, okay? She still asks about you *all* the time—maybe you could stop by? I know she'd love that."

"I will, I promise." He nodded.

They finished eating, moving on to lighter topics, going back and forth between laughter and heated glances.

"Wanna watch a movie?" Josh called from the kitchen after they had cleared the table, while Avery browsed through his impressive book collection, wine glass in hand. Before she could answer him, her phone buzzed in her pocket.

Brooke [8:12 pm]: What are you up to tonight? Want to do a movie night with us? I got wiiiiine

She replied right away.

Avery [8:12 pm]: Can't. Already doing movie night at Josh's

"Only if I get to pick," she shouted back. Everybody knew Josh had the worst taste in movies and she doubted this had changed over the years. He'd once made her and Brooke watch three *Transformers* movies back to back in *one night*.

She heard his smooth laughter even through the mess he was making with the dishes. Brooke's reply appeared on her screen.

Brooke [8:14 pm]: First, offended that I didn't get invited.
Brooke [8:14 pm]: Second ARE U KIDDING ME GET IT AVE
Brooke [8:14 pm]: Third, please don't let him choose the movie. We all know how that turned out last time. K, love you!

Avery laughed and shot back.

Avery [8:16 pm]: First, you said you were busy with Alice tonight when I texted you earlier
Avery [8:16 pm]: Second, you're a child. Third. The day Josh gets to pick the movie again, something really bad will have happened to me.
Avery [8:16 pm]: Enjoy your night and say hi to Al for me. Love you

She placed her phone on the table, and after a few minutes, Josh joined her in the living room, palms up. "Alright, alright, you can choose but let's settle this right now, because I know you're going to pick a holiday-themed one so just so we're clear, *Die Hard is* a Christmas movie."

Avery gasped. "It is *so* not! See?" She waved her finger at him. "This is why you can't be trusted."

They settled into his L-shaped couch, Avery lying on the long side of it, and Josh close to her, his feet propped up on his coffee table. She sank into the fluffy cushions.

"Ugh, this feels so good."

Out of the corner of her eye, she saw him swallowing, the muscles in his neck slightly flexing.

"Here, pick one," he said, handing her the remote.

She opened Netflix and selected her favorite movie without hesitation.

Josh snorted. "Again?!"

"Shh, it's a holiday classic."

"Like *Die Hard*," he mumbled.

"I heard you, and *Die Hard* doesn't have Jude Law." *The Holiday*'s title music filled the room as Jude Law's name appeared on screen.

Josh tilted his head to peer at her, and raised an eyebrow, amused. "And?"

"Aaaaaaand ..." Would he notice if she changed the subject in a very subtle way? "Nothing." She shrugged, attempting to be very casual. "I just think his acting is far superior to Bruce Willis'."

"Uh huh, sure, his *acting*." Josh smirked. "Come here." He draped one arm on the back of the couch as an invitation for Avery to slide against him. She willingly gave up the soft cushions for the hardness and warmth of his chest.

Josh hummed and dropped a kiss in her hair. "Better."

A shiver rolled down her body as he pulled her closer to him, his hand spread flat on the curve of her hip. It felt like it weighed a hundred pounds against her jeans.

Unable to resist, she ran her hand up and down his abdomen, feeling the muscles twitch and clench under her fingertips. She hid her smile in his shirt, and continued her exploration, sliding her hand under his shirt, the hair on his lower belly brushing against her fingers.

"Avery," Josh grunted under his breath, a warning in the timbre of his voice.

"Hmm?" She lifted her head to look at him.

His eyes were ten shades of blue darker, mischievous, and far from their usual peaceful blue. Storm on the horizon rather than calm sea. He gripped her hip tighter, his fingers digging into her skin.

The movie was still playing in the background, Avery recognized Cameron Diaz's voice but quite frankly, she wasn't sure she wanted to watch it anymore. She was suddenly more interested in the waistband of his sweatpants, into which she could easily wiggle her hand if he let her.

Slowly, she moved her fingers lower, drawing circles on his taut skin before reaching the line of his sweatpants. Josh caught her wrist abruptly. Before she could apologize for crossing his boundaries, he pulled her onto him with her legs on each side of his thighs, spread over him but not pressed against him yet.

"What do you think you're doing?" he whispered, pulling her flush against him. She let out a small noise at the contact with his already hard length. His fingers trailed down her spine, the small of her back, down the curve of her ass, squeezing both hands in her flesh and rocking her even closer. How stupid of her to think she'd had this under control.

"Is that what you wanted? To feel how out of control you make me?" Josh breathed.

She closed her eyes and tilted her head back, enjoying the delicious pressure he was causing between her thighs, losing herself in the sounds coming from his throat.

One hand still grinding her against him, Josh used the other to explore her body more gently, his fingers traveling down her neck, her collarbone, grazing the tip of her perky breast through her shirt. She arched under his touch.

Being here with him felt *so* right, natural. She started rolling her hips against him, and felt him grow bigger and harder under her, if it was even possible.

"I need to kiss you," he muttered before clasping his hand around her neck and bringing her down to his mouth. There was no mercy for her as he ravaged her with every stroke of his tongue while she held on for dear life, literally gripping the collar of his shirt.

"What do you want, Avie?" Josh breathed against her mouth, thrusting his hips forward, as if he couldn't help it. He might as well have been naked, given that the thin material of his sweatpants did nothing to conceal his erection or the feel of it.

Avery unclenched her hands around his collar and dragged them down his chest before tucking them under his pants, curling her fingers above his briefs and around his cock. Josh groaned and dug his fingers into her thighs when she gave him one single stroke before whispering in his ear.

"You."

The word made him lose his mind and all sense of self-restraint. He scrambled to undo the buttons on her jeans, trying to peel off her sweater and kiss her at the same time. His movements were frantic, urgent, as if he wanted it all and right away. In terms of efficiency, she had seen better. But his impatience did something to her heart, because it told her he was feeling the same way she was: she needed him, right here and right now.

The sound of her phone interrupted his work, while Avery had her arm caught in her sleeve, her sweater halfway over her head, and her jeans slung low over her hips.

"It's just a text," Avery panted.

"Okay, yeah, good." Josh resumed his task, but another ping stopped him in his tracks. And another. And another. Avery's phone began to ring this time and she grumbled, burying her head into his neck.

Josh laughed, a hint of frustration in his tone. "I think you should go see what's going on."

Her phone had stopped ringing. "Maybe it was a mistake? It's so late, nobody calls me at this hour."

But her phone rang again, shutting out any chance of picking up where they'd left off. The moment had passed.

She reluctantly got up from his heat, vowing as she went to get her phone that she would never leave it on loud again. Who needed to be reachable 24 hours a day anyway?

But when she saw her screen, her jaw dropped.

"OHMYGOD Josh," she called out. "Claudia is in labor, it's happening right now!"

She hurried to get her clothes back in order and spun in all directions, trying to gather her thoughts. Claudia wasn't due for another two weeks!

"Now?!" Josh scrambled to his feet. "What can I do? Hey, Avie." He planted his hands on her shoulders, making her halt for a second. "Calm down, take a breath. What can I do? What do you need?"

She was trying to get the rush of adrenaline from Josh's mouth and the unexpected turn of events down, and his serenity was all she needed to see this through.

"I need to get there as soon as possible; Claudia wants me to photograph the birth."

"I'll go start the car and drive you there, okay? You take care of your equipment and just fix your hair, maybe?" Josh looked at her softly, cupping her face. "Even though, if you ask me, I like this wild look on you." He planted a quick kiss on her lips.

"Be downstairs in five!" he said before flying out the door.

Thirteen

Treacherous

The drive to Claudia's was quiet. Josh was focused on the road, while Avery grew nervous that she wouldn't make it in time. She had texted back and forth with Sonia, Claudia's midwife, since she got the call. Claudia's contractions had started in the afternoon right after the photoshoot, but she hadn't thought much of it, being two weeks early. It was when they'd grown closer in the evening that she had dialed Sonia and asked her to call Avery.

Avery took a deep breath. Right now, the only thing that was keeping her grounded was Josh's hand sprawled across her knee, warm and comforting, squeezing her every now and then.

"We should be there in five minutes, okay?" he said calmly as he glanced at her with a little concern dancing in the blue of his irises.

"Perfect." She smiled tightly.

"This is her first kid, right?"

Avery nodded.

"Well, it's going to take her several hours then, don't worry." He gave her knee another squeeze.

He was right. Rationally, the labor had slowly started in the afternoon. She'd certainly be in for the night, but knowing Claudia, she was going to want every step documented.

Josh barely had time to park in front of the massive residence before Avery was already leaping out of the car.

"Thank you, thank you so much, J. I'm sorry, but I gotta go."

"Go, go, go. Hey, wait, Avery! How are you going to get home?"

"I'll take a cab! Thanks again!" she shouted, halfway to the front door.

Inside, the living room had been transformed into a delivery area, with a round inflatable pool sitting in the middle of the space.

"Avery, thank god you're here!" Claudia said before wincing and taking several short breaths.

"Contractions are five minutes apart," a small woman in nurse's attire informed Avery. She held out her hand. "You're the photographer? I'm Sonia, Claudia's midwife."

Avery shook her hand. "Hi, yes, pleasure to meet you."

She settled in while the midwife explained to her how the birth would proceed, letting Avery know when to give her space when she needed to get to work. Claudia's husband was there beside her, doing his best to help in any way he could, which apparently was to have his fingers crushed with each new contraction.

"Avery, I hope you're well rested," Sonia said. "It's going to be a long night."

♪♫

Around 5 a.m., the contractions were only a minute apart and Claudia was fully immersed in the water-filled pool. Exhaustion was building in Avery's body, but she told herself to suck it up because Claudia was the one doing all the work.

When Sonia asked Claudia to start pushing, it took about an hour before they saw the crown of the head. The excitement in the room was buzzing as she made the final push.

"It's a boy!" shouted Sonia, hurrying to scoop the baby up to clean and wrap him in a warm towel. When he let out his first cry, the entire room breathed a sigh of relief, along with the new parents' choking sobs.

It was the first time in her career that Avery had witnessed a birth, and her emotions were overflowing. She let herself shed a few tears over the beauty of the moment unfolding before her. The blend of tenderness, sweat and chaos all around her was creating an aura that she was so grateful to be able to capture.

Once the baby was thoroughly cleaned, the umbilical cord cut, and Claudia was comfortably settled in her bed, Avery packed up her equipment and joined her in her room.

"Knock, knock," Avery said softly.

"Come in, come in."

Claudia was snug in her bed, her features drawn but blissful, her little boy asleep next to her.

"I know this sounds clichéd, but isn't he beautiful?"

Avery smiled and sat on the edge of the bed. "He really is."

"Thank you," Claudia said, "for coming on such short notice. You must be so tired, you should go home."

Avery patted her hand. "Don't worry about me for one second, you did all the heavy lifting out there. I already got a few shots of this sweetie while he was sleeping, but I can come back in a few weeks to take newborn shots if you'd like. I'm sorry I can't come sooner; I'm already booked with a wedding."

Claudia closed her eyes and hummed in agreement. "Yes, that would be perfect, Avery."

"Okay, great. I'm going to let you two rest. I'll send you the photos as soon as they're ready. Text me if you need anything, okay?"

"Mmmh." Claudia was already half-asleep.

Closing the door quietly behind her, Avery retrieved her belongings and opened her app to order a cab.

It was 8 a.m. and she was *exhausted*. She had been up since 7 a.m. the day before, had already worked all day on Claudia's maternity shoot, and this all-nighter was the final straw. Nothing was more exciting to her at this moment than the thought of collapsing into her comfy bed.

She was walking down the porch steps when she stopped short, squinting her eyes. *Was that Josh's car parked over there?*

It couldn't be. Because if it was, it would mean he'd been there all night, and while he was a thoughtful man, she didn't think anyone would go through the agony of sleeping in a car. Her whole body shivered at the thought. Her sleepy brain was probably playing tricks on her.

Still, she approached the black Audi, and saw Josh, his head tilted toward the window, his mouth hanging open and drool coating his chin. How could he look so cute drooling?

Maybe it was because he'd been sitting in his car all night in the cold waiting for her, or maybe it was because he was fiercely loyal, showing her over and over again that he wasn't the same man he'd been, that she could trust him, that she *should* trust him again, but Avery felt her heart melt at the sight of him soundly asleep. She had a sudden urge to tell him all about her fears and beg him to never leave her side. And this time, to follow through.

She knocked on the window, startling him. He rubbed a hand over his face and opened the door.

"Hi," he said, still sleepy. "Are you all done?"

"Yes, everything's good. What are you still doing here?"

"Uh, I was waiting for you?" As if it was obvious. Well, it was pretty obvious, but Avery needed to hear him confirm it.

"You must be freezing," she whispered.

"Meh, a little bit but that's okay." He got out of the car and stretched his long legs, followed by his arms over his head, revealing the tanned skin of his hip. "How did it go?" He grabbed her by the waist and tucked her against him.

"Very good," she said as she slid her arms around his neck to return his embrace, as if it were the most natural thing in the world to do. "It's a little boy."

"I'm glad it went well." He traced the lines under her eyes with his thumb. "You must be exhausted, baby."

Baby. The term of endearment made her heart skip a beat.

"I am, yeah." Her stomach rumbled at the same time. "Maybe I should eat first though," she chuckled.

Josh pressed a kiss to her forehead. "Come on, I know just the place."

♫

"Mmmh, my god," Avery said, her mouth full.

She had been making those obscene sounds for the past ten minutes, or every time she bit into the buttery croissant. Josh had ordered her a plate full of different French pastries, pain au chocolat, croissants and brioches of all kinds. She had never tasted anything that good, and even though she could fall asleep on the table at any second, at least her belly was full and happy.

Josh was looking at her, amused, while sipping his hot cup of coffee.

"How did you know about this place?" Avery asked, still salivating. They were in a little French café she had never seen before, near the university. Josh informed her that the owners were a couple in their sixties who'd emigrated to Canada forty years ago and still spoke French between themselves.

"Perks of having connections in Europe." He winked.

She laughed. "Cocky is not a good look on you, Josh."

He grazed his feet against hers under the table.

"You sure about that?"

The intensity of his stare as it moved up from her hands, lingering a second too long on her chest, her lips, before boring in her eyes, made her heart flutter and heat rush straight down.

"Joshua!" someone shouted in a thick French accent from behind her. The spell was broken.

Josh flashed a wide smile at the man who walked up to their table and rose to greet him, European-style: a firm handshake and a kiss on each cheek. Avery quickly identified him as the owner of the café.

"Robert, how nice to see you again!"

Robert gave him a pat on the shoulder. "Pas d'anglais avec moi, mon ami, tu le sais!"

Oh well, that was unexpected. Damn her for only paying half-attention to her French classes in school. All she had understood, at least what she thought she understood, was "no English" and ... "friend."

"Ah, Robert, je sais, je sais, désolé!"

Avery slowly rotated her head toward Josh, eyes wide. *I'm sorry, what?* Since when did Josh speak the sexiest language in the world?

"Je te présente Avery. Avery, this is Robert, the owner of the café," Josh said smoothly.

"Enchanté," she sputtered with the worst French accent possible. The audacity of this man to hide something like this from her.

Robert smiled, taking her hand in his. "Me as well, mademoiselle." Turning to Josh, he switched back to French, a little mischief in his tone. "Est-ce que c'est ton amoureuse?"

Whatever Robert asked him was enough to make Josh blush and pique her curiosity. There were too many *sss*'s sounds for her to catch the whole question, but she managed to get the last word. *Amoureuse.*

Didn't it mean lover? *Was Robert asking Josh about his lover? Oh my god*. The alarms went off in her head, driving her anxiety up. Did Josh have a girlfriend that Avery didn't know about? He would have told her, right?

Rational, Avery, think rational. Evidence only, don't start spinning out of control.

Up until now, all he had shown her was loyalty, devotion, tenderness. *But he never said he was single*, a small voice whispered in her ear. *He said he wasn't* married. She immediately shut it out. No, it was true, he'd never said it, but he had always been honest with her, ever since he'd been back. That had to count for something, right?

Seeing that she was mulling over something, Josh struggled to keep his focus on Robert. "Euh, c'est un peu compliqué mais j'aimerai bien, oui. J'espère en tout cas."

Robert gave him a knowing look. Whatever his answer was, Avery decided it was not for her to hear, so she shifted her attention back to her breakfast and let the two men finish their conversation. She was too tired anyway to focus on a discussion that wasn't even in her language.

"À bientôt!" she heard Robert say a few minutes later. "I hope you like our croissants!"

She thanked him more or less correctly and watched as Josh slid back in front of her.

"Everything all right?"

"Are you single?" The question came out way more directly than she had intended, surprising even herself that she couldn't wait more than a second before asking what was burning her mind.

Josh stared at her for a long moment, and she feared she had gone too far, before he finally said, "I'm not going to pretend your question doesn't hurt me, because it does. Haven't we already talked about that?"

He sighed, and Avery's heart sank down in her boots. Had she asked him already? She had a vague memory doing so during the night at the bar, but events were foggy from all the alcohol they had. In no way did she want to hurt him, but trust didn't come easy for her. He should know that better than anybody else.

"I thought it was pretty clear after last night. I'm not a player, Avie, and never have been. Ten years away from you hasn't changed me, what matters to me."

He took her hand, and she breathed a bit easier, glad he wasn't upset with her, and that she wasn't the other woman. "Look at me." He waited for her eyes to meet his before continuing. "I'm not interested in anyone but you, okay?"

She nodded. This gorgeous man in front of her wanted her for who she was, and he knew her so well, she had no doubt that he understood what he was walking into. It was almost too much to wrap her anxious mind around.

"Okay, well, I'm glad we settled this."

Avery wanted to tell him everything, so he could understand where she was coming from, but she hesitated at how much she wanted to share with him now, while she was almost drunk with exhaustion. She decided to rip the band aid.

"I just got out of a nine-year relationship." Well, when she said 'just,' it had been almost a year ago but hey, when you spent nine years with the same person, a year was nothing in the grand scheme of things.

"When he graduated, he interned for one summer in Washington working for a representative in Congress. It was supposed to be temporary, but his internship eventually turned into a job. He was so successful, a natural charmer." She shook her head, the thought leaving a sour taste in her mouth.

"He asked me to move in with him, when I had just started my own business, and I agreed because I was foolish and in love, without really thinking about what I was leaving behind." Her friends, her family, her career.

"My boxes were all packed. Two days before I left, he sent me a text that wasn't meant for me, and that's how I found out he was seeing someone else over there." Her throat thickened and tears filled her eyes.

"Avie ... I'm sorry, I ... I didn't know." Josh looked as though he didn't know what to do, whether to comfort her, touch her, or not. He seemed at a loss.

She shook her head quickly. "No, no, I'm sorry. I'm just angry. I'm okay. Ugh, fucking emotions."

She wiped her cheeks with a flick of her hand. "I'm sorry, I'm not crying because I'm sad, or because I'm not over him. Believe me, *I am*. He doesn't deserve me to cry for him."

"Don't apologize, please," he said softly, and Avery offered him a faint smile.

"I'm just angry, you know? For not seeing it coming and for blindly agreeing to turn my life upside down for him, without thinking it through."

It was hard for her to admit that, but the situation had made her realize—after several months of not getting out of bed—that she had to live for herself and not for others, and that above all, she was the only one she could rely on.

"I just thought he was it, that we were going to get engaged, and it was going to be me and him till the end ..."

Josh turned his focus on his coffee, an Avery saw what those words did to him. *Why did you have to leave, J.?*

"But I'm glad I knew that before—"

"He didn't deserve you Avery," he said roughly.

"I know that now. But ..." How did she always end up in dangerous territory when it came to him? She needed to take a step back before it was too late.

"Even if it's in the past, it still left a mark. And I don't think I'm ready to get back into anything serious."

The real truth was that she was ready—damn she *was* ready. If Josh pushed her even a little bit, she would give in right then and there. But she was too afraid of what it would do to her if he were to leave again, if she gave him her heart and he stomped on it on his way out of Toronto the first chance he got. That would be it for her. She couldn't risk losing him as a friend, and she couldn't risk losing herself again.

"But I'm not blind either, I can see there's something going on here." She waved her hands between them. Josh's gaze flicked back to her, the blue of his eyes boring their way into her heart, expectations on full display again.

"What are you saying?" he whispered.

"What I'm saying is ..." She took a big inhale and let the rest out. "What I'm saying is, why don't we just take this as it comes, no pressure, no strings attached. No commitment from either of us, no feelings. Like a friends-with-benefits kind of deal. So neither of us can be disappointed when it ends." Something flashed through his eyes, too fast for Avery to catch.

"I just need you to promise me that, whatever happens … you won't forget to keep calling me." The last words trembled out of her mouth as emotion grabbed her throat again. No, she couldn't go another ten years without seeing him, not now that she knew the wonderful man he'd turned into.

"So," he said carefully. "And correct me if I'm wrong but … you want us to be, what … together?"

"Well, yes and no. You wouldn't be my boyfriend. That's the opposite of no strings attached." She laughed somewhat forcefully, because if Josh had been someone who could settle down and stay in one place more than a few years at a time, then her answer would have been totally different. "We'd be doing the same thing, I guess. Watching movies, going out for dinner and a drink, but with …" The words stuck in her mouth, and she felt the heat of embarrassment creep up her neck. *Really, you can't get the words out?*

"Sex?" He cocked an eyebrow and crossed his arms over his chest, the muscles of his biceps stretching the fabric of his shirt.

"Yeah," she said, flustered by the image of a sweaty Josh between her legs, lips parted and wet from her.

He appeared to think about what she had just offered. The look on his face was indecipherable and she began to wonder if she had just said the stupidest thing of her life, so she tried to justify it.

"Josh …" She didn't want to hurt him, but she needed to be selfish right now. "Not that I think you're going to disappear tomorrow, but you and I both know damn well that at the first opportunity for your career, you'll leave." She quickly added. "And you should, absolutely. I just don't want to suffer for it."

His lips tightened. Of course he was allowed to be hurt. Even pissed. She could feel his leg bouncing under the table and all she wanted to do was put her hand over it, pull him into her arms.

"Josh, if I said—"

"Okay, let's try it," he interrupted her. "No strings, no feelings, no timeline."

She looked at him, dubious. "Is this really what you want?"

"I do." He leaned over the table, lowering his voice when he said: "and if you don't believe me, the only reason I'm not dragging you out of the restaurant right now and taking you right there in the car is because you're completely exhausted and you need to sleep."

Her mouth formed an *O*. She tried to reply but nothing came out, only her mouth opening and closing like a fish. Well, she had her answer.

Josh smiled, smug and satisfied. "Okay, now eat so I can tuck you into bed."

They finished their breakfast, back on their usual banter. Avery wondered for a second if the conversation had actually happened or if she had dozed off at the table and dreamed up their deal.

When Josh spoke next, she was almost sleeping in her plate. "Should we go? You need to sleep, Avie."

She hummed in approval. "Yeah, let's go."

Josh paid the bill while she put on her coat, shivering from the cold and the strain of her night. When Josh met her outside, he wrapped his arm around her shoulders to steady her and guide her to the car, and she let herself lean against him, no longer having the strength to handle it all on her own.

Fourteen

I Guess I'll Just Lie Here

"Avie." Josh shook her gently. "We're outside your house."

Avery groaned, groggy with sleep, and slumped against his shoulder. *Aaah, there, so much better.* Josh grinned.

"Come on, baby, let's get you inside." He removed her seatbelt and helped her out of the car.

Inside, he helped her take off her coat, fed Simba and tucked her into bed.

"Call me when you're awake, okay?" he said, stroking her hair

"Mmmh, m'kay," she mumbled.

The last thing she felt was his lips on her temple, the loveliest thing to fall asleep to.

♪♫

When her phone rang over and over, Avery scrambled to get out of bed, still drowsy from sleep. What if Claudia had a problem and needed her? She blinked when she saw that it was still light outside, meaning she hadn't slept long. Forcing her eyes open, she sighed with relief when she saw Brooke's name on her phone.

"What?" she answered, a little cranky.

"What's up with you?"

"I was sleeping for—" she looked at the time, *ugh*— "thirty minutes, so this better be worth it."

Silence lingered on the other end of the line.

"B.?"

"Yeah, sorry. Well, I'll skip over the fact that it's almost noon and you're still sleeping, you weirdo." Avery heard Brooke sigh. *Oh, that didn't sound good.*

"What's up?" her heart rate picked up. Did something happen to Brooke? Was Alice okay?

"Um ... little update for you ... So, I'm at my parents' house right now and my dad just got a call from the tenant downstairs and looks like they have termites."

"*What*?!" A chill of disgust ran down her spine.

"Yeah ... turns out the house is full of it. They found some crawling on their kitchen counter and when they followed their path, they saw the whole wall was infested."

So that's why Simba was being weird lately, staring at walls and the floor ...

"Anyway," Brooke continued, "my dad just called a company to take care of it, they're coming in three days. The only thing is the house needs to be empty ..."

"Oh, yeah, of course." Which meant—

"I don't know how long it's gonna take, it looks like the house is in really bad shape and there might be some structural work that needs to be done ..." Brooke's voice faded into the background. All she could hear were muffled sounds she couldn't make out.

"Ave?" Brooke sounded worried.

"Yeah, yeah, sorry."

"Do you have a place to stay?"

Did she? "Yes, I'll figure it out don't worry, I'll be out of here by then. Hey, listen B., I gotta run, I'll call you later, okay? Love you, bye." She didn't give her the chance to answer and hung up.

She dropped her phone and sank to the floor. She didn't really have a place to stay. Miles didn't have enough room to accommodate her, and her grandmother was too far away from the city to make the commute every day.

Heaviness pressed on her lungs, as if a herd of elephants were stomping on her. Her breath quickened. *Breathe, breathe, you'll figure it out. One thought at a time.* And how the fuck was she supposed to pack her things in three days? *One breath in, one breath out.*

Things had been finally starting to look up, but now she was left temporarily without a home. *Damn it, Avery, one breath in, one breath out.*

Her throat tightened, and no matter how many breaths she took, the air wouldn't come out. It was like she was underwater, her lungs flooded with fear and uncertainty. She was drowning. She was drowning and there was nobody to help her and save her from the rising tide. She tried to breathe, but it was too late. Her head was already spinning, her vision swimming through the growing darkness and her whole body was shaking. Dizzy with her anxiety that coursed through her faster than her own blood, she reached for her phone lying next to her and dialed the last number she'd called.

He picked up at the first ring. "You're already awake?" he asked surprised.

She didn't have time for formalities. "Can you come over, please?"

Bless him for not asking questions. "I'll be here in 20, okay?"

"Yeah, okay."

And like he said, twenty minutes later, Josh was banging on her door. Avery wobbled toward the sound.

When she opened it, Josh cupped her face in his hands, his eyes searching hers in panic. "What's going on? Are you hurt? Did someone break in?"

She shook her head between his hands. "No, no, everything's fine."

She eased into the warmth of his skin. "I mean, everything is *not* fine, but I'm not hurt." Well, she was. Just because she was fine physically didn't mean her mental state hadn't taken a hit. *Ugh, this was so complicated.*

"Talk to me."

"The house is infected with termites and I have to move out so they can clean it. Brooke called to tell me just before I called you." She was still a bit dizzy, but his hands kept her from vacillating, and the room wasn't spinning anymore.

He sighed sharply, pulling her into the comfort of his arms. "I was so worried. I was so scared something … someone …"

Avery didn't know how it was possible, but she could feel him everywhere around her, and he was shaking. "I'm pretty sure I left my door open when I rushed out."

"I'm sorry," she said, her voice muffled in his chest.

"Don't be," he said softly. "I'm glad you called me. I'm glad you're okay."

He stepped back just a little, squeezing her arms. "I know it's not ideal, and I know it goes a little bit against the rules we talked about this morning but ... you can crash at my place in the meantime."

"I—I can't, Josh. I can't put this on you." She was grateful that he'd offered, but she couldn't accept. Could she?

"You're not putting anything on me, I'm the one offering. It doesn't need to mean anything, and it's just until they finish cleaning your apartment. Okay?"

"Where would I sleep?" She didn't want to intrude in his space and disrupt his life, but she had to admit that the idea of waking up every morning next to him sounded pretty appealing.

"I was hoping in my bed, with me. But if you're not comfortable with that, I'll take the couch."

Hell no. "No." She swallowed a bit loudly, making his gaze fall on her throat. "I'm fine with your bed ... and with you."

Josh nodded. "Okay. Okay, good. What do you want to do now?"

She thought about it for a while. No need to delay the inevitable, and might as well use Josh while he was here. "Can you help me move out today?"

"Of course. Let's get your stuff."

They spent the rest of the day gathering her things, mainly clothes and her photography equipment. Simba was already in his carrier, frightened by the commotion around the apartment.

"Hey, Ave?" Josh called from her room. She was in the middle of packing Simba's food.

"Yeah?"

In the doorway, Josh held her souvenir box. "I didn't mean to pry, but this fell out when I was packing your clothes." She froze, heart faltering. "You kept all of this? All these years?"

"Well, yeah," she whispered.

He picked up the photo her mom had taken of them. "I've never seen this one." He studied the photo for a second before looking at her with glistening eyes.

"My grandma took it." It felt like they were saying so much more. *Can you see how you looked at me? Did you love me then?*

"I love it," was all he replied, and Avery found herself fantasizing that he wasn't just talking about the photo.

♪♫

"I think it's the last one," Avery shouted as she pushed one of her dozens of bags into the trunk of the car. Simba, in the backseat, was meowing as if the world was ending. She rolled her eyes. What a drama queen.

Well, here was her life. Packed in the trunk of one car. Her mind was still struggling to grasp what was going on. Was she really saying moving in with Josh?

"I can confirm," Josh said as he walked out and pushed the door behind him. "What are you doing with these?" He dangled the keys in front of her.

"Put them in the mailbox. Brooke's parents are supposed to come by to pick them up."

Avery was physically and mentally drained. She still hadn't slept more than thirty minutes in the last 48 hours, and she looked like shit, her dirty hair in a ponytail, and rocking her old sweatpants. Trunk closed, she turned and found Josh beside her.

"Thank you," she said, rising on her tiptoes to kiss him. "I never would have made it without you. I don't know where the hell I would be." His legendary poise had once again soothed her in no time.

Josh tightened their embrace, rolling a strand of her hair around his fingers. "You don't have to thank me for anything, Avie. That's what friends-with-benefits do."

She laughed and he smiled, leaning down to kiss her gently, his tongue skimming over her lips.

"Okay, get in the car and let's get your cute ass to bed." He dropped his hands down her spine and gave her butt a squeeze.

"Sounds absolutely perfect to me."

Fifteen

Good As Hell

It took a little bit of time for Avery to figure out where she was when she opened her eyes. The sun filtering through the heavy ivory curtains bathed the bedroom in a peaceful morning light. Beside her, the sheets were scattered and the pillow slightly sunken from where Josh had laid his head.

She rolled over and buried her nose in his pillow, breathing him in. She would never get over his scent, so deliciously him. It soothed her better than any anxiety medications or essential oils ever could. And how she needed it, now that she was temporarily without a home.

She had talked to Brooke since she'd settled in Josh's apartment several days ago. Brooke had been worried the move had impacted Avery's mental state, apologizing over and over for something Avery knew wasn't even her fault. Apparently, the whole cleaning process and construction work would take at least a month. Avery had reassured her best friend that she was all right, and everything was okay, letting her know she was staying with Josh for the time being. And Brooke must have been completely stunned by that piece of information, because she hadn't even joked about it. Not wanting to give her a chance to recover, Avery had let Brooke know she'd be busy in the next few days with Julia's bachelorette party and had hung up after making plans to meet up once everything slowed down.

Avery inhaled another deep whiff of his scent. Since she'd temporally moved in, Josh had made her feel so welcome, cooking for her, making sure that Simba was settled properly, and attentive to her boundaries and what she wanted.

Intimacy didn't come easy to her, Josh knew that. But there was something about him being forever mindful of her needs that made her relax and enjoy sharing a bed with him. And the guy slept shirtless for christ's sake. She should get a gold medal for not jumping him every night.

Since they had talked and more or less defined the boundaries of their 'relationship,' she felt more comfortable letting go and embracing it for what it was: two friends having fun together for as long as it lasted. They were both well-aware that it couldn't go anywhere, so might as well scratch the itch and get it over with.

She knew that the friends-with-benefits thing never worked, but that's where her rom-com training came in handy. Golden rule: never for fall each other.

So that's how she found herself this morning in his bed, in her favorite t-shirt of his. They had spent the evening getting to know each other in new ways, with their hands exploring the other slowly, tentatively. And this morning, she woke up in his arms, to the feel of him hard and warm against her ass. She had pressed herself further into him, making him groan and grip her hip to still her. It was what she was comfortable with right now, even though her skin responded to his touch like it was the only thing it had been craving all along.

But there was a divide between what her body wanted and what her mind allowed her to do. She needed time. Time to allow her mind to catch up with her body, to understand that it was not in danger, that it wanted this.

And because he was the only one who knew what had happened at Brooke's sixteenth birthday, he understood why. The memory was still fresh and painful, as if it had happened yesterday.

The music was getting louder, or maybe it was just in her head, and the room was slightly spinning. Avery didn't know how many shots she'd had but one thing was certain, it'd been too many.

At some point in the night, she had lost track of Brooke, who'd been whisked away by her high school math team for a 'secret birthday surprise,' right before some college guys crashed the party with booze and everything had gotten out of hand.

Avery was dancing in the middle of the sweaty, drunk bodies, a dangerous mix of gin and vodka flowing through her veins and obliterating every ounce of self-consciousness. Was Josh here tonight? She couldn't remember. He must have been, he would not miss their best friend's sweet sixteen.

Swaying her hips to the lively music, she let herself go. Eyes closed and arms in the air, her head was tipped back until two hands grabbed her by the waist, snapping her focus right back to the living room.

The guy holding onto her and moving to the rhythm of the music was looking at her with a teasing smile, his baseball cap backwards on the blond hair curling around his ears. He was cute, although he looked a bit older than her. Maybe in his early twenties? She was too drunk to care or to even be freaked out that a complete stranger was putting his hands on her.

She ignored the way they brushed her skin and lost herself in the beat once more. When the song switched to a slower one, Baseball Cap Guy drew her closer to him and draped her arms around his neck, settling one hand on each side of her waist.

He leaned in, grazing his lips against her ear. "What's your name?" The sound of the music was so loud he had to shout.

"Avery!" she shouted back.

Baseball Cap Guy pointed to his chest. "Ashton. Nice to meet you, Avery." He grinned. "You know the birthday girl?"

She nodded a little bit too quick. "Yep, best friend!" she slurred.

"Ah, I see," he laughed. "My little brother is in her math club." Ashton pointed to a guy chugging a beer outside. "Doesn't look like it right now, but he's a smart ass."

His eyes were focused on her, full of mischief. God, he was hot.

Avery tightened her grip around his neck, still rocking her body to the sweet melody.

"Well," she said, "I'm not part of their club, so I'm not a smart ass."

Ashton cocked a brow. "Is that so?" Looking over her shoulder, he said, "I'll be right back, okay? Don't move."

A few minutes later, Ashton was back with two shots and handed one to Avery.

"To not being a smart ass," he said, clinking his glass to hers. They downed their shots as people around them cheered when Katy Perry's "California Girls" started playing.

They danced together and flirted all night, a tango of loose hands and intoxicated bodies pressing against each other. The alcohol removed any boundaries Avery would have had sober, and she gave in to the vibrating pull of Ashton.

"Do you want to go somewhere quieter?" he asked a moment later, shouting above the music. "We can't hear ourselves think here!"

"Sure!"

Ashton took her hand and led her upstairs, steadying her when she almost tripped on the last step.

"Wow, easy," he laughed. "You okay?"

"Yep, perfect!" she said. Or something close to that.

He led them to what she thought was the guest bedroom, where a pile of coats were strewn on the bed and closed the door behind them.

"Ah, better, isn't it?" He took a step closer to her, and another, until he was back in her space. "Hi, gorgeous."

Avery blushed, but it was unclear if it was because of the nickname or the alcohol.

"Hey," she simply said. He bent down and kissed her, and she kissed him back because the guy was a Greek God. Damn, who was she right now?

His lips were sweet and smooth against hers until they weren't anymore. Ashton tightened his grip around her back, pulling her to him and pushing his tongue in her mouth. An unsettling feeling crept over her. How old was he again?

Avery broke the kiss. "Woah there, slow down," she said, breathless.

He chuckled. "A little bit hard when you're teasing me like this." He slid his hands down her back and gripped her ass. Wait, what? *She was flirtatious, sure, but she was not teasing* him.

His mouth was back on hers and before she could register what was going on, the back of her knee hit the edge of the bed and Ashton pushed her on top of the coats lying on the bed.

She struggled as best as she could against the strong hold he had on her wrists, being drunk and scared shitless.

"Ashton, let me go, this isn't funny anymore."

"Shhh," he said, hovering above her before pressing himself down against her body. "It's okay, we're just having a little bit of fun."

I'm not, I'm not, I'm really not, *her mind was screaming inside but no words came out because his tongue was invading her mouth, one hand holding her wrists above her head, and the other pushing her dress up over her hips.*

She tried to free her hands from him, but it only made him grip harder, as he pulled her at the edge of the bed and knelt between her legs.

Half her brain understood what was happening, the other half was still drifting in the alcohol she'd had that night.

She felt his fingers curl around the hem of her underwear and push the fabric down.

"Ashton, wait... I don't want ..."

This could not be happening. *She wanted to scream, to kick, to fight but the fear, alcohol and shock paralyzed her. She felt his breath against her skin and before she could say or do anything, his mouth was on her.* Why aren't you screaming. Fucking scream. *But nothing came out.*

She heard him groan between her legs, his mouth and tongue still intruding the most intimate part of her body, while his hand was sprawled on her belly, pinning her down. She couldn't move if she wanted to, her whole body was numb from the terror that washed over her.

Avery closed her eyes as Ashton ceased his assault and lay on top of her, all his weight pressing down on her.

"So fucking good," he said, before sliding a hand between them and unfastening his jeans.

The sound had the effect of sobering her up. No, no, no, no, she had to do something.

"Ashton, you're hurting me," she said, trying to get him off of her but he was too strong for her.

"Don't worry, love. I'm gonna make us both feel very good in a second."

Panic flooded her senses as his words sank in. He couldn't ... he couldn't do that to her, this was not how her first time was supposed to go. Her heart banged against her chest and for a moment she thought she was going to die because no air was getting into her lungs anymore.

The sound of a condom wrapper ripping echoed through the room, and the next thing she knew, he was pushing himself inside her.

The pain was so intense that Avery thought that she was dying. She closed her eyes, hoping it would be over as quickly as possible, tears streaming down her cheeks as Ashton jerked hard into her, cursing loudly. His fingers were digging into her hips, further paining her damaged body.

His head buried in her shoulder, he pushed one last time, putting his sloppy mouth on hers, before straightening up and zipping up his pants.

"Wow, that was ... amazing," he said while discarding the condom in the trash next to the desk. "Hey, I'm gonna go grab a beer, so I'll see you later, okay?"

He didn't wait for her response, not that Avery was able to give him one anyway, and left the room, leaving the door opened.

She didn't know how long she stayed immobilized on the bed, lifeless and incapable of moving. It could have been minutes, or hours, when she heard a familiar voice call her name.

"Avie?"

In here! She wanted to shout but nothing came out.

The footsteps came closer and so did Josh's worried voice.

"Avie? Avie! Oh my god, Avie!" Josh rushed to the bed, panic all over his face. His eyes frantically looked at her body as to check if she was okay.

"What happened? Are you o—" His words died in his throat when his gaze caught on her underwear wrapped around her ankles.

Shame surged through her as understanding dawned on his face.

"Oh my god," he whispered. "Oh my god, Avie. Who did this to you? Tell me!"

The tears flowed again. She sobbed openly and without restraint, the sound of her voice finally breaking through her sore throat.

Josh stood by her side, helping her sit up. When she looked at him, she saw the horror and anger in his features.

"I'm so sorry, Avery. Please, tell me who it was. Please."

She whispered his name, leaving the most bitter taste in her mouth and Josh muttered something she didn't hear.

"I'm gonna get you home, okay? And tomorrow, we'll go to the police."

She shook her head. "No."

"What do you mean, 'no?' Avery, you need to—"

"I don't want to!" she cried. "I want to forget. It's okay, I won't even remember it tomorrow." She had heard enough stories of women trying desperately to get justice for sexual assaults to know she didn't want to subject herself to that. Didn't want to do tests and have to recall every detail to cops who wouldn't move a finger anyway.

Josh didn't press further. "Okay, okay. Let's get you home, then, is that okay?"

Avery nodded. Josh helped her on her feet. Her shaky legs were barely supporting her.

"We have to get these back on," he said, pointing to her underwear still around her ankles.

She pressed her lips together and nodded again. Josh quickly pulled her panties back on, careful to not touch her skin. Avery winced when his fingers brushed her thigh.

"I'm sorry," he whispered before pulling her dress down. "Come on, let's go."

She didn't make it far. Avery took one step before her legs gave out under her, but fortunately Josh was faster and caught her before she fell.

"Why don't you wait for me here, I'll be back in two minutes, okay? I'm gonna get the car closer."

Avery clung to his shirt. "No please, please don't leave me here alone, J. I can't stay here alone," she sobbed.

Josh put his arms around her, holding her tight and rubbing her back. His familiar scent relaxed the muscles of her throat a bit.

"Okay, okay, I won't go, I promise. I will never leave you again, Avie, you hear me? It's over, you're safe now. I'm here, always will be. I promise."

She hadn't realized she was crying until she felt the wetness on her cheeks. No matter how many years had passed, the pain never went away, she would never get that part of herself back. Josh had slept on the floor of her bedroom that night, but Avery hadn't been able to close her eyes. She had cried in her pillow until dawn, careful to not wake Josh up each time a sob had broken free. In the morning, Josh had brought her a steaming cup of coffee, and had held her till her body, bruised and exhausted, had finally given in to sleep. And throughout the whole day, and the days and weeks that followed, he'd kept repeating the same words, over, and over, and over again: *I promise I will never leave you, Avie, I'm here, always will be.*

A loud noise outside the bedroom caught her attention and pushed the memory out of her mind.

She stretched and reluctantly climbed out of bed, following the smell of fried food and spices coming from the kitchen. When she got there, she didn't know what came as a bigger shock: Josh with morning bed hair, wearing nothing but his gray sweats, hanging low on his hips and fitting him just right, or her cat clinging to his shoulders, ready to jump on the kitchen cupboards.

Avery snorted, amused by the terror in his eyes.

"I'm sorry, I didn't mean to wake you up. Simba just jumped on me. It scared the shit out of me. How the fuck do I get him down?"

Josh stood still, his shoulders mauled by Simba's claws as he clung onto him.

"Simba, down." The cat jumped on the table and came to rest against Avery's belly. "Good boy," she said, scratching between his ears. "I'm sorry, he's a weirdo. He likes heights and will consider you furniture when needed."

"Noted," Josh said, a smile tugging his lips.

Rounding the table, he wrapped his arms around her waist and pressed her against him. Avery let her fingers run over his naked torso before sliding them back up into his already mussed curls. Josh shuddered under her touch. Every time she touched him, she saw him lose his mind and grow hot under her fingertips. This wasn't something normal right? She'd never felt this pull with anybody else, and it was kind of scary to see the power they had over each other.

"Good morning," he said softly. "I made us breakfast."

She rose to her tiptoes and planted a light kiss on his lips, his approval reverberating between them.

"I can see that," she said as she let her hand trail on his left pec. "What's this?" she said, following the lines of the red poppy tattooed on his chest.

"It's a tattoo."

She made a face. "I *know* it's a tattoo. When did you get it? What does it mean?"

The poppy was wrapped around his whole left pec, like it was hugging his heart in a way. The lines were fine, delicate. It was gorgeous.

His voice was calm, soft when he explained the meaning behind it.

"I got it when I was in Spain. It was my mom's favorite flower, and favorite color."

Of course. Of course, he'd do that for her. She couldn't stop her fingers from caressing the red petals, drawing goosebumps on his skin.

"I love it. It's beautiful," she said before dropping a soft kiss just above his nipple. She heard his heartbeats growing louder under her lips and Josh humming a sigh. She could have stayed like this forever, as long as his arms were holding her.

"Thank you, baby," he said as he kissed her hair. "Are you hungry?"

"Starving!" She suddenly remembered all the delicious smells in the kitchen. She could get used to this, someone taking care of her for a change. "What's on the menu?"

"Well, it's Saturday, and Saturdays are brunch days in the Harding household. You'll see." He pressed his lips to her temple before resuming his cooking.

What a sight. Josh was giving her a show, and she had a front row seat and all the time in the world to enjoy it. Her eyes traveled down his broad shoulders, watching the defined muscles of his back work and roll under his sun kissed skin as he whipped something in a bowl.

Josh glanced over his shoulder, amused. "Cup of coffee? Or are you already having your fill?" *Oops, busted.*

Mortified, she ducked her head, using her hair to hide her embarrassment. "Yes, please."

Josh chuckled and poured freshly brewed coffee into a mug. He settled a plate in front of her.

"Here you go. Huevos rancheros, coffee and ..." he grabbed a bag and took out a little sugary bun that he placed next to her plate. "Concha!"

Avery looked at the feast in front of her. A fried egg was nested in a warm tortilla, above what looked like beans and salsa. Josh had sprinkled cilantro and cheese on top, and cut an avocado on the side, with a small spoon of sour cream.

"Did you just make this for me?" She could not believe her eyes and was actually salivating.

"I did! Well, I did make a plate for me too."

She took a bite, careful to have a little of everything on her fork.

"Oh my god," she moaned, her eyes fluttering.

It was the perfect balance between sweet and spicy, mellow and hot.

"This is *so* good Josh, wow. I didn't know you could cook like that!"

"Do I have to remind you that my dad owns a Mexican restaurant?" he said, cocking an eyebrow. "Plus, my grandma used to cook this for me and my cousins every morning during the summers I spent in Mexico."

"Fair." She smiled.

"My dad had taught it to my mom and she used to cook it for us every Saturday and I would help her every time. I never stopped doing it, even if it was just for me."

Nostalgia clouded his tone, but when he looked at Avery, it was with eyes full of tenderness.

She reached across the table and placed her hand on his. "I absolutely love it, it's delicious. Thank you for allowing me to be part of your tradition. It means a lot."

He gave her a small smile. "Always, Avie. Now eat before it gets cold."

Avery complied and marveled at almost every bite.

"Oh my god, what is this?!" she said after taking a bite of the pastry, which tasted like what she assumed heaven would. She could have sworn she moaned aloud.

"That's a concha. Dad makes them for the restaurant and always bakes a few more for Julia and me."

"Mmmh ... I'm never going to fit in my dress for the wedding." But she didn't care because right now she was on cloud nine, thanks to a pastry. There were worse ways to live her life. "What time did you get up to do all of this?"

Josh laughed again. She loved hearing this sound. Especially this particular laugh that she seemed to hear only when it was just the two of them.

"Not too early, I promise."

"Well, I don't think I'm going anywhere today." She patted her stomach.

Josh finished clearing the table and walked over to her, pulling her to her feet and wrapping her arms around his neck.

"As much as I'd like to keep you here with me and take care of you the way I want to—" He slid his hands down her back and cupped her ass, squeezing it gently. Avery's back arched at his touch. "My sister will destroy me if we don't pick her up on time for her bachelorette party."

He bent down and kissed her, softly at first and then more hungrily, his tongue coaxing her mouth open and invading her in the best way possible.

"Okay, let's go before I can't stop myself."

He kissed her one more time and released her from his hold, head spinning and heart humming.

♪♫

"Where are you taking us?" Julia's impatience was bubbling as Josh drove them to an unknown destination for the first part of the bachelorette party. He glanced in the rear-view mirror.

"Come on Jules, it wouldn't be a surprise anymore if I told you. We're almost there."

Julia slumped back in her seat, scowling. She was wearing a small tiara and a sash with "Bride-to-be" written on it that Josh had forced her to wear when they picked her up.

"The girls will already be waiting for us there," Josh informed his sister. His gaze slid to Avery. "Are you going to be okay for two hours alone with them?"

Julia scoffed and leaned on Avery's shoulder. "Of course she will be! She has me, right? Plus, the girls are the sweetest, you'll see."

"Yeah, I'll be fine," Avery said, while trying to give Josh her most convincing and reassuring smile. She didn't fool him one second, she knew that.

If she was honest, she was a bit anxious to spend time with Julia's girlfriends, who she knew nothing about. She wasn't the best in unfamiliar settings with unfamiliar people, but Josh had to take care of a few other things for the party tonight, and she didn't want to be a burden. And two hours in a spa didn't sound *that* bad.

They pulled up in front of the spa entrance, where four women were waiting for them, and Julia squealed.

"A spa day?" She grabbed her brother's shoulders from the back seat as he tried to park. "Thank you, thank you, thank youuu."

Josh laughed. "Okay, okay, get out of the car now. Everything is planned, so you just have to show up at reception and they'll take care of you guys. I'll be back in two hours to pick you up." Julia jumped out of the car to hug her friends, which left Avery alone in the car with him.

"You sure you're okay?" Josh asked.

"Positive." She smiled. "Thank you for adding my name to the list for today. I know it was last-minute so let me know how much I owe you, yeah?"

Josh twisted in his seat so he could see her. "It's on the house. Julia wants to thank you for stepping in at the last minute, and you deserve to relax, especially after the month you've had."

He placed his large hand on her knee, gently stroking her black tights with his thumb. She had opted today for a butterscotch suede mini skirt with a simple black turtleneck top tucked into it. She covered his hand with hers and squeezed lightly.

"Thank you," she said softly.

"You're welcome," he said in the same tone. "Now go, before my sister starts asking you a thousand questions." He retrieved his hand. "Have fun!"

She hurried to join Julia and her friends, who were waiting outside the spa lobby.

"Guys, this is Avery ... she's my wedding photographer and Josh's best friend. Avery, I think you might remember Ashley and Hannah, my oldest friends," she said, pointing to two women Avery vaguely remembered seeing a few times years ago. "And this is Rachel and Spencer, who you haven't met yet, but I *know* you will love!"

Once the introductions were made, the women made their way to the reception desk. An employee directed them to the dressing room, where Avery changed into a bathing suit and slipped into a robe.

Josh had booked them thirty-minute facials, followed by mani-pedis, where they enjoyed some champagne and Avery got to know Julia's friends a bit better.

Spencer was married with two children. Rachel was also married, but to her job as marketing director for a large luxury brand. Avery recognized herself in Rachel's ambition and drive, and admired her for working twice as hard to get what she wanted. She was a woman in a senior position and those were not easy to come by, especially in her industry.

They spent the rest of the afternoon in the outdoor thermal baths, since fall was the best season for that; the heat of the baths was like a slap on the skin after braving the freezing temperatures. Avery's muscles, which she hadn't noticed were so tense, immediately relaxed at the contact of the warm water and the steam that created a dense cloud around the girls.

"So, Avery, tell us everything," Rachel said. "How did you end up getting dragged into this one's wedding?" She pointed at Julia playfully.

Avery chuckled. "Actually, Jules is the one doing me a big favor," she said. "But it was Josh who told me his sister needed someone, and it worked out perfectly for me!"

"Oh, Josh you say ..." Hannah teased, turning towards Julia. "Is he still single? Because *damn*, that man is hot, and now that he's back ..."

Julia studied Avery for a second before replying.

"First, ew. This is my brother we're talking about. He is *not* hot. And I don't think he is single, actually. I know he's been talking to this girl he's been dying to ask out forever, so I hope he's finally taken his shot." She winked at Avery discreetly. *Oh shit.*

"Ugh, why are all the good ones always taken?" Hannah pouted. "Look at you and Paul. The dream couple. I don't know where you found him, but I'd like to get one too, please."

"First, get off the apps because you won't find one on there," Rachel said. "Then, stop reading romance novels. You're hurting yourself with all your dreamy 'book boyfriends.'"

Everybody laughed and sighed because, yeah ... real-life men could never measure up to book boyfriends.

Avery was happy to be surrounded by this group of girls today, who had immediately welcomed her with open arms. For the first time in months, she didn't feel stressed, anxious or irritated. And knowing that Hannah saw Josh as 'one of the good guys' made her feel better too. It wasn't just her and her usual poor judgment.

Feeling spontaneous, she raised her glass. "Julia, thank you for allowing me to be part of your bachelorette party today and letting me capture your special day. Cheers to the future Ms. Walsh!"

"Cheers!" everybody echoed, clinking their glasses together.

♩♫

By 3 p.m., Josh was waiting for them outside like he had told them he would, to drive them to the next activity.

"How was your afternoon, ladies?"

"AM-AZ-ING," Julia said, planting a big smooch on his cheek. "Well done, Joshy!"

Josh blushed at the mention of his nickname. *Oh, if looks could kill.*

He clapped his hands. "All right ladies, we're off to the next location! Avery, Jules, you guys are with me, and we'll meet the rest of you there, okay?"

"Actually," Julia said. "I'm gonna ride with the girls if you don't mind. Some last-minute bridesmaids' duties I need to take care of." She looked at Avery and smiled. "You guys go, and we'll meet you there!"

If Avery didn't know any better, she would have sworn that Julia was trying to give her and her brother some alone time, which she wasn't mad about. At all.

She'd barely made it inside the car and closed the door before Josh's hands were cradling her neck, pulling her closer to him.

"Hi," he said, his lips just an inch from hers. His warm breath whispered across her skin. "I missed you."

Could she admit to him that she had missed him too? It was so silly considering that she was with him a few hours ago. But she'd be lying if she said she hadn't thought about him more than once, wishing he were there with her too. *Don't overthink this, just tell him the truth.* "I missed you too."

He grinned and captured her lips with his own, pressing them against hers as if he hadn't kissed her in years. Avery reciprocated, sliding her hands into the mass of curls, trying to get closer and closer to him. Josh grabbed her waist and dragged her onto his lap, straddling him. She gasped in surprise, but the sound was quickly followed by a moan when her center made contact with the bulge in his pants.

"I know, baby, me too." He pulled her against his hips as his hands gripped her ass under her skirt that was now rolled up her hips. The thin material of her tights was not helping.

"These fucking tights ... it's like I can *feel* you against me."

She liked blunt Josh. She liked him very, very much. She grabbed his hands and pushed them under her sweater, letting him do the rest.

His mouth traveled down her neck, and she whimpered when he raked his teeth against the skin just above her breast, before kissing it.

"You need to stop making that sound, Avie, or I'm gonna come in my pants like a fucking teenager."

His hands started moving, making their way up to the curve of her breast, brushing the tip of her nipple still covered by her bra with his thumb.

"Josh," she moaned, breathing hard.

He grunted, kissing her harder while his hand struggled with the clasp of her bra and hit the horn on the wheel. Avery jolted and came to her senses. Julia. *Another kiss*. Her friends waiting. *Another kiss*.

"Josh," she said, trying to slow him down. "Josh ... we can't ... your sister ... and her friends ..."

Finally, he stopped. He rested his forehead against hers, his breath shallow.

"Fuck. Me."

Avery laughed. "I know, trust me. *I know*."

His hands were still gripping her hips and as if with reflex, he pressed her against his length again.

"Josh!"

"I know, I know, *ughhh*! Why do you have to be so tempting, uh?"

Avery chuckled. Slowly, she eased herself out of his embrace and climbed back into the passenger seat. She pulled her sweater back into her skirt and used the small mirror to fix her hair.

"You look gorgeous," Josh said.

He took her hand and kissed it, like he had done on the front porch of his sister's house, before placing it on his thigh. "Come on, let's go."

♫

The rest of the afternoon went by smoothly between tea tastings and all kinds of biscuits and cupcakes.

Josh had arranged for them to have the entire room at a fancy hotel in Toronto that hosted traditional tea parties, where Julia opened her presents. Good thing the room was just for them, because the gifts ranged from rated R to adults only: sex toys, delicate lingerie, massage oil and a beautiful bathrobe with "Mrs. Walsh" written on it. Josh had been red-faced the whole time, switching between grumbling and flushing with embarrassment.

Even though she had tried to focus on the moment, Avery's mind kept going back to what had happened earlier in the car. If she hadn't stopped them, who knows what would have happened. Well, she knew.

Who even are you?

It was so unlike her to do something like that, but Josh was bringing out sides of her that she didn't remember existed. Wild, carefree.

There was a time when she used to be like that, but the years and disappointments rolled over her and shaped her into the person she was today. Being with him made her feel a little more like her old self, which was a really dangerous thing. She had to remember to keep it casual. No expectations and no promises.

But a small voice in her head, the one she tried not to give too much attention, kept reminding her that all the stolen glances during the tea party, all the moments where Josh had sought her contact, whether it was when he walked behind her and let his hand brush against her back, or when he leaned his knee against hers below the table, were not meaningless. And maybe, those little things were like small promises, telling her that he wasn't going anywhere.

Well. Shit.

♫

As night started to fall, Avery headed to her hotel room to change into something more fitting for a night out and met the group in Julia's bedroom.

"Avery!" Julia shouted. "Daaamn girl, you clean up nice!"

Avery chuckled. "So do you, look at you!"

Julia had given them instructions regarding their outfits tonight. She wore a short, tight white dress with thin straps, and the rest of the girls, including Avery, had similar dresses but in black. Avery had paired her outfit with black strappy high heels and gold bracelets, and for once, she had let her brown hair completely loose.

When her eyes landed on Josh, he was devouring every inch of her. He too had changed into a black suit and crisp white shirt. Very classy, timeless, and impossibly sexy.

"Okay so ladies," Josh said, commanding attention on him. "Before we head out, I have a few surprises for you, including a classic little drinking game to warm us up for the night."

His speech was met with some "woooos" from Rachel and Hannah.

He laughed. "Okay, okay, let's settle on those couches there." He gestured towards the living room area. "We're going to ease into it slowly because I don't want to be drunk in ten minutes. So, let's start with 'How well do you know the bride!' Every question you get wrong, you have to take a sip; each one you get right, Julia has to drink." Everybody nodded in understanding. "Ready? The first question goes toooo...Spencer!" Josh pointed in her direction.

"Spencer, which Jonas brother was Julia so in love with she had her entire bedroom covered with his face when she was a teenager?"

Spencer answered right away. "Easy, Joe!"

"And that would be correct!"

"To be fair, emo dudes were *hawt* then." Julia laughed, taking a sip of her wine.

"I'm totally on the Joe train now," Rachel said. "He can ask me to have his babies anytime."

Julia patted her knee. "I think you're a little bit too late on that front sweetie, but I like how you're thinking."

"Alright, next question," Josh said. "Ashley, wanna take this one?"

Ashley straightened up and cracked her neck as if preparing to fight. "Let's do it."

"Who did Julia dump on the night of prom during her senior year?"

"Wow Julia, cold," Hannah said.

"Ugh *fuck* what was his name again? Ben? Brendan? ... BLAKE!" Ashley shouted.

Julia snorted.

"Poor guy spent the whole night watching her dance from the stands," Ashley added.

"He gave me *a ring,* guys. I was not ready for that level of commitment."

"My sister, breaker of hearts since 2011," Josh teased her, and Julia flipped him off.

Everybody answered several other questions, taking turns with sips. The alcohol was slowly flowing through their veins, with the exception of Josh, who was handling the questions.

"Josh you're not drinking, it's not fair," Julia whined. "Let's switch games!" She thought for a minute. "Oh, I know! What about a good old 'never have I ever'?"

"Ooooh my favorite," Hannah squealed.

"Okay, I'll start us off. Never have I ever lived in Paris for four years." She winked at her brother and Avery stifled a laugh.

"So not fair," but Josh took a big sip anyway.

"You're a few behind so you need to catch up!"

"My turn then. Never have I ever peed my pants on a flight to Mexico." Josh looked at Julia with mischief.

"Asshole. I was six!" Julia downed the rest of her drink. "You want to play?"

Josh cocked an eyebrow as if to say *bring it*.

"Never have I ever kissed someone in this room."

Oh. *Ooooh*, shit. Julia was looking at Avery and Josh, waiting to see who would break first. No, no, no, Avery didn't want her sweet little oasis she had with Josh to become a whole thing and for everybody to make a big deal out of it, because it was *everything* but a big deal.

She glanced at Josh who mouthed *sorry* and reluctantly brought his drink to his lips, and so did Avery.

Ashley, Spencer and Hannah gasped. Rachel smiled.

And Julia screamed, "I KNEW IT!"

"Julia, please sit down, let's not make a big deal out of this."

"*Not a big deal?!* You've only wanted this since *forever*! Oh my god, Joshy!"

I'm sorry, what?

Panic crossed Josh's face as he registered Avery's expression. He could read her all too well. But before he could say anything to calm her down, someone knocked on the door.

"Perfect," he mumbled. He went to the door and stepped aside to let in ... three firefighters?

Julia gasped, a big smile on her face. "You *did. Not!*"

"We heard there were some pussycats on fire tonight," one of the firefighters teased, "but don't worry ladies, we brought our big hoses to put it out."

The girls giggled and squealed in delight, cheering on the three beefed-up men as they swayed their hips in front of them. Avery snapped a picture and sent it to Brooke.

Avery [10:40 pm]: Look how horribly my night is going

Brooke replied with a pouting gif and Avery chuckled, slipping her phone back in her purse.

Josh was still standing at the other end of the room with a bottle of whiskey in hand, amused to see one of the dancers rip off his shirt as he took Julia's hands and pressed them against his massive chest.

One of them approached Avery and opened her legs in a single motion before slipping in between them to roll his body against her. Glancing at Josh, she saw him immediately close off, still as a statue, his jaw clenched and ready to pop. *Interesting*. Was he … *jealous*?

She wanted to see how far she could go before he reacted, so she put her hands on the guy's ass, as he made a whole show of removing his shirt and suspenders. He hooked one leg on the couch where Avery was sitting and grinded his hips a few inches from her face, giving her a clear view of his crotch.

Out of the corner of her eye, she saw Josh take a pretty big swig from the bottle he was holding and cross the room to exit through the glass doors leading to the balcony. *Uh oh*.

"Thank you, thank you, Mr. Fireman," she said, trying to escape his suggestive movements. "Here you go," she dug into her purse next to her and slipped a twenty-dollar bill into his waistband.

She got up and tiptoed toward the balcony where Josh had run off to, leaving the rest of the group enjoying the strippers for themselves. Judging by the sound level alone, they seemed to be having a lot of fun.

"Oh my god, it's freezing!" Josh turned to see her exit the party before returning his attention to wherever he was looking.

"Everything okay?" Avery asked, as she leaned next to him on the balcony railing.

"Everything's perfect," he quipped, taking another pull of whiskey.

"Wow, easy on the alcohol," she laughed, resting her hand on top of his.

"Did you enjoy yourself in there?" He looked pissed off and so different from what she was used to.

Okay I get it, I might have pushed it a bit too far but come on, caveman.

"I did! It was just some fun."

"I didn't like it, Avie." Another swig.

"Well, you don't have to like it. But I'm still allowed to do whatever the fuck I want. You and I are not in a relationship anyway, right? This is supposed to be fun and simple."

"Right ..." His eyes wandered off to the city skyline. Tonight was game day for the Blue Jays, and the CN Tower was lit blue and white to support the home team.

It felt weird to say that because of how they'd been acting for the last several days. They were sleeping in the same bed, eating dinner together, watching movies, and cuddling. In fact, the more Avery thought about it, the more she realized that they were really acting like an old married couple, and not at all like two people having fun and enjoying each other's company.

Josh sighed and turned to her. "Except ... except no. *No*. You may not want to be in a relationship with me Avie, but don't act like what we have going on between us is nothing more than *fun*. Because to me, it's real."

He stepped closer, his voice dropping dangerously low. "And honestly, I don't want to share. Not tonight, not tomorrow, not ever. I don't want another guy's hands on you."

"You're drunk. You don't know what you're saying." Avery chuckled forcefully. "Let's go inside."

"I may be a little drunk, but that doesn't stop me from telling the truth. You're insanely gorgeous, smart, funny, passionate, sexy. I'd be the fucking dumbest man on earth not to be completely crazy about you."

Her heart skipped a beat. "You don't mean that."

Josh reached for her waist and yanked her to him. The hardness of his chest took her breath away in the most delicious way possible. When he ran his fingers over her shoulder, lingering when they reached the strap of her dress, she thought he was going to tear the fabric.

"I've been wanting to rip you out of this dress all night." He lowered his head and kissed her collarbone, biting the top of her shoulder where the strap was.

"Josh ... your sister's inside." Avery was already starting to get drunk on his touch, his scent, and she knew that before long her mind would be too fuzzy to think clearly.

"I don't fucking care," he said, his voice huskier than normal.

His hot breath was trailing on her neck, licking at her skin in a way that made the tip of her breasts spring to attention under the thin fabric of her dress, and want pool between her legs.

"I should have been the one between your legs, not that guy," he whispered in her ear as he grabbed her hand and placed it on his crotch. "This is what you do to me, Avie."

Her breath hitched in her throat when she felt his cock swell under her fingers.

He released her and slid his hand between her thighs, pressing his fingers against the soaked fabric of her panties. "Fuck. This is what *I* do to you. Not him, not anyone else."

Her legs went completely slack from the sudden onslaught, and she had to hold on firmly to his arms to keep from collapsing on the floor.

The glass door creaked, and Julia stepped out, her hair disheveled, and the straps of her dress halfway down. Josh pulled his hand away and positioned himself next to Avery, one hand on her lower back, always seeking contact.

"Hey lovebirds! The hot guys just left, and the girls and I are going to a bar to finish the night. You guys coming?"

Avery was unable to speak. Her throat was completely dry, and her mind flooded with arousal and the memory of Josh's fingers pressed against her clit.

Josh cleared his throat. "Yeah, sure, why not! Avery?"

Avery blinked and struggled to get the words out.

"Uh, no I'm ... I'm okay, thanks. But you guys go ahead, don't worry about me. I think I'm gonna call it a night and go lie down, I'm exhausted. You guys have fun."

Josh frowned "Are you sure?"

"Absolutely."

She stood on her tiptoes and kissed his cheek. "See you tomorrow."

She said goodnight to Julia and the girls and disappeared into her hotel room. She didn't sleep at all that night. All she could think about was what Josh had said to her while drunk, and how happy she had been to hear his words, no matter how hollow she thought they were.

She knew what she was doing. Looking at the moment from every angle, examining every inch of it, replaying it over and over in her head. That was her anxiety at play. But still, the understanding sank in. She was falling in love with him. *Shit*.

Sixteen

I Feel It Coming

The days following the bachelorette party were a whirlwind of work for Avery, between scheduled photoshoots and the finishing touches on Julia's wedding, plus dinners and lunches with Miles and her grandmother.

She had barely seen Josh since, even though they were living together, but they had exchanged texts or called each other when they each had some free time in their busy days. When Josh wasn't working on projects, he was helping his father out at the restaurant, trying to ease the tension between them. They worked at different hours of the day, which didn't make the whole 'with-benefits' thing especially rewarding.

Avery would usually get up early and by the time she got back to his apartment, Josh had already left for the restaurant. When he would come home, Avery would already be asleep, exhausted from her day, and in the early morning, Josh would still be sleeping. An endless tango.

This was not an ideal situation, considering that Avery needed to talk to him about what was going on between them. She knew they had both agreed that this was just a little no-strings-attached fling, but Avery wasn't sure she could pretend anymore. The bachelorette party had shuffled the deck and she needed to know if it was just on her side, or if there had been a shift for him too. So yeah, a discussion was definitely called for, ideally before they left for Niagara-on-the-Lake.

Just as she was parking in Brooke and Alice's building for a long-needed happy hour at their place, her phone pinged.

Josh [4:30 pm]: Will be home tonight around 6. Want to go out and grab some food?

Warm feelings tangled in her heart. He finally had a night off and he wanted to spend it with her.

Avery [4:30 pm]: I'll be there at 6. It's a date
Josh [4:31 pm]: It sure is!

Smiling like an idiot at her phone, Avery pressed the elevator button that was taking her to the fourteenth floor and knocked on their door.

"Ave!" Alice said, opening the door. She gave her a warm hug. "Long time no see, friend!"

"I know, it's been forever!" She took her coat off and hung it on the rack. "What's up with you?"

Alice was a lean woman, cut exactly as one would expect a ballerina to be. Her features were sharp and delicate, her hair always loose when she didn't need to have it pulled back into a tight bun. Alice was the epitome of grace and elegance and just overall incredibly beautiful.

It really wasn't hard to understand why Brooke had fallen for her so fast.

"Well, actually, I've got some news, so come on in!"

Avery walked further into the apartment and found Brooke in the kitchen uncorking a bottle of wine.

"Baaabe, hiii!" Brooke settled the bottle on the counter and gave Avery a Brooke-like hug, which meant that Avery didn't have a lot of room to breathe.

"Hey B.," she said, chuckling. She returned her embrace. "It's so good to see you, I feel like we haven't talked in forever."

Brooke took a step back, staring at her. "We literally called each other yesterday."

"Calling me to tell me you saw Beyonce's doppelgänger doesn't count, B. Besides, I have some interesting things to tell you."

Brooke gasped. "Are you and Josh finally boning?!"

Avery rolled her eyes and turned to Alice. "Has she had wine already?"

Alice laughed and slid her arm around Brooke's waist, pulling her closer against her.

"Not yet. You know it's her way of saying she missed you too."

Alice winked at Avery, and they all moved to the living room. Avery sat comfortably in an armchair, while Brooke and Alice settled on the other end of the couch, Brooke snuggling against her girlfriend.

"So, Alice," Avery said, putting her glass of wine on the table. "What's the big news?"

"Well." She looked proudly at Brooke and back at Avery. "You know how every Christmas the National Ballet runs the Nutcracker?"

She nodded.

"I just got a call today letting me know I just got the lead role this year!"

"Oh my gosh Alice!" Avery squealed, jumping from her seat and crashing against Alice. "I am *so* proud of you!"

Alice wrapped her arms around her. "Thank you, lady."

"She's going to blow everybody away and some big company is going to steal her from us," Brooke said, her gaze full of love.

Avery picked up her glass. "Well, if that's not cause to down the entire bottle of this delicious cabernet, I don't know what is!" She raised her glass. "To Alice, congratulations on always impressing the shit out of us with your talent!"

"Hear, hear!" Brooke said, before dipping for Alice's mouth and kissing her like nobody else was watching.

Avery laughed at her shameless friend. She was completely transfixed by the love those two had for each other, and some part of her in that moment envied her. She wanted that, and maybe, if she played her cards right tonight, she might be close to having it.

"Okay, what's up with you?" Brooke asked, when she finally let go of Alice.

"Er... okay don't be mad ..."

Brooke snorted. "Great way to start."

At the face Avery pulled, Brooke said, "Sorry. Please continue."

"So, Josh and I kissed after his show and ..."

Avery paused because Brooke held out her hand to Alice and Alice placed $10 in it, rolling her eyes.

"Um, what the fuck?"

"Your best friend bet you and Josh would kiss before his sister's wedding and," she placed a dramatic hand on her chest, "*I* was deeply against it, Ave."

Brooke scoffed and kissed her cheek. "*Liar.* You're just bitter you lost, honey."

"You guys are the worst." Avery shook her head, smiling. "*Anyway*, as I was saying, since we're temporarily living together now, we kind of … grew closer I guess and, well…" She sighed. *Out with it, Avery.* "What I'm trying to say is I think I'm starting to have real feelings for him." *There.*

Brooke was looking at Avery like she was waiting for something else.

"Why are you not saying anything?" Avery was confused. "You usually jump everywhere and gasp and squeal. What's happening, did you not hear me?"

"I did."

"And?"

"Aaaand … wait." Brooke frowned. "Girl, you've been looking at him with hearts in your eyes since he came back. You've been a goner since day one, I've been telling you this *every day*." She dragged out every single syllable. "I'm glad you finally decided to act on it, but this is not news to me. Because I know you too well. And I'm pretty sure deep down you knew it too."

Did I? Avery had been so confused and trying to wrap her mind around the fact that he was back in the beginning, and then, protecting her heart, that she hadn't stopped to think about *why* she had felt that way, except for the obvious reason that hello, she hadn't seen the guy in ten years.

"I ... I don't know. Maybe?"

Alice laid her hand on her knee and smiled gently at her. "You should tell him how you feel."

Avery exhaled. "I know. The thing is, we've both agreed to not make a big deal out of this," she gestured, "thing we're doing, because we both know it's not going to lead anywhere. So, me catching feelings was really not part of the plan."

Brooke narrowed her eyes. "Whose idea was it to have a casual thing?"

"I don't know, it's not important. Me, I guess. But we were on the same page."

Brooke and Alice exchanged a look that told her they knew something she didn't.

"What?" she said flatly. "What are you not telling me?"

"I think you should have a real talk with Josh, Ave. It's not my place to say," Brooke said. "*But* I will tell you this: go for it. You know he's not like Scumbag Alex. You have to get back out there, and I *know* he left but it was a long time ago. Give it a real shot. Tell him how you feel. Maybe you'll be surprised."

"You're torturing me," Avery whined.

Brooke put her hands up. "Hey, you're the one that always says I shouldn't meddle."

"Ha! Only when it suits you apparently." She downed her wine and got up. "I have to go anyway; he's waiting for me at the apartment."

"Ooooh yes, get it babe!" Brooke winked.

"You're hopeless, but I love you." She hugged them both and flew out of the door.

♫

You're doing this. You're going to tell him you were stupid and didn't hold up your end of the deal and that you've caught feelings for him. He's going to freak out but at least he'll know, and you'll feel better ... right?

Avery had been standing in front of his door for the past five minutes, pacing the floor and going back and forth on what to tell Josh, or rather *how much* to tell him.

She fiddled with the key he had made for her a few days ago, took a deep breath and opened the door.

Josh was sitting on the edge of the couch, dressed and ready to go. When she walked into the apartment, he smiled widely as soon as his eyes landed on her, making her knees wobble in response. His chestnut hair was neatly styled, a few rogue curls still falling over his forehead. Just how she liked it. His jawline was further accentuated tonight by a light stubble that made her think he hadn't shaved in a few days and would definitely scrape her thighs. He wore simple dark jeans, a black sweater with a gray shirt underneath and a black overcoat. In other words, he was fucking gorgeous.

"Hey you," he said, getting up to greet her.

They hadn't seen each other properly in a several days so she was not surprised when he picked her up and kissed her senseless. Oh, how she'd missed the taste of his lips, the feel of his tongue invading her mouth. His possessive hands were pulling her waist flush against him, like he wanted her closer than physically possible.

"Hi," she laughed against his mouth.

"I missed you," he said between kisses on her lips, her cheeks, the tip of her nose. "I made a reservation at your favorite sushi place for 6:30 so you have ..." He checked his watch. *The man had a watch. If that didn't scream put-together.* "Ten minutes if you want to change?"

"Actually." She lifted her chin so she could look at him. "Can we talk?" Seeing the alarm all over his face and his body tense under her hands, she rushed to clarify. "Everything is fine, don't worry, I— I just want to talk to you about something."

"Okaaaay? Not gonna lie, feels a lot like you're going to tell me you don't want to see me anymore." He took her hand and guided her to the kitchen stools.

The fact that he was worried about her leaving him actually gave her the courage she needed to push the words out.

"I know this is not what we agreed on and I totally understand if this is not something you want but ..."

Her nervousness was palpable, and she started frantically massaging her fingertips, like she usually did in anxious situations. Josh lowered his gaze to her hands and pulled them between his, stroking her palm with his thumb to soothe her. She let out a labored breath.

"It's okay, Avie, tell me. It's just me here."

"I know, I know. And it's also why it's scaring the shit out of me. We've known each other forever and your friendship means everything to me. I lost you once and I don't want to relive that again. But the truth is ... the more I spend time with you like this," she said, pressing her hands on his chest, "the more I wonder how it would be if we were actually doing it for real."

He swallowed, his gaze focused on her. "What are you saying, Avery?"

Come on, help me out here.

Summoning all the courage she had, she blurted it out. "I want to try it. Us. Like, *really* want to give it a shot. I don't want this to be a fling, I'm not even sure I could do casual sex." She laughed. "Have you met me? I want us to be together and figure it out as we go."

And because Josh was still looking at her silently, she added, "I know this is not what we agreed on. I completely understand if you didn—"

"Are you fucking kidding me?" he growled before crushing his lips against hers.

The kiss was anything but gentle. It was urgent and all consuming, clutching her against him like she was his lifeline in the middle of a storm, his mouth possessively taking what he wanted, his tongue stroking hers furiously. They had no space to breathe, not that they needed it anyway. Avery sank into him, letting herself drown in his intoxicating smell, as he tilted her head to dive deeper, a groan vibrated deep in his throat. The sound sent a bolt of pleasure straight to her core, just as Josh broke their kiss.

"I ..." He was breathing hard against her mouth. "I only accepted what you suggested because I thought it was what *you* wanted, Avie. It was never what I wanted. I didn't want to push and be a selfish bastard and have you all to myself." His words kept echoing while he kissed her again, more tenderly this time, the weight of his words heavy on every brush of his tongue.

"So, to answer," he said, grinding his hips against her—*damn, he was already hard as a rock.* "Yes. I want to try this for real."

He tipped her chin up with one finger so she would look at him. His gaze was full of tenderness as he delivered his next words. "And I'm not going anywhere, okay?"

The words threatened to break her on the spot and, empowered by his admission, she grabbed his coat and pulled him to her, pressing a sloppy kiss to his lips.

"Bedroom, now."

It didn't take him long to scoop her up and wrap her legs around his waist, letting her feel how turned on he was, before putting her down gently on his bed. He discarded his coat and shoes and carefully, he hovered over her, leaving enough space between them for her to put a stop to it if she wanted to.

"Are you okay?" Josh asked.

"Yeah, I think so," she said, pulling him down to her.

Josh kissed her but was still making sure to not crush her with all his weight. He slowly kissed her jaw, traveling down her neck, and letting his hands roam freely under her shirt. His fingertips were exploring her flesh like they'd already had, but tonight Josh was more daring and slipped his hand under her bra, grazing her already hard nipple with his thumb. She arched her back at the touch.

"Fuck," he hissed, grinding himself against her thigh. His head was still buried in her neck, switching between licking and kissing and nibbling her.

Lost in the thrill, Josh completely forgot that he was no longer holding his weight and was fully pressed against her, and the dawning realization hit her. *Oh*, maybe she wasn't *that* okay.

Feeling her pull away, Josh froze and removed his hand immediately. He looked at her, trying to read her face.

"Talk to me. What's happening in that beautiful head of yours?" he asked, still a bit breathless from a few seconds ago.

"I thought I was ready but ..." Avery cleared her throat, disappointment and shame washing all over her and extinguishing the blazing fire in their path. "I guess I'm not." Admitting it out loud brought up tears that she struggled to swallow back down.

Josh sat back on his heels, lifting her up with him. She could see that his cock was straining uncomfortably against his zipper and Avery wanted to do something about it. She really, really wanted it. But mind and body were two different things, weren't they?

He cradled her face, his thumb brushing her cheek. "Hey, listen to me. Baby, look at me." Avery lifted her gaze to him. "Hi," he said softly and kissed the corner of her lips. "You don't have to feel guilty about anything, you hear me?"

She nodded, not trusting herself to not burst into tears if she opened her mouth.

"Okay, good. Let's take it down a notch, okay? We can have sex in a lot of different ways. I don't need to be inside you. Even though I very much want to be."

He kissed her again, this time more tenderly, his tongue just grazing the skin of her lips, drawing a whimper out of her.

"I need to know what I can and cannot do, okay? You need to show me. Guide me."

"Okay," she whispered, not entirely sure about what he had in mind.

"Lie down," he asked gently, and she obeyed. "First I think there are too many clothes between us, so I'll start."

He took his sweater off and unbuttoned his shirt, before dropping it to the floor, revealing the full glory of his chest. His tattoo glistened slightly under a thin film of sweat, making the poppy look as if it had just awakened in the morning dew. Avery wanted to lick him from top to bottom, to savor every dent and dip of his smooth skin, to run her fingers over his toned stomach.

As she let her gaze wander over the spectacle in front of her, she simply couldn't help herself. She reached out and carefully placed her hand on his chest, making him shudder under her touch. She traced the lines of his pecs, contouring the ones from the flower, then moved down, feeling the tightness of his abs. Further down, she trailed the path of hair that dipped under the waistband of his jeans. Feeling brave, she kept going down above his jeans, and gripped his erection, her hand finally taking in the magnitude of his size. Josh caught her wrist and stopped her.

"Avie, if you keep this up, I'm not going to be able to hold back." He let out a jerky breath. "Slow, remember?"

"Yeah, okay." Loosening her grip, she fiddled with the buttons on his pants. "Can you at least take these off?"

He swallowed hard. "Sure."

Standing up, he unfastened his jeans, removed them, and returned to his place between her legs.

The view in front of her was breathtaking. His pants didn't do justice to his muscled thighs, nor the thickness of his cock pulsing against the now-damp fabric of his briefs, begging to be set free.

"Okay, now your turn," he said, reaching for her jeans. "Let me?"

His constant need to make her feel comfortable was pulling at the strings of her heart. If he kept this up, she was going to propose in about two minutes.

"Yes."

He pushed her pants down, leaving a trail of kisses on her legs as he uncovered her skin.

"You are so soft," he whispered against her skin. "So soft. Better than I imagined."

She was down to her underwear and t-shirt, her heart quickening at his every touch. Too much and not enough at the same time. She wanted to feel him on her now, but knew that she could have another episode at any moment. *Take it slow, Ave.*

Breathing hard, she hooked her trembling fingers in her underwear and slipped them off.

Josh's jaw clenched and he closed his eyes for a second. Standing between her legs, he could so easily pull down his boxers and thrust into her in a heartbeat. And yet here he was. Patient. Caring. Earning her trust bit by bit.

"You're so fucking beautiful," he said, his voice hoarse. Taking her hand, Josh guided it to the heat between her legs. "Show me what you like."

It took Avery a second to realize what he meant. Was he really asking what she thought he was asking?

"I've never done that in front—"

He pressed his hand against hers, creating a light friction on her clit that made her muscles clench.

"It's okay. Show me," he said.

Nodding, she exhaled and closed her eyes, unable to look at him. She started to rub her clit in slow circles, her hand shaking from being this vulnerable in front of him. She could feel the tension building up slowly, Josh's breaths growing more ragged by the second. Keeping the sweet pressure on her center, Avery cracked one eye open to see his eyes riveted on the motion of her fingers, teasing and stroking her sensitive flesh, while his hand was sliding along the length of his cock, still tucked in his briefs.

"Josh," she moaned as he visibly tightened his grip around himself, groaning.

"I won't last long baby, not when you're touching yourself like that." His voice rippled through her straight down her thighs, where she increased the pace and easily slid one finger in.

"Jesus, Avie," Josh whispered, looking absolutely wild with his disheveled hair, as he involuntarily jerked his hand towards her.

"Please, yes," Avery said, grabbing his hand and pushing it against her already swollen nub.

The feel of Josh's warm breath between her legs and his touch triggered a whole range of sensations Avery hadn't anticipated, pleasure soaring through her at an unexpected pace.

"You're completely drenched," he said, trailing his fingers down and pushing one inside. Feeling her opening up, he pressed a second one, making her gasp his name. Teasing her at first, Josh began to pump faster, curling his fingers slightly to hit her spot perfectly.

"Oh my god, Josh, don't stop," she panted, digging her nails in his shoulders. Increasing the speed, each of his strokes were pure, delicious torture, driving her closer and closer to the edge. His face was only inches away from her. One lift of her hips and he'd be sucking on her.

As if he had read her thoughts, he rasped. "Please, baby, let me taste you. I need you on my tongue."

She barely nodded. "Just ... don't hold me down, okay?" she managed to say.

Placing his hand gently under her thigh, Josh lowered himself and slid his tongue from his already buried fingers all the way to her throbbing clit.

"Fuck. Fuck, fuck," he said, not wasting a minute before taking her fully in his mouth, sucking and licking and feasting on her like he hadn't eaten in days. "Ten years I've been wanting to know what you taste like." Her senses were too overwhelmed to register what he had just said. All she could feel was Josh's ravenous mouth on her sex.

Avery was gripping his hair, pulling him closer and Josh was willingly following her every demand. And she had guessed right: his five o'clock shadow rubbed against her delicate skin, adding to the already thrilling friction of his mouth and nose against her. She was almost there, every single one of her muscles pulsing against his mouth.

"Josh," she moaned again, arching her back.

"I got you, let go, Avie." Josh thrust two fingers inside her again, his mouth still busy doing mad things to her clit.

The combination was too much, and Avery felt her walls clench around his fingers. She cried his name one last time before convulsing and shuddering under him, completely limp.

La petite mort. The little death. *Here's something you remember in French,* she thought, as she slowly regained consciousness.

While he slowly removed his fingers, Avery watched, half-conscious and utterly spent from the life-altering orgasm she'd just had, as Josh brought them up to his mouth, sucking them clean.

Had she ever felt anything remotely close to what she'd experienced tonight? Sex with her ex had never been bad, far from it, but she didn't remember him at any time worshipping her body as Josh had tonight.

"I could spend my days buried between your legs and never even need to come up for air," he said, bending to kiss her, letting her taste herself on his lips. "And I would be the luckiest man alive."

She laughed as happiness overwhelmed her. *See? You can still feel it.* She peered at him, still slightly bent over her, when the bulge of his cock straining against his briefs caught her eyes. She could do it. She had done it before, there was nothing to be afraid of. She reached for him and palmed his length through the fabric.

Josh gritted his teeth. "Avery ..."

"Let me, please."

Josh gently pulled her hand away, shaking his head. "Taking things slow, remember?" He cupped her face and kissed her softly.

Searching her eyes, he added, "I appreciate it, I do. But tonight was about you learning to trust me, being confident enough in us, right?" She nodded.

"Good. I don't want you to be terrified every time I want to touch you or be inside you, because if I do things right, I plan on doing it *a lot*. I want you to be comfortable when I'm on top of you, and not thinking of ten thousand ways to run away." He locked a strand of hair behind her ear as he brushed her cheek.

"Next time, okay?"

"Next time," she agreed, kissing and losing herself in him. *Every time*.

"Okay, okay," he chuckled against her lips. "Just, let me collect myself a bit. I'm gonna take a shower, okay?"

"Sounds perfect," she said, smiling, because a little something in her had finally clicked.

Seventeen

Close

"Okay, I think we have everything," Josh said, closing the trunk of his car. Well, 'car' might have been a stretch, Avery thought, seeing the whole thing tremble from the impact.

"Are you sure we shouldn't rent a newer car? Where's your Audi?" she asked, side-eying the old rusty truck as she hung her dress and Josh's suit on the grab handles. If she was a betting woman, she would definitely put all her money on them not making it to his family's house alive.

"Are you insulting Louise?" Josh gasped, one hand on his heart. Yes, he'd given his car a name. He tapped the hood of his car. "This gal has been with me since I started driving, and not once has she let me down. My dad took the Audi last night." He leaned in and brushed his lips against her ears. "Have a little faith."

Avery snorted, closing the door. "Well, we'd better get going if we don't want to be late to your sister's fun day."

The Niagara region had quickly become an international tourist destination for wine and cheese lovers in Canada and around the world. Bordering the scenic Lake Ontario, some 50 wineries offered guided tours, tastings and accommodations, and Julia had scheduled their entire day around visiting with a wine expert.

That's why Avery and Josh were on their way to Niagara at 7 a.m., after she had barely slept the night before.

Last night. *Oh god, last night.* Something she couldn't quite pinpoint had changed inside her. Having Josh between her legs, his tongue and fingers on and in the most intimate part of herself, reverent, attentive, had been a profoundly life-altering moment. It was as if all her life she'd seen the world through blurry glasses and suddenly, someone had adjusted the lenses.

Josh had somehow already known her body like the back of his hand before even splaying his wide palms on her, letting her relax under his touch, and in doing so, offered her the possibility of letting herself go. Her heart, her skin, her blood, her whole body had buzzed under him. And now she needed more. She craved it so badly, each of her thoughts was chanting his name. It was a nice change from her usual anxious spiral.

She looked at him and took a minute to study him, to memorize every line of his face, not that she didn't already know them all too well. How handsome he was in the soft morning light, the rays of the sunlight dancing through the strands of his hazel hair that fell over his forehead, giving it an almost honeyed hue. The same hair that she clutched yesterday when she'd held him closer, coming alive under the pressure of his tongue.

His face was serene, relaxed. Trained on the road ahead, his eyes were especially vibrant today, the glow of the day giving a warm color to his blue eyes, like a sunrise on the ocean.

Josh hadn't had the time to shave this morning, and his stubble had transformed into a light beard, outlining the sharp lines of his jaw. She was dying to kiss him again.

Her gaze drifted down to his defined shoulders, which Josh had dressed today in a simple olive shirt rolled up to his elbows, making her drool at the display of veins, muscles and hair.

"What's going on over there?" Josh said, intercepting her checking him out with a smirk tugging on his lips.

"Nothing." Color tinted her cheeks. "I'm just ... happy."

His smile grew wider, lighting up her whole world. He reached over and took her hand, brushing his lips over her knuckles. "I'm happy too, baby." He didn't let go of her hand and instead, placed both of them on his thigh, squeezing lightly when she splayed her fingers.

"Are you nervous for the long weekend? Spending it with my family?"

Avery thought about it. "Not really, no. I know everybody already, and I know they like me." She stroked his thigh with her thumb, allowing it to wander and graze the inner part of his leg. "I'm more worried about you, actually. Are you going to be okay being with your father for four days straight?"

His grip on the wheel tightened, his long fingers curling around it. "Yeah, yeah it'll be fine. And Jules has packed the weekend with so many activities and then there's the wedding, so I'll barely spend time with him."

They spent the next hour driving down the highway, blasting 2000s music they'd listened to when they were kids. Beyonce, Rihanna and the sounds of other pop queens filled the truck, and Avery sang at the top of her lungs, her walls completely knocked down.

The surge of freedom coursing through her was like nothing she'd ever felt. It empowered her. She didn't feel like she had to hold back or hide her emotions because they were 'too much.' No, Josh pushed her to be the most honest version of herself, and it was *liberating*.

They had only thirty minutes left on the GPS when the smell of grease and burning clouded the space.

"Are you smelling this?" Avery asked, a little panic in her voice. "Is it coming from the car?"

They were out of the highway and driving on smaller country roads now, so Josh pulled over on the side, rubbing his brows together.

"What's happening?"

"The temperature warning light just turned on," he sighed. "Fuck!"

That couldn't be good right? She was very tempted to tell Josh 'I told you so,' but from the look on his face, Avery thought better of it.

"What does it mean?" she said instead.

He didn't answer and popped the hood of his truck open, letting a cold chill flow into the car.

"Looks like we're going to need to be towed and have a car loaned to us while we wait for it to be fixed. The engine is overheating. We shouldn't drive with it like this."

Oh, that was definitely not good. They could be here for hours waiting for the tow truck, stuck here in middle-of-nowhere, Ontario.

Josh was already on the phone with a towing company when Avery joined him outside, bundled up in her winter coat. She called to let Julia know that they were probably not gonna make it in time for the winery tour, which prompted her to call her brother.

"I know, Jules, I'm sorry. There's nothing I can do right now. In about forty-five minutes, they said." His frustration was growing by the second, pacing in front of his poor dead Louise. "Okay, I'll keep you updated."

"What did she say?" Avery asked, stepping closer to him.

Josh dragged a hand down his face and sighed. "She's a bit pissed and said we were not going to make it in time, and frankly, she's probably right."

She wrapped her arms around his waist and pulled him close to her, her chin resting on his chest.

"It's going to be fine, okay? Maybe we'll be a little late, but we'll catch up with them. Come on, let's get warm in the car, I am *freezing*."

He leaned in and kissed her, gently at first, before his tongue swept over hers, and his teeth nipped at her bottom lip.

Avery laughed against his mouth. "Josh, I'm super cold. We can pick this up in like two seconds."

He rested his forehead against hers. "Okay, okay. Come on."

♪♫

Turned out, waiting for the towing company, filling out the paperwork at the garage and having a car lent to them took about two and a half hours.

So, when they arrived at the house almost four hours late, it was no wonder it was empty. Josh had texted his sister, and they had both agreed that there was no point in joining them so late.

Being in Josh's family's country house brought back a lot of memories. Avery had grown up here too, in a way. When they weren't at her grandmother's house, they'd spent the rest of their vacations diving into the lake or building snowmen. Josh's mother had always been cooking tons of food, and that's how they'd spent their time—laughing and stuffing their faces.

It was when she walked into the house that she realized how much she had missed it, especially the family atmosphere that hung in every tastefully decorated room. The entire house was decorated in a beachy style, with neutral tones blending with more daring colors like turquoise blue and yellow. Avery's favorite room had always been the living room, with the grand white piano sitting right on top of a blue and white woven Moroccan rug beside the fireplace. She had spent so many nights here, listening to Josh play, or curled up on the couch reading a book.

She must have been lost in her memories for a little while, because she didn't hear Josh coming up behind her. "Do you want to take your stuff up to the room?"

"Yes, but first, caffeine please. I'm already exhausted."

Once the coffee was brewing, she turned to Josh, who was leaning against the counter, and placed her hands on his chest, a teasing smile on her lips.

"Are we sleeping in separate rooms?"

"Are you insane?" he huffed, grabbing her arms and linking them behind his neck. She sank her fingers in the curls of his hair.

"I don't know! What about your dad?"

Josh slid his hands down to her waist. "Frankly, I don't really care. I'm allowed to sleep in the same bed as my girlfriend."

"Oh, girlfriend? Is that what I am?" she said, feeling her heart flutter in her chest.

"I thought I made it clear after the talk we had last night," he said, nibbling her jaw with his teeth. "*And* in my bed right after." His voice had dropped several octaves, feeling the vibration rumble low in her belly and making her whole body shiver.

"Well, about that," she said, pinning him between her and the counter. God, just feeling him against her like that was enough to make her dizzy with want. Wasting no time, Josh reached for her hips to keep her grounded against him.

"We still have two hours before your family comes back and I thought we could maybe ..." She dropped her hand from his neck and gave his cock a gentle squeeze, feeling him already hard and ready. "Pick up where we left off yesterday."

"Avie ..." Josh closed his eyes and hissed. He didn't get the chance to say much else, because she unzipped his pants and pulled them down with his boxers, laying her eyes for the first time on him, taking in the full measure of his size.

Getting on her knees, she ran her fingers along the smooth skin of his length, feeling the twisted path of his swollen veins under her fingertips. Josh sucked in a breath and trembled when she reached the most sensitive part of it. She grazed her thumb over the tip, splaying the liquid that was already starting to build up.

She lifted her eyes to him. "Can I?"

"Mmhmm."

Taking her time, she swirled her tongue over the head, licking his salty taste, before closing her mouth around it and gliding her lips almost all the way down.

"Fuuuuck," Josh groaned, threading his fingers into her hair.

Empowered by his praise, she sucked harder, and pumped faster, until she was completely full of him, not able to fit an inch more. She'd never thought she would be here one day, the most intimate part of him heavy in her mouth, but at this instant, she lost herself in the feeling of deep connection reverberating between them.

"Harder, Ave," he panted. And she obeyed.

Josh started moving on his own accord, fucking her mouth with one hand tangled in her hair, and one gripping the kitchen counter. *Fuck, it was hot.* He guided her head over him, sliding in and out of her mouth while Avery gladly gave into it, letting him take full control and showing her what he liked.

When she peered at him under her lashes, the sight knocked the wind out of her lungs. Josh was coming undone under her touch, his eyes clouded, lips parted, his muscles taut and his breath shallow. The sight of him like this, unguarded and full of lust, sent a pang of warmth straight between her legs.

"Avie ... baby ... you have to ... you have to stop." Josh tried to hold her head back, but she was lost in the taste of him invading her senses, her mind chanting his name.

"Avie," Josh rasped, more forcefully. The urgency in his voice brought her back to the kitchen. She saw his abs tensing and twitching as she gave his cock one last lick before releasing him with a loud pop.

"I need to feel you," he said, tugging her up on her feet. Lifting her easily, Josh positioned her on the kitchen counter, lining her up perfectly with his hips.

"Those need to come off now or I'm gonna lose my fucking mind." He yanked her jeans off before grabbing her panties, almost ripping them in the process. When was the last time she'd turned a man on like that?

"Avie ..." he whispered as he brushed his finger over her slit, his gaze focused on her. She should feel embarrassed, exposed like that, but no. She felt powerful. Powerful because the man in front of her would get on his hands and knees if she asked him to.

"Look at you, so perfect, so ready for me already." He rubbed himself against her and she swore under her breath.

She was ready. God, she was and couldn't wait another minute. Her blood hammered and rushed down, her legs shaking at that simple touch. She needed more, *more*. She arched her back, lifting her hips slightly, looking for more pressure, more friction. But Josh grabbed her ass, tugging her closer to the edge of the counter and gently pushed her down.

"You're gonna have to wait just a bit longer, baby," he said, pressing small kisses over her knee, her inner thighs, her hip bone. She could feel his erection brushing against her pussy as he was trailing kisses up her body, and it was torture.

"Because there's no fucking way I'm going inside you without making you come first."

She wanted to complain, tell him that she would probably come if he just continued to grind against her like that, but that was before he sank one finger inside her and obliterated all her thoughts and surroundings. For a moment, everything blurred and Josh was the only one that was in focus. She gripped his shoulders as he hovered over her, pushing her shirt up and unclasping her bra with one snap.

"You're so beautiful," he said, before drawing her breast into his mouth, rolling her hard nipple with his tongue. "So fucking perfect for me."

She moaned, aching to be touched more and everywhere at the same time, Josh's mouth working on her like pure magic, sucking, biting, before soothing with his tongue, exploring her body and setting it on fire, leaving her burning for more. He awakened parts of her body she'd never known to be sensitive, and yet there she was, gasping when his teeth scrapped her collarbone, sucked her earlobe, his finger still inside her, pumping in and out, and curling just enough to hit her spot. He kept his thumb busy, stroking her swollen clit.

"Right there, yes!" she panted, so close to the edge.

"Squeeze my fingers, baby, yes, that's it, that's it," Josh panted as he plunged another digit, moving faster, deeper inside her.

"Josh!" Avery cried as her whole body convulsed under him. Pleasure rippled through her like a thousand tidal waves crashing one after the other, sweeping away all thoughts and senses in their wake.

Josh kissed her tenderly, leaning his forehead against hers.

"Watching you come is my new favorite thing in the entire world," he whispered. "But don't you dare think I'm done with you yet." Wrapping his arm around her, he hauled her up against him and carried her spent body to the couch, laying her gently between the cushions. They discarded the rest of their clothes quickly, Avery eager to finally be free of any layers separating her from the heat of his skin. The air caught in her throat as her eyes settled on him for the first time, completely naked. It was as if seeing it all together was too much at once.

"Are you eye-fucking me?" He smirked. His eyes were liquid fire roaming over her own naked body.

"Maaaaybe??" *This is mine. This is all mine.* "Please …" She was so desperate to feel him against her, *in* her, that she was not above begging.

Josh spread her legs open, standing in between, before pausing abruptly. "Shit."

"What? What's wrong?" Avery rose on her elbows.

"I left the condoms in the car. The car, which is now at the garage."

Avery hiked her legs around his waist, pulling him against her, his cock hard against her stomach.

"It's okay. I'm on the pill and I got tested recently. You?"

Josh nodded. "Same."

"Okay, so can you please, *please*, fuck me Josh, because I really, *really* want you to."

Josh bent down and sucked her breast in his mouth. "So demanding. So impatient."

He let out a curse as he angled himself at her slick entrance and closed his eyes, exhaling sharply. Avery moved against him, inching closer, pressing herself just a little more when one of his hands fell like a shot on her hip and stilled her.

"Jesus, Avie, you have to give me a second or it's gonna be over before it starts." His eyes were still shut and he was breathing hard. She clasped her fingers gently around his wrist, feeling his pulse drum under them.

"I'm sorry." She didn't want to rush him.

"Don't apologize, please. It's me, it's ... what's happening right now ... this is big. I don't want to mess it up."

He leaned down and kissed her, gliding his tongue between her parted lips and finding hers, twirling and dancing together. Slowly, Josh sank into her, inch by inch, letting her adjust to him, and take what she could. His fullness was almost too uncomfortable to endure, and yet it was the most delicious kind of pain.

"Christ, Avie you're so tight, I barely fit," he rasped, his face buried in her neck. She felt his ragged breath skimming over her shoulder.

"More," she whimpered, rocking her hips to try to pull him closer.

And he did.

He pulled all the way out, making her feel suddenly so empty, before pushing back into her in one hard thrust, so deep, so perfect, Avery could have cried from pure bliss. Maybe she did. She surrendered herself to him, at his merciless pace that dug deeper and deeper into her, each thrust bringing her closer to losing her damn mind.

"Fuck, baby," Josh grunted. "You don't know how many times I've thought about this."

She replayed his last phrase again and again in her lust-hazed brain. *He's wanted me for a long time.*

"You thought about this?" her voice was hoarse.

"Hundreds of times," he whispered.

Bending down to kiss her, Josh grazed his thumb over her nipple, pinched it gently before taking it in his mouth, sending a thousand shockwaves down her belly. If she didn't cry out before, she was certain the moan that filled the room was hers, loud and full of need.

"Josh ... I need ... please. God," she begged as she grabbed the couch cushion, trying to get a hold on her sanity.

"There is nothing god can do for you here; this is all me. All me, Avie."

He picked up his pace, one hand gripping the back of the couch and the other flying where they were joined, rubbing and circling her clit in a delirious rhythm. It was madness. That's what it was.

In a desperate attempt to regain a bit of control, Avery burrowed her nails into the flesh of his ass, bringing him as close as she could and rubbing his hips against her most sensitive spot. But Josh was the conductor, and Avery's body hummed to the music. He moaned her name as he gripped her hips to bury himself even deeper, his abs clenching with every powerful thrust, and the wet sound of their bodies smacking together growing louder and louder. She would bruise from his grip, but she didn't care. She *wanted* to.

"Give in, baby, I can feel you pulse around my cock. Come for me," he demanded, breathless.

And she listened. Because she couldn't hold it any longer, because she never saw him like this, wild, and unrestrained, and that made her dissolve into a million pieces.

She finally let herself go and let her orgasm roll all over her, screaming his name again and again as she clenched around him, gripping him so tightly that he toppled with her the next second, pumping one last time before shuddering over her, his body still twitching inside her as they both came down from their high.

Nuzzling his sweaty face in her hair, Josh pulled slowly out of her, and circled his arms around her, flipping her onto his chest. He was all sticky, but so was she, and the idea of their damp skin blending together, that he still wanted her so close to him afterwards, made her chest tight from happiness

She exhaled a happy sigh as Josh trailed his fingers along her spine. Up and down. Up and down. She could spend the rest of her life lying on him and be content. She had everything she needed right there.

"Are you freaking out?" Josh whispered in her hair. "I can hear your mind working from here."

"I don't think so," she said honestly as she traced the lines of his pecs with her fingers, watching his tanned skin react to her touch. *He was so responsive.* "Are you?"

He tightened his arms around her, answering her question. "I had time to think about this moment over the years. What it would mean, what it would be like. So, if I'm freaking out, it's not because I regret it. It's because it *finally* happened."

She raised her chin on his chest to peer at him. "Since when?"

"Mmmh?"

"You said you've thought about it over the years. I'm just curious to know since when."

"Oh." He did a small sit-up to kiss her, and Avery felt every muscle under her flex.

"Well, if we're being honest here, the thought did cross my mind a few times before I left. You remember when we were here during the school holidays? In the fall? I played you that song while B. was in the kitchen." She heard his heart racing.

"The one from the gala? And the concert?"

He nodded. "That song was the only thing that kept me going when everything seemed to go against me when I was in Europe. Every time I felt down, I played it and closed my eyes, and saw you lying on the rug here, looking at me like you knew exactly what I was trying to tell you." He swallowed hard. "If Brooke hadn't interrupted us, or if she hadn't been here at all, I would probably have taken my shot with you. If you had wanted it."

It was a lot of new information to process all at once, especially with her mind still foggy from the sex they'd just had. She didn't want to start exploring what it meant, not now, not while they were still basking in the post-sex glow. So for once, she went with honesty.

"I would have."

"Yeah?" Josh smiled tenderly, his hands still caressing her bare back.

"Yeah," she said simply.

And it was true. She would have said yes without thinking about it twice. Even at eighteen, Josh had already been the sweet, handsome boy everybody loved, who cared about the people around him and who poured himself into everything he did. Not much had changed since then.

"I guess," he sighed, "we had a few missed opportunities. A lot of 'almost' moments. Every time I thought about you when I was in Europe, I thought 'what if,' you know? I'm just glad we found our way back to each other."

"Me too," she said as she snuggled closer in his arms.

The real world could wait a little longer, while she enjoyed these last few stolen moments with him before his family returned from their tour. Because once she opened the door to the outside, she knew that this conversation and its implications would come back to her full force.

♪♫

They were all sitting in the living room, Josh and Julia's father, David, Julia, Paul, and the bridesmaids Ashley, Hannah, Rachel, and Spencer back from the winery tour. Avery was cozied up on the couch next to Josh, who had his arm slung around her shoulders, her cheeks on fire as she thought back to what they had done in that very spot a few hours earlier.

Huddled against him, her feet on the couch under a soft blanket, she took a sip of her coffee, listening to Julia recount the events of the day.

"We met a couple there who are also getting married this weekend and guess what?" she said, laying her hand on her brother's knee.

"What?"

"They're going to the same place we are for their honeymoon, on the same week! Isn't that crazy?"

"Crazy, yeah," he echoed. Since his family had returned, the mood in the house had shifted and so had Josh's demeanor. He was more closed off, on edge.

"What is up with you today?" Julia asked, a bit annoyed by her brother's lack of enthusiasm.

Josh ran his fingers through his hair. "Nothing, I'm just really tired by the day we had with the car and everything." *And everything.* "And just thinking about the last things I have to do before the rehearsal dinner tomorrow."

"Look at you, being more anxious than the bride herself," Julia teased. "Don't sweat it, Joshy, everything is going to go am-azing. Dad, do you have everything you need for lunch tomorrow?"

David nodded. "Everything is already ready to go in the fridge, *mija*. Who do you think I am?" He laughed. "Which reminds me. Josh, I haven't had time to talk to you about the restaurant yet, but Paul and I decided we needed to make a few changes."

Avery felt his body stiffen against her. Julia pursed her lips and Paul quickly turned his attention to his cup of coffee while the girls were engaged in a separate discussion. Suddenly, she was acutely aware of the tension in the air. Should she excuse herself and leave?

Josh locked his eyes on his father. "Paul told me about it."

"Then it's settled. After the wedding, we can discuss the transition. Paul will help us and look at how we can leverage investments over the long term." His tone was firm and definitive, leaving little room for Josh to object. And yet ...

"I don't think it's settled, no. You know damn well I won't take over the restaurant, Dad."

David waved his hand casually. "This is not the time or place to ramble on about your hobby, Josh. If you like music, you can always pursue it on the side. We've talked about it. It's time to move on. I want to retire, and your nonsense has gone on for long enough. End of discussion."

Josh straightened up, resting his elbows on his knees. "I'm sorry, but you were the one who brought up the subject just now. Not end of discussion, Dad. I'm not a kid you can boss around anymore and my career, *Mom's career*, is not a hobby. It's time you show me some respect."

Josh was starting to shake, his knee jerking. Paul glanced at Avery, a pinched smile on his lips and mouthed *sorry*.

"Respect? What about your family history? Your Mexican roots? The restaurant is your legacy, you need to honor it."

Avery ran a hand down his back, just so he wouldn't forget that she was right there with him, but startled when

Josh raised his voice, surprised to see a side of him she had never seen before.

"So was the piano for Mom! Or have you forgotten how passionate and thrilled she was about me playing it too?"

"Don't you dare tell me I forgot anything about your mother," David said, pointing his finger in his direction. "We'll talk about that later; your sister doesn't deserve the scene you're making right now. I'm sorry, *mija*," he said, turning to Julia.

Julia shook her head, her eyes glued to the floor. "I can't believe you're still talking about this, and just before my wedding." When she looked at her father, her eyes were wet. "For just *one day*, you couldn't help yourself." She stood up and stormed out the door, Josh in tow. When he walked by his father, Josh stopped and patted his shoulder. "I'm not the one making a scene, Dad."

They left the room, while David grumbled back to the kitchen, leaving Avery, Paul and the girls, who had stopped their discussion at some point when the voices were raised, in an uncomfortable silence.

Eighteen

Father & Son

"**I**s this okay for tonight?"

Avery was standing in their room in her lacy bra, looking at herself indecisively. Should she go with the cozy cream turtleneck sweater, or would it be a more formal type of dinner? After spending the day going over the last details for the wedding tomorrow, the rehearsal dinner—well, lunch—and more sideways glances between Josh and his father, she couldn't wait for the day to be over.

Josh stepped out of the shower, a towel wrapped around his waist and water dripping on his chest from his still-wet hair. Did they really need to go downstairs for dinner? Seemed like she had plenty to eat. Right. Here.

"What's okay?" he asked, drying his waves with another towel.

Avery showed him the sweater. "Do I need something more dressy than this?"

Like a feline rounding its prey, Josh slowly closed the distance and gripped her waist, biting his bottom lip. "I'd argue that you should be *less* dressed. In fact, my vote goes for you to be completely naked 100% of the time."

He dipped and kissed her playfully. First her mouth, then her neck, sliding the straps of her bra and ….

"Josh," Avery laughed, pushing him away gently. She should get a gold medal and a high five for this, because his proposition was pretty appealing. "We have to get dressed and meet everybody downstairs." She poked her finger on his chest. "*You* need to behave, mister."

He snatched her hand and brought her flush against him. "How can I behave when you're standing right here, almost naked and looking so delicious?" His breath was hot against her cheek.

"Well," she said, clearing her throat, "it's not like you're a whole lot more dressed than me." She stood there, tugging playfully at his towel.

She held the towel firmly in her hand, her fingers brushing against the skin of his lower belly and the trail of dark brown hair paving the way to her new favorite thing.

"My point exactly," he said, grinning. "I say let's get rid of all those unnecessary obstacles and we can come back to the sweater dilemma in a few hours."

Avery sighed. It wasn't that she didn't want to. But she could read him like an open book. "If I didn't know you better, I would think you're trying to avoid the family dinner."

Josh grunted and raked his hand through his hair. "It's all *a lot.* I don't know how many jabs I can take. Lying in bed with you sounds like a better idea."

"I'm sorry." Avery wrapped her arms around his neck and dropped a light kiss on his mouth. "I know it hasn't been easy with everything going on with your father, but you are handling it so well. Better than I would for sure, and it's almost over." She kissed him again, nipping at his lip. "Come on, J. And I'm here with you, right? You know I'm Team Josh all the way."

"I know. You're right." He exhaled. "Okay let's do this." He headed toward the walk-in. "And definitely sweater. It's super casual tonight, family only." Avery's heart grew ten sizes, her chest cramping from the sudden happiness his last words provoked.

"I know you said it's nothing fancy, but you know I—" She choked on her words when Josh dropped his towel on the floor, giving her a full view of his perfectly rounded ass.

"Not fair!!"

He gave her his most devastating smile. The one that made her want to climb mountains and run marathons. And she was *not* into sports at all.

"Who said I was playing fair?" He pulled on his briefs, molding *everything* to perfection. *Close your mouth idiot, you're drooling on the floor.*

"Are you checking me out, Avie?" Josh said, chuckling.

She swallowed hard. "Oh, I *definitely* am."

She turned to the mirror as she slid her sweater on, brushed her hair and hooked some gold hoops in her ears. She was about to ask Josh if he was ready when he came up behind her, encircling her waist with his arms and holding her close to him.

"You are the most beautiful woman I've ever laid my eyes on," he said, pressing his cheek against hers.

They were looking at their reflection in the mirror, arms and fingers intertwined. Avery could just see it. How happy they were, how happy *she* was. For a second, she let her mind wander to places she never allowed it to go. What if she followed him if he had to leave Toronto again? She knew the mistake she had made the first time, but the truth was, Josh was nothing like Alex. He had proven that to her the past few months. Could she go through with it? Could she bring herself to change her mind, get over her fears and her past? She'd be terrified, but was that reason enough to end what was happening between them?

For once, Avery wondered if she should listen to her heart and take the leap. If she was strong enough to move past her anxiety and change her whole life.

Josh had shown her over and over in recent weeks his commitment to her, and maybe it was time she started to trust him. But even though she felt like that now, while she was on cloud nine and filled to the brim with happiness, it wouldn't always be that way. What would happen when they got into a routine, and she started resenting him for making her abandon the career she was building? Or when they got into a fight, and she had no one to turn to? Would he be enough then?

The truth was, she was having a hard time hiding her feelings from him. She had tried the last few days not to dwell on it, but it was time to face the music. Avery was in love with him, and there was no doubt about it. She loved him with every fiber of her being, and every fiber of her body ached with the urge to confess it all to him. She just needed more time. But fuck, she didn't really know how much time she had. That was the problem, wasn't it? She didn't know the second he'd take off, so she was kind of playing it day by day. This whole situation gave her a headache. *One thought at a time.*

She really needed Brooke right about now. Her best friend always knew what to say, and right now, Avery felt like she was at a crossroads and was deciding on way more than just a relationship. She was deciding who she wanted to be.

♪♫

Downstairs, Julia was reading, curled up against Paul on the couch by the fire, while David was busy in the kitchen.

Should she ... No. *Not your business, Ave.* The relationship Josh has with his dad was a minefield, and Avery was too scared to say the wrong thing. But at the same time, David was alone, and...

"Knock, knock," Avery said, before entering the kitchen. *Looks like you're doing it*, she sighed inwardly.

"Ah, Avery, come in." The same spicy smell that Avery had become familiar with at Josh's place tickled her nose and helped her relax her tensed muscles.

"Can I help you with anything?"

"Well, why don't you set up the table over there?" he nodded towards the living room.

"Sure thing!"

She knew this house like her own, so if nothing had changed in the last ten years, plates should be in the cupboard next to the fridge. *Bingo.*

"Is Josh coming down soon?" David said a little too sharply.

"Hum, yeah I think so? He was finishing a few things for his surprise for Julia tonight." At David's puzzled face, Avery clarified. "He, uh … He worked on a song for her." *Way to put your foot in your mouth and stay out of people's business, Ave.*

"Ah …" Disappointment washed over David's face. "Well, good for him," he mumbled and turned his back to Avery to resume his cooking.

Oh no no no. She was not going to leave things on this note. Maybe she could help him see how brilliant his son was? Maybe he just needed a little push. Okay, she was definitely meddling now, but she couldn't help it, not when people she loved were involved.

She cleared her throat. "David? Listen, I know it's not my business, and I'm obviously not aware of everything that has happened between you guys but …" She took a deep breath. "I want you to know that you have a *very* talented son who loves what he does more than anything in the world and who strives *every day* to keep the memory of his mother alive and to make you proud.

"I know that you want him to take over the restaurant when you retire but he would be *miserable*. It doesn't mean that he does not respect or value his legacy or his origins, and all you've done for Julia and him." She took a step closer and put her hand on his arm, giving it a gentle squeeze.

"There is so much of Nora in Josh, but I know how much he values your opinion of him. Your son is brilliant at what he does, David. He works hard, harder than anyone I know. And if you give him the smallest chance, you'll realize how exceptional a man he is. Listen to him tonight.

Please. I know without a doubt in my mind that you'll be the proudest father in the world."

Not wanting to stay a second longer to hear him tell her she had overstepped her bounds, and should just pack up her bags and leave, Avery picked up the plates and disappeared into the living room, her heart hammering in her chest.

♪♫

Shit, shit, shit, what had she done? She hadn't just crossed the line, she was so far over it that she couldn't see it anymore.

They were all sitting around the table, Julia and Paul across from her and Josh and David at the head. There wasn't an inch of the table that wasn't covered with food, all of which looked delicious. Too bad Avery's stomach was too tied up in knots to enjoy any of it.

Julia was of course chatting about the wedding, completely oblivious to what had happened in the kitchen half an hour earlier. Josh's father listened diligently to his daughter, but sometimes let his eyes drift to Avery. And each time, she averted her gaze, terrified of what she might see.

Sensing her tense at his side, Josh reached over and gently stroked her knee with his thumb. He probably thought she was stressed about being with his family, and not because she had just lectured his father. Fuck, put it like that, it was not good *at all*.

They ended up having a nice dinner thanks to Julia making conversation with everyone. Josh and his father barely exchanged a word, and when they did, she could see his shoulders stiffen.

"What has been up with you tonight, girl?" Julia asked Avery once they were in the kitchen, cleaning the dishes. "You look like someone just told you they were dying."

Avery dropped the plates in the sink, sighing. Pinching the bridge of her nose, she said. "I think I fucked up, Jules."

Julia cocked her eyebrow, leaning against the counter and crossing her arms. "I'm listening."

"Okay, *ughh*. I had a chat with David just before dinner. Talked to him about his relationship with Josh and how he should be proud of him and give him a chance to prove how incredible he is." She shook her head and grunted. "It was soooo not my place to say anything, but I don't know, in the moment, I just spilled everything out." *Damn big mouth*.

Julia's eyes were wide open, her hand covering her mouth. The next second, she burst out laughing.

"You ... You said what ..." She couldn't stop laughing. "... You said *what* to my dad?"

"I knoooow," Avery said, mortified.

"Oh my god, I wish I would have been there to see his face." She was wiping her eyes with her hand. "Oh, Avery, thank you so much for this, but you don't have to worry one bit." She walked towards her and grasped Avery's shoulders.

"My dad is the most stubborn man I have met. And that should tell you a lot, considering you know my brother." Avery chuckled at this little dig.

"But I'm glad you stood up for Josh and you called my father out on his bullshit. This has been going on for too long and trust me, I have been telling him the same thing for *years*. I honestly don't know if it'll change anything. But, if he needed to hear it from someone else, someone who cares about Josh deeply, well, hopefully, this was it."

Avery cared about him so much it terrified her. "Thank you, Jules. I ... I honestly don't know what came over me. I guess I felt a little ... protective?"

Julia puffed. "Don't sweat it, okay?" She gave her a quick hug and whispered quietly into her ear. "I'm happy my brother has you in his corner."

When they were done, they made their way back to the living room, where the fire was crackling, and candles warmed the atmosphere. Josh looped his arm around Avery's waist and drew her closer to him.

"Everything okay?"

"Everything's perfect," she said, standing on her toes to kiss the corner of his mouth.

Josh squeezed her waist and released her before addressing his sister. "I actually have a little something for you, Jules." He made his way to the piano. Avery scanned the room, seeing still no sign of David. *Come on, show up.*

"What are you *doing*?" Julia said, straightening up on the couch. Josh smiled his beautiful smile of his and looked at his sister with so much tenderness it made Avery choke up.

"I've been working on this for a little while." His voice was soft when he spoke as he sat behind the piano. Avery saw him shift his gaze towards the door and she immediately understood who he was looking for. *Come on, come on.*

Sighing, Josh began to play.

The sweet melody filled the room and Julia burst into tears on the spot. Something was lost on Avery. The song was beautiful, no doubt about it, but both Julia and Josh had tears streaming down their cheeks, their eyes glinting in the dimmed light. Paul pulled Julia closer to him, and Avery sat on the rug, listening intently as the man of her dreams poured his emotions into his music.

A movement in the corner of her eye startled her out of her focus. She spotted David in the doorway, his eyes bright with tears too. Josh, too absorbed in the notes he was playing, didn't see that his father was watching and listening to him for the first time since his wife's passing.

There was not a dry eye in the room when Josh hit the last note. Julia threw herself in her brother's arms, almost making him lose balance.

"This was the most beautiful gift you could have given me," she said loud enough for everybody to hear. Josh hugged her tightly and buried his face in her neck. When he looked up, his eyes met those of his father, who was still looking at him, almost as if in shock.

Josh let go of his sister, choking back another wave of tears. Carefully, he stood up and stared at his father, who took a tentative step in his direction. Avery joined Julia by the fireplace and took her hand, giving it a little squeeze as Julia leaned against her and whispered, "Thank you," her eyes still wet.

Josh was still standing by the piano, looking unsure of what to do next. It was David who ended up taking the lead, crossing the room to pull his son into his arms. Avery saw the surprise in his eyes but after a few seconds, he clung to his father and let out years of tension as he cried his heart out. The two men were sobbing in each other's arms and the sight was too much for Avery to contain her emotions.

Taking his son's face in his hands, David said, "You may have her eyes, son, but it's her talent that burns the brightest in you." His voice was shaking with the weight of the words he was finally speaking out loud. "You are just like your mom. And if she were here tonight, listening to you play the lullaby she played to you guys when you were kids, she would tell you how proud of you we are."

Avery could see Josh's throat bobbing hard, his father's words no doubt cutting through layers and layers of loneliness and grief, and go straight to his heart. Years of rejection were healing in front of them all.

"But she's not here, so I will be the one to say it. I am so sorry it took me this long to say it, but I am *so* proud of you, son. No," he said, shaking his head. "Pride is not the word I'm looking for, because there's so much more. And I can see it now."

Avery looked around, emotion vibrating in every corner of the room. Maybe a few people were missing to make the moment perfect, but being surrounded by Josh, after ten years of not being around him, and sharing such an intimate and significant moment now with him, she felt her heart burst with love.

She knew that as long as she was with him, she was home.

Nineteen

Adore You

A very closed their bedroom door behind them.

"Are you okay?" she asked, slumping on the bed. The sheets were still unraveled from the restless night they'd spent doing anything but sleep.

Josh sank down next to her, burying his head in her neck and inhaling. "I am. Or getting there." He cupped her cheek so she'd face him.

"I talked to my dad tonight. Afterwards. Things were definitely laid out on the table—it's far from being settled, but it's a start." He stroked her cheek tenderly. "He told me you talked to him before dinner tonight. Or 'yelled at him like I was a five-year-old,' in his words." He laughed softly, before turning serious again, his eyes filled with molten lava that made her turn liquid in his arms.

"There's not a day since I've been back that I don't thank my lucky stars for placing you back on my path. But what you did tonight …" Josh choked back a sob and Avery placed her hand on his arm, squeezing it. *It's okay, I'm here.*

"What you did tonight for me, baby, no one has been able to do it before. And you just ... you *actually* did it. Because it's who you are, no one can stand up to you. I've been trying to talk sense into my dad for years and it only took you ten minutes to start the conversation. I am in complete awe of you. I love you. I love you so much and it was unavoidable because the truth is that I fell in love with you years ago, but I only have the courage to tell you now. Now that I'm holding you in my arms, I'm never letting you go, because I know I cannot go ten years again without you by my side."

She wasn't prepared for this. It was too fast, too soon, she wasn't ready to tell him—she'd barely had time to understand her own feelings and put a name on what they were. Yes, she loved him, more than she could ever possibly admit to him. But she wanted to be sure of herself, and be sure that he wasn't going to run away. Because once those three words were out, so was her heart. There were no take-backs. And she was going to be certain that he would take care of it.

Seeing that she was internally freaking out, Josh grabbed her wrists and brought them to his lips.

"Hey, hey. Listen to me." She lifted her eyes to him. "I didn't tell you this so you could say it back to me, okay? I've had this in my heart for a long time, it needed to come out. Whatever you want to say to me, good or bad, you take your time. I'll be here if and when you're ready."

Her heart stumbled and fell face-first in front of this understanding and patient man. She had to hold herself back really hard not to say it. But she still needed to let him in on what she felt.

"I care about you so much, and if you had asked me a few months ago if we would be where we are today, I would have said you were out of your mind. I'm just … cautious, I guess, because I can't take another heartbreak, J. I can't, it's physically and mentally impossible. And I can't lose you again. I'm sorry." She slid her hand across his chest.

"You have nothing to apologize for, baby. You take your time, I am not going anywhere."

"I like the sound of that." She fisted his shirt in her hand.

Josh raised an eyebrow. "Yeah? Let's see if we can figure out what else you like …" he murmured, his hand sliding from her cheek, down her back to her ass, squeezing it hard and pulling her closer to him. "Tell me."

Her breath caught in her throat. "I like when you hold me so close it feels like I can't breathe anything else but you."

Josh pressed her against him, letting her feel how much he liked the sudden shift in the mood. "Like this?"

"Yeah, like that," she whispered, her need quickly growing.

"What else?" he rasped, nipping at the lobe of her ear, his warm breath spreading down her spine.

"I like when you touch me here …" Avery said, guiding his hand to her breast.

Josh closed his eyes and exhaled as he slipped one hand under her sweater, unclasping her bra and cupping her left breast. Slowly, at first, the tip of his fingers tracing the lines of the rosy skin, circling her nipple. And then with more intention, rolling the sensitive peak between his fingers, teasing and torturing her.

"What else?"

"I like … when … when you …Josh, oh my god …"

"What else?" he demanded, increasing the pressure of his touch, the rhythm.

"I like when I can hold you in my hands," she whimpered.

"Oh, baby. I do too."

In no time, he undid his pants and threw them on the floor with his underwear. Standing in front of Avery, who sat on the edge of the bed, he grabbed her hand and guided her around his cock, holding her hand with his and squeezing, showing her exactly how hard he liked it. The heat of his skin under her fingers consumed her whole body.

"Oh god it feels so good when you touch me," Josh groaned, his hips already moving, thrusting harder in her fist.

"Look at what you're doing to me, Avie. Look." She did, and the sight of her hand around him shot a pang of desire straight between her legs. She kept the rhythm as she grazed her thumb over his tip, making him tremble with pleasure.

"What else?" he panted.

"I like when you put your mouth on me."

"Fuck … where?"

What a silly question. As if she had one place where she didn't crave him. "Everywhere."

He helped her strip out of her clothes before she settled back on the bed, Josh crawling over her like he was going to make an entire four-course meal out of her, dropping kisses on her navel, below the curve of her breast, before drawing her nipple between his teeth. She arched her back, pushing herself in his mouth, because she was greedy when it came to him and wanted more, always more. And she wasn't the only one apparently, because as she was already panting his name, Josh glided two fingers inside her, making her discover a whole new constellation of stars she hadn't seen before.

But it was the sight of Josh stroking himself, his fist squeezing hard around his length, up and down, up and down, his head swelling with the pressure, that consumed her. Her muscles tightened under the unexpected orgasm that rolled over her.

Josh paused, his hand still firmly gripping his cock, and studied her a second. "Did you just ... come?"

Avery let out a faint laugh, still coming down from her high. "I think I did."

"That's ... fucking incredible," he said, teasing her nipple with his tongue before releasing it. He grinned. "I want to do it again."

He sealed their mouths together, plunging his tongue to meet hers, his lips soft and warm as his heavenly taste ignited her fire once more.

"Come here," he demanded, rolling on his back. His hands were firmly gripping the dip of her waist and she loved it. She surrendered all control. He angled her on his stomach, with one leg on each side of him, the feel of his erection rubbing against her pussy a blissful agony. He gave her ass a little slap, making her whimper.

"Scoot closer. You said you wanted my mouth everywhere, right baby?"

Avery nodded, just as he pushed her up to his mouth, aligning her above him perfectly. Trying to find some semblance of balance, she steadied herself by sinking her fingers in his curls, holding on tightly for what she knew was probably going to be the end of her. Josh pulled her down slowly, only brushing the tip of his nose and tongue against her flesh, unleashing that wild side of herself that she'd kept buried away for years.

Josh hummed in pleasure. "Your taste, baby ..." he inhaled sharply, "it's making me wild. Lose all my control. I don't know how long I'll last, I'm sorry."

And before she had time to understand what the fuck he was apologizing for, he pushed her all the way down on his mouth. His fingers bore into the flesh of her ass as he dove his tongue inside her with a deep groan. Avery gasped and twisted her fingers in his hair, her head falling back as he kept lapping every inch of her, sucking her clit between his lips.

And like that, rocking on his face, her hips rolling from the pleasure Josh was giving her, she felt like the queen of the fucking world

For once in her life, she was in control, holding the power that Josh gladly handed over. She was not held back by anything, completely free to let herself go, to let her body relish the thrill it was feeling. Her brain was no longer in the driver's seat, only her need was running the show and it was exhilarating. He gave her power and was telling her to fucking own it.

She kept moving back and forth, another whirl of pleasure building as Josh kept increasing his pace.

"Jesus, Josh ... don't ... don't stop ..." She went off, coming apart on his mouth, her legs wobbling as she rode every last pulse.

Josh licked her one last time, like he was unable to help himself, before sliding her down gently on his chest and kissing her eagerly, her own taste melting in her mouth.

"I'm a total goner, Avie," he said in between kisses. "Your taste, your sounds, your scent, your skin." He inhaled the hollow of her neck, as if in withdrawal. "I will never have enough of you." He massaged her ribs, her ass. "I need you."

"Then have me," she whispered, pressing a kiss to his swollen red lips.

He placed his palms on her waist as he guided her down until she felt his cock pushing slowly into her, stretching her inch by inch. She exhaled as he settled fully inside her.

"You feel so fucking good," he groaned. "Stay here."

She did as he asked, and within seconds, he started to move, oh so slowly, each thrust crashing into her like like waves on the shore.

He was rolling his hips into her, slow, deep, unhurried, purposefully taking his time while keeping his eyes locked on her.

This wasn't just sex.

He was making love to her right now and she felt it with each long and deep thrust he made.

Josh cradled her neck with one hand and claimed her mouth, swallowing her gasps and moans, sucking on her bottom lip, all the while keeping his leisurely tempo. He threaded his fingers through her hair, and let them trail down her back, caressing the curve of her ass, before dipping his middle finger between her cheeks, teasing her back entrance.

"I want to have all of you," he said, before pressing his finger in, opening the door to a sensation she'd never experienced before, and one that made her eyes roll to the back of her head. Full of him, she let herself fall to his mercy, letting him do to her whatever he pleased.

"Ride me, baby. C'mon, take what's yours."

She righted herself, once again taking control and moving at her own pace, rolling her hips as a moan escaped from his throat. She used his hip bone to rub herself, building up her pleasure tenfold. She was so close to bursting, but not just yet, no. She wanted to make it last as long as possible.

She marvelled at the sight of Josh lying beneath her, lost in a hazy trance, his lips parted, his neck completely exposed, and his eyes closed in pure ecstasy. So beautiful. She placed her hands on his torso for support, and began to move faster, sinking him deeper into her each time.

"You want more? Is that what you want?" Josh breathed, locking his gaze on her.

He didn't wait for her to answer.

He pinned her against his hips, slamming himself into her, one hand on the dip of her waist, and one at the base of her neck, holding her in that divine position that made her forget her name.

"Josh," she panted, helpless against the carnage he was unleashing over her.

One more thrust.

"I can't, I can—" She cried out his name as her orgasm detonated, ripping through her and dripping down her thighs and all over him.

"Oh fuck, Avie." Josh pumped one last time before following her into the deep end, pouring his release inside her.

Josh remained inside her for a moment, his chest heaving from the effort, Avery sprawled over him, unable to move. Never in her life had she experienced this level of physical connection with someone else. It was like he understood her body better than she did, knew exactly what she loved and craved. And the same was true for her.

"I love you," he said, running his hand through her hair. Her heart squeezed inside her chest like a stress ball.

I love you, too. So fucking much I'm scared I won't survive it.

But all she did was kiss him, and hope with all her being that she was conveying what she couldn't yet articulate.

Twenty

The Luckiest

"Oh my god," Julia whispered, looking at her reflection in the mirror. Paul's mom was fastening the last buttons of her beautiful long-sleeve A-line gown that dipped just under her chest and left her back almost completely bare. *Absolutely stunning.*

Today was finally Paul and Julia's wedding day, and Avery could feel the typical buzz of excitement in the air. Everybody was busy with the final preparations, from the bridesmaids' hair and makeup to Julia's dress.

The champagne was already flowing copiously, luckily for Julia, who drank her glass in one gulp, trying to soothe her growing nerves.

"Rachel?" she called, handing her the empty glass. There was an edge to her voice that told Avery the stress was getting to her. "Can you refill this, please?"

Gently, Avery snagged the glass from Rachel's hands and put it down on the table next to her.

"Hey, Jules?" she said in her most calming voice. Knowing Julia well and the fact that it wasn't her first rodeo, she knew exactly how to handle the situation.

"I think we should go easy on the champagne, just to make sure you don't stumble down the aisle, okay?" She smiled warmly at her, hoping to convey as much reassurance as she could. "I know this is a very stressful day, so here's what I suggest: you finish getting dressed, and in the meantime, I'll go check on Paul and then report back to take some pictures before you go downstairs. Does that sound good?"

Julia nodded and whispered, "Thank you."

"You got it," Avery said, gently squeezing her arm.

Camera in hand, she walked down the hall and knocked on Paul's door, laughter and chatter coming from the other side.

"Everybody still alive in there?" she asked through the door.

She had to pick her jaw up off the floor when Josh opened the door, impossibly sexy in a mouth-watering black tuxedo.

"Hi," he said softly, visibly drinking her in too, his gaze sweeping down her body.

Julia had insisted a few weeks ago that Avery wear a bridesmaid dress to blend in with the crowd, so here she was, in a burgundy velvet floor-length gown with cut-out off-the-shoulder sleeves and draped with a faux-fur cover-up one tone darker, perfect for the winter weather.

Josh let out a breath, one hand stroking his jaw. "You look ... fucking incredible."

Avery blushed as he leaned in and dropped the lightest of kisses on her lips.

"Don't want to mess up your makeup right away. But tonight though ..." He winked.

She laughed, patting his chest fondly and goosebumps spread all over her at the firmness under her fingers. *Damn, every time.*

"I like this look on you too. Very classy," she said, fidgeting with his bowtie. "Hey, shouldn't you be over there with your sister?"

He shrugged. "I figured it was easiest like this, so the girls could be comfortable getting dressed without me around."

"Always so considerate," she said and leaned in close to his ear, whispering. "Is Paul alright? Not freaking out?"

"No, why?" he asked, and she appreciated that he kept his voice on the same level.

"Well, your sister has the jitters. Just wanted to reassure her."

She felt his mouth turn into a smile against her ear. "Thank you, baby."

"Of course. I'm just going to take a few shots while I'm here."

Josh let her in, but not without brushing his fingertips against her waist as she walked past him. *This man.*

Avery surveyed the room, her camera looped around her shoulder. Paul was standing in front of a floor-length mirror in black pants and maroon velvet tuxedo jacket, adjusting his sleeves and fastening his cufflinks. There was an apprehension in the air, but the excitement overcame every worry or nerve Paul could have.

She took the opportunity to snap a few photos of the groom and his groomsmen getting ready together, putting on their tuxedo jackets, lacing their polished black shoes, straightening their bow ties.

The soft morning light barely filtered through the frosted windows, casting a hazy glow across the room. Shooting in the morning was Avery's favorite thing to do. There was something almost magical about morning light that gave a very distinctive quality to the atmosphere, without having to make any effort at all.

She made an all-good sign to Josh as she was heading out.

"See you downstairs, boys! Don't be late!"

♪♫

The no-phone policy ended up being really useful during the ceremony. Avery didn't have to worry about the annoying aunt's arm or the obnoxious nephew's iPhone in her angle of view, and could let her creativity roam free. The results were simply amazing.

Julia's tulle and crepe dress was perfect for a winter wedding, the slightly puffy, flowing skirt of her gown creating a fluffy cloud among the snowflakes, like she was one of them. Paul's tuxedo jacket contrasted with the pristine white around him. Avery loved to play with different textures, colors, and contrasts, because it was in these settings that she felt fully in control of her art.

She hadn't smiled this much in a long time, or cried for that matter, when Julia and Paul had exchanged their vows, promising themselves to each other for the rest of their lives.

It had snowed a fair amount the day before, which gave the landscape a true winter wonderland feel that was perfect for the contest theme. Fortunately for everyone, the temperature was mild today and the sky was completely clear, allowing the hundred or so guests to enjoy the ceremony in the big open venue to the fullest.

For Avery though, the task was slightly trickier. The sun's reflection on the white snow forced her to be as steady as possible and to further manipulate her settings to account for the bright conditions.

Throughout the ceremony, she had tried to be as discreet as possible, only the click of the shutter giving away her presence. Had she taken the opportunity to take an unhealthy number of pictures of Josh? Yes, she had. Her camera loved him. The guy was born to be photographed, a masterpiece of sleek lines and symmetrical shapes.

And he was returning it well. More than once, she had caught him glancing at her and smiling when their eyes met. She knew he was attentive to her every move, as if he was trying to learn everything about her, taking his own mental pictures.

She was wrapping up the shots from the ceremony and preparing to move to the newlywed photoshoot when Josh strode up to her, a smirk plastered on his face.

"Everything going okay over here?" he said, resting his hand on her lower back and pulling her closer.

"Perfect! The ceremony was incredible, and I'm pretty sure your sister will cry when she sees the photos."

"I'm positive she will." Josh planted a peck on her temple, and lingered there for a few seconds, the feel of his soft lips making her quiver.

"Have I ever told you how incredibly attractive you are to me when I see you in your element? Sure of yourself, confident, passionate?"

Avery's heart melted just a little bit more. "You've never said it, but I wouldn't mind hearing it again."

Josh laughed. "Look at you being all bossy and demanding." He kissed her softly, cradling her face in his hands. His thumb drew small circles on her cheeks. "I am so attracted to you right now."

How could she be anything but in love with him? He was her best friend, her confidant, the one who knew every single part of her, and now, he was adding champion and supporter to the list. Frankly, it was a scandal she'd taken this long to realize it.

"As much as I'd love to stay here and let you compliment me all day, I need to pull Julia and Paul away from the champagne for their photoshoot before they're unable to stand straight. I'll catch you up later, okay?"

"Can't wait."

♫

The party was in full swing, music and laughter echoing through the old barn overflowing with white flowers and green foliage, where the rest of the wedding was being held. The sun was already setting, forcing Avery to adjust once again her settings to the dim lighting that warmed the barn.

Guests were gathered at their tables, still enjoying the incredible array of food Julia and Paul had put together when a familiar voice boomed through the loud chatter of the barn, clinking a spoon against his glass. She would recognize it anywhere.

"Excuse me everyone." Slowly, the room fell into a quiet hush.

"Good afternoon, everyone," Josh said. "My name is Josh, and I am Julia's incredibly handsome brother." He turned and grinned at his sister who rolled her eyes. "And today, I also have the immense privilege of being her man of honor."

Someone in the back of the room whistled, making Josh chuckle. "Thank you, Brian." A slight shade of pink colored his cheeks, giving him a boyish look that Avery found very endearing. She captured the moment, knowing she would always want to remember him this way.

"When Julia asked me to do a speech at her wedding," Josh continued, "I was very surprised because I'm not known to be a great public speaker. You see, my true passion is the piano, not the microphone, but I'm gonna try my best tonight to not embarrass my little sister, because if there is one person I know who, without a doubt, deserves to find happiness and love, it's her.

"Most of you already know this, but Julia and Paul met in high school." A ripple of *awws* spread across the room. "Yes, these two are the very definition of high school sweethearts. What you didn't know is that for several months Julia would come home and complain about how this guy named Paul, or Annoying Paul—yes that was Jules' nickname for him at home—was always trying to hang out with her."

Avery saw Julia suppress a laugh, and Paul smiled. She snapped a photo.

"Until one day he invited her to a Backstreet Boys concert, and according to my sister, who'd been talking way too loudly on the phone with her best friend that night when she got home, 'French-kissed her like there was no tomorrow.'"

Avery snorted with laughter while Julia sank in her chair, blushing a bright shade of red. "Oh my god, you heard that?"

"Hard to miss when you were going on and on about how it was the greatest kiss of your life, Jules." Josh grinned affectionately.

"All this to say that despite a rocky start, they eventually found their way to each other and the love they have today is infinitely more powerful. They share a closeness that is rare to find nowadays and when you do find it, trust me, you hold on to it."

Josh regained his seriousness, and it had the effect of sobering Avery up when he glanced intently at her, making her insides twist from his sudden scrutiny.

"I invite you to raise your glass in celebration of Julia and Paul," he said, raising his champagne. "Jules, witnessing your happiness is the most priceless gift you could ever give me." He turned to Paul. "Paul, I know you will take care of my sister. I can't tell you how happy I am to finally be able to say: welcome to the family, brother."

Cheers, whistles and claps erupted in the barn, as Josh gulped his drink and sat back down, dropping a kiss to Julia's wet cheek.

Several other guests made speeches, while Avery continued capturing the evening. After half an hour, the music resumed, and the crowd quietly returned to chatting and dancing.

Josh's words were still buzzing in Avery's mind. It was true that their past, the fact that they were best friends above all else, deepened the bond they had today. There wasn't another person on this earth who knew her better than he did, who could read her as well as he could. Most of the time, she didn't even need to speak for him to already know what she was feeling, what she wanted. And Avery had been surprised at how comfortable and natural being intimate with Josh had been, when she would have thought that the years of friendship would have made it awkward.

It was as if she'd opened a door that had always been there, but that she'd never dared to step through. And now that she had, she couldn't close it again. Josh saw her for exactly who she was, her qualities, her strengths and talents, but also her flaws, her fears, and her insecurities.

And despite all that, despite the fact that he knew all those sides of her, he was still here. He helped her be who she truly was deep down, and it made her feel like she could have and do anything she wanted.

She couldn't wait to get to him and wrap her arms around his neck, shower him with kisses and never let him go. To tell him that she loved him deeply, and always had. That she too saw him for who he truly was, an impossibly talented, caring, handsome and passionate man.

Ecstatic, she made her way through the crowd, looking for him. She found him just outside the barn doors, one hand to his ear and the other holding his phone. He hadn't seen her coming, and when she realized he was talking to someone on the phone, she backed away slowly. She didn't want to eavesdrop on him, but the excitement in his voice was too evident to ignore.

"I got it? I can't believe it, thank you." A pause. "In three weeks? Uh, well, I'd have to see, I have some things to take care of here, but, sure." A pause. "Tuesday, 7 p.m., noted."

It was when Josh concluded with "Thank you, looking forward to it," and hung up, that Avery slipped away before he could see her, her stomach in a bundle of knots as she realized what had just happened.

Twenty-one

It'll Be Okay

The rest of the wedding played out in a blur, forced smiles and fake laughter, something Avery had perfected throughout the years. She knew she wasn't fooling Josh, who kept glancing at her when they were not together. He was worried, the lines on his forehead creased tightly together.

"I got it?"

The question Josh had asked kept ringing in her ears. She couldn't just drop everything and think about what she'd heard. She was a professional and had a job to do. But at the same time, she was incapable of focusing on anything else. She didn't want to jump to conclusions and wanted to talk to Josh before she went into panic mode, even though she'd already felt it starting to bubble up inside her. *Rational thoughts, Avery. You know the drill.*

It was starting to get late, some people were slumping into chairs, tired from dancing all day and night to the band's boisterous music while some guests started to head out slowly.

When Julia and Paul exited the night and left for their honeymoon, Avery packed up her equipment, ready to finally be alone with Josh and clear the air.

Back in their room, Josh paused and drew her against him, tipping her chin up so he could kiss her gently. "Have I told you how stunning you are?"

Avery chuckled quietly, but it rang hollow. "Once or twice, I think?"

"Well, that simply won't do. You're stunning."

She nuzzled her face into the collar of his shirt as he cupped the nape of her neck, inhaling his scent that she couldn't get enough of, the notes of citrus and fresh soap that had become so familiar to her.

"I'm going to go take a quick shower, and then maybe we can find a way to pass the time. I have a few interesting ideas in mind."

"I'd love that," she murmured, not trusting herself to say more without breaking.

Josh kissed her again before disappearing into the bathroom. She heard the sound of water running in the shower as she plopped down on the bed, her face pressed into the cover. There had to be a logical explanation. She was probably wrong, because Josh had told her over and over that he would never leave her again.

His phone rang, interrupting her thought spiral.

"J., your phone is ringing!" she yelled loud enough for him to hear.

"Can you answer it please?"

"Sure." She picked it up. "Hello?"

"Hi, is this the number for Josh Harding?"

"Uh, yes. I'm his— his girlfriend. Can I take a message?"

"I'm calling from The Chase restaurant to let him know that a reservation has been made for 7 p.m. Tuesday for five people. Mr. Davis asked me to let Mr. Harding know a few executives from the studio will also be there."

Her heart dropped. She cleared her throat. "Got it, thanks."

"I hope you have a wonderful evening."

"Thanks, you too." She hung up, almost dropping the phone on the floor.

Josh popped through the door. "Who was it, baby?"

"The Chase confirming a reservation for Tuesday at 7 p.m.?" Avery said, matter-of-factly.

Josh's face fell. "Oh. Shit ... give me a second, I'll be right there."

When he emerged from the bathroom, he had changed into his sweatpants and a lightweight white t-shirt. A real contrast to the tux he had worn all day.

She was still standing by the dresser, staring into space. This was not happening. Josh took her hand and guided her to the bed, both sitting on the edge so they could face each other.

"I got a call during the reception," he told her, exhaling. Although he was looking at her, she could see his eyes were evasive. "I didn't tell you about it because the chances of me getting that call were very small, but apparently, I must have made a good impression."

Go ahead and get it over with.

His thumb stroked the back of her hand, but she didn't even feel it. All she could actually feel was the brick wall she was rebuilding bit by bit, and the sound of her heart pounding in her throat.

"Just before the gala, I auditioned for a job in Los Angeles to work on feature film scores. They called me today to offer me the job, and they want to discuss the details on Tuesday over dinner."

Los Angeles. The room started to spin as her mind went into freefall. Of course he would go, what an incredible opportunity for him and his career. Who was she to stand in his way?

She should have known better and been more careful. Why did she let herself get carried away by his eyes, his mouth, his hands, *by him?* She knew better, and yet there she was, suppressing sobs that were threatening to come out. But she wouldn't break down in front of him, because that would be admitting that she had already given him her heart.

"Oh ..." She swallowed, the air barely getting to her lungs. There was no oxygen left in the room. "That's great Josh, I'm really proud of you. Congrats."

Well, she was never going to be an actress, that was for sure. Even if she tried to feign the slightest enthusiasm, her performance was a total flop and Josh saw right through it.

"Can we talk about this, before we go to the worst-case scenario?" he asked, a hint of nervousness in his voice.

What more did they have to talk about? She had gotten attached to someone again, she was getting left again.

Story of her life.

Josh had promised her that he wouldn't abandon her a second time, and like a fool, she had believed him, because never in her worst nightmares could she have fathomed saying goodbye to him once more. It was 2012 all over again, but this time they had gone further, and they couldn't take back what happened.

"Yeah, let's talk …"

"I don't want this to end, Avie," he said, squeezing her hands. "I know this is going a little bit fast, but I know how I feel about you won't go away. Please. *Please*, look at me." He tipped her chin up, so she would meet his eyes. She could *not* handle him begging her right now.

"Come with me to LA."

"Co…come with you to LA?" she stammered, incredulous.

"Yeah, I want you with me. You can pursue your business from there, get new clients, there's nothing keeping you here."

"*Nothing* keeping me here?" Obviously, shock had taken over her brain because she was stuck repeating whatever words he said. "Josh, my family is here, my mother who just got divorced is here, my grandma, my brother, Brooke. Is that *nothing* to you?"

Her breath hitched as she listed all the things that kept her in Toronto, not out of obligation but out of *love*.

"I'm sorry, that's not what—"

"Maybe you don't mind leaving on a whim and abandoning your family, but I'm not like you."

He flinched as if she had slapped him, shooting his eyes to the floor. She immediately regretted her words.

"I … I'm sorry, J., I didn't mean what I just said. This whole thing is just catching me a little off-guard … I'm not wired the way you are, I guess. I can't just take off to the other side of the world overnight. I have people depending on me."

"So do I, but I don't stop myself from living because of it!"

If they were keeping score, it was one-for-one. She heard the quiver in his voice and all she wanted to do was close the small distance between them that was growing wider by the second and forget that they were heading straight for the wall.

"I love my family, Avery, you know that. But I'm living this life for myself first. That doesn't make me selfish, though. Maybe you should try it, for once. When was the last time you did something spontaneous, or something for yourself, that you wanted to do, without thinking about anything else but you?"

She remained silent, because not only was he right, but the worst part was that she couldn't see herself ever changing that.

"That's what I thought," he murmured. "Trust me, *please*, and come with me. We can come back to Toronto as often as we want. I can't lose you, baby."

"Then *stay*," she implored him. "You said you wouldn't leave me a second time." At those words, the tears she had been trying so hard to hold back spilled down her cheeks, a stream far too powerful for her to control.

"And I'm not! I'm asking you to come with me!" he almost shouted.

"And what about the contest? If I win the contract, it's for a year in Toronto. That's loads of new clients, a golden opportunity for me. Did you think about that?"

Josh scrubbed his face, frustrated. "Of course, I thought about it. But you could have ten times that in LA. I know I'm asking a lot of you, and it means you'd be starting over.

I know. But I'll be there to support you. Every day." He took her face in his hands, trying to chase away the tears that were still flowing.

"Don't cry, baby, please. It's killing me. We'll figure something out."

Avery pressed her hand against the one that cradled her face, knowing that her next words would spell the end.

"I can't start over again, Josh. I can't. I don't have it in me. You don't know the sacrifices I've had to make to get to where I am today. I can't go back. I know I'm talented, and I *know* I have a chance to win this thing. I can't jeopardize that. I can't leave."

Josh's hand fell to his side as his eyes filled with tears. "And I can't turn down this offer Avery, you know that. I've been waiting for this for years; this is my chance to keep my promise to my mom. To show her that I've finally done it."

If there was one thing they had in common, it was their drive, their desire to be the very best at their passion, and to give it everything they had. How could she fault him, when she was doing the same?

"I know. And I understand. I'm happy for you. I just can't be part of the rest of your story."

They were both messes, allowing the tears to freely flood their hearts and souls, dealing with this awful twist of fate.

"Avie ..." he whimpered, letting his pain speak for him.

"We always knew it would come to an end one day, remember?"

"I don't want it to."

Neither did she. "I don't see either of us giving up our dreams for the other."

She backed away a little—being so close to him was physically hurting her.

"I'm going to go pack my things and call Miles to come get me." She choked back a sob and resolved herself to utter the last words she wanted to say. "I need you to get out of the room, please, or I'll never be able to leave."

"Stay. Please, Avie. Baby, *please*." His beautiful face that always looked at her so tenderly was full of sadness.

She got up. She couldn't be strong for both of them, he had to meet her halfway. Her heart was breaking too, though he would never know how much.

She'd been foolish to think that because she hadn't told him *I love you*, she'd protected herself enough from the pain that was ravaging her from the inside and tearing her apart.

"We're over, Josh. *Please*, get out."

Without looking at her, Josh got up and paused a few feet away from her, his eyes reddened by tears.

Not breaking eye contact, he took the two strides that separated them and crashed his mouth against hers, his tongue working its way between her lips. Avery tasted his pain, his helplessness on the tip of his tongue, his anger in every stroke he delivered, every kiss more brutal and desperate than the last. His hands gripped her hips tightly in an attempt to hold her against him, and she let herself be swept away one last time in the bliss of his embrace, drunk on his smell and his touch on her body.

When he broke their kiss, both breathless, he locked his eyes with hers. With one hand curled around the nape of her neck, he whispered. "We're not over, baby. We can never be. As long as I'm breathing, my heart is yours. It always has been."

With that, he stormed to the door and walked out just as quickly, letting the emptiness of the room and the absence of his presence swallow her whole.

Emptied of all her strength, Avery sank to the floor. The tears she had thought were drained grew heavier, leaving a pool of water around her.

She had really thought this time would be different, but she was the most naive of all. She had always felt unlovable: Alex uprooting their entire life and ending up cheating on her, her father choosing his job and affairs over his family, Josh leaving her ten years ago and not uttering a single word the whole time. Who could love someone as damaged and broken as she was? Her past had left scars, some that would never heal properly. It took a special kind of person for her to be comfortable, to open up, someone she could give her trust to.

This time around had felt different, though. Josh had told her he loved her, and she hadn't questioned it. She had really wanted to believe him and get over her fears.

But tonight, Avery realized she had been looking at it completely wrong. It wasn't that she was unlovable, it was that she wasn't worthy enough to sacrifice anything for.

Twenty-two

Hold On

Miles [8:47 pm]: Be there in 10

Avery tucked her phone into her pocket, and bundled up in her coat, shivering from the cold December night and from the emptiness of Josh's revelation.

Right after he'd walked away, she had texted her brother to come get her, and bless him for not asking any questions. She had cried her eyes out on the bedroom floor, her face was red and puffy, her nose sore.

She was just a big fucking mess.

Like a snake shedding its skin as it aged, she had left her bruised one behind, forced to grow a thicker one. Again.

From a distance, she could hear the muffled sounds of the remnants of the party where Josh was, probably drowning his sorrows in champagne or whiskey. She ached to get to him, but kept herself firmly rooted where she was. It had taken her years to get over the first time she had lost him, and when she'd seen him again a few months ago, she'd realized that maybe she had never fully recovered.

But the worst part was that now she knew the taste of his lips, the sound of his moans, the scent of his skin, the delicious weight of his body on her, and she would never be able to wipe it from her mind. Or how he had just begged her to go with him a moment ago.

Stop thinking about it, it's over, you knew you shouldn't have gotten into this and now it's over. He's out of your life for good, and you need to deal with it.

Out of the corner of her eye, she saw headlights approaching, and recognized her brother's car as it pulled into the driveway.

When he got out of the car and saw Avery, his face dropped.

"What did he do?" he roared. He took Avery in his arms and cradled her, stroking her hair. "Avery, where is he?"

"It's okay Miles, come on, I just want to go home."

"Avery," he hissed, pinching the bridge of his nose. "Tell me where he is."

She snapped impatiently. "Miles, damn it, I want to go home. Enough with your overprotectiveness. I'm a grown woman."

He huffed. "Avery, it's 9 p.m. I drove an hour and a half to pick up my sister in the middle of nowhere because some guy broke her heart for the second time. Not once, twice!" He was fuming. "I was the one who picked up the pieces the first time and I'm the one who's still doing it now. So, excuse me if I feel like beating the shit out of him so he doesn't think about trying for a third."

Avery looked at him, stunned. "First of all, tone the toxic masculinity down a smidge. Second, how do you know he broke my heart?"

He shrugged. "I called Brooke."

"You did what?!"

"I called Brooke. Oh, don't look at me like that. You called me all freaked out, without giving me a reason. Did you really think I wasn't going to ask your best friend what the fuck was going on? She told me you were with him this weekend. I guessed the rest on my own. Looks like I was right."

"Well, congratulations. A real detective," she quipped, "Now take me home, please."

She didn't give him time to respond and got into the car, slamming the door to end this puerile conversation.

They had been driving for about thirty minutes on the quiet country roads of Ontario when Miles broke the silence.

"Okay, listen. I'm sorry about before, I lost my temper. It's just ..." He drummed his fingers on the wheel. "What do you see in him, Ave? I don't get it, he doesn't deserve you."

Outside, the ice-covered lake stretched as far as the eye could see, looming in the darkness of the night. It looked so peaceful. Quiet. She liked the quiet. Could they go back to it?

"He's got some shit to deal with on his own, but he's not a horrible person. We're just not on the same path." Her breath blew out over the chilly window.

"I wish you'd let me introduce you to Dom. I know you guys would hit it off right away."

Dom was Miles' new co-worker, but Avery wasn't exactly thrilled with the idea of her brother playing matchmaker.

"We'll see, okay? My head's not in it right now." She sank into her seat and closed her eyes, resolved to forget the outside world, but Miles gently squeezed her shoulder.

"You're going to be fine, and I'll be here for you whenever you need me."

"Thank you," she murmured, before slipping back into the depths of her thoughts.

♫

"Um, Ave? Why is your house under construction?"

Her brother pulled her out of her numbness.

"Mmh?" Oh. *Ooooooh, shit.* Miles had just parked in front of Brooke's parents' house.

"Oh, yeah, um ..." *Uuuuugh he was about to freak out.* "I forgot to tell you ... I don't live here currently." She gave him a coy smile. "Termites."

His eyes widened. "*What?* Where do you live then? I don't understand."

She rubbed her forehead. Oh, this *was not* going to go over easily, she already knew that.

"I'm temporarily staying at Josh's."

Miles took a deep breath. "Avery." He said her name as if he didn't know what to do with her anymore. "Why didn't you tell me? You could have stayed with me."

She scoffed. "You don't have enough room for me."

He started the car again.

"Give me his address. We'll go get your stuff and you're sleeping at my place tonight. I'll take the couch. And tomorrow we'll go to Mom's." How humiliating to go back and live at home at 28. *Not* the direction she'd seen her life going in.

When they walked into Josh's place, her whole body ached as his scent hit her full-force. Tears prickled the corners of her eyes, which she tried to quickly wipe away with the back of her hand. It was funny how quickly she had scattered her things around his house. Everywhere she looked, she found a little piece of her. A sweater. A camera. Her iPad. Some shoes. In the bathroom, her toothbrush was next to his, and he'd even made room on his shelf for her toiletries. To an outsider, they certainly looked like a couple, and no one would think she was just passing through. And maybe deep down she had hoped that she wouldn't have had to pack again for the second time in a month.

"Where's your stuff?"

Avery huffed at the bitter irony of the situation. "Everywhere."

They spent the evening repacking everything, her life reduced to five poor boxes, and Simba, who Brooke had visited a few times since they had left for the wedding, back in his carrier.

In the bedroom, as she packed up the last of her belongings, Avery stopped short when she caught a glimpse of a photo on Josh's nightstand. Shaking, she picked up the photo her grandmother had taken of them and her throat squeezed until she couldn't breathe anymore. She didn't know that having her heart broken would lead to having it *physically* broken, shattered into little pieces in her chest, each shard cutting into her a little bit more.

"Hey, Ave, is this yo— Hey, hey, hey, what's going on?" Miles rushed over and threw his arms around her.

She began to weep uncontrollably, her sobs choking the words out of her mouth. Miles took the picture from her hands, which she let go without resisting. He sighed.

"I know you're hurting, Ave, and I hate him for it," he said, rubbing her back. "But there's one thing I'm certain of, and that's that you're going to bounce back from this. You have done it before, and you're going to find someone who will put you first. It may take weeks, or months, but the Avery I know doesn't stay down for long. She's a fighter, she's got attitude, and she sure as hell isn't going to let a guy who doesn't see her worth destroy her. We'll get through this. You and me, okay?"

His words felt like a small band-aid on one of her hundreds of cuts. It helped, but it didn't heal. She was a fighter, it was true, but how many battles could she lose before she surrendered forever?

"Okay," she simply replied.

"Come on, let's get out of here." He placed a kiss on her forehead and hugged her, as he had done a million times before. It was his signature move when it came to her, and at this moment, she needed nothing more than a little bit of home.

♪

"Mom?" Miles called as they stepped inside their childhood home in the middle of the afternoon.

Earlier that morning, Avery had edited the wedding photos, being very careful not to open the ones of her and Josh. She hadn't been able to avoid him completely and had closed her computer several times when his devastating smile had filled her screen, but somehow, she'd managed to get through it. She'd ended up selecting six photos, two from the ceremony, two from outside, and two from during the reception, and she couldn't be more pleased with her work.

"In the kitchen, honey!"

Avery noticed the tone of her voice. She sounded in a good mood, cheerful even.

"Hi Mom!"

"Hi sweetie!" Her mother came over and gave her a hug. She had the same long hair as Avery, though a little darker and with bangs framing her face. Today, she had her hair styled, her makeup done, and Avery felt the buzzing energy surrounding her mom. She couldn't remember the last time she had seen her mother like this. Most of the time she was at home in sweatpants, cooking something or reading a book. But today she looked more like someone who was ready to take on the world.

"I haven't seen you in forever. Busy as a bee?"

"Yeah, something like that," Avery mumbled. "You look good today, Mom."

Rebecca blushed and motioned for them to take a seat.

"Okay, guys, I have some news for you." She took a breath and Avery recognized the routines her therapist had given her to manage her stress. Avery was holding hers, because surprises weren't her forte and when it came to her mother, she downright hated them.

"I want to start by saying that I have not felt this good *in years*. I know you guys will have many questions, and I understand." Rebecca took another deep breath. "I have my weekly appointments with my therapist and I'm sticking with my medication that we monitor closely with my doctor. It's really helping this time around. I'm not happy all day every day, but I'm more stable. Less of the extreme highs and deep lows."

"I'm really happy to hear that," Avery said, squeezing her hand.

"Now that the divorce is behind me, I called an old friend of mine from college who works at an architectural firm. She is amazing. So, here's the news, guys." Avery saw the excitement in her eyes. "I met with her this week and pitched her the idea of us partnering up and starting our own interior design firm together!"

Avery squealed. "Mom! That's fantastic! I'm so proud of you!"

"That's really great, Mom." Miles hugged their mother, who looked so tiny in her son's embrace.

"Thank you, kids. With the money from the divorce, our combined talent, and my friend's roster, I think we've got a real shot at it. I came prepared and had everything ready. She just couldn't say no."

Avery was brimming with pride. This was a giant step for their mother, and one she would support however she could. As far as she could remember, her mother had always had ambitions and ideas, but married life and her mental health had always held her back from achieving them. And here she was now, finally owning the strength she always had.

"I'm really proud of you, Mom," she said, her voice thick with emotion.

Rebecca looked at her with a tenderness she missed so much. "Thank you, honey. How's work for you? Miles told me you were entering a contest?"

"It's going. Yeah, I am. I'm actually submitting the photos from the wedding today."

"This is great, honey! I'm sure you're going to win. I always say you're the artist of the family. Do you have the photos with you?"

"Uh, yeah I—"

"Actually, Mom," Miles cut in, "Ave had to move out of the house she was staying in, so do you mind if she stays here for a while?"

Her mother looked at her, a smile spreading across her face. "You're staying here? Here, here? With me?"

Avery tucked her hair behind her ear. "Is that okay?"

"Of course, my love! Oh, I'm so happy, come here."

Rebecca pulled her into her arms and Avery let herself go into her mother's familiar scent.

"I still want to see those photos, though. You know me, I love weddings."

"I'll go get your laptop," Miles said, mouthing *I tried.*

"Whose wedding was this again?"

"Julia's. Josh's sister." Avery moved to pour herself a cup of coffee. If they were going to have this discussion, she'd better be fueled with caffeine.

"Josh! Long time since I've heard that name," her mom said. "What has he been up to? Still playing?"

"Yep, mmhmm, still playing." She took a sip of coffee that burnt her throat. Good, maybe that would stop her from talking.

"I remember you guys were as thick as thieves when you were younger. You should tell him to stop by some time. I miss him."

Avery gave her a tight smile. "Will do."

Miles interrupted the inquiry. "There you go," he said, setting the computer down in front of Avery.

As they gathered around her, Avery wondered if she could get away with just showing the pictures she was going to submit to the contest. Might as well try.

She opened the file and scrolled through the photos, earning a series of "wows" and gasps of approval.

"Oh, I have no doubt you're going to win, Avery, they're beautiful," her mother said, overcome with emotion. *The apple didn't fall far from the tree.* "What a lovely bride! Where is Josh?"

Reluctantly, she opened the folder that included all the photos. Miles, who was standing next to her, put his arm around her shoulders, holding her close.

She scrolled through the photos one by one, until she came across one that she had taken in selfie mode, with Josh planting a big kiss on her cheek as she was giggling. A lump rose in her throat, making it really hard for her to breathe. The picture definitely didn't do him justice, but even then, she wanted to run her fingers across the screen, hoping that maybe she would feel the fullness of his lips through the photo.

She remembered exactly what had happened just after she snapped the pic. She'd turned her head and Josh had kissed her, capturing her lips between his and making her want to drag him out of the room to their bedroom.

"Oh my goodness, look at that handsome guy!" Rebecca yelped. She swatted Avery's arm. "You didn't tell me you guys were a thing!"

"Because we're not," she replied, a bit dryly. "We're just friends." The word left a bitter taste in her mouth, because that too was probably a lie.

Rebecca kissed her hair. "Well, you guys look like you had a lot of fun. I can't believe he's back and hasn't called me yet! Maybe we should call him right now and tell him to stop by."

"Mom, no I ... He's very busy. He's moving soon and has a lot of stuff to figure out." Although their relationship wasn't one of them.

Her mom looked at her confused. "What do you mean? He just came back, right?"

Miles stood up, dropping a kiss in Avery's hair. "I'm gonna go get your stuff out of the car, okay? I'll be right back."

With her brother leaving in the middle of the conversation, Rebecca grew more suspicious. "Honey, did something happen between you two?"

Ugh, she didn't want to do this. She just wanted to submit her photos and crawl back to bed. She wanted to forget that she'd fallen in love with her best friend and that she would never see him again. And she certainly didn't want her mom's pity.

When Avery didn't answer, Rebecca pushed a bit more. "You know you can talk to me, Avery."

She grumbled. "I know. It's just … it's nothing. He got an offer for this great opportunity in Los Angeles. And he's going. I just thought, because we had kind of decided to give it a try between us … I thought this time he'd stay, you know?"

Her mom raised an eyebrow. "What's keeping you from going with him?"

"I can't leave Toronto, Mom. My life is here."

She smiled softly. "Why not? Don't get me wrong, there's nothing I want more than to keep you close to me, but you have to live, honey."

This was the second time in 24 hours that someone had told her she had to live, and she was getting tired of it. Especially coming from her mom, who hadn't done any of that said living in twenty years.

"I am living!" Avery snapped, and immediately wished she hadn't. "I am living, Mom. For the first time in my life, I am living for myself. *This* is the reason why I am staying, because I am choosing myself. I don't want to resent him for making me leave my career behind. Or be fifty and only just starting my life because I've put everything aside for someone who will ultimately leave me like—"

She stopped short before saying something she knew she'd regret. It wasn't fair. She knew it, but it was too late because Rebecca understood where she was going.

"Like me?" She looked pained, her soft features tensed under the weight of Avery's cold truths. "You can say it, it's true."

"I didn't mean it, Mom. I'm sorry."

Rebecca shook her head with a heavy sigh. When she spoke her tone was harder, more definitive. "You've got it all wrong Avery, and even though I do have regrets, putting in the time to raise you and your brother certainly isn't one of them."

"But—"

"Let me finish please," she said, raising her hands in front of her, and again, there was no room for negotiation. "I know I haven't always been a role model to you guys. I wasn't always there for you and I could have done a better job taking care of myself. But my mental health and my journey with depression has *nothing* to do with what happened with your father. Or maybe I should say, that is not what triggered it. Did you know that grandma's sister had depression too? You may not remember her. Back in her day and honestly in mine too, you know, mental health wasn't something that people cared about. We didn't talk about it. You had a fractured arm? You went to the ER. You couldn't get out of bed and you didn't know why? Were you physically hurt? No? So, what was wrong? There was no room for invisible pain. Now we're getting there, but trust me that even just ten years ago, it was a whole other story. And we have also learned that it's something that can be passed on from one generation to the next. And sometimes, well, sometimes it skips one."

Rebecca placed her hands over Avery's. "All I'm saying, honey, is this. I made my choices. I *chose* to dedicate myself to you guys, in the best way I could. Was my life perfect? No. Did I wish your father was around more? Of course. It wasn't the kind of marriage I expected to have. But no one ever pushed me to make that choice."

Avery let her mom's confession sink in, piecing together a new reality she'd never considered, reshaping the memories of her childhood.

"Mom, I … I didn't know. I thought you were depressed because of Dad, and because you had to stop doing the things you loved and wanted to do."

She smiled. "No, honey. I wish it would have been that easy. I would have left his ass if it was only that, trust me. He certainly didn't help. But *I* was my own obstacle."

Her mom lifted her chin with her fingertips. "My daughter is strong, independent and ambitious. I know you well enough to say you'll never let a man walk all over you or your dreams. And I doubt Josh would even let you lose sight of yourself or your goals. That man adored you ten years ago, and he still seems to be just as madly in love now, judging from those photos. Don't let your past or fear get in the way of your future. Don't be your own obstacle, honey."

Tears in her eyes, Avery squeezed her mom's hands. The strength her mother was showing her now knocked the wind out of her. Avery had never seen her mother be so honest, so open, and vulnerable. When was the last time they had a mother-daughter talk? Totally uninhibited and unabashed. It was as if she was catching a glimpse of some version of her mother that she'd known years ago, but had been pushed under layers of depression.

And even though she wasn't out of the woods yet, and likely never would be, Avery couldn't help but hope. Hope that she would reconnect with her mother. The one with whom she had exchanged laughs, tears, love stories, anger. The one she had spent evenings snuggled up with, watching rom-coms. The one she had spent so many times cooking with when she was still a kid. It had only taken this much. That little conversation had opened up this big world of possibility, like an electroshock that had restarted their dormant relationship. For the first time since her childhood, Avery felt like she had her mom back.

Thinking about her mom's last words, she said, "I'll think about it. I promise."

"That's all I wanted to hear, honey."

They spent the afternoon together, Miles, Rebecca and her, going over her mom's business plan and submitting the photo Avery had chosen for the contest. And before Miles left for his apartment, they shared a dinner, like they hadn't done in a very long time.

As she watched her brother tease her mom over her business name ideas, Avery felt her lips curve into a smile. Her heart was so full, despite the big missing piece still in the hands of a particular pianist. But what was left of it? It was filled to the brink with love.

And maybe her family wasn't perfect. Maybe they were broken. But they loved each other so fiercely that Avery realized she would never change a thing. And surrounded by her mom and brother, the little spark of hope she'd felt inside her earlier today slowly grew into a more permanent gleam.

Twenty-three

The Fools who Dream

Over the week following The Wedding, Avery kept her mind busy between her work and her mother, by planning every minute of every day.

There was no down time between preparing for Luc's vow renewal, helping her mother with her design firm project (she had a little bit of knowledge in building a website) and visiting Claudia and her little guy. And in the evenings, she'd free-dive into the gripping world of thrillers, leaving her stack of romance novels untouched for the time being. Cute love stories were not what she needed right now.

With a few exceptions, she had sort of managed to shove aside the two things she didn't want to think about: the man who need not be named, and the result of the contest.

The only time she allowed herself to think about it was when her mom's words popped into her head. She had promised her that she'd think about it, and she was a woman of her word, though honestly, she could have done without it.

Not only had what Rebecca shared messed her up, but it had led her to see another path for herself. One where she could perhaps consider leaving with Josh, to build her business elsewhere, with his help, as he had so gently suggested. *I'll be there to support you, every day.* And she knew he would be. That meant that she could maybe be happy elsewhere, as long as she had him by her side. That she wasn't doomed to follow her mom's path when it came to love, because the root of the problem came from somewhere else entirely. She had her own mental health issues, and who knew what might come up in the future. But Josh would never be the source. And *that* had changed everything.

But what if she won the contest? She couldn't leave Lisa hanging when she'd helped her so much over the last few years. And she didn't know when Josh was supposed to leave, if he was even already gone. Did she have time to prepare if she decided to go? Or would she have to pack up everything right away, say goodbye to her family overnight?

She was not the kind of person who liked to do things without planning, her anxious nature made the unexpected terrifying. So she was faced with an impossible impasse, and needed her best friend now more than ever. Brooke always knew what to do.

A bit annoyed, Avery grabbed her phone and texted Brooke.

Avery [2:10 pm]: Where are you?

They were meeting at this cute cafe where cats roamed freely, rubbing their little heads against customers' legs in the hopes of charming them into adoption. If she listened to herself, she would adopt them all.

True to form, Brooke was late. Avery hadn't seen her since before Julia's wedding, and hadn't updated her on the latest developments—she wanted to fill her in in person rather than by text. Either way, she knew Brooke was going to bombard her with questions, whether she brought it up or not.

Brooke [2:12 pm]: Coming, coming, I'm five minutes away. You can order now if you want. I'll have a matcha latte.

The order placed, Avery returned to sit at the table, a small gray and white kitty waiting on the chair next to her.

"Hey there," she said, scratching her head. The kitten began to purr right away, seeking the touch of her hand. She was so tiny, with her fur creating a lovely pattern of white spots, as if she'd fallen into a can of permanent paint.

"Her name is Troopie," one of the waiters told her. "You're lucky because normally she's pretty shy. Even with us!"

"Oh, really? Well, it doesn't look like it," Avery said, as Troopie jumped into her lap and rubbed against her belly.

If Avery wanted to see it as a sign of fate, maybe she'd believe that Troopie sensed her need for love and comfort. Animals had a way of picking up on moods.

"Sorry I'm late!" Brooke said as she walked in, and the kitten took refuge on Avery's shoulders, hiding behind her thick hair.

"The day you arrive on time, that's when I'll worry."

Brooke rolled her eyes. "Ha. Ha. At least *I* didn't stand you up."

"That happened *once*, you're never going to let that go, are you?"

"Nope," Brooke said, popping the p.

"You're insufferable," Avery said, taking a sip of her vanilla latte.

"But you still love me." Brooke plastered a bright smile on her face before it dimmed slightly. "Who's that little guy on your shoulders?"

Avery scratched Troopie's ear. "*This* is a little gal, and her name is Troopie. She might be Simba's little sister."

Brooke gasped "Are you adopting her?"

"Maybeeee? I feel like we get each other."

"Mmhmm, 'k, Ave?" Brooke looked nervous. *Not really her style.* "I feel like I need to get this off my chest. Ughh, okay listen, and please don't be mad." Has anyone ever started admitting something by in this way without the other person getting angry? Doubtful.

Avery raised an eyebrow.

"I know what happened last weekend with Josh, he called me. And I know he's been in love with you forever."

"Wait, what?"

"When you told me you ran into him at the gala, and seeing how messed up you were, I texted him. Just a little text to warn him that if he did what he did ten years ago again, he'd have to deal with me. He told me then that he hadn't expected to see you again, especially that night, and that it completely threw him off."

The text she'd seen on Brooke's phone the next morning. That was why Josh had texted her!

"Why didn't you say anything to me?" Avery whispered, annoyed.

Brooke shrugged. "It wasn't my place to do so. But I tried to nudge you in his way whenever I could, because, babe, I truly think he's crazy about you. Besides, honestly. You'd have to have been in real denial not to see that he was smitten with you."

"And so, I guess you know what happened then ... Why did he call you?"

Brooke stared at her dead in the eye. "Ave, he's my best friend too, you know. He's heartbroken, I've never seen him like this."

"I'm heartbroken too, B."

"I know!" she said. "I know, and I'm here to tell you that you are both idiots. You found each other and you're seriously going to pass up what could be a beautiful love story just because of your fears and ambitions? Come on. I've never seen you this in love. Even with Alex."

"I never said—"

"Oh, cut the bullshit, Ave. Not with me."

Avery fell silent for a moment, Troopie still perched on her shoulders.

"Ughhh okay, fine! Did you all talk and agree to tell me the same thing today or what?"

Brooke chuckled. "Who's 'all?' No, I haven't talked to anyone. I'm not surprised I'm not the only one who thinks that though."

"It's not that simple B., okay? I have a commitment here if I win the contest."

"And if you don't win? Not that I think you won't. I'm just speculating a little."

Avery thought for a minute, thinking back to her mom's words.

"I guess," she said carefully, "I guess I could consider it. But that's just guessing, B. And what if he's already gone? I'm not going to chase after him."

Brooke shook her head. "You're both as stubborn as the other, I swear."

"But you still love me, right?" Avery stuck her tongue out as Brooke rolled her eyes once more.

She'd be lying if she said her mom's and Brooke's words didn't make her reconsider her decision. But all she knew for sure at the end of their coffee date, was that Troopie was coming home with her.

♪♫

As she drove home to her mom's, her phone rang, and Lisa's number appeared on her screen. Were the contest results already in? Her heart raced as she pressed the button on her steering wheel to answer.

"Hey Lisa!" she said, trying to control the tremor in her voice. *Be confident.*

"Avery, darling, I have some news. Listen, I'm not going to beat around the bush. It was between you and someone else, and the jury went with the other person. I'm really sorry, but you didn't win."

Avery felt her world and everything she'd worked for collapse. Not to be cocky but she had been so confident in her own skills that the thought of losing had barely crossed her mind.

"Oh. Okay, well, I tried. I knew it would be hard." She really needed to work on her convincing skills.

"I'm sorry, darling. You know I adore you. Don't be too disappointed, your passion and talent shine through your work. Maybe an opportunity will present itself to work together in the future, who knows?"

"Absolutely, thank you Lisa." Eyes stinging, she needed to end this call now before she could humiliate herself. "Listen, I'm driving right now. Can I call you back later?"

"Sure thing. Be safe."

She hung up and burst into tears at the bitter failure of both her professional and romantic life.

Twenty-four

Wild

She slammed the front door and let out a cry of frustration. Luckily, no one was home—her mother was away at a meeting with her colleague, and her brother wasn't coming to see her until later that night.

She made a stop in the kitchen to grab a bottle of wine, climbed the stairs and stepped into the bathroom, ready to do nothing besides take a hot bath with a bottle in hand.

She opened her music app and blasted Adele on shuffle in her speaker as she shed her clothes and slipped into the tub, because who better to help her through this moment than the Queen of Hearts.

She felt like Zooey Deschanel in *New Girl,* watching *Dirty Dancing* over and over again whenever she had a breakup, crying like crazy every time.

She turned on the faucets and let the scalding water run over her skin, the sensation almost numbing. Perfect, it was exactly what she needed. Taking a big swig of wine straight from the bottle, she let out a long sigh. Her muscles slowly relaxed, and closing her eyes, she sank into the peaceful sounds of water trickling over her body.

She wasn't one to give up, but fuck, that setback had really hurt. She had put all her energy into the project that could have been a major turning point for her business and here she was, soaking in a bathtub that was half-water, half-tears, at her mother's house. *The dream.*

"Really nailed that one, didn't you, Avery?" she mumbled to herself.

No matter how hard she worked or how much she wanted it, nothing was ever good enough. Right at that moment, "Million Years Ago" started playing.

"Oh, perfect!" she scoffed. *Just perfect.*

The lyrics echoed in her ears, as another sob escaped. How did Adele always managed to press *just* where it hurt? Maybe it was time for her to live a little more, indeed. Right now, she was more Cameron Diaz in *The Holiday*, soaking in her bath of sorrow while a voiceover narrated about how miserable her life was.

Finding a balance when starting a business wasn't an easy task, and she had been so obsessed with the success of it that she had lost sight of the most important thing of all. Her own happiness. Maybe losing this contest was the wake-up call she desperately needed. Maybe it was a sign from the universe that said 'get off your ass and follow your instincts for once,' instead of always thinking about doing the 'right thing.'

And her instincts were telling her to drop everything and beg Josh to give her a second chance, that she was dumb and paralyzed by fear but the only thing that mattered was her love for him.

She was done wallowing in self-pity or making excuses for not going after what she was dying to. She was going to call Josh, or better yet, go to his apartment, tell him everything that was on her mind and own up to her feelings, and for once in her life, trust someone other than herself.

Filled with her newfound resolve, Avery rinsed off and wrapped herself in her bathrobe when her phone rang with a number she didn't recognize.

"Hello?"

"Hi, is this Avery Clark?" a feminine voice asked on the other end.

"Yes, this is she."

"Fantastic! My name is Maggie Porter. I was one of the judges on the wedding photo contest?"

"Oh, yeah, hi." *Uhhh, what the fuck?*

She heard Maggie chuckle. "I'm sorry for calling you out of the blue, but I would have hated myself if I didn't reach out. I loved the photos you submitted. For me, you were the clear winner, but it was a majority vote and unfortunately, well, you know how it went. If it can make you feel any better, the vote was very, very close."

"It does a little bit, thank you." She still didn't understand the reason for the call, though.

"Anyway, I'm rambling. As I said, I loved your photos. You have an eye for capturing emotions and bringing them into focus that I have rarely seen in any photographer I've worked with."

Pride rushed through Avery at that. "That's what I've been really trying to focus on, so I'm happy you noticed," she said, still trying to put the pieces together. "I'm sorry, what did you say you worked in again?"

"Oh, I didn't, I'm sorry!" Maggie laughed. "That's what I get for thinking about a million things at the same time, you know? I work for a big European advertising company, AFocus. We just opened offices in North America. We help our clients with their advertising needs and usually handle everything from coming up with the idea to the execution. We started working more and more with influencers last year and adapting to the new technologies. I bet you must have a few requests for Instagram photoshoots, am I right?"

Avery chuckled. "Yeah, I've had a growing number over the past two years, it's true."

"Doesn't surprise me! Anyway, I would love to meet for a coffee next week, if you have some free time. And maybe talk about working with us."

Had she just gotten offered a job? Wow, this 'stop feeling sorry for yourself' thing was really working for her already.

"That's, yeah, um, for sure," she stammered. Super eloquent. Professional. Perfect. *Gold star, Avery.* She cleared her throat. "I'm free on Wednesday morning if that works for you."

"I'm writing it in my calendar as we speak," Maggie said. "And I know a great place. I'll text you the details, sounds good?"

Just as she was about to answer, the front doorbell rang.

"It's perfect, Maggie. Thank you very much, I can't wait to discuss it further," Avery said as she ran down the stairs to open the door. Her mother was expecting an important delivery today and had told her to keep an eye out for it.

"So am I, Avery. Talk soon."

She hung up and opened the door. "Sorry, I—"

The words died in her throat when she saw Josh standing outside on her front porch, still the most gorgeous man she had ever seen, his hazelnut hair tousled, deep blue eyes always glowing with a little bit of mischief, and ... shock all over his face as he let his gaze slowly travel down her body.

Shit.

She'd forgotten she was still in her bathrobe when she'd rushed downstairs. Awkwardly, she wrapped her arms around her waist, still trying to comprehend what he was doing there.

Can I just manifest shit like this now?

"Hey."

"Hi," Josh said at the same time.

Avery chuckled. "Um, do you want to come in?"

"I would love to," he said, while offering her one of his dazzling smiles as she closed the door behind them.

"Listen, Avie I—"

"I'm sorry," she cut in. "Can I say something first, please?"

"Of course."

They were standing apart from each other which was totally unfamiliar to her. Just one or two strides and she could be in his arms.

"I lost the contest," she said bluntly. Josh was about to say something, but she stopped him before he could get a word out. "Wait, let me finish. I'm okay. Well, if you had come a few hours earlier, I wouldn't have had the same answer, but I promise you I'm fine." She saw the concern dissipate across his features.

"Turns out, a lot can happen in a day, and I just got off the phone with one of the contest judges who wants to talk to me about working with her company." She raised her hands. "But wait. There's more, and more importantly, this is what truly matters."

She took a step closer, hesitant to invade his space considering she didn't know where they stood.

"I've done a lot of soul-searching over the past week, and trust me when I say that what happened that night between us was probably one of the hardest things I've ever gone through in my life. And believe it or not, you have quite the fan club between my mom and Brooke."

Josh's shoulders loosened and he let out a small laugh, still listening closely to what she had to say.

"Though you might have some work to do with my brother. Anyway," she said, shaking her head. "This is so not the point. What I'm trying to say here, and very poorly at that, is that I am done letting my fears get the better of me. I have been hiding away my whole life from the things I truly wanted because I was scared of being rejected, abandoned, never good enough. I'm done letting them dictate my choices and always going with what's safe and predictable. And I'm done doubting the people I love."

Josh's eyes sparked at her last word. "Did you just—"

"I love you. I love you like I've never loved anybody, and that scares the shit out of me. I'm scared to lose you, to give my all to you and lose myself along the way. I'm terrified of so many things, but I love you more than the fear that weighs on me constantly. I'm coming to LA with you. I don't know if the company who wants to work with me has offices there, but I don't care. I'll start over if I have to. I need to trust in myself and my talent. And above all else, I need to trust you."

"Can I say something?"

She exhaled, relieved that the words were finally out. She hadn't realized the true weight that she had been carrying all this time. "Yeah, go ahead."

"First of all, can I touch you, because this," he said, gesturing to the empty space between them, "is killing me right now." She nodded, because she was desperate for his arms too.

In one stride, he swooped her into his strong arms, holding her tightly against him, their racing hearts humming in harmony. *Home.* That's where she was. She missed the feel of his jaw against her neck when he buried his head like that, or the feel of his smooth hair curling around her fingers.

"I fucking missed you." His breath was hot against her skin, his lips brushing against her neck.

He straightened up and cupped her face in his hands, like he had done plenty of times before, his thumbs drawing circles on her cheeks. "I'm not going to LA."

"What do you mean?" Avery almost yelped.

Josh shook his head. "I'm not going. See? You're not the only one who did some thinking. I haven't been able to sleep all week, and I couldn't even get myself excited about the job because all I could think about was how close I'd come to having you in the way I've always wanted, and how I let you go, *again.*"

Her heart was pounding against her chest, each time a little harder as Josh continued to spill his own truth.

"And I know my mom is looking over me and approves of my decision. If she was still here, I'm sure she would have smacked me in the head for reacting like I did on Sunday." Glimmers of tears shone in his eyes and Avery placed her hand on his wrist. *I'm here.*

"I called Tom at the conservatory and he agreed to let me teach for the next year. I'll be working in the same place that made my mom the brilliant artist she was. Sounds pretty great to me."

"That's…That's amazing, J.," Avery murmured.

He nodded. "I agree, pretty amazing." He inhaled and continued as his eyes dove into hers. "I won't regret passing on Los Angeles, but I *know* I will forever regret not giving everything I have to get the woman I love back. You're it for me, Avie. So, I'm asking. No. I'm begging. Will you please, *please*, have me back?"

Josh didn't know that he'd always had her—it had never been a question, but as his own fears crept out, Avery realized she had the chance to get both of them on the same page for the first time in all those years.

"I've always been yours, J.," she said simply.

Josh closed his eyes in relief, his chest rising and falling hard.

"Does that mean I can kiss you?" he whispered, his lips only inches away from her mouth.

"I'm just wondering why you're not doing it already," she teased.

His hands already holding her face, he brought her lips to him, overflowing her senses and thoughts with the feeling she missed so much. *Ugh, finally.*

It seemed like forever ago that she had last felt his full lips work their magic against hers. How could she have thought she could go without it completely?

Starved from his absence, she grabbed the front of his shirt and pulled him closer to her as she deepened their kiss and slid her tongue between his lips, daring him to deny her request. Startled by her attack, he dug his fingers into her hips to steady himself and groaned against her mouth. The sound reverberated in every bone and muscle, making her light and jelly in his arms, when he opened to let her in.

Avery reveled in their kiss, devouring every bit of the man she loved so deeply, capturing his lips between hers as she dropped her fingers down his chest, dipping them in his waistband and giving it one tug, her message perfectly clear.

"Stay here," she ordered, as she broke their kiss.

And because she felt like teasing him, she took a step back. And another. And another, until her back was against the wall.

Would this feeling ever go away? Always wanting him, being absolutely consumed every time he put his hands on her? It was new to her, and it was exhilarating.

She had always been cautious, the one who didn't dare too much but still enjoyed it, on a, let's say, healthy level. Even if 'healthy' didn't really mean anything. But with Josh, it was like he'd lit a fire inside her that was just waiting to set everything ablaze. She wanted to try things, to be bold and fearless, to see what he wanted to do to her and agree without batting an eye. It was as if his confidence in her was fueling her flames, allowing her to surrender herself completely.

Josh studied her with hooded eyes, staying right where he was, as if to see how far she would go. Slowly, and with her gaze holding his, she pulled on her bathrobe belt, letting it fall on the floor with a light thud. The garment parted, showing him that she was completely naked underneath.

Josh sucked in a sharp breath, his bulge already pressing against his pants. He bit his lips, taking his time to go over every nuance of her body, as Avery brushed the curve of her breast with the back of her hand, trailing lower, around her navel, until she reached the most sensitive part of her body and started stroking herself.

Josh let out a strangled noise, and in less time than it took her to blink, he was pushing the rest of the robe off of her, pinning her against the wall.

"You didn't listen," she said breathlessly, while Josh wasted no time roaming his mouth and hands all over her, swirling his tongue around her already hard peak and squeezing her other breast in his hand.

"How the fuck did you expect me to when you're standing here like this," he whispered roughly, pushing himself against her and letting her feel the effect she had on him.

He unbuttoned his pants and pulled them down along with his briefs, before lifting Avery into his arms and wrapping her legs around him.

"You okay?" he asked

She nodded and dove for his mouth as he pushed inside her in one hard thrust, burying himself as deep as he could.

"Oh my god, J.," she yelped, clutching his shoulders and sinking her nails in his skin as he delved once more, rocking into her with a frantic rhythm. Wanting to feel him closer, she pressed her heels in his ass, allowing him to go even deeper.

"Fuck, fuck, fuck," he groaned as her muscles clenched around him, her orgasm growing rapidly inside her.

In three final thrusts, it was game over for her. She cried out his name in pure bliss as she rolled her hips around him, her legs shaking, until she was utterly limp in his arms. Josh gave in a few strokes later, spilling every last drop of himself inside her.

His chest heaving, he pressed a soft kiss on her lips. "I fucking love you."

"I fucking love you too," she said, smiling as he dipped to kiss her once more.

"Don't move," he said as he carefully let her down.

He climbed the stairs quickly and she heard him fumbling in the bathroom. A minute later, he was back with a wet towel and bending down to clean the inside of her thighs. The gesture was so intimate that it tugged at her heartstrings.

"Thank you," she said when he stood up, holding her bathrobe open in his hands and helping her put it back on.

"I assure you that it was entirely *my* pleasure," he grinned, and laid his forehead against hers. "I'm never letting you go again, baby. Ever."

He squeezed her hip and she wrapped her arms around him, resting her head on his solid and comforting chest as she let herself drift off into the overwhelming happiness she felt in this moment.

♫

"Avery, you home?" her mom called out from the front door.

"In the kitchen!" she replied, as she winked at Josh, who was busy getting dinner ready.

"Oh my god it smells delicious in here," she heard her mom's voice coming closer. "Don't tell me you—"

Here we go.

"Josh!" she screamed. "Oh my god, Josh!" Her mom threw herself at him, and thankfully Josh was robust enough to absorb the impact and catch her.

"Hi Rebecca!" he said, hugging her close. "It's so good to see you."

"I can't believe you're here," she said, squeezing his arms before swatting it. "Don't you dare disappear on us like that ever again!"

Josh chuckled. "I won't, I promise." Taking a step back, he whistled. "Damn, Beck! Are you planning on putting Bezos in his place with that outfit?"

"Oh, stop! Always the charmer, this one. No, I was just in a meeting with some prospective clients."

Avery swirled her head. "Already?"

Her mother looked proud. "Yes! Told you my friend had good contacts!" She looked at the stove. "I see you're trying to get back into our good graces with ... what is it you're cooking for us tonight?"

Josh flashed his most handsome smile. "A little French dish I picked up while in Paris. It's called boeuf bourguignon."

Her mom raised her eyebrows. "Fancy! Well, don't get your hopes up just yet. I need to see for myself if you've earned my forgiveness. And my daughter," she said, while coming to Avery and dropping a kiss in her hair.

"Mom!" *What game was she playing?!*

"Don't worry, honey, I'll be nice." Her mother winked at her, and Avery groaned.

Josh put the lid on the pot and took Avery by the waist, standing behind her, and kissing the spot where her neck met her shoulder.

"Actually Beck, that sounds like an amazing plan. And I can't wait to show you how madly in love I am with your daughter."

Avery swore her mother's jaw hit the floor and by the time she'd recovered, she was already completely smitten. Who wouldn't be, though? He just knew exactly what to say, but most importantly, she knew he meant every word of it.

They spent the rest of the evening around the meal Josh had prepared, laughing, chatting and reminiscing about childhood memories.

Rebecca was overjoyed that her daughter and her beloved Josh were finally a couple, and Avery felt a rush of happiness crash over her. She hadn't seen her mother like this in years or heard so much laughter in their house since Miles' failed improv show back when he was 12.

And, as Josh's thumb gently stroked the inside of her thigh under the table, as if he was always in need of her touch, Avery met her mom's gaze, who gave her a knowing smile and the tiniest of nods—everything she needed to finally   start   living.

Epilogue

Malibu

ONE YEAR LATER

"Come back to bed," Josh groaned. "It's way too early to be up on a Sunday."

Avery was standing in front of their large bedroom windows overlooking the ocean, dressed in one of Josh's shirts that hung just above her knees, and holding a steaming cup of coffee.

"But the sunrise, J.!" she said. "I will never get used to it." She wanted to capture every second of it, but her camera was already full of the morning light shots she'd taken since they'd moved to Malibu a week ago.

She turned to look at him, sprawled out in their bed, the white sheets ruffled and hanging low on his hips, his naked torso on full display. She had to admit that this view was pretty spectacular too, and one she was never going to get used to either.

"Can you at least watch it from here?" he said, patting the empty space next to him. "Promise I'll keep you warm."

She laughed, but made her way to their bed, sliding under the covers. "Oh, I have no worries about that."

She nestled in the hollow of his arms, resting her head on his shoulder as he pulled her close against him.

He sighed in contentment. "Way better." This man. His devotion to her knew no bounds and he had repeatedly proven it to her over the past year.

She placed a kiss on the lines of his pecs. "Are you nervous for tomorrow?"

"Not one bit. I am so excited," he said, squeezing her against him. "I'm so happy to see Mark again. We hit it off so well last year. I'm sure we'll work really well together too."

Mark was the guy who had reached out to Josh at Julia's wedding about the job offer in Los Angeles. They had stayed in touch while Josh worked at the conservatory, and when his teaching contract had come to an end, Avery had encouraged him to go for it and ask Mark if he was still willing to work with him. The answer had been a resounding *yes*.

"What about you? Nervous?"

"Would you be surprised if I said yes?"

Josh chuckled. "Not at all. In fact, I'd be concerned if you said you were feeling very relaxed. But if you're tense, I can probably help you with that," he said, the mischievous gleam in his eyes sparkling as he rolled her over him.

"Hey! I can't watch the sunrise anymore!"

"You can watch it tomorrow morning. I'm sure you'll be pacing the floor around 3 a.m.," he said, running a hand through her hair and tucking a strand behind her ear, leaving the rest to spill over his chest.

She leaned to kiss his delicious lips. "It's a big deal, you know."

"I know it is, baby. But I also know that you're going to crush it, like everything you put your mind to."

When Avery had met with Maggie last year, it had been like everything finally coming together all at once. She'd been offered the opportunity of a lifetime: keep her business and work as the main photography partner for AFocus.

She had been the primary source of contact, hired the help she'd needed, photographed hundreds of ads and done many photoshoots with models and influencers with a budget she'd never thought she would have. The best part? Total and absolute creative control. Maggie had told her they had hired her because of the uniqueness of her style, and they weren't about to get in the way of it.

Well, they had kept their promises, so much so that when they'd decided to open their next office on the West Coast, they'd asked her if she would be willing to assist with the move and run the photography division. It had taken her a few days to think about it, discuss it with J., because this shift hadn't only meant moving to another country, but also putting her own business on the back burner for some time.

In the end, she went with her gut, something she had learned to do more and more since getting the call about the contest. She'd accepted the job, and the amazing raise that went with it. After struggling to make the ends meet for several years, she was finally able to breathe. She had worked, and worked, and worked some more, and it had paid off. Literally.

With Josh working for one of the major Hollywood studios, they had managed to buy a beautiful two-bedroom villa in Malibu, with a view of the Pacific. Their master bedroom was her favorite part of the house, with its white walls that made the light wood beams really pop. It was so peaceful.

Out of the corner of her eye, she saw Simba and Troopie snuggled together in one of the armchairs, sleeping soundly. The rescues had become inseparable the moment Avery had brought Troopie home.

"Are we doing anything tomorrow night?" Avery asked, her head laying on his heart. She heard his heartbeat pick up. Weird. "I was thinking maybe we could go celebrate our first day at our new jobs somewhere fancy. With lots and lots of champagne." She raised her head to look at him and smiled. "And lots and lots of celebratory sex."

"Mmh, the best kind. That sounds like the perfect evening to me," he said, bending to kiss the tip of her nose.

Uh. No teasing? No sexual joke or attempt to make love to her right here, right now? What was with the sudden weirdness?

A theory formed in her mind, and she decided to try it out.

"Do you want me to take care of the reservation?"

Josh's hands that were lazily brushing her back stilled.

"Um ... No, no, no, I'll ... I'll find something, don't worry."

Okay, he definitely had something planned. His whole nervous vibe was very far from the casual Josh she knew. And he wasn't nervous about his first day. If he had been, he wouldn't have been so secretive about it. So truly, if she thought about it, there was one reason and one reason only why this man would have his hands sweating on her back right now.

Oh my god he's going to propose, isn't he? Don't get your hopes up, Avery, you're extrapolating right now based on very little evidence. Ohmygodohmygodohmygod. This was so the opposite of keeping her cool, but fuck it. She knew him like nobody else, and as much as he was trying to keep his cool and act all nonchalant right now, he couldn't keep a thing from her.

The thought of him getting on one knee obliterated every other thought in her mind. The past year they'd spent together had been like nothing she'd ever experienced. Josh had showed her what it truly meant to be loved, every single day. He hadn't lied when he'd sworn to be by her side and lift her up in any way he could. He was her biggest and most ardent supporter, always finding new ways to show her how much she meant to him. And boy had he found the most delicious ways sometimes.

She had thought that when she'd finally moved back into his apartment (for the second time in less than a month) and fallen back into a routine, the wanting him would eventually dim a little bit. But to her utmost delight, she couldn't have been more wrong. His needs were insatiable, and he'd kept on worshiping her and her body like she was the most precious treasure in the world.

So much had changed in a short period of time, and if the Avery from a year ago could see her right now, splayed over a naked Josh, only wearing a shirt, in their own gorgeous home in another country, she would've probably had a hard time comprehending it.

It had taken them years, but they were finally there, ready to go through life together, supporting and loving each other unconditionally.

"What are you thinking about, my love?" he whispered softly, his hand trailing down her back and slipping under her shirt. The feel of his touch on her bare skin still sent a burst of electricity to her nerve endings.

She nuzzled her face under his jaw, feeling his weekend stubble graze her skin. "I was thinking about how for the first time in more than ten years, we are finally in the same place, at the same time, on the same page."

Their love story reminded her of encores artists did during shows, leaving the stage for a while, the crowd going wild, only to come back with one final song that would end the evening on the highest note. That's what this was. Their last encore. One last song that would last for the rest of their lives, after an eventful, thrilling, heartbreaking show.

He wrapped his strong arms around her, holding her tight. "Twenty years of joy, heartaches, tears and laughter, for a lifetime of happiness together."

Josh tipped her chin and kissed her tenderly, sealing with his lips yet one more promise she knew, without a doubt in her mind, he would hold above all else.

Enjoyed Avery & Josh's story?

Stay tuned for Miles & Riley's book coming up next year!

Acknowledgments

They say write what you know. I didn't know this story would end up being the one it is, in your hands, when I first started thinking about it. I wanted to write a cute love story between friends who lost touch over the years, but I hadn't planned to include heavier topics like mental health issues or sexual assault.

In the end, this book is an intimate and deeply personal one, that I hold very close to my heart. I hope that by reading it, readers who understand these experiences will find comfort in the story and relate to Avery's tenacity and resilience.

Strong women is all I have known all my life and it was only fitting that the first woman I wrote about would be stubborn, independent and unwavering. All my life I have been told that my sensitivity was a weakness, but I hope that you were able to see that despite her emotional ways, Avery is anything but. Women are so often reduced to their feelings and discredited because of it. It's time we celebrate female characters that aren't afraid to wear their hearts on their sleeves, all the while leading the way.

That is why I first want to thank my mom. Even though we don't always understand each other, she has always supported me to chase my dreams, even if those dreams happened to be on the other side of the Atlantic.

Writing this book would not have been possible without the understanding, patience and unwavering support of Pierre. Thank you for always cheering me on and for being my very first reader. Thank you for taking care of everything else in our lives so I could focus on this. I will forever be grateful.

Thank you to my editors Dominic, Britt, and Julie, whose guidance and support helped me get this story where it is today.

Thank you to my beta readers Amelia, Chelsea, Nikki, Stephanie, Jess, Jocelyne, Lacey and Kathrin for taking the time to read over this book and provide me with your most honest and helpful feedback. I love you guys.

Thank you to my book cover artist, Leni. It was such a pleasure working with you. Trusting you with my debut novel was honestly the easiest choice I had to make during this entire process, and I am still obsessively looking at this gorgeous cover at least once a day.

Thank you to my friends, Kevin, Heather, Mark, Matt, Emily, for supporting me during this crazy time and checking on me when I would go completely mute (sorry!!)

Thank you to Ashley Winstead for giving my book a read and supporting me through this entire experience. You, my friend, are one of a kind.

Thank you to Elena Armas, my romance queen, who paved the way for aspiring authors like me, and made me believe anything is possible if you just try.

Thank you to my Booksta sistas Rachel, Carol, Jules, Breanne and Kelly, for your invaluable feedback on some of my favorite scenes in this book. I knew I had the perfect people for those.

And finally, a big giant thank you to the Bookstagram community. I don't know where this book will be in a few months or years. I don't know if it'll be loved, or if it'll even work. But one thing I know for sure is that the support I have received from this community is unlike anything I have ever known. I know that this book has been eagerly awaited by many of you. And that alone is the greatest gift and made it all worth it. This is truly the best corner of the internet.

About the author

Originally from France, Elodie moved to Montreal, Canada in 2014 to pursue her studies in politics.

An avid reader since her childhood, it wasn't until 2021 that she rediscovered her love for books, especially romance novels. Because she never does anything halfhearted, Elodie has shared her love for reading with other book lovers on her Bookstagram (@elosreadingcorner) where she has found an incredibly supportive and inspiring community.

When she's not immersed in reading or analyzing public policies during her workdays, you can find Elodie baking sweets for the whole neighborhood, cuddling with her cats or behind her keyboard, trying to create a world and love stories that everyone can dream of.

The Last Encore is her first novel.

 @elosreadingcorner
🌐 www.elodiecolliard.com

Made in the USA
Las Vegas, NV
02 November 2022

58615725R00215